A RELUCTANT SPY

A RELUCTANT SPY

David Goodman

HEADLINE

First published in 2024 by
HEADLINE PUBLISHING GROUP

3

Cataloguing in Publication Data is available from the British Library

Hardback ISBN 978 1 0354 1601 1

Typeset in 12.76/16.82 pt Adobe Garamond Pro by Jouve (UK), Milton Keynes

Printed and bound in Great Britain by Clays Ltd, Elcograf S.p.A.

Headline's policy is to use papers that are natural, renewable and recyclable
products and made from wood grown in well-managed forests and other
controlled sources. The logging and manufacturing processes are expected to
conform to the environmental regulations of the country of origin.

HEADLINE PUBLISHING GROUP
An Hachette UK Company
Carmelite House
50 Victoria Embankment
London EC4Y 0DZ

www.headline.co.uk
www.hachette.co.uk

For Valerie, without whom, nothing.

Part One

LIKE A GLOVE

I

Jeremy

Bishkek, Kyrgyzstan: June 2003

Even six hours later, Jeremy Althrop could still see the twin furrows in the dust where they'd dragged him in. His head ached. The repeated punches to his face were the main reason. But dehydration was a factor too.

The sun had moved around enough that even this benighted basement had a sliver of dusty light to spare for his one functional eye. It lanced in, making him squint and groan. He tilted his head back. His chair creaked. The concrete ceiling pressed down on him.

A single strip light flickered overhead. Vauxhall Cross was full of lights like that. They made his eyes twitch, even when he hadn't spent most of a working day being punched in the face.

Jeremy coughed and closed his eye, then flexed against the plastic biting into his wrists, trying to keep the circulation going.

'Water?' he said, for the fifth time in the last hour. The word came out low and husky, dry as the mountains and steppe that stretched out around the Kyrgyz capital.

'Water is for those who cooperate,' said a low voice. 'I am getting tired of saying this.'

Jeremy grunted and shuffled back on the chair. He coughed again, tried to wet his lips with a tongue that was just as dry. 'Well, that makes two of us. I'm getting tired of being called a liar.'

'You are a field handler for MI6. You are here to falsely plant evidence of nuclear material on Kyrgyzstani soil. Perhaps so you can do to us what you have done to Iraq, yes?'

Jeremy inhaled slowly, fighting the urge to correct the man sitting across from him. It hadn't been 'MI6' officially since 1920.

London: four days later

'*Terrible* luck in Bishkek,' said Winston Bascomb, section chief for the Central Asian Desk. The older man steepled his fingers and gazed over his rumpled tie at Jeremy. His hair was very carefully arranged into precise, lacquered grooves.

The swelling around Jeremy's eye had gone down, leaving a purpling bruise. The headache was still there, although a few hours of jolting half-sleep in the back of an RAF Hercules transfer from Cyprus had taken the edge off it. The debriefs in windowless, fluorescent-lit rooms downstairs in the intervening time hadn't helped, but he'd finally got a full eight hours the night before. Or at least, he'd lain in bed for eight hours. Thinking about what he'd say in this room.

'Yes, sir, it was.' He reached out and picked up his coffee cup from the desk. A droplet soaked into the splinted bandage around his third and fourth fingers and he swore under his breath.

Bascomb winced. 'They did a number on you, Althrop. I read your debrief from Akrotiri. Why'd your joe make a run for it, you think?'

Jeremy shrugged again, affecting a nonchalance he didn't feel. He'd been asking himself that since he'd heard the thump of secret police boots on the stairs of his hotel.

'Could have been a million things. Joes run. They panic, they get out of their depth. Bakiyev is on the ropes, clamping down hard. Perhaps Ruslan thought he saw which way the wind was blowing. But that's not why I asked to see you.'

Bishkek

The interrogator on the other side of the table was a slim, bearded man in his forties, wearing a dark grey suit. His hands were unblemished by blood or bruises. He'd been leaving the punching to the soldier looming by the heavy steel door. There was someone else behind Jeremy, who he hadn't seen yet, typing. Always typing.

The interrogator sighed. 'Your cover is . . . paper-thin, is that the phrase? Your name is not Daniel Tait. You are not a salesman for a water-well boring company based in Somerset. That company does not exist, and neither does Daniel Tait.'

Jeremy sensed movement, then the mysterious typist resolved into a young woman. She stepped into his peripheral vision and placed a bulky laptop on the table, then pointed at the bright white screen.

'There are no results,' she said, close to his ear, her English crisp and clipped. 'The address does not exist. It is not on Mapquest.'

Jeremy coughed, trying to project the bafflement of a drilling engineer who had started his career in the punch-card era. 'I don't really understand computers. I drill wells. I dig holes in the ground. I know about drill bits, pressure flow, pipe linings. I haven't even got an email.'

She leaned forward and turned the laptop away, then sat in a chair to his left. Her fingers tapped at the keyboard. 'Very well. Please tell me whether you favour a tricone bit or a PDC bit for drilling in Kyrgyzstan's soil?'

London

Jeremy took a deep breath. 'I had to break cover, sir, as you know.'

Bascomb sighed. 'Yes. Regrettable. Chaps in the Foreign Office don't like it when we do that. I suppose it was necessary?'

'It was, sir. Things got . . . rough. I told them I was Foreign Office and claimed diplomatic immunity. They dumped me at the British embassy the next morning. Persona non grata'd my diplomatic passport too.'

Bascomb nodded. 'Well, you have diplomatic cover for a reason. If they PNG'd you, we can always issue another. But what happened with your primary identity?'

'That's what I want to talk about, sir. Cover identities. And why they're about to stop working.'

Bascomb frowned, sipped from the cup of Earl Grey in front of him. He swivelled his padded chair and gazed out of the rain-streaked window at the grey waters of the Thames. A rubbish barge headed for landfill in Essex chugged slowly under Vauxhall Bridge, bright-jacketed figures moving on the foredeck.

After a moment, Bascomb spoke, still staring out at the water. 'In 1971, I was dropped off by a Trabant near Magdeburg with a paper driving licence and ID book, a couple of hundred Ostmarks and a Browning with fourteen rounds of ammunition. I had three weeks to pick up the accent in a suburban safehouse, then I was out in the field for nearly nine months. Passed many a VoPo cordon with those papers, let me tell you. I'm led to believe the work of the forgers and backstory specialists has only grown better. So what, pray, do you mean by "stop working", exactly?'

Jeremy rubbed his forehead. How was he going to explain this? He looked at the clean, leather-topped expanse of Bascomb's desk, the blotter, the neat in-tray and stack of correspondence.

'Do you have an email address, sir?'

Bascomb cleared his throat. 'No, I do not. I receive my mail the correct way, on paper. Bloody computers give me a headache. They've given Samantha one though. A computer, I mean. She prints things out for me.'

Jeremy's head turned to spot Samantha Brookner, guardian of the Bascomb domain, perched behind the smooth, pine-effect sweep of her desk. The glow of her monitor lit her face as she worked.

'I'm afraid you're in a minority, sir. Most section chiefs have email now. The analysts downstairs work digitally most of the time too. They go into the paper archives when they're working on something more' – he paused, swept his gaze across the empty desk – 'old school.'

Bascomb's face darkened. 'If I'd wanted a critique of my working style, Althrop, I'd have asked for it. What's your bloody point?'

Bishkek

Jeremy blinked. 'Miss, what are you looking up there? I don't think we've got a website.'

He peered sideways at the young woman. She smiled, dark hair swept back into a tight bun under a sheer headscarf; plain green fatigues, a slim watch. It ticked lightly against the casing of the computer as she typed. 'An online encyclopaedia. Quite new. Very useful. Tell me, Mr Tait, do you subcontract primarily for Ulterra or Schlumberger?'

Panic rose behind Jeremy's breastbone, heart fluttering. His cover was two wrinkled pages of notes on the fictional Somerset Borehole Company, a landline number that redirected to Enquiries on the fourth floor of Vauxhall Cross and a wallet with standard pocket litter: expired Tube travelcard, a voucher for a sandwich shop in Taunton, his flight ticket stubs, scribbled notes about drill line pressure. Perfectly convincing.

Once.

London

'My cover fell apart as soon as their interrogators gave it the slightest digital prod. Non-existent addresses, no email or website for the company I was supposed to be working for. No breadcrumbs. No history. They picked my story apart like they were deboning a chicken. My briefing materials may have passed muster five years ago. Not now, when anyone can just use Google.'

Bascomb's brow creased in confusion. 'What the hell is a "Google"? Are you pulling my bloody leg, Althrop?'

Jeremy sat forward, the urgency he'd felt in Bishkek rising again. 'It's a search engine, sir. You can ask it anything you like: addresses, company websites, contact information, Wikipedia entries about any subject you can imagine.'

'Wicket . . . pedia? Is that something to do with cricket?'

Jeremy waved a hand. 'Doesn't matter. The point is that these tools are getting better, every day. Counterintelligence research that used to take months now takes *minutes*. I did a little digging this morning. This kind of thing has happened *six times* so far this year alone. It's going to change everything. And we're behind, sir. Very *far* behind.'

Bishkek

Jeremy pulled himself up. 'I'm a British citizen. I'm here to do work in the communities around Bishkek. Bringing water. I don't know why you're treating me this way.'

The interrogator sighed. 'This is as unpleasant for me as it is for you. I know you are not Daniel Tait. So tell me *who you are*, or we will begin even more' – he rippled his fingers in the air – 'unpleasantness. Your name?'

Jeremy flexed his wrists again. He'd lost the feeling in his fingers. Perhaps that would make the next part hurt a little less.

'Daniel Tait. I'm a water well drilling specialist. I'm from Taunton, in Somerset.'

The interrogator stood up and fastened his suit jacket. 'Very well. I am tired of this. Goodbye. It has not been a pleasure.' He nodded to the guard at the door and spoke quickly in Kyrgyz, then left. The young woman closed the laptop and followed.

Jeremy looked up as the huge soldier closed the door behind them both. He picked up a pair of pliers from a tray by the door and turned around, face still perfectly blank.

'Now, look, my friend, we don't need—' he started. The beefy hand that clamped over his mouth muffled everything, including the screaming that started shortly afterwards.

London

Bascomb drummed his fingertips on the leather of his desk. 'So we add some new items to the list. Websites and such. False addresses.'

Jeremy shook his head. 'It won't work, sir. There are ways to tell these things, to see how long a website's existed, who registered it. You can fake them, but if your opponent is determined, they'll see through it eventually.'

Bascomb sighed. 'Why do I get the feeling you're about to suggest something expensive?'

'I think, sir, you'll be surprised at how cheaply we can solve this problem.' Althrop reached into the laptop bag by the side of his chair and pulled out a manila folder. Bascomb immediately looked more comfortable. He knew a programme proposal when he saw one. On paper, as it should be.

Jeremy slid the document across the polished wood of Bascomb's desk. The proposal was the result of a feverish two days of work, as soon as he'd been able to see properly. His hands still throbbed from trying to type with only eight functional fingers.

Bascomb picked up the folder and peered at the title printed on the cover. ' "The Legends Programme". What on earth's that?'

Jeremy smiled, lopsided, peering out at his boss from under his swollen eyebrow. 'It's how we'll keep our people safe, sir.'

2

Jamie

The day started at the worse end of the spectrum, by London transport standards. Delays on the Circle line, packed carriages on the Central. Pissing rain at street level.

Jamie Tulloch took a Piccadilly Line trek to King's Cross, then a Northern back *south* to Old Street, followed by a damp shuffle to the office through the backstreets off the junction, awash with last night's smashed pint glasses and damp, corrugated patches of brown sludge that had once been pizza boxes.

The extra travel was the price of living in Chelsea. A Terence suggestion, of course. A little nudge from the Legends Programme. His former, semi-affordable place in Chalk Farm wasn't *quite* the right image. But the red-brick mansion flat in Cadogan Gardens was very nice. Quiet.

When he left Old Street station he *did* notice the young man in a tracksuit leaning nonchalantly against the railings by the side of the road, eyes flicking across the commuters. They lingered for a half-second on Jamie. The head turned away, white earbuds flashing in a ray of low, golden sun that had briefly slipped under the cloud lying over the city like a damp, grey blanket.

Jamie filed it away, same as all the other false alarms. Years ago, he'd seen his benefactors every time he locked eyes with someone on the Tube escalators, convinced they were always watching. Now, part of him thought his activation might never actually happen.

At the office, Jamie shook off his umbrella, waved to Carla on reception, got an over-roasted latte from the machine, then crashed into his Herman Miller chair and booted up his computer.

Another day, another fifteen go-nowhere tentative sales queries. Another two mandatory bi-weekly status calls added to his calendar.

At least it was Thursday. More than halfway through the week.

Calls all morning. Reeling off the benefits of enhanced enterprise resource planning, the customisation options they could consider, the many different ways that a data-driven business could outcompete and outmanoeuvre those without the foresight to buy the products of Tacitech Plc.

Around half past one, the gloom began to lift a little from the grey towers and slate roofs outside.

'Lunch? Couple of new places on Old Street I fancied . . .' he said across the sales desk to Sanjeev, his opposite number in back-end integration sales.

'Nah mate,' said Sanjeev. 'Thursday's my day to meet Leeanne. Gonna have to have a sad sandwich on your own.'

He was leaving Pret fifteen minutes later, his usual lunch swinging in a white paper bag, when he spotted the man in the tracksuit for the second time. The same casual lean, same earbuds, same sharp jawline turned away from him, hair buzzed short. A white guy, trim inside the tracksuit jacket, looking anywhere but at Jamie.

He stopped mid-stride, recovered, rifled through his memories for the next part. It had been a long time since his extremely minimal training: a weekend in the Brecon Beacons well over a decade ago, with precious little since, aside from the bi-yearly scheduled meetings.

What if this was something else? *Someone* else? Terence had assured him, years ago, that he wasn't a target.

But then, he would say that.

Jamie turned and walked away, heading south towards Bunhill Cemetery. He glanced back. The young man followed, well back, apparently staring at his phone. Best to keep heading for the cemetery. If this wasn't one of Terence's people, the cemetery was always busy at lunchtime. Lots of exits.

Jamie turned off the Old Street roundabout, quickening pace. Drops of rain spattered his jacket. Into the cemetery, following a small gaggle of office workers toting their own Pret bags.

He walked faster, wondering if he should stop, eat his lunch, stay in sight of other people. The wide stone slabs under his feet were slick with morning rain. He passed two benches, glanced back again. The tracksuit was at the gate, strolling along. But definitely following him.

Then, a familiar figure sitting four benches along. A man he'd last seen nearly a year before in Regent's Park, suggesting the move to Chelsea.

Terence Stringer. Of course.

It was finally going to happen. On a random Thursday in March. While he was holding a bag with a soggy sandwich inside, with six unclosed sales queries still in his pipeline and a hundred and forty-six unread emails.

'Hello, Jamie,' said Terence as he approached. 'Sorry if young Gavin gave you a scare. Needed to make sure you were coming to your usual lunch spot. It's this bench, isn't it?' Stringer was white, early fifties, mid-length greying hair swept behind his ears. Dark jeans, Chelsea boots, a black raincoat over a sensible jumper. He patted the damp bench beside him. Gavin, the tracksuited follower, settled on to the next bench along, still apparently engrossed in his phone, next to a young woman gently rolling a pram back and forth.

'You scared the shit out of me, Terence,' said Jamie, sitting down, lunch on his lap. 'I thought you were supposed to give me a heads-up. A text or something.'

Terence leaned back and nodded. 'Yes, sorry about that. New

protocol. Don't want to leave too much of a trail. So we prefer to do things in person. That's changed a bit, since last we spoke.'

Jamie looked down at the white paper bag on his lap and felt his stomach rumble. 'Mind if I . . .'

'Not at all. You've had a busy morning. Best to face things with a bit of food in your stomach.'

Jamie was two bites into his sandwich before the last sentence fully sank in. 'Face what, exactly?'

'The next phase of our fruitful partnership, young man. You're being activated.'

3

Jeremy

Pembroke College, Cambridge: May 2013

Old Court was a pool of yellowish light, early-afternoon sun shining full on the limestone walls of the Old Library and the college hall. Jeremy Althrop clasped his hands behind his head and leaned back against the grey, weathered wood of a quadrangle bench. The neat lines of the college lawn stretched in front of him, dotted with the scarf-muffled, dark-coated figures of undergrads moving between lectures. The sun was bright, but without much heat in it. It lit the rising breath of the students as they talked in low voices. A sharp guffaw of laughter rang out across the flagstones. Jeremy pulled his coat a little tighter.

When Tulloch arrived, three minutes early, he wasn't hard to spot. He sidled into the quadrangle like he might be spotted by a porter and kicked out. A leather satchel on one shoulder, over a charity-shop pea coat buttoned against the cold, pink blooms on both cheeks of his otherwise pale, angular face. He'd been here for the better part of three years, but hesitance still lived in every bone of Jamie Tulloch's body.

Perhaps he was simply disquieted by the invitation from his tutor to meet 'an old friend with an interesting proposition'. When Jeremy's own tap on the shoulder had come, it had been over gin and tonics on a very pleasant pub terrace by the side of the River Cam. He'd half expected it, after three years of Central Asian languages and two summers of non-profit work on the steppes.

Tulloch had no such expectations, that much was clear. Why would he? Born to a single mother and an absent father, raised on a pebble-dashed estate of four-in-a-block social housing on the outer edge of Edinburgh, everything Jamie Tulloch had won for himself had come hard. An autodidact loner with a library card, a couple of supportive teachers and the sense to mostly cut ties with his deeply troubled mother and her extended family. Adrift in the south of England, with an accent that had hardly mellowed and a chip on his shoulder the size of Greenland. Precisely why he'd been singled out.

Jeremy raised a hand as Tulloch approached. This would be his thirty-eighth programme recruitment approach since his run-in with Bakiyev's thugs in '03. He'd taken some small pleasure in seeing that particular regime tumble a couple of years later, but he was still persona non grata in Bishkek, even now.

Jeremy half rose from the bench, extending a hand. 'Jamie. A pleasure. I'm Stuart, Stuart Brown.'

Tulloch shook his hand and sat down, hunched forward, the satchel a barrier between them. He looked like he might make a break for it, hands shoved in the pockets of his peacoat. 'What's this about? Dr Farley said you were a friend of his, something like that.'

Jeremy nodded slowly. 'Something like that.'

Tulloch's roots were still evident in his accent, even after three years surrounded by the scions of the British upper classes. He hadn't adopted the protective colouration so common to scholarship students, the extended vowels, the ice-cut 'T's and 'H's. *Bu'er* and *wa'er* becoming *buttah* and *woahta*. After reviewing his academics, Jeremy wasn't surprised. Tulloch's schedule in the computer labs left little time for the usual socialising, clubs and societies. He was a navy-jacketed ghost, moving silently from college rooms to dining hall to lectures to labs and back again. Now he had a postgraduate offer from

Stanford, internships on the table from two major consultancies. Quite the thing, for a lad from the far end of the bus routes.

'So?' said Tulloch, eyes sweeping across the manicured grass. 'What'd you want to talk to me about, exactly? I've got labs in half an hour.'

Jeremy turned his body halfway towards Tulloch, laid an arm along the back of the bench. 'When a similar approach was made to me, a few streets over at Trinity, we danced around the topic for a good hour. But I get the sense you're a big fan of directness.'

Tulloch glanced sideways at him under dark eyebrows, brown eyes searching his face for mockery. When he saw none, he sat back, relaxing a little. The hands came out of the peacoat pockets and began to fiddle with the buckle on his satchel.

'Aye, you could say that,' said Jamie. 'You Security Service?'

Jeremy smiled a thin smile, noting the correct nomenclature. 'No. The other one. I'm not supposed to directly confirm things like that, but I *also* prefer directness.'

'Is this a tap on the shoulder, then? I thought that kind of thing was over with, these days. Old-boy networks.'

Jeremy shook his head. 'It's not the *only* route, any more. But a certain contingent still believes in that kind of talent-spotting.'

'Look, Mr *Brown*,' said Tulloch, the emphasis showing exactly what he thought of that little subterfuge, 'I suppose I'm flattered, but I haven't exactly seen myself going into government service, y'know?'

Jeremy shook his head. 'No, indeed. Not with the prospects you have in front of you. Twenty-three and already on the glide path to considerable success.'

Tulloch looked away again, eyes tracking a small gaggle of first-years, college scarves artfully draped over greatcoats and chunky cardigans. Another ripple of laughter, more fogged breath in the air. 'If it was going to be anybody, I thought it'd be GCHQ. But I hear they only want the real numbers guys.'

'That's not where your passion lies, though, is it, Jamie? You care about application, not theory.'

Another glance, a grudging half-smile. 'That's why I'm thinking about Stanford. Maybe an MBA as well. Where would SIS fit with *that*, exactly? You're not exactly early adopters. I heard you only got a *website* in 2005. Government procurement isn't my idea of a good time.'

Jeremy crossed one leg over the other and straightened the hem of his coat. 'No. Not mine either. But I represent a different kind of programme at SIS. We're not recruiting agents, or analysts, or field operatives, or any of the things you might expect. It's something a little different. And it would be almost entirely to your benefit.'

Tulloch was smiling, but there was a hard edge to his eyes. 'If I've learned anything in my life, Mr Brown, it's that fuck all is "entirely to my benefit". Give me your pitch. But dinnae lie to me.'

Jeremy laughed, a genuine, bottom-of-the-stomach laugh that seemed to take Tulloch by surprise. Yes, Tulloch would be an excellent candidate. Exactly what they needed.

'Fair enough. The programme I run recruits what we call authentic data producers. That's the official term. Mostly we call them Legends.'

It was Tulloch's turn to laugh. 'What, like, "he's a fucking legend"? That kind of thing?'

Jeremy nodded. 'In a way, yes. The Legends are talented individuals with good prospects, out in the real world, living their lives. We provide . . . support. Guidance, opportunities, leaving a few doors ajar. Gentle direction. A few very limited restrictions.'

'Why?' said Tulloch. He was interested now, the satchel by his side forgotten, arms folded, body half turned towards Jeremy. 'What do these "authentic data producers" do for you?'

'At SIS, we put field operators into dangerous situations, often pretending to be someone else. For a long, long time, we got by with false papers, fake business cards, a few front business phone numbers and faxes, an email inbox or two.'

'But?' said Tulloch, eyes narrowing. 'Something's changed?'

'You know yourself. You're studying it. Software, hardware. Storage. Computerisation. The *internet*.'

Jamie raised his eyebrows. 'Didn't think you lot had your finger on the pulse like this, to be honest. This thing your idea?'

Jeremy smiled, suddenly somewhere else. 'You could say that. It came to me in a flash of inspiration, when I was in a basement somewhere, regretting my life choices.'

Tulloch nodded. 'The best ideas come from necessity, right enough. So, what, you need . . . "authentic data", right?'

'I knew you were a sharp one, Jamie. That's why I approached you.'

'So, how do I fit in?' said Tulloch. 'You're writing some kind of software to generate fake information? You want me to work on it?'

'Far simpler than that,' said Jeremy. 'The Legends Programme asks real people to lead lives that lend themselves to effective cover. Then, when the time comes, a trained agent who resembles you, who knows everything about you, will step into your life. We'll swap images of you online, give them falsified papers that match yours. Then you'll go on a nice holiday for a few weeks. Maybe months. It depends.'

Tulloch sat back, bemusement written in the frown on his face. 'And in return, I get a helping hand into plum jobs, stuff like that? What's the catch? And why me?'

'We need people with real talent, who will have access, later in their careers. In return you will have a safety net, of sorts. Think of it as the network you never had, coming from where you do.'

Jamie bristled. 'What's that supposed to mean? You think I don't deserve to be here?'

Jeremy gave a slight shake of the head, then gestured at the stone walls of the college quadrangle. 'Not at all. You got to this point entirely on your own. That's admirable. And I can see how hard you've worked. And continue to work.'

'So what do I need you for?' said Tulloch. His shoulders were hunched again. 'If I'm such a bright young thing.'

Jeremy gave a small sigh. This was the inflection point. About a third of his candidates walked away, and he respected their reasons for doing so. Perhaps they felt it was a betrayal, or a short cut. Something that would dog their steps through the rest of their life, undercut their own sense of themselves.

But the temptation was a strong one. They'd designed it that way.

'You asked me not to lie to you, so I won't. Look around you. Most of the people here are *awash* with opportunities, connections, silent helping hands. They don't see it that way, of course. An uncle with a flat in London they can stay in for their unpaid internship, which they can only afford to do because they don't have any bills to pay. A car, when they need one. Rent paid, when they've gone overboard with the socialising. And that's just the sons and daughters of middle managers from the Home Counties. A few of your fellow students go home at the weekends to *literal* mansions.'

Tulloch slumped a little deeper on the bench. 'Aye, I've met them. Been invited, once. Uninvited, with lots of excuses, once they realised I didn't have shooting tweeds.'

Jeremy winced in sympathy. 'I remember a few moments like that. But I'm *one* of those comfortable Home Counties types, Jamie. Never had to worry about failing, not *really*. Insulated, in so many ways.'

'What's your point?' said Tulloch. He was closing himself off, lip twisting in anger.

Jeremy took a breath. This was it. The core pitch. 'Bluntly, you're not. Insulated, I mean. Failure *means* failure, for you. It means the bottom dropping out and the *not insubstantial* loans you've taken out coming due. One serious job loss, one mistake, and it's all over for you. Back to where you came from, zero-hours contracts and pre-paid electricity meters and Tesco Value spaghetti.'

Tulloch snorted with what might have been disgust or recognition or both. He settled back on the bench.

'Lidl's better, these days,' he said, his face closed and impassive. 'So, you're offering, what? Security? A guarantee?'

Jeremy nodded. 'Yes. Repayment of your student loans, for a start, through a scholarship you'll be awarded.'

Jamie's eyes snapped up at that.

Got him. Time to reel him in.

'Then there's internship opportunities and graduate scheme places, after Stanford. And a safety net. Roles can be found for you, if the economy falls over again.'

'Money?' said Tulloch, eyes still on the gaggle of first-years across the quad.

'Not directly. But it will be a continuous stream of *opportunities* to make money. Bites at the cherry, if you like.'

'And what am I giving up?'

'A little freedom, in your relationships, mostly. Who you associate with and how close you get to them. Keeping online images of yourself to a minimum, to make the insertion process easier. If you agree to discuss this further with us, we'll take you to the Brecon Beacons for a weekend, lay it all out. Give you some . . . basic training so you can interact with us. If you don't want any part of it, I'll ask you to sign the Official Secrets Act regarding this approach, then you'll never hear from me again.'

Tulloch nodded slowly, tapping a finger against his chin. 'This is some offer you're making, Mr Brown. But I like to know who I'm actually dealing with. You gonna keep lying to me about your name?'

'Jeremy. It's Jeremy.' He held out a hand. 'Do you want to become a Legend, Jamie?'

The younger man clasped his hands and looked down at the flag-stones. There was a long moment of silence, punctuated only by another distant laugh from the dining hall.

Tulloch looked up and extended his hand. 'Aye, Jeremy. I think I do.'

4

Jamie

London: now

'So, what's next?'

Jamie swirled the dregs of his overpriced smoothie. One bench over, Tracksuit Gavin stretched luxuriously in a patch of dappled sunshine.

Terence stood up and tugged his jacket down. 'Come on, let's walk. You've got eighteen minutes left on your lunch break.'

Jamie gave a low chuckle. 'I haven't taken a full hour for lunch in years, Terence. Targets to hit.'

'Nothing to be proud of, young man,' said Terence. 'Poor time management. You don't get it back as credit on your next life, you know. And I say that as someone who's spent more of his life than he'd like sitting in cars, watching buildings.'

Jamie balled up his Pret bag and tossed it into a litter bin. Gavin rose silently as they passed, slotting in a few metres behind them.

'Is he armed?' said Jamie, flicking his head back towards their shadow.

'In central London? Are you mad? That'd be a very quick way to piss off SO19. And we're not authorised for that kind of thing on home turf anyway.'

Jamie glanced back again. 'But he knows, like, kung fu or something?'

Terence gave a small snort and shook his head. 'An extendable baton and a good strong right arm are all he needs, Jamie, believe me. He was mainly along to ensure you came here. Since it's strictly "leave no trace" on contacts these days.'

'Why is that, exactly?' said Jamie. They left the cemetery gate and turned towards Old Street roundabout, then cut across the road and down a side street, taking the long way back to the office.

'We always knew a digital history would be important, just not *quite* as pervasive as it's become. Even so, you're minimally online. Very few pictures, very few things we need to update, once you're activated. But it's still a bad idea to leave unnecessary footprints when we contact you. Texts you might forget to delete. Emails. Phone records. Speaking of which, we'll need you to ditch your personal phone here in London. We'll give your replacement one of his own and you'll hand over your work phone to him.'

Jamie rolled his shoulders, a chill blast of March air whistling down the street at their backs. He bit his lip. 'I've got a lot on. At work. What's going to happen with that?'

Terence nodded. 'Very diligent. But it won't be your problem. You're about to get an enquiry, from a company operating out of Kenya and Tanzania. Major manufacturer looking to modernise their enterprise resource planning. They're going to ask for you, specifically. Personal recommendation from someone they trust. Later today, you'll be asked to book yourself a flight to Dar es Salaam, in Tanzania. Lovely city. Maybe a month's initial trip, including some negotiations, a little light networking. It'll be a big contract. A career-maker. Fifteen facilities in two countries, a couple of hundred warehouse terminals, nearly a thousand hand scanners. A few follow-up trips required as well.'

'But I won't be there?'

'You will. Just not *you* personally. This is it, Jamie. Your chance to take that little backpacking trip we specifically told you *not* to take after Stanford. Off the grid, under an assumed name, for as long as we need you to be. I hear South America is extremely pleasant this time of year. A week from now you'll be in a hammock on Copacabana beach. Doesn't that sound lovely?'

Jamie walked on in silence for a moment. 'Would have been nice to do that when I was twenty-three.'

Terence *tsked* lightly. 'Don't look a gift horse in the mouth, Jamie. Enjoy the trip. You'll come back to a sizeable bonus and the congratulations of all your peers. And you'll have a tan that matches your story of being in East Africa for a month or two.'

'Never understood that phrase, "looking a gift horse in the mouth",' said Jamie, as they turned towards the office. 'If the Trojans *had* done that, they wouldn't have been caught by surprise.'

Terence smiled, lips thin. 'No tricks or hidden Greeks here, Jamie. Think of this as a little thank-you gift. A few weeks away from everything, no responsibilities, nobody asking anything of you. How many people get that in their lives, once they're in the daily grind? Damn few.'

Jamie nodded. 'I suppose so. It just feels . . . well, like an anticlimax. Almost thought you were never going to actually pull the trigger.'

'Oh, it was always coming, Jamie. Our mutual friend doesn't ever waste an asset,' said Terence, referring to the man Jamie had met only twice, the first time on that bench in the Old Court. The second time had been the long weekend in the Brecon Beacons, at a windswept farmhouse a mile from the nearest road.

'What about the deal?' Jamie asked as they turned the last corner, heading towards Jamie's office. 'If it's really that big, well, not everyone can deliver a deal like that. There's estimates to be done, commercial negotiations. My job is . . . well, you can't just drop into it.'

Terence smiled. 'This deal will be easier than most. We've arranged it that way – rush ISO certification. Bit of a fait accompli, since your company is the only real option they have. But the man who'll be using your identity has been studying up. He'll do what needs to be done.'

Terence reached into his jacket pocket and extracted a brown envelope, thick with paper. He handed it to Jamie. 'There's the details. We need you to connect through Charles de Gaulle, outside Paris. That's where you'll meet me and, briefly, GARNET.'

Jamie stopped and frowned. 'Garnet?'

'Your opposite number, that's his cryptonym. Code name. When you leave that airport, you'll be him and he'll be you. And you'll be off to beaches and hammocks and jungle trekking, while GARNET goes to Dar in your stead. He'll step into your shoes and nobody will be any the wiser.'

5

Jeremy

South Wales: June 2013

On the third day of Tulloch's induction briefing, the Americans arrived.

Jeremy Althrop waited at the end of the long, switchbacked road up to Y Bwthyn Glas – 'the blue cottage' – an SIS safehouse among the windswept mountains of the Brecon Beacons National Park.

It was mild and lightly breezy for the Brecons, the kind of spring day that the paratroopers, marines and special forces who trained nearby would dream of when they were halfway up Pen Y Fan in the more usual sideways rain.

Tulloch was inside, beginning to relax finally, running through the basics again with Bob Davis and Terence Stringer. Contact drills, essential countersurveillance, how to check he wasn't being followed.

A black Range Rover turned off the main road a mile down the valley, bumping and rolling up the tight turns leading to the cottage, roofline bobbing as it negotiated the potholes. No US embassy plates. So Alex was here unofficially. Interesting.

The Range Rover ground to a halt on the expanse of stone chips already half occupied by two SIS vehicles.

A dark-haired white woman in her mid-thirties stepped out and gave Jeremy a wide grin. Alexandra Bowen: a career field handler just like himself, but on the Yank side of the pond. They'd met in Lebanon in '06, both trying to extract their operatives from the slow-rolling clusterfuck at the southern border. Ad hoc cooperation there had turned into a series of joint operations elsewhere. Now she was here to witness exactly how the Legends Programme recruited its assets.

'Jeremy. Thought you said it was always raining in Wales?' she called, striding across the stone chips with a steady crunch of booted feet. She wore jeans and a chunky woollen sweater under a light jacket.

Jeremy returned her smile and they hugged on the steps of the cottage. 'Wonderful to see you, Alex. It usually is raining, to be fair. You just bring the sunshine wherever you go.'

Bowen punched him lightly on the arm. 'Good to see you, man. Wanna show me this new recruit of yours? You got him in the bag yet?'

Jeremy shook his head. 'Not quite. We sign the Act on the last day, once they have a . . . fuller understanding. Works best that way.'

She followed him inside to the low-ceilinged kitchen. An oak table dominated one side of the room, a cast-iron range the other. Bowen looked around her and shook her head.

'Why is everything so fucking charming over here? Even your safehouses are cute. When we're doing a debrief we get some tract home in the 'burbs.'

Jeremy smiled. 'Brits think a hundred miles is a long way . . .' he began.

'And Yanks think a hundred years is a long time,' Bowen finished. They both laughed. That joke, in a Beirut hotel bar, had broken the icy reserve between them. They'd been stuck together for three days while the Israelis shelled the border and had emerged from the experience as friends.

'Fair point. Guess I just like old shit. Must be why we're friends.'

Jeremy pantomimed offence, hands held up. 'Ouch. Tea, coffee?'

'Tea,' said Bowen, taking a seat at the battered oak table. 'What do I need to know before I meet this kid?'

Jeremy filled the kettle, then leaned back against the counter. 'Well, you know the basics. But it's essential to see the final bargain we make with these assets. They get a lot, but they give up a lot. And they're not *trained*. We're not investing in them, in the way we might with a field agent.'

Bowen looked thoughtful. 'I guess that was my next question. Why not just train these people up? Make 'em field agents?'

Jeremy shook his head. 'We can't. The cover has to be *perfect*. They have to have *real* careers. Real lives. None of the usual indicators that might point towards us. Unexplained absences, long training courses, encrypted comms.'

'Why this particular kid?'

Jeremy frowned, considering. 'Jamie? He's a bright spark with computers. Loves big, complicated problems. We're going to steer him into enterprise software development, I think. Give him the kind of industrial connections we can lean on in a decade or so.'

'How do you choose them? Are they . . . reliable?'

Jeremy filled two cups, steam rising.

'To a degree, they don't have to be. They sign the Act and we keep light tabs on them. But if they tell anyone or break our agreement in any other way, they're cut off. All the nice things go away. It's . . . a bit of a devil's bargain. Designed that way. We need them to stay in place for a long, long time, ten years at least, I'd guess. We only activated our first asset last year.'

Bowen nodded. 'And how'd that go?'

Jeremy smiled as he fished the tea bags out of the mugs, teaspoon clinking. 'Impeccably. Successful insertion, retrieval and re-entry. It went so smoothly the asset signed up for another five years. They got a month-long holiday on us; we got access to a target in China we'd have had zero chance with twenty years ago. So far as we can tell, the Guóānbù were none the wiser. Milk?'

Bowen nodded. She took the mug and stared through the steam for a long moment. The mention of Chinese state security had clearly struck a chord. 'I won't lie, Jeremy, the CIA is extremely interested in this approach. Can't confirm or deny what we're thinking, but I'm glad you agreed to let us take a peek. It'll help, a lot.'

Jeremy sipped his tea and smiled. 'Anything for our dear cousins over the water. Come on. They'll be finishing up. Time to make the last pitch.'

Jeremy walked through to the next room, Bowen close behind. The room was bare, only a dented aluminium table and six chairs, white-washed walls, flagstone floor. Tulloch was sitting at the far end, a folder of documents in front of him, looking a little dazed. It had been a busy weekend.

Terence Stringer looked up as they entered, then turned to the other man in the room, Davis, the street work specialist. Jeremy nodded to him, marvelling at just how nondescript a human could be. Davis was so blandly forgettable it was like he wasn't there. He looked like the manager of a deli counter in Nottinghamshire. Or a call centre in Leeds. He certainly didn't look like someone who could break your arm in sixteen different ways.

'That's us, Bob, thanks,' said Stringer.

Davis shook Tulloch's hand. 'Nice to meet you, Jamie,' he murmured, then slipped out of the room.

Jeremy sat down, Bowen beside him. 'Jamie, this is Elizabeth. She's here to observe.'

Tulloch's eyes darted to Bowen and back to Jeremy. 'Uh . . . okay,' he said softly.

Jeremy gave him a smile. 'Today's our last day. You now have some very basic field skills. Enough to work with Terence here, over the next few years. He'll be your main point of contact. It's likely you'll never see anyone else in this room again, including me. So, it's crunch time.'

Tulloch shifted in his chair. 'Seems like it.'

Jeremy pointed at the folder in front of him. 'You've read it all?'

Tulloch nodded. 'Aye. No serious relationships. No close friend-ships. As few pictures online as I can manage. Continue to *not* talk to my mother, which won't be difficult. Don't tell anyone about the programme. Don't try to use being in the programme to get out of trouble. In return, you lot are my benevolent secret fucking uncles.' He said it with a tight smile, but hesitance lay behind it.

'You can still walk away. But this is the last chance for that. Sign today and we'll begin developing a field agent. That takes time. It's a *commitment*. If you decide you're bored in five years' time, you're fucking us, and yourself. Do you understand that?'

Tulloch nodded. 'And you'll make life difficult for me.'

Jeremy nodded. 'Within the bounds of the law, of course. We'll remove all support. Place you on the watch list as a security threat, because you will be, with knowledge of this programme. No-fly list too. Probably tax investigations. Jury service citations arriving every other year. Difficulties renewing your library card. It's amazing how *inconvenient* life can be, if we want it to be.'

Tulloch waved a hand, the hesitance fading. 'Jeremy, you know enough about me to know this isn't a *sacrifice* for me. Not really. I like to be . . . by myself. This way I get to be who I am anyway *and* get a wee helping hand. A safety net, like you said. Sounds perfect.'

He said it with a hint of bravado, but Jeremy heard the resignation underneath it. He remembered that same conviction, in his early twenties, that he'd never figure some things out. Friendships. Relationships. It was precisely the emotion they relied upon, to recruit the Legends. He pushed down the guilt that he felt more keenly with each recruitment. Tulloch would get his rewards. And if Jeremy's own marriage was any guide, perhaps Tulloch was right. Maybe this life *would* be better for him.

Jeremy glanced at Alex, who was watching the young man with an unreadable intensity. She flicked her eyes to him and gave him a barely perceptible nod. She could see it now. The devil's bargain. How they got the assets on side and kept them on side.

'Well then,' said Jeremy, producing a pen from inside his jacket and sliding it across the table, 'make your mark, young man, then start your new life.'

6

Nicola

SIS Headquarters, Vauxhall Cross: now

The conference-room door opened with a hiss of air from the privacy seals. Nicola Ellis looked up from the laptop in front of her and half stood out of her chair.

'Sit, please sit,' said Stephanie Salisbury, her section chief, smiling benevolently. 'Nicola, this is Jeremy Althrop. I'm sure you're aware of his reputation.'

Nicola leaned across the table and shook Althrop's hand. His palms were warm and whisper-dry, like shaking hands with a leather couch. He smiled and gave her a small nod. He was in his early fifties, she guessed, slightly greying hair in an elegant side-part, a sport coat and blue shirt, open at the neck. A field man, once.

'Nice to meet you, Nicola. I've certainly heard of *you*,' he said.

She sat back in her chair and closed her laptop, neck prickling. 'I'm afraid you have me at a disadvantage,' she said. 'I didn't get an agenda for this meeting.'

'Stephanie tells me you have extensive experience in Sub-Saharan Africa, particularly Kenya, Tanzania, Somalia, Ethiopia and the CAR,' said Althrop. 'You were part of that business in Nairobi last year, correct?'

Nicola nodded, eyes flicking to Salisbury. She gave a small wave of the hand. 'Jeremy is cleared for all of that,' she said, smile never wavering.

Nicola took a sip of water, remembering the dusty go-down in Embakasi where they'd found the crates. Shots ringing out in pre-dawn light. The dead civilian. She swallowed the water and nodded, but her mouth stayed dry.

'Yes, sir. I was. Some deeply unpleasant people trying to sell an S-300. Fell off the back of a Black Sea transport, during the Russian withdrawal. We nailed them in the city and traced them back to the drop-off in Embakasi. Rolled up a disconcerting amount of heavy-duty hardware apparently destined for mercenaries in Bangui. Dregs of the Vityaz Group.'

'So you've come across Vityaz before?'

Nicola nodded. She'd never considered herself a violent person before Vityaz. But afterwards, during the interrogations, she'd have happily shot most of them in the face. And that was just from what they'd admitted to doing in the Central African Republic. Never mind Ukraine. 'They're . . . pieces of work, sir.'

A police siren wailed past on the Albert Embankment. Even through the blast-proof glass that faced the river, she heard the pulse of the city outside.

'We're targeting them, as part of a larger operation. We want you to run one of our Legend assets.'

Nicola widened her eyes. She'd been on the edges of a couple of Legend ops. But never primary. Never in the hot seat. 'On my patch?'

Althrop smiled and nodded. 'Correct. We've just activated one of our Legends. He's heading for Dar in the next couple of days, but on the way he'll switch out with an operative, callsign GARNET. We want you to be GARNET's field handler. You know the ground. You've got the local contacts and the experience.'

Nicola glanced at Salisbury. The smile was still there, but the older woman raised a single eyebrow, just a fraction. This was something big. The next step up from the gun-running and anti-piracy ops of the last few years. Perhaps even a chance to come back to London more often. To Rachael. If they ever spoke again, after last time.

She pushed down the thought. 'What's the target?'

'You'll be investigating one of the primary buyers of Vityaz services in East Africa. Specifically, one Arkady Bocharov.'

Nicola narrowed her eyes. 'Ex-FSB. Ran Wagner units in Ukraine?'

Althrop looked impressed. 'You've heard of him?'

She nodded. 'He ran a lot of guys through the bush wars in the CAR, before and after Bakhmut. When your primary patch is the illegal arms trade, the same ugly bastards pop up again and again.'

Althrop conceded the point with a nod. 'He's come a long way since he was "managing" the morale in the Donetsk trench lines. All the reshuffling in Moscow has given him some pretty prime money-spinners. He's the recently installed chairman of the Ulan Manufacturing Concern, UPK in Russian. Steel and precision component manufacturers. Big investors in East Africa.'

Nicola nodded. 'I know UPK. We've had an eye on some of their container shipments for a long time. Nothing concrete yet, but they ship a lot of heavy-duty hardware. A lot of which could be weaponised.'

Althrop nodded. 'You'll be backstopping GARNET's infiltration of his inner circle. Bocharov is living the Instagram lifestyle on Zanzibar, mainly, with some trips to Dar. He's relocated to Tanzania and he's nominally in charge of all of UPK's East African operations. But we think he's doing something else.'

'How is GARNET making the approach? Does his Legend counterpart have some kind of connection?'

Althrop nodded. 'Of a sort. Senior sales for a major vendor of warehouse management and manufacturing plant software. We've leaned on a few sources to push for a major overhaul. He needs it done quickly to comply with some new ISO regulations his numbers people forgot to tell him about.'

'But something else is going on?'

Althrop nodded. 'We think so. Bocharov's compound on Zanzibar has had a *lot* of visitors in the last month. It's building up to something. But we don't know what.'

Back to Tanzania, then. It had been a while, since the gun-runners and pirates had kept her so busy further north. But Dar was her turf too, though she hadn't worked deep cover there before. Only a few days at most. Nothing like this. 'I'll need a lot of context on Bocharov. Full work-up on the compound and analysis on what GARNET might be walking into. Most of my ops have been shorter. Street moves. Rooftop OPs, that sort of thing.'

Althrop grinned. 'Mine too. But sometimes you have to actually get in a room with these guys. Look them in the eye. And with your help, that's exactly what GARNET will do.'

'And GARNET – who is he? What's his background?'

Jeremy smiled. 'William Price, thirty-six years old, twelve years in the Service. He's been assigned to this Legend for the last ten, building his knowledge. On other ops of course in the meantime, but he was one of our best people in Belarus and Ukraine before and during the war. Fluent Russian. Three years in the Rifles, made captain at twenty-five, then he was late-entry Foreign Office fast-track, before we got our hands on him.'

Nicola nodded. 'I've heard the name. Not my patch, but he's got a good rep and we've overlapped on some Russian arms-smuggling ops.'

Althrop slid a USB stick across the conference table. 'This should get you started. Basic mission package. We'll get a full work-up to you by the time you're on task.'

Nicola slotted the stick into her laptop. 'And the civilian? Where will he be?'

'Nowhere near Dar es Salaam or Zanzibar. You'll get an outline on him too, of course, in case you need to support GARNET with a particular detail. But he'll be off the board. Enjoying a little trip, well away from both of you.'

Nicola finished copying the stick, then closed her laptop. 'Good. Nothing worse than collateral risk.'

Althrop stood and held out his hand again. 'Thank you, Nicola. I'm happy to put GARNET in your hands for this operation.'

Nicola stood too. 'I appreciate the opportunity. I'll keep him out of trouble for you.'

Althrop gave her hand one last firm shake, then dipped his head. 'I'm rather hoping Bocharov will be the one who ends up in trouble. But we'll see what GARNET digs up.'

7

Jamie

London: now

Terence's envelope nestled in his jacket pocket all afternoon. When the email about the 'Tanzania opportunity' came from his Head of Sales, he spent more time than he should have trying to inject his reply with the right tone of surprised enthusiasm.

Now, at home, sitting at his six-seater kitchen table, he opened the packet and spread it all out in front of him.

They'd thought of everything.

There was a suggested packing list, all he might need for a month in Tanzania. Well, not him. Whoever would be picking his case up off the luggage carousel in Dar es Salaam.

Next was a map of Charles de Gaulle airport. The location of the airside toilet where he'd meet Terence and GARNET was marked with a slash of red Sharpie. Someone had written at the bottom of the map in block capitals, using the same pen:
BURN AFTER READING

Jamie held the map in front of him, trying to fix the corridors and escalators and shops in his mind, the ranks of seats, the gate numbers.

What would it be like to look into the face of a man who was going to pretend to be him? Would it be like having a twin you'd never met?

With the map was a set of instructions. Transit times. The meeting point. A code to knock on the door. The start and end of his handover window.

The rest of the packet was about afterwards. Onward flight itinerary, starting in Brazil. Backstory documents for his new name, Paul McKenzie. A battered copy of the Lonely Planet guide for South America. The same red Sharpie slashes highlighted items he was supposed to destroy.

He pored over the documents, trying to take them in. Paul McKenzie had led a life similar to his own, though with a lot more travel. There was enough of an overlap that Jamie felt like he could answer the kind of casual questions that might come up in a hostel or a bar or on a long bus ride. He'd travelled a little, before Cambridge. But never for long. Never getting close to anyone.

Jamie sighed and piled up the documents in a ceramic Ikea salad bowl. He opened a window, then lit each document, watching it burn down to curling ash.

He laid the packing list out on his bed and followed it to the letter, carefully rolling shirts and khakis into packing cubes. Would these clothes fit GARNET? Had they found someone so like him he could shrug on his shirts, stride out of the lobby of his hotel and simply *be* him? What was Jamie, really? A digital shell, ready to be inhabited by someone else. An empty glove, waiting for the hand of an agent to fill it.

Once he was packed, he sat at the kitchen table and looked around the elegant marble countertops and brass taps of his refurbished kitchen. There was always music playing in here, the coffee machine gurgling in the mornings before he left for work, laptop and keys waiting where he'd left them the night before. Always movement and life. Sometimes a glass of wine. Two, if he'd met someone. But never for long.

The life of Jamie Tulloch had to be real, but limited in scope. Verifiable, but not vibrant. GARNET could not afford to be outed by a casual acquaintance, cover blown by a photo from a birthday party or a night out. The only photos online were his LinkedIn profile, with sunglasses of course. A picture on the company website on the 'Our Team' page. A single slightly blurry image of a talk he gave once at a sales conference. He was a ghost inside his own life, alive but barely there.

It had been this way since Cambridge, then Stanford afterwards. He'd drifted through both of those great institutions with barely a ripple. Money slowly accreted in his bank accounts like stalagmites growing from the dark, cold floor of his life. He donated some to charity. He read expensive, leather-bound books, listened to rare vinyl, went away on the odd trip on his own, but mostly he worked and he slept and he spent his time in this simulacrum of a life, this kitchen with the radio always quietly playing.

If he didn't have the murmuring voices there, he was fairly certain he wouldn't be able to stand it.

Packed and ready, Jamie turned on the television and stared at it for a while, then stood up and paced the length of his lounge, eyes sweeping across the six-seater couch and out to the darkened city beyond. He ran a finger along the shelves of records, the Bang & Olufsen stereo that cost more than a small car, the leaves of the beautiful houseplants he paid someone else to water and tend.

What if he never came back? Just stepped out of his life for good. Would anyone notice? His mother might notice, when her semi-annual guilt-trip emails bounced back. He hadn't been home for the better part of eight years, not since the last argument. There was nobody else.

He sat down and looked at his packed case, lined up neatly beside the sofa, thrumming with possibility. He'd have the chance to withdraw from the programme after this, to live a different life, without the restrictions he had agreed to as a much younger man. They might ask him to keep going, if the mission went well. But all these years later, he wasn't sure the bargain had been worth it.

What if he'd walked away from that bench in the Old Court? Who might he have become? One thing he knew for certain – if he *had* walked away, he wouldn't have this ashy aftertaste in his mouth every day, the constant doubt that he was worth anything at all. He would have stood or fallen on his own.

It was time to see who he really was. All he had to do was walk into Charles de Gaulle as himself and walk out again as someone else. Then he'd be free, for a few weeks or months, to assess his own life from the outside.

A gift. A fresh start. A real life.

He checked his watch. Eight p.m. His flight wasn't until early morning the next day. But the sooner he slept, the sooner he would be free of this.

He lay on his bed for some time before sleep eventually took him.

8

Nicola

Dar es Salaam, Tanzania: now

Julius Nyerere International was near-empty when the overnight flight from Cairo landed two hours before sunrise. Nicola Ellis swept through the Arrivals terminal with nothing but her usual small backpack, bypassing the exhausted backpackers clustered around the silent luggage carousels.

She slipped through border control with muttered Kiswahili pleasantries, hand on her heart and head bowing with polite nods. Smiles and swift stamps of her cover passport, then 'Karibu Tanzania' as she stepped through into the half-dawn of the terminal.

Nicola sidestepped the gauntlet of cab drivers at the Arrivals gate with more polite nods and the ritual call and answer. 'Mnaendeleaje?' She left with a dozen calls of 'Vizuri' in her wake.

Ali was waiting for her just beyond the cab rank, engine running. She slid into the back seat and groped for her water bottle, sweat already prickling at the nape of her neck. Ali pulled out, swiftly joining the flow of traffic on the T24. Dar stretched away, low and bright under the purpling sky.

'Anything, at the airport?'

'Nothing, mukubwa. I was there since midnight. Nobody watching.'

She sipped from her water. It was already warm and tasted faintly of metal. 'And at the hotel?'

'Nothing there either. Kanai was there yesterday, all day. Nobody came.'

She leaned forward and palmed a handful of US dollars into Ali's hand. He glanced down, then back up at her, his smile broad in the mirror.

'I appreciate your efforts, as always, Ali,' she said. 'Hotel Samora, then. Let's see if we can get there before sun-up.'

Ali's eyes drifted back to the road and he gave a slow nod, then tugged the bill of his baseball cap down a little and shifted up a gear. Nicola suppressed a smile, then checked her field phone.

Nothing from London yet. The asset wouldn't be here for some time. She had time to check out UPK's offices, circle their hotels. Drink a lot of very strong homegrown coffee. Then she'd be ready to shadow GARNET as he made his approach, standing by to extract him, or the intelligence he was gathering, or both.

Ali came off the highway and turned down Samora Avenue. The call to prayer echoed across the city as the mosques began their day. Soon enough they were on busy streets, figures moving in the half-light, their clothes white and pale yellow and dark, kanzu tunics and skull caps and long, colourful patterned shirts. The foot traffic thickened as they crawled along until they reached her hotel.

Nicola gave Ali's shoulder a light squeeze and threw him another quick smile, then slung her bag over her shoulder and stepped out into the damp heat, dust and traffic fumes of the city.

She was across the pavement and up the steps of the Samora before the doorman had fully roused himself, but he gave her a short bow and opened the door with a sweep of the hand. At the polished wooden expanse of the reception desk, her key was waiting for her, as always.

Usually, she would avoid staying in the same place too many times. But her diplomatic cover as Kate Askwith, a field officer for the Foreign Office, meant a degree of comfortable routine was expected. She hid in plain sight, moving around the city from meeting to meeting, dropping in at the High Commission. The identity fit her well. She had to be watchful, but it was a small reassurance to stay in the same room, to nod to the same people each time she landed in the city.

She found herself thinking of these places, her cover identities, as the fixed points her life rotated around now. The flat in Wandsworth certainly wasn't any more, especially this last time. At least they'd finally had the argument. Rachael had had enough. And Nicola found she could hardly blame her.

She showered and changed into khaki trousers and a light shirt, then repacked her bag with everything she'd need for her day on the streets of Dar.

Nicola opened the double doors and stepped out on to a tiny balcony overlooking the street. The sun was a thin yellow line, still half hidden among the rooftops and minarets of downtown Dar, the sky a whiteish blue as night quickly faded. Wisps of high cloud would be gone in a few moments as the sunlight began to bake the city. Across the street she saw shutters rolling up, skull-capped youths leaning on doorframes, tapping on the screens of their mobile phones.

Another day in Dar.

One day to prepare the field. Less time than she'd like. More than she needed.

9

Jamie

Charles de Gaulle Airport, Paris: now

Jamie started awake as the Airbus tyres screeched on the runway. Cabin lights flickered on, engines roaring. His weight shifted forward as the aeroplane braked heavily.

The sleep that had eluded him at home had crashed over him in a wave as soon as he'd boarded. A different flight, it turned out. He'd woken at four in the morning and stared at his packed bags for a while, then decided he'd rather wait at the airport. When he tried to check in, the woman on the desk had frowned apologetically.

'This plane is no longer flying. It is cancelled.'

Jamie's stomach had dropped, but her bright smile had swiftly re-assured him. 'You are here *very* early though. There is another flight in one hour. I will put you on this one. You will have longer stop in Paris, but this is okay?'

Relief washed through him. 'Yes, that's absolutely fine. More than fine. Time for a French espresso.' She'd smiled as she printed a fresh ticket and slapped it on the counter.

Now they were landing, an hour before he'd planned to be in Paris. He wiped his face and stared out of the tiny window by his elbow. The grey morning light was half masked by sweeping curtains of rain.

A few people began to get up, unbuckling and muttering to each other about transfers and trains in French and German and Spanish.

Eventually he heard the whump and hiss of opening doors and people began to file out of the cabin, business class first. At the door, the steward's eyes passed over him as though he wasn't there, a perfunctory 'Merci' dropping from his lips as Jamie shuffled past.

The jetway was already mostly clear. A couple of rumpled business-men lingered, heads bent over phones as they caught up on emails and alerts, suit jackets hanging from their arms, wheeled bags pulled in tight by their feet.

In the terminal itself, most of the coffee shops, tabacs and duty-free electronics stores were still closed, shutters rolled down. One kiosk was doing a brisk trade in espressos, a queue already forming.

The meeting point was at the other end, a broad curve of glass and steel. Here and there small groups of early travellers sat hunched over laptops or curled up with headphones in. Some were trying to sleep, jackets balled up as pillows or laid across shoulders to fend off the chill of the mostly empty terminal.

Should he go straight there? He was pretty early. Yesterday, Terence had patted his arm gently. 'Just follow the directions. Plenty of time, so don't rush. We've got a good two hours and it's the same terminal, so all you need to do is find us, make the handoff, then walk away. We'll take care of the rest.'

The two-hour margin was more like three now. But there wasn't any harm in taking a look, to see if Terence had already arrived. Perhaps even GARNET would be there. Doing some kind of complicated spy things, no doubt. More terms rose out of his hazy memories of Wales. Countersurveillance. Back-checks. Front-running. Not that he'd need any of that on a beach somewhere in South America.

The slight curve of the building meant he didn't see the sign for the washrooms until he was quite close. He fingered the key in his pocket. How on earth Terence had come into possession of a French airport toilet master key, Jamie had no idea. A bribe, perhaps. Or maybe that was just the kind of thing you could get your hands on, if you were a spy.

At the washrooms, there was nobody around, hallway empty and echoing. LED lights glared.

He felt a twisting thrill in the pit of his stomach. Jamie ran his thumb over the serrated edge of the key, scanning the beige toilet doors, looking for the correct one. He hadn't felt like this since that first and only weekend in Wales, the lonely farmhouse.

He turned another corner, a few paces beyond the main male toilets.

There. Toilettes Accessibles. The door was closed, the lock flipped to red. Occupé.

Jamie looked left and right along the narrow corridor. No cameras he could see. He had to be quick.

He leaned against the wall and rapped on the door, three quick knocks, a pause, two slow. He caught himself smirking a little. Secret knocks and codes. Like a child's game.

No response. Maybe he *was* too early. The rendezvous window didn't start for another forty-five minutes.

It wouldn't hurt to check. If there was nobody inside yet, he'd go and get a coffee. Clear his head a little.

He slid the key into the lock and looked left and right one more time, then turned it with a loud snick. The heavy wooden door, faced in more beige laminate, sagged a little as the tension of the lock released. He stepped inside.

Blood shone dully in the glare of the LED lights. Flat, lifeless eyes gazed at him.

Jamie's hand slipped from the door handle with sudden perspiration. He turned around, facing the door, his breath hitching in his throat, then shoved it closed. He twisted the lock, heart hammering, blood hissing in his ears. Up close, the veneer of the door was scuffed and worn, hundreds of hands polishing it smooth near the handle.

Jamie took a long, shuddering inhalation, suddenly aware he'd stopped breathing for a moment. He closed his eyes, opened them again, then pushed himself away from the door and turned around.

Terence Stringer was dead.

He was slumped back against the rear tiled wall, one shoulder jammed awkwardly against the sink, the other lower down, in a parody of a shrug. Blood pooled under him, his shirt soaked with it.

His eyes were open, mouth slightly ajar, as though he was calling out. But the pallor of his skin, the perfect stillness, told Jamie that his main contact with the Legends Programme was definitely dead.

His throat had been cut, a ragged slash from ear to ear. The wound was dark with sticky, half-dried blood, the tiles around him spattered with a few drops of spray.

There was a pervasive smell of blood, metallic and hot, sliding in under the floral tones of toilet cleaner and air freshener. It felt oppressive in the tiny, self-contained bathroom, air-conditioning units pumping in a steady flow of warm air.

The air-freshener unit on the wall bleeped and sighed, spraying a fresh dose of chemical scent into the cramped space.

His stomach churned. Terence continued to lie there, eerily, perfectly still.

Jamie doubled over and vomited into the toilet, turning his head away from the sight of the dead man in the corner, his stomach clenching and unclenching.

Once he was finished, he scrabbled for tissues from the dispenser and wiped his mouth, then slumped back against the wall, as far away as he could get from the body. His head fizzed, a solid scream of unanswerable questions.

For a little while, he went away, inside his head. He leaned against the wall, fistfuls of hair in his hands, moaning softly. What the *fuck* was he doing here? He hadn't agreed to this. To a dead man on a toilet floor. To the acrid sting of bile in the back of his throat. His eyes roved across the tiles, following the lines, looking anywhere but the body.

He took a breath. Another one.

Okay. He was in *deep* shit.

Should he walk out of the airport, take his chances on the streets of Paris? Try and get back to London? The return ticket he was supposed to hand to GARNET was for a flight in just under a month, from Dar. If he went to the ticket desk, he'd leave a record, CCTV, ticket changes. That would invite questions, and questions meant suspicion. The same if he went through passport control, tried to get back on the Eurostar.

Should he wait here, find GARNET? Try and do the handover? Clearly something had happened. *Someone* was following him, or following Terence, or both of them. They were compromised. There had been drills, things he'd been taught in Wales. How to break contact if he was recognised by an acquaintance. How to leave a chalk signal on a particular wall in Finsbury Park that meant 'don't approach, come back in a week'. There had even been notes in the file Terence had given him, about what to do if he saw the same chalk mark at the airport. But there had been nothing about what to do if he found himself locked in a toilet with the corpse of his only contact.

Could he go to airport security? Report what he'd found? He couldn't see that ending anywhere except an interrogation room then a French jail cell. If Jamie claimed to be part of a secret government programme, SIS would deny all knowledge. They'd made that clear, in the Welsh cottage. It's not like he had a contact number for SIS, or for the man he knew only as Jeremy. His only contact with the programme since that weekend in Wales had been through Terence. The man lying a metre or so away, in a pool of his own blood.

Christ, could he . . . could he google a phone number for SIS? Call for help somehow? Fill in a contact form on the website? How exactly *do* you get in touch with spies when the only one you actually know properly is dead?

Where was GARNET? Was he dead too? The agent would have Jamie's world trip luggage, his backpacker clothes, the passport in the name of Paul McKenzie, ready to exchange. But if GARNET wasn't here, Jamie was locked inside his own life, trundling towards a destination he'd never been intended to reach.

Dar es Salaam.

Maybe he could go there. GARNET must have contacts, people who were supposed to meet him. Maybe Jamie could warn them that someone had killed Terence. That Legends was compromised. Maybe GARNET was already there, could protect him somehow, get him home.

Maybe . . . maybe the only way out was through.

He felt a brief, absurd stab of disappointment that all of this might have been for nothing. That the slow cultivation of an entire life wouldn't, in the end, make the difference that Althrop had told him it would.

But he wanted to live. And maybe he could warn SIS.

First, he had to get clear of Charles de Gaulle airport. And that meant getting out of this blood-soaked bathroom without being spotted.

Then he had to go to Dar. Every other option tied him back to this dead body, lying there like the lead weight at the end of a fishing line, ready to drag him under.

10

Nicola

Dar es Salaam: now

The offices of UPK, Arkady Bocharov's company, were on a side street to the north of Samora Avenue. It was the kind of place that could be difficult to observe, simply because the quarters were so tight and the eyes so many.

Nicola eventually found a café with outside seating that extended just far enough to give her a view of UPK's front door.

Awnings stretched across the pavement, rustling a little in the mid-morning breeze. Vehicles muttered past in the flat, dusty light of mid-morning.

It took nearly an hour before she saw anything worth noting. She had waved off three offers of safari tours to the Serengeti or Kilimanjaro, the guides leaving her alone after she responded in fluent Kiswahili. Eventually the silent, white-shirted waiter began steadily supplying another coffee almost the second she put down the empty cup, whisking away the previous one as she muttered 'Shukrani' in his wake. She was mulling a trip to the toilet inside when two black Toyotas swung into the side street and pulled over.

Russians. You could spot them a mile off in Africa. Especially the ex-military ones, shaved heads red under baseball caps, jackets hanging oddly. If these weren't Vityaz mercenaries, she'd eat her sun-bleached hat.

Nicola leaned slightly over, getting a better angle. She picked up her point-and-shoot camera and fiddled with it, playing the part of an oblivious tourist. The mercenaries scanned the street with bored indifference, heads turning behind black Ray-Bans and Oakleys.

Nicola zoomed in slowly, glancing back to check the position of the waiter. He was busy serving another customer, so she took the risk of zooming in a little further, slumping back in her chair and angling the camera down the street.

The back door of the second Toyota swung open and a heavy-set older man in safari vest and khaki trousers clambered out.

Bocharov. He was in his mid-fifties, head shaved like his men. Unlike them, he was deeply tanned, clearly enjoying the benefits of his African sojourn.

The guards braced themselves as Bocharov swept his eyes across the street, backs straightening, eyes snapping front. Even after so many years out of the FSB and the killing fields of Donetsk, he still inspired both loyalty and fear.

On the other side a tall, slim figure in black emerged. Thinning dark hair, small round glasses, a sallow, hollow-cheeked face that had clearly not been in Tanzania long.

Nicola inhaled sharply as she peered down at the screen of her camera. She had to make sure. No question, once she'd zoomed in, as the dark-haired man loped around the back of the Toyota and followed Bocharov inside the building. Yevgeny Olenev, one of the most prolific arms dealers and private military contractors operating in and around the Black Sea.

But he was way the hell off his patch. And apparently operating alongside his main competitor.

Nicola sat back and finished her coffee, frowning into the middle distance. The waiter silently provided another small cup, and she took it gratefully. She was going to need the caffeine.

What the hell was Yevgeny Olenev doing in Tanzania?

II

Jamie

Charles de Gaulle Airport: now

Twice, just as he was about to open the door and slip out, Jamie froze at the sound of approaching footsteps. While he waited, channelling half-remembered spy films, he steeled himself to search Terence's pockets, just in case there was something he could use.

He searched quickly, trying not to look at the man's face, conscious of the still, slack weight of Terence's limbs. Nothing. No wallet, no passport, no phone. Just an anonymous body, stripped of everything but his clothes.

Another moment of silence stretched outside the door. Time to go.

Jamie stepped out, pulled the door tightly shut and fumbled the maintenance key into the lock, damp hands slipping. He blinked a couple of times as he tried to force the key over, suddenly thinking about fingerprints, about evidence. But it was too late for any of that. The lock snicked home with a cold finality, imprisoning the horrible, visceral truth of Terence and that ear-to-ear black-encrusted gash.

Someone was just turning the corner, a young businesswoman in a skirt suit, neat roller case rumbling behind her. She wore headphones, eyes on the phone in her hand. She didn't look up as they passed each other.

Jamie concentrated on putting one foot in front of the other, vision narrowed to the pale polished concrete under his feet, flecks of mica glittering in the harsh LED light.

He reached the end of the bathroom corridor and looked along the broad sweep of the terminal building. Far more people now, arranged in ranks at each gate, pacing up and down, gazing at the departure monitors.

He could still give himself up. But he'd already fled the scene. He'd locked the body of a murder victim in a toilet in a French airport.

A lingering distrust boiled up from his teenage years, the stab-vested, black-uniformed men and women who had haunted his housing estate. He'd had a friend once, briefly, back in Cambridge, a cheerful rugby player called Tim from somewhere in Surrey. He remembered watching in astonishment one day as his friend simply walked up to a copper in the town centre and asked him for directions. For Tim, police were bastions, figures of authority and assistance, standing ready to guide and support and protect. Not simply the biggest, best-equipped gang on the block.

No. Absolutely no way he was putting himself in the hands of the cops. Especially not *French* cops. Without even a common language to smooth his explanations, he'd be banged up within ten minutes.

Jamie kept walking. Hundreds of people, most wholly absorbed in their own small worlds, just the phone or food or book or laptop screen in front of them. The few that were looking around stared briefly as he passed, but their eyes slid over him and straight to the next moving point of interest.

He blinked, suddenly aware of how he was walking. Jerky and nervous, head darting. He took a slow, shaky breath.

The inhalation slowed him down, oxygen lighting up the deeper cognitive patterns that seeing a corpse had shut down so comprehensively.

He took a seat in a quiet corner of the terminal. He'd been on the ground for forty-five minutes. There was still over two hours until the flight to Dar departed, via Istanbul. Two hours in which someone might open that bathroom door. But maybe Terence had taken care of that, ensured they would be left undisturbed for the handover. If he stayed where he was, tried to blend in as a bored business traveller, perhaps he could make it.

He rubbed at his eyes, hiding the tremor in his hands with fidgety movement. Now that he was clear of immediate danger, his brain began to fire questions at him.

Where the hell was GARNET? They were in the handover window now, but there was no sign of him. If he was watching nearby, surely he would have approached Jamie by now, given him some sort of signal. He had to be delayed, missing or maybe even dead just like Terence.

More to the point, was the murderer still in the airport? Why hadn't they stayed with the body, waited for Jamie to arrive, then done him in as well? What were they trying to achieve?

He spun out theories, testing and discarding, the way he might do for a particularly thorny client-requirements document. It calmed him, somehow, the logical exercises giving him something to focus on that wasn't his own thudding heartbeat or slippery palms.

Perhaps they wanted to see where Jamie went, to follow him? Maybe the killer was a novice who'd panicked and made a run for it after their first killing. Perhaps this was even some horrific coincidence, a mugging gone wrong, a case of mistaken identity. He shook his head. Not many muggers in airports, you absolute lemon.

The departure boards ticked over slowly, minutes sliding by at a glacial pace. Finally, his flight number came up on the screens, then inched its way towards the top.

Perhaps fifty people waited at the gate, a mixture of Western business travellers, backpackers and Tanzanians heading home, all looking equally exhausted. The red-jacketed Turkish Airlines staff clustered at the check-in desk. Weary travellers looked up expectantly.

Jamie kept walking. As the panic receded, some of the lessons from his trip to the Brecon Beacons resurfaced. He needed to do a back-check, look for someone following him who might try to board the same flight. Keep watching for anyone who might be watching him.

Would they try to kill him in the air? Bring down the whole flight? Surely not. Surely there were limits to what they might do to murder a moderately successful technical sales manager?

Why had they done this? Did it have something to do with UPK, who Jamie was supposed to meet? They were some kind of high-end precision component manufacturer, website full of stock photography of ball bearings and shiny cylinders. Why would that lead to a murder in an airport?

Jamie reached the other end of the terminal and bought a bottle of water from a tabac. Then he doubled back, looking for anyone trailing behind. Nothing. Certainly nobody obvious like the tracksuited minder who had flushed him out like a rabbit just yesterday. Where was that minder now? Why had Terence been unprotected? Was there *another* body in a janitorial cupboard somewhere? Was this airport just full of dead British field operatives?

He reached the gate and sat down, hands clenching and unclenching. He could still leave. He was out of the bathroom now. Maybe he could tell the ticket people he was sick, that he had to go back to London on the next flight. Maybe they wouldn't tie him back to the body, or SIS could help him out somehow. A lot of maybes. But he'd be home and safe. He could walk up to reception tomorrow at the big building by the Thames he'd seen in James Bond films, ask for someone called Jeremy, explain who he was and exactly how much trouble he might be in.

Jamie closed his eyes. As soon as he did, he saw Terence's face, the open, staring eyes, flat and dead. Quite unlike the flashing, avuncular, friendly eyes he'd grown used to over the past decade or more. It occurred to him then that Terence Stringer was probably the closest thing he'd had to a real friend, in all those years since Wales. And now he was dead. And if Jamie did nothing, if he ran away, well, then maybe more people would die. Including a man who happened to look like him, who should be sitting right where Jamie was.

He couldn't do it. He had to warn them.

When the tannoy announced the flight, Jamie stood and joined the priority queue. A bored flight attendant gave him a tight smile and flicked his eyes over Jamie's passport. Jamie slipped past and on to the jetway, shoulders dropping a little.

He glanced back. Two people were looking at him. A young Black woman with two children in tow and a small herd of roller cases. Her gaze flicked to the next person on the jetway.

Five people back from the young family, a gaunt, shaven-headed white man in a black raincoat lingered, gaze fixed on Jamie. He caught the returning gaze and snapped his eyes away, back to the front of the queue.

The killer, or just someone embarrassed at being caught staring? Jamie clenched and unclenched his fists, his feet carrying him on automatic towards the aircraft's hatch and his seat. He sat down, belted himself in, gripped his bag tightly on his lap.

The others filed aboard, agonisingly slowly. Jamie stared out of the window at the shining wet asphalt of the flight apron. He'd been in Paris less than three hours, but his entire life had been flipped on its head.

The young family passed him, then, a few moments later, the gaunt man in the raincoat. He glanced at Jamie with little curiosity as he passed. Jamie tracked the man's progress until he disappeared behind the standard-class partition.

Maybe the gaunt man was just some guy, boarding a plane, whose eyes had lingered a little too long on someone having the most para-noid airport transfer of his entire life.

Jamie looked down at his hands, clenched tightly around his bag, knuckles whitening. He relaxed them and took another long, shudder-ing breath. The pilot murmured something incomprehensible over the intercom, then the flight attendants swung the aircraft's doors closed with soft thumps.

He'd done it. He was getting away from Terence, dead on the tiled floor.

Maybe it was going to be okay.

Well, for at least as long as it took to get to Dar es Salaam.

Part Two

MISTAKEN IDENTITY

12

Nicola

Dar es Salaam: now

Bocharov was inside the offices of UPK for nearly three hours. After the first hour, Nicola used one of her burners to call in Ali.

He pulled over just down the street from the café, tucking his battered white Toyota behind a delivery truck. Nicola recognised the vehicle a moment before her throwaway Nokia buzzed with a single-word text message.

ARRIVED

She paid the waiter and left a tip in line with her cover as a diplomatic officer on expenses. He gave her a small smile and a nod as he cleared the table.

The back of Ali's car was blessedly cool. Nicola felt the light sheen of sweat on her neck and forehead begin to evaporate almost as soon as she slid on to the leather seat.

'Thanks, Ali,' she said, peeling off a couple more bills from the stack inside her cover wallet. Ali Omary was a good guy and a reliable driver. She paid him enough that he always turned up when she needed him and kept her abreast of what was happening in the street life of Tanzania's largest city. But she needed to keep the money coming.

Ali leaned back and smiled at her. 'What now, boss?' he asked in Kiswahili.

'We wait, my friend. I'm interested in the fellows currently inside that building. Let's see where they go.'

Ali nodded and they lapsed into a companionable silence, broken only by the low beat of a zenji flava track that Nicola didn't recognise. She'd spent so many hours on ops with local drivers she had briefly prided herself on an encyclopaedic knowledge, for a white Westerner, of Tanzanian and Kenyan pop. But it had been a while.

Fifteen tracks later, plus at least half an hour of Kiswahili in-jokes by the morning DJs that made both her and Ali snort quietly, there was a flurry of movement.

The bodyguards emerged first. Ali clicked his tongue against his teeth and jerked his head towards the building.

'Hao ni watu wa Urusi,' he said.

Nicola smiled. Just like she had, Ali had picked out the Russian mercenaries instantly. 'Ndiyo, Warusi,' she replied.

The Vityaz gunmen formed a tactical square in the street, two either side of the door, two at each corner of the black Toyota. She saw one merc turn towards the café, eyes scanning behind his aviators. If she'd still been sitting there, would the Vityaz thug have taken note?

After a moment, the one closest to the door spoke into a hand-held radio. Bocharov emerged. He'd changed his clothes, swapping the safari vest and trousers for a light linen suit. It was cut too tightly for his bulky frame, but he carried it off with the same brutal confidence he'd shown in the trenches of Donetsk. Nicola remembered footage from the closing stages of the war, Bocharov standing next to a mass grave, a carbine AK in his hands, gesturing at the camera and threatening further 'disciplinary retributions'.

Now here he was, a few short years later, blending in with the Dar expat business class, just another slightly gauche capitalist. Most of the men and women who sipped drinks around the private hotel pools of Dar had some blood on their hands, but it was usually at a few removes, matters of policy and regulation. She wondered how they'd feel if they knew the big Russian beside them at the bar had once shot a dozen

POWs in the back of the head, personally, to make a point to another local commander.

Bocharov climbed into the back of the Toyota with his men. Olenev didn't emerge this time. Interesting.

The black four-wheel drive pulled away from the kerb. The driver was a local and drove like one, pulling out confidently into the busy main road. Ali glanced back at her, and she gave him the nod. Anything Bocharov's driver could do, Ali could do better.

He nosed out into traffic, long arm extended out of the window, fingers rippling in mixed apology, dismissal and acknowledgement. Horns followed their progress, but they hardly stood out among the constant din of beeps, whistles, shouts and laughter. To most tourists, Dar traffic sounded angry, incessant, a humming buzz of annoyance. But it was a swift and delicate dance, full of unspoken convention, permission and refusal. A constant, careful balancing of priority and speed.

The traffic picked up as they turned on to Uhuru Street, then slowed again as they reached busy Samora Avenue.

Ali got into a loosely organised left lane of traffic, bumping along at just above walking speed. Bocharov's vehicle was four ahead in the centre lane, negotiating its own stop-start progress.

Nicola leaned forward and peered through the gaps in the traffic, frequently interrupted by rattling trail bikes cutting through the lanes of cars, the bulk of dala dala minibuses and smaller, imported tuk-tuk-style motor rickshaws called bajaj. Each time she got a clear sightline, she could see Bocharov's broad shoulders and shaved head, flanked by two guards. They weren't looking for following vehicles like Ali's. But if the local driver had been working for Russians for a while and valued his own skin, he'd have got into the habit.

'Easy now, easy,' said Nicola as Ali pulled forward. 'Watch his mirrors.'

The driver nodded and slumped lower in his seat, arm cocked over the steering wheel. Just another bored Dar cabbie with a mzungu tourist in the back.

With little warning, the Toyota cut across the rightmost lane, the driver's hand waving in the same way Ali's had, then turned into another, broader street.

Ali swore under his breath and started to cut across to make the turn. More horns followed their progress.

'Sorry, boss, sorry,' he murmured with each turn of the wheel and gunning of the accelerator.

Nicola shook her head. 'Don't worry. I think I know where he's going. Five-star place down this street. Near the ferry terminal. Let's cruise past. Get eyes on them.'

Ali nodded and turned into the road, followed by a final blast of horns. The bright, aquamarine expanse of the Kizinga estuary lay ahead of them, low and shining between the concrete buildings. A fishing dhow and a pair of low motor skiffs crossed from left to right, the curved sail of the dhow slicing through her memory, back to darker ocean waters and anti-piracy ops off the Horn of Africa. She shook it off. She wasn't there, with salt in her pores and the grip of a carbine rifle in her hand. She was here, now, in Dar, skin chilled by air con, eyes flicking across the road ahead.

At the end of the street, the Toyota had pulled over to the left, Bocharov climbing out.

'Straight forward. Past them. You're just dropping me off at the ferry terminal, like any other tourist. Look bored.'

'Got it, got it,' Ali murmured.

The bodyguards, back in their tight tactical formation, swept their eyes across Ali's vehicle as it approached, hands hovering near jackets and belt holsters. They relaxed as they saw Ali, saw the white woman in the back, recognised a local cabbie going about his business. Bocharov didn't even look up. He was standing in the centre of the pavement, tanned neck and shaved skull bent over his phone.

As they passed, Nicola noted the name of the glass-and-steel hotel. The Yakuti, or Sapphire Hotel. New, since her last visit. Very high end. A place to stay for the more adventurous social media influencers who wanted to visit Dar. Or bored executives with travel budget to burn who wanted some home comforts. Or, of course, murderous ex-FSB officers growing fat off a state-sanctioned monopoly. Even in the New Russia, there were still rewards for the loyal.

A group like this was a tough nut to crack. Suspicious and insular by default. But GARNET was as well prepared as an agent could be. And with the real-life identity of Jamie Tulloch to cloak who he really was, the odds were good that he'd be accepted as the civilian software salesman he was pretending to be. Maybe even assigned a little less security. She spun out possibilities in her head as they drove on, working the angles and the opportunities.

Nicola twisted in her seat as they reached the end of the road. Directly opposite the Yakuti was a bank building of some kind, stone and concrete, its doors closed. But one street back and far higher was another apartment block, also high end, probably with a rooftop pool. Somewhere she could rent a sea view, hopefully high enough to look down on the Yakuti's entrance. And, if she got lucky, perhaps even see the room where Bocharov would meet with GARNET.

13

Jeremy

SIS Headquarters, Vauxhall Cross: now

One thing he did miss, from the old days, was the clacking of keyboards.

Every department was a little different, but until a few years ago the one thing they'd all had in common was the rattling of the old standard-issue keyboards as analysts and desk officers wrote report after report.

Now there was mostly silence and murmured conversation, the soft pattering of laptop keys and slim, low-profile desktop keyboards. Occasionally the squeak of an ergonomic chair. Rank after rank of flatscreen monitors in dual or triple configurations, heads half hidden. Even one at the end with five monitors arranged in a semicircle. Quite how Sally Lime had got that past Purchasing he had no idea. But there was no doubt she could work wonders with the set-up.

Jeremy swung around in his own ergonomic chair and gazed out of the window. They were high enough here that he had a good view of the river. The dome of the Tate nestled among spring leaves on the opposite bank, just along from the unpleasant monolith of Millbank Tower. He could even see the white stone facade of Thames House, where the busy bees of the Security Service plied their trade.

He was distracted. He was always distracted on the first day of an op. Especially when it was in the hands of literally everyone but him.

Bocharov and his dreadful friends in East Africa weren't the only thing on Jeremy's plate. There were assessments to do on six more potential recruits, for starters.

He'd once thought Legends would be his ticket to promotion, perhaps one of the big Desks. Maybe even Bascomb's. But then Winston had retired and Central Asia had gone to someone else and Jeremy Althrop had become a victim of his own success.

For any mission that required deep infiltration of opposition locations or organisations, the Legends couldn't be faulted. They had a near-perfect record, with the only screw-ups so far being factors well outside of the programme's control – a single flaky recruit in the early years, who had prompted the carrot-and-stick approach he'd taken since. And a field agent forced to break cover during a particularly out-of-the-blue military coup.

Otherwise, it was hit after hit. Expert, highly trained agents with impeccable backstories, slipping in and out of missions with barely a whisper, extracting intelligence and defectors and key evidence that had paid for the programme many, many times over.

Jeremy had stayed at the helm throughout, trapped in the role by the sudden demand, from every Desk, for the Legends. Well, perhaps 'trapped' was too strong a word. He still loved it, even this many years in. But he would be lying to himself if he didn't admit there were some days, much like this one, when Vauxhall Cross felt like a very shiny prison.

Perhaps he just needed a little field trip. He had some recruitment visits coming up. He could flex his field muscles then, do some on-the-ground reconnaissance.

Yes, Jeremy, that's the ticket. Pretend you're still a field man on a university campus full of oblivious first-years. Ridiculous.

He snorted and turned back to his laptop, then sighed and scrolled to the end of the recruitment report he'd been working on, a candidate who'd declined. Jeremy completed the GCHQ watch warning for him, authorising metadata extraction for the next five years. In Jeremy's experience, if they didn't blab in that time, they weren't likely to in the future.

Perhaps a cup of tea would make him feel better. Although it was after twelve. If he wasn't careful with the caffeine, he wouldn't sleep. Next thing on the list was his initial report on the Bocharov op. By now, GARNET should be headed to Dar and Terence should be on his way back to London for his debrief. No check-in from Terence yet, but that wasn't unusual after a handover.

He checked the recruitment report over one last time, then hit save.

A warning popped up. Something about the file save location. Jeremy swore and saved the document locally, although that would only last until the daily purge of files on his local desktop. He got up and walked to the end of the floor, to the five-monitor nest of Sally Lime, data analyst, and the one person he couldn't run the Legends Programme without.

'Sally, bit of a weird one,' he started as he got closer. Lime was sitting cross-legged in her chair, eating a bag of Doritos. The days of skirt suits for the ladies and sports jackets for the chaps were long gone at the Cross, but Jeremy was still quietly admiring of just *how* far Lime had managed to push the dress regs. She was typing with one hand, swathed in an oversized hoodie, jeans and a pair of brightly coloured trainers that careful observation of his daughters led Jeremy to believe were extremely fashionable.

Lime looked up at him from under a mop of short brown curls. Her normally pale skin was splashed with fresh freckles, legacy of a recent snowboarding trip she'd bored him with extensively by the coffee machine. It had sounded exhausting.

'You called IT? Cos that's the first step, Jez. Calling IT.'

Jeremy grinned. 'Well, I mean . . .'

Lime pushed her glasses up into her curls and sighed. 'I'm a technical analyst, Jez. Not a support person. Literally just finished the image swap for your Tanzania op. Highly sophisticated white-hat computer intrusion. Traceless digital manipulation. You know, my real job?'

Jeremy gave her an ingratiating smile and a comically exaggerated shrug. 'I'm at a loss without you, Sally, you know that.'

Lime inhaled deeply through her nose and rolled her eyes skyward. 'One of these days you'll regret taking advantage of my generosity. What's the issue?'

'I was working on a debrief doc. Can't save it. Something about the file save location?'

'Checked connections, yeah? These thin clients sometimes have dodgy network sockets.'

Jeremy hadn't. He grimaced.

'No . . . but I still have network access. Email and such.'

Lime tilted her head, the smallest of frowns flickering across her face. 'All right, let me check the server.' She put the Doritos down and dusted off her fingers, then shuffled her seat forward by shifting her weight back and forth, feet never touching the nylon carpet.

'Terrible for your back, you know, sitting like that.'

Lime snorted. 'Yeah, if you consider walking down to the cafeteria for a muffin a key part of your exercise routine.'

Jeremy narrowed his eyes. 'I believe the phrase is "I feel both seen and attacked", correct?'

Lime pointed a finger at him like a pistol and made a soft *ptchoo* sound. 'Bingo.'

Her hands went back to the keyboard. Jeremy circled around. Windows flashed up and disappeared, arcane queries unspooling from her fingertips.

'Huh,' she said softly, leaning forward and pulling her glasses down. 'That's weird.'

Jeremy peered at the query results: an ASCII table of text that might as well have been in Latin for all Jeremy understood it. Indeed, if it had been Latin, he might have had a chance.

'Please define "weird",' he said.

'Give me a second. Need to try a few things.' She typed a little more, hunching over her keyboard. A steady stream of commands. More windows.

A slow drip of disquiet began at the very nape of Jeremy's neck, creeping downwards to leave an acid emptiness in his stomach.

As she typed, Lime kept up a steady muttered commentary to herself. 'Caches? No. Nothing in the buffer. Right. Not even seeing it. Okay, what about the secondary tier. Nope. Right, if I power cycle . . .'

She paused, eyes fixed on a progress bar inching its way across one corner of her screen. Jeremy noticed how rapidly she was blinking. Her breathing had picked up. She took a long, slow breath. Jeremy couldn't read ASCII tables, but he could read people, and Sally Lime was not happy.

'Can you—' he started.

Lime held up one finger, not even looking at him. 'Wait. Just trying something. If it's not this . . .'

The vague sense of something not quite *right* was blossoming into the kind of clanging internal alarm bells that had saved his skin in the field more than once.

The last time he'd felt like this, the blue lights of the Kyrgyz police had cast jagged fingers of flashing light across the ceiling of his second-floor hotel room in Bishkek. By then, it had already been too late.

Something was very, very *wrong* here.

Lime sat back, rubbed at her eyes, then put her glasses back on. She stood up quickly, hands unplugging laptop cables with practised speed, then tucked the device under her arm and strode away.

Jeremy was caught flat-footed, still staring at the now-blank monitor. Lime was already fifteen metres away, standing in the doorway of a secure meeting room. She jerked her head, impatience in every angle of her body, eyes widening so he'd get the point. He followed her, and the heavy, soundproof door hissed closed behind them.

Jeremy stayed standing while Lime plugged her laptop into the wall display. He hated these rooms. The sonic baffling always made him feel like his head was wrapped in cotton wool. Like the few moments just before you passed out from blood loss, which he'd been unfortunate enough to experience twice in the course of his career.

'Sally, what's going on?' he said, finally taking a seat opposite her.

'Something bad, boss. Something really fucking bad. The RAIDs for Legends aren't mounting. But *just* the ones for Legends.'

Jeremy knew enough about both servers and Sally Lime to know she was truly rattled. 'That *does* sound . . . bad.'

'It's weird *and* bad. RAID is a redundant array, right? Redundant Array of Independent Disks, that's what it means. It's our air-gapped storage, because none of this stuff can be on an open network, even a protected one. Too sensitive.'

'And they're not working?'

Lime drummed her fingers on the tabletop. 'They're not *mounting*. The internal network can't see them or access them. That can happen, if a whole RAID enclosure has a hardware failure. But Legends is important, right? Grade Emerald. It's *multi*-RAID storage, duplicated across the production server and three back-ups.'

'And *none* of them are mounting? What does that mean?'

Lime nodded, her face almost grey with the implications. 'It means bad things. There's weekly tape back-ups, but we need to physically go and check them.'

'Aren't they in big crates in a basement somewhere?'

'Yeah,' said Lime, typing more queries. 'We might be able to salvage something, if this wasn't a drip-feed attack of some kind.'

The pit in Jeremy's stomach turned into a gaping chasm. 'Wait, are you saying this was deliberate?'

Sally Lime looked up from her laptop. 'RAIDs *don't* fail like this, Jeremy, four completely independent units at once. The odds are astronomical. And there's gaps in the logs. This morning, between about 0500 and 0620, someone got into the Legends system, purged every RAID we have and fried the units.'

Jeremy gaped, mouth opening and closing. 'It's . . . it's all gone?'

Lime typed a little more. 'All of it. Local copies on devices get wiped every day. Everything's in the production servers and the back-ups. If I can get a clean disk out of one of the RAIDs there might be something I can salvage, if they didn't spin them until the fucking things melted.'

He wiped his face. 'Jesus Christ. We've got assets out there. People, on the ground in Tanzania, right now. And the Legends, they're civilians . . . if someone's after them? Fuck. *Fuck*.'

Lime stood up, still pale. 'I'll go and look at the racks, see if I can salvage anything. But this was a deliberate attack, Jeremy. Someone's trying to burn Legends to the ground.'

14

Jamie

Dar es Salaam: now

By the time he got off his final connecting flight from Istanbul, Jamie had sweated deep circles into the armpits of his light blue shirt. Adrenaline had kept him awake most of the way to the Turkish stopover. Once he'd switched planes and the gaunt man in the black raincoat had not followed, he'd crashed hard, slumping into an exhausted sleep for the second flight. As he cleared customs and rolled out into the whirl and bustle of the Julius Nyerere airport concourse, he realised he hadn't eaten anything since he'd left his flat in London, nearly sixteen hours before. Too nervous before Istanbul, too unconscious after.

But he was here now. Incredibly hungry, sweating, terrified. But here. He'd made it without getting murdered in an airport. Now, perhaps, he could find someone from SIS and get out of this mess.

He stopped, squinting in the harsh white light of the concourse. Dozens of men and women stood in tight knots around the Arrivals barriers, holding signs or calling out taxi fares over the noise of the terminal.

'Mr Tulloch? James Tulloch?' said a loud voice to his left. Jamie turned in a daze, looking for the source of the voice. A local man in a leather jacket and grey chinos held a small dry-erase board in his hands with Jamie's name in block capitals on it. He was in his mid-forties perhaps, broad-shouldered, with close-cropped dark hair. But he had a friendly smile.

Jamie approached, his steps faltering as he realised he had no idea who this man was. A local driver or a field agent? Did he work for SIS or UPK?

'You've been sent to . . . pick me up?'

The man placed his hand over his heart and gave a small bow. 'Yes, yes. I am Noah Alawi, I will be your driver. Come with me, please. I take your bag.'

For a half-second, Jamie thought about darting away, about losing himself in the terminal crowds and trying to find another driver to take him to the British consulate. But perhaps this smiling Noah was armed. Or there were other eyes watching him. Best to go with the flow, for now.

Noah had already wrested the bag from him and turned towards the terminal doors by the time he completed the thought.

Jamie let himself be led through the crowds, Noah waving away three or four cab drivers who thought it would be worth trying to poach a passenger. Two of them spoke into their smartphones, Kiswahili swiftly translated into a toneless American drone. 'I can give you a better deal' floated out after Jamie as he stepped into the heat outside, as though he'd been followed to Dar es Salaam by the smart speaker he used to turn down his lights at home.

Noah pointed to a black Toyota Land Cruiser pulled up just ahead of the busy taxi rank, then opened the rear and loaded up Jamie's bags. 'Sorry about that. These drivers are very . . . what is the word. They do not stop.'

Jamie blinked, light-headed in the sudden heat. He really needed to eat something. A marine haze lay over the city in the distance, lights twinkling, half hidden in curling fog. He instantly felt sweat begin to trickle down his spine. 'Persistent?'

Noah smiled. 'That's the word. Please. Take a seat.'

Jamie opened the front passenger door and climbed in. Noah was already in the driver's seat by the time Jamie had found his seat belt, looking at him quizzically. 'You don't prefer in the back?'

Jamie shook his head. 'No. Like to see where I'm going. Used to get car sick when I was a kid. I don't any more, but I still like to sit in the front.'

Noah considered this for a moment, then gave a small nod. 'It is a good view, coming into Dar. You will like it. Mr Bocharov is looking forward to welcoming you.'

Jamie clicked his seat belt home at the same time as his stomach lurched. Well, that answered one question.

When they came off the highway, Jamie sat up, his exhaustion forgotten. They weaved through densely populated streets, busy even in the evening, flashes of colour, rattling motorbikes, billboards everywhere. He gazed out of the window, taking it all in. An old flicker of curiosity bubbled up in him, immediately followed by the sourness of regret. So many countries, so many whole *continents* he'd never visited. All to keep a job he was good at but barely cared about, and a flat in Chelsea he spent most of his time being miserable in.

'Here we are, sir,' said Noah as they turned on to a street that led towards the ocean. He blinked, looking for their destination.

'Where—' he started. Noah nodded at an illuminated glass-and-steel cube on the left side of the road.

'The Yakuti, sir. It means Sapphire. These gentlemen will take you to Mr Bocharov.'

Four men waited for him on the pavement. None was *visibly* armed, but they all stood as though they were; a certain straightness of back and watchfulness. Russians, he guessed, by their skin colour, shaved heads and sunburn. UPK security. Serious customers.

All he had to go on was the briefing his Head of Sales had sent him, a few notes about UPK, a short profile of Bocharov. None of the real details. Nothing like what GARNET would have, if he'd been here, as planned. What the hell was he doing? He wasn't ready for, well, any of this. He climbed out of the Toyota. A guard stepped forward, huge and looming.

'Mister Tullok?' said the Russian, eyes hidden behind a pair of Ray-Bans, his upper lip twisted by a pale scar, head shaved to a half-millimetre fuzz. All the men wore khaki trousers, light green safari shirts, dark, lightweight jackets, desert boots.

'Jamie Tulloch, yes. Here to see Arkady Bocharov.'

The guard nodded, then jerked a head towards the vehicle. 'These will take your luggage. I must search you before we go inside, okay?'

Jamie nodded and raised his arms, allowing the bodyguard to swiftly and expertly pat him down. Two of the other guards went ahead, carrying his laptop bag and his rolling case.

'I am Vitaly. Mr Bocharov's security lead. You are a welcome guest, Mr Tullo— Tulloch?' Vitaly said the name correctly and raised one eyebrow behind his sunglasses.

'That's right. Thank you, Vitaly.'

Vitaly didn't smile, but the eyebrow rose a fraction higher. 'Welcome to the Yakuti. Follow me.'

Vitaly turned and strode through the rotating doors into the brightly lit lobby of the hotel, Jamie in tow. Jamie felt rather than saw the remaining bodyguard following close behind and briefly saw himself as he must appear to everyone else in the lobby: a pale, sweaty Anglo in a stained shirt being frogmarched through the cool marble and glass by two paramilitary security goons. What exactly had he got himself into?

The building's lobby was long and wide, high windows to the right with clusters of low sofas, armchairs and hardwood tables, mostly occupied by small knots of businesspeople in suits or skirts with impeccably styled hair. Here and there someone stuck out, clad in a hoodie or high-end athleisure gear. Tech people, Jamie guessed, familiar with the look from his quarterly trips to the Bay Area. The hotel was clearly a favoured meeting spot among both the expats of Dar and the local elite. There were enough Savile Row suits and handbags the price of a small family car to put Bond Street to shame.

He was led up a glass staircase to a bank of elevators. The sweat dried on his neck in the powerful air conditioning, sending a shiver across his shoulders.

Vitaly pressed the call button and then stood at ease, hands crossed in front of him, perfectly still. The other guard did the same on Jamie's right. Jamie stood between them, unsure what to do with his hands, watching the green numbers count down. When the lift arrived with a low ding, Vitaly ushered him inside. He thumbed the button for the very top floor.

'Penthouse, eh?' said Jamie, aiming for a chuckle but landing on a dry squeak.

Vitaly glanced back over his shoulder. 'Whole floor. Mr Bocharov likes privacy.'

Jamie felt his eyelid twitch. Christ, he really needed some food and water inside him. Even if he hadn't been here in the place of a deep-cover SIS agent, this was not a great way to start a business deal. If the Legends Programme was burned, if he was on his own again, he had to make this work. Terence had said it would be an easy deal, but he still had to make sure it landed. Without Legends, there was no more secret helping hand for him. No more Terence with his sage advice and steady hand on Jamie's shoulder. Thinking of Terence made his stomach twist, bile with nowhere to go.

As the lift slowed, his neck prickled in warning. How much did GARNET actually look like him? Years ago, in Wales, they'd told him the few images of him online could be replaced untraceably, server logs edited, a blurry shot of him in sunglasses replaced by a smiling picture of GARNET. What did those replacement pictures look like though? Were they like the originals? Or clear shots of GAR-NET's face? What if Bocharov had seen clear pictures of GARNET and it was Jamie who walked in? Would the carefully constructed illusion mean Jamie was taken for an imposter in his own life?

The doors slid open on a dimly lit corridor, large windows at each end looking out over the city. Vitaly led him down the corridor to

Suite 1, which seemed to take up half of the southern side of the whole floor.

Inside, Arkady Bocharov waited, leaning back on a huge, cream-coloured sofa that curved around a circular coffee table. He had a laptop open in front of him on the glass surface, a tablet in one hand and a phone on the sofa cushions beside him. He was thoroughly engrossed in the tablet, flicking slowly through something.

'Sir, this is Mr Jamie Tulloch. From Tacitech. The software people.'

Bocharov grunted and pointed to the opposite side of the sofa. He didn't look up. Jamie hesitated, then took a seat while Vitaly went to a small bar area by the door, returning with a large bottle of water and a glass with ice and lemon.

'You want something to eat?' said Bocharov, looking up from his tablet finally. 'Airline food is shit. You came with two stops, yes?' Bocharov was in his early fifties, jowly, head and jawline shaved clean. Piercing green eyes swept Jamie up and down, taking in the damp shirt, the pale face. 'You look younger than your photo. On LinkedIn.'

Jamie blinked. 'I never look good in photos.'

Bocharov nodded. 'Secret is to hold the phone *up*, for selfie. Makes you look good. I do it for my Instagram.' He tapped the large iPhone on the table in front of him. 'You have Insta*gram*?' He pronounced the word with a rolled, guttural 'r' sound.

Jamie shook his head and swallowed. 'Not my thing.'

Bocharov shrugged. 'I like it. The videos are funny.'

The green eyes took in the sweat in Jamie's hairline. 'I think you should eat. You look like you need some food.'

Jamie was halfway through uncapping the water. He began to smile, then remembered a colleague saying that Russians thought Westerners smiled too much. That it made them look like halfwits. Glaikit, as the folks back home would say.

He nodded. 'It was a long trip. Something to eat would be great.'

Bocharov nodded. 'Vitaly, get this man a fucking sandwich.'

15

Nicola

361 Golden Heaven Apartments, Dar es Salaam: now

'I suspect . . .' said Graeme Sylvan from the other side of the room, 'that this is our boy.'

Nicola looked up from the room's double bed and squinted over at Graeme. He was a street-work specialist, one of the best surveillance guys she had in the region. Early forties, former Army like herself, a white guy who had been in Africa long enough to develop a deep tan, rangy and lean in his neat shirt and trousers. Dark brown hair that had lightened with the sun, trimmed short. At a glance, you'd take him for an NGO worker or embassy staff. He was hunched over a spotting scope, currently pointed at the top floor of the Yakuti.

Sylvan swung the scope a little to the left. 'Bloody thick windows, but I've got a positive ID on Bocharov, and someone new just came in.'

She stood up and took a pair of powerful but compact binoculars from the bedside table. The top floor of the Yakuti snapped into focus, three figures visible through the huge glass picture windows of the penthouse suite. Say what you like about the ultra-rich and their hotels, their preference for expansive views made them easy to spy on. Especially at night, when they lit the place up like a football pitch.

'Want to use the big scope?' said Sylvan, holding out a hand for the binoculars. Nicola nodded, and they swapped. The eyepiece of the scope was slightly warm to the touch. They'd been here for hours, watching and waiting.

She focused, getting Bocharov's crew cut as sharp as she could. He was leaning back now, one hand gesturing, the other holding a tablet.

'Any luck with getting a bouncer?' she asked Sylvan in a low mutter. She always found herself talking quietly on surveillance ops, even though their targets were over a hundred metres away, through two sets of windows.

'I've asked for one,' said Sylvan. 'In case we get into closer quarters. No chance it'll work at this range, though, boss.'

She nodded. 'Worth having in our back pocket anyway. And no joy with getting a live mic in?' She glanced across at the veteran surveillance man. He shook his head.

'This place is too new. And they're fully staffed, so we'd struggle to get someone in there for weeks. We could do a straight drop-in ourselves, but it's risky.'

Nicola nodded, acknowledging the difficulty of infiltrating a modern, high-security hotel like this one, getting into the room, placing a microphone and getting out again. Tough even without the Russian mercenaries.

Sylvan continued, nodding towards the third figure, standing to one side. 'Those Vityaz boys are ugly and there's always at least two of 'em on the premises, even when Bocharov's out and about.'

She looked up. 'You've been keeping tabs on him pre-op? I didn't know Dar station had those kinds of resources.'

Sylvan chuckled. 'We don't, normally. But he got a priority marker on him when he first arrived in Dar. He shifts around a lot, hotel to hotel, a couple of private places. Definitely more security and more caution than you'd expect for a precision engineering company, even a Russian one. Cobalt, oil, maybe. But not bloody ball bearings.'

Nicola chuckled. 'I suspect Mr Bocharov has minimal interest in precision ball bearings, Graeme. So, this is our guy? Operative GARNET?' She twitched the scope to the right, focusing on the dark-haired man sitting side on to her. The combination of distance, multiple panes of glass and the darkness outside made him a little fuzzy and indistinct. She focused tighter, trying to reconcile the image with her briefing notes. He was the right height, hair colour, build. What she could see of his face looked like the images she'd memorised, induction photos of GARNET from his initial briefing. But those photos were several years old. The man on the sofa looked similar to the Legend who was safely out of the way in South America by now. That was the point, after all.

Sylvan nodded. 'He matches the description I've got. So he's one of them "Legends", right?'

Nicola shook her head. 'Not quite. He's a trained field operative. This guy did a lot of work around Ukraine and Belarus. I never crossed paths with him, but I've heard his name. Ex-forces. Ex-Foreign Office. Fluent Russian. More than equipped to tangle with Bocharov.'

Sylvan frowned. 'So who's the Legend then?'

'The Legend is the civilian component. But they're paired. So GARNET took over from this' – she tapped her knee, momentarily blanking on the Legend's real name – 'Jamie Tulloch. Sales manager. He's off somewhere else entirely by now. The operative slips in, pretends to be him. *Is* him, for all intents and purposes.'

Sylvan grunted. 'Clever stuff.'

She sat back from the scope, pushed down a strange feeling. It was a factor of distance. When she saw him up close she'd be sure. 'All right, I need to tell the Cross I've got eyes on our boy. Ping my burner if they show signs of going anywhere.'

Nicola stood up and headed for the door. Halfway there, Sylvan grunted.

'What is it?' she said, half turning back.

'The big Russian bloke just brought in room-service sandwiches and they look amazing. Any chance you could grab us something? I'm starving.'

She grinned. 'I was just thinking the same thing. Honestly, if this op is just a couple of weeks watching hotel windows, I'll be more than happy. Makes a change.'

Sylvan looked up from the scope. 'Bit different from the Horn, eh?'

She laughed and opened the suite door, heading for the rooftop terrace, where the phone signal was better. After that she'd head to the food stalls on Samora Avenue and pick up something for them both.

Sylvan was right though. Nicola had made her name working in the Somali borderlands with Kenya, watching dusty containers in Mombasa's port, tracking Vityaz and Wagner leftovers as they moved guns, drugs and worse along the Juba corridor into the Central African Republic. By contrast, this was easy street.

So why was there a note of uncertainty in the carefully planned orchestration of her operation? Something wasn't right, but she'd be damned if she could tell what it was.

16

Jeremy

SIS Headquarters: now

For the fifth time in the last ten minutes, Jeremy Althrop swore and scribbled out the name he'd been writing. He was up to thirty-five Legends that he could remember in some detail: full names, where they lived, what they did. But it was the absolute bare minimum. Everything else was gone. Their signed Official Secrets Act documentation. Dossiers. All the prepwork and analysis on their future careers. And, crucially, their linked operatives. All gone.

He wrote another name, then realised he'd got the surname wrong. It wasn't Wilson. It was something else. He scratched it out. The flickering overhead lights in the conference room he'd holed up in were hurting his eyes.

Why couldn't he remember them all? Was he getting old? Was this what happened when you offloaded the important stuff to databases and spreadsheets? When he'd been a young field officer in Azerbaijani oil towns and tiny villages in the Caucasus, he'd prided himself on never referring to his briefing notes. He'd commit them to memory, using the near-perfect recall that had served him so well at Cambridge.

But now, when he really needed it, when his whole programme was hanging in the balance and there were dozens of people at real risk, he couldn't *remember*.

Sally Lime came in with a laptop dangling from one hand and two mugs of coffee clutched in the other, swearing under her breath as the heat got to her knuckles. She thumped the mugs down on the conference table, spilling a little, then unfolded the laptop and sat down opposite.

'Good news, bad news.'

'Bad news first, get it over with.'

Lime nodded. 'Drives are toast, as suspected. Tape back-ups are, well, they're bloody *gone*. Someone walked out of here with the whole crate. I found gaps in the logs for the physical access controls to Secure Three. No logs from 0622 to 0744. In and out, nice and quick. Someone was *in the building*, Jeremy.'

'Jesus Christ.' He hunched forward, took a breath, then reached for the coffee. It was hot and strong. The pit of dread that had opened inside him a few hours ago had begun to settle into a kind of acidic acceptance. This was real. His programme had been targeted. Vauxhall Cross had been infiltrated. He'd wished for a little bit of excitement, and now he had as much as he could handle and more.

'So, we have absolutely nothing?'

'That's about the size of it,' said Lime, leaning back in her chair.

'What about email?'

She shook her head. 'The programme's well over a decade old at this point, so the earliest stuff will have been purged; we only have to retain seven years of ephemeral stuff like email, unless it's to or from a ministerial account or section-chief level.'

'Fuck.' Jeremy rubbed the back of his neck, trying to massage away the rapidly growing tension in the muscles there. 'And since 90 per cent of programme communications have gone through me, and I never got promoted to that level, as well as doing most things in person by habit . . .'

'Yeah, there's sweet fuck-all in your email. I did a metadata search, and we've got maybe 1,100 emails, but 95 per cent of those are one-liners or you accepting meeting requests. It's all in your head, mate.'

Jeremy tapped the sheet of paper in front of him. 'Except it's *not*. I haven't had to really *remember* any of this in years. I feel like a dull pair of scissors. I've got a few names, but it's maybe two-thirds of our Legends at most, I think. We've been recruiting these people for a long time.'

Lime typed a few lines then swivelled the laptop around. 'The next bit is good *and* bad news? Our attacker was a real clever-clogs, wiped the logs on their way out after launching the attack that took out the servers. But they didn't account for our *logs* having tertiary back-ups. We do a primary back-up every five minutes, then a secondary full snapshot every hour. The attacker got both of those. But there's a third level, transcribing every log event as it happens in two other places. Hidden process. It's a security measure, so we can see if someone is messing with the logs themselves.'

She pointed at scrolling text in a black window on one side of her screen. 'Look, you can see them wiping the compressed back-up logs. Really neat and quick. Probably used a script of some kind to find the right timestamps and IDs.'

Jeremy squeezed the bridge of his nose. 'So we can see the crime in progress. What does that give us?'

Lime grinned. 'More than that, Jezza. We can see *exactly* what they did. They *copied* the files, before they burned the servers.'

'What?' said Jeremy, hope rising in his chest as quickly as fear had made his stomach curdle. 'So our entire operative list is out there? All the files? How did they get that much data out?'

Lime shook her head. 'It's really not that much. About three terabytes. Half of that is document scans and images. Legends had a dedicated RAID set up for security reasons, not because it was a lot of data. You could lift it out on one decently sized SSD. Two, if you're being careful.'

Jeremy stood up and went to the window of the conference room, fighting the surges of adrenaline coursing through him. 'So, someone walked out of the building with my entire programme in their back pocket?'

Lime grimaced. 'Not quite. There *was* definitely someone else in the building to lift the tape back-ups, but the security team reckon that was a different attacker. No way they could have got from the workstation that launched the server attack down to Secure Three in the time allowed. You can't teleport down six floors in under a minute. They also wiped the cameras for Secure Three from the same hotdesk. We did find this though.'

She leaned across the conference table and slapped down something that looked like an oversized USB stick.

'Is that . . .'

'A 5G mobile internet dongle, yes. Someone did some serious prepwork for this. They found a gap in the building's electromagnetic shielding. It wasn't as important in 1994 when this pile was built, and a lot of it was retrofitted later. They managed to find the *one* place in the building that some contractor hadn't lined up the shielding panels quite right. Two bars of 5G signal. Enough to get three terabytes out, slowly. Looks like it's been there a while. Probably a fortnight or so. That was the last time that floor was swept for unauthorised devices.'

'Christ,' said Jeremy. 'So we've got a full copy of all of the programme data out there?'

Lime nodded. 'Two, technically, with the tape back-ups, but they'll probably ditch or burn those. We've got our friends at Thames House working on tracking down the other end of that 5G connection. So far they've narrowed it down to the Greater London area. Looks like it's being bounced through a couple of VPNs.'

'Great, only three or four million possible places they could be hiding, then,' said Jeremy. 'If they even stay in one place for long.'

Sally shrugged. 'On the plus side, all of it's encrypted. You need serious hardware to read the tapes, hence why they'd probably destroy them. But the logs they tried very hard to delete show us they didn't get out with the encryption key. So they can't read anything they got. Yet.'

Jeremy sat back down at the conference table. 'So we might have a little bit of time, then. To warn our field teams.'

A memory surfaced: Winston Bascomb, in his cups one night, telling a story about losing a whole network in Hungary in the late seventies. Gone overnight, disappearing into cells and gulags and shallow graves. His carefully lacquered hair had come loose, along with his tie, the whisky glass clutched in his hand. 'We didn't see it coming, Jeremy. That was the thing. Didn't bloody see it coming.'

Jeremy looked down at his hands, the piece of paper, the scribbled names. It couldn't happen to them, to his people. *Must* not.

'No encryption is unbreakable, but Grade Emerald is pretty good,' said Lime. 'Right now they've got a big chunk of data they can't do much with. Maybe there's time to extract your teams, get them out before they're blown. But the clock's running.'

Jeremy felt his phone buzz in his pocket. It was his issued one rather than his personal, connecting to the Vauxhall Cross mobile network cell that SIS ran themselves, with every call and byte of data subject to logging and archiving. The number on the screen was a mission phone in East Africa, one issued to Dar Station.

Ellis.

He answered. 'This is AEGIS Actual, identify please.'

Nicola Ellis's voice was fuzzy and indistinct. He could hear faint traffic noise in the background. 'AEGIS Three One. Identifying, Papa, Romeo, Mike, Three, Three, Six.'

'Acknowledged, go secure.'

The phones exchanged encryption keys with a brief hiss of static, then the line was crystal clear, only a very slight delay caused by the distance indicating that Nicola Ellis wasn't in the next room.

'GARNET is on site and on task. I'm observing with local station assets. He's made contact with the primary target.'

Jeremy felt a tiny portion of his stomach unclench for the first time that day. At least *something* was going right. Terence had made the handover with GARNET, Tulloch was safely out of the way and the mission might not be compromised. He stood up and walked to the window, looking out over the Thames. Behind him, he heard Sally Lime pick up her coffee and leave, the conference-room door sighing closed behind her.

'Acknowledged and very glad to hear it.' He paused for a long moment. 'I'm—I'm afraid I have some bad news . . .'

17

Jamie

Dar es Salaam: now

Arkady Bocharov was remarkably considerate, for the subject of an active SIS investigation. More than once in the hour or so he spent in the penthouse, Jamie found himself wondering what exactly GARNET was here to do. Bocharov seemed no different to a dozen senior executives he'd met over the course of his career. There was the common mild sociopathy, the tendency to see people as units of production or pawns to be moved. That seemed to be true of both the owner of a washing-machine-parts warehouse in Swindon and the Russian former mercenary owner of a precision engineering manufacturer in Dar es Salaam.

In some ways, it was reassuring. He'd half expected some kind of Bond villain. Unusual fashion choices, a chair with buttons along the arm for the despatching of deficient henchpersons. Obvious evil.

Instead, he had supper with a slightly blunt Russian. It fitted well with his natural selling style. When Jamie finished his sandwich and told one of his classic ice-breakers, a gag about the voice-control unit not understanding his Scottish accent, it went down very well.

'. . . and I said, no, *activate* the locking clamps.'

Bocharov slapped his knee and bellowed a laugh that shook the glasses on the coffee table. 'That is funny. That is fucking funny. Vitaly, don't you think that's funny?'

The taciturn bodyguard raised one corner of his mouth a millimetre and assented to the hilarity with the briefest of nods.

Bocharov indicated his guard with one hand. 'Vitaly thinks it's funny. This is a great achievement, my friend. When he started working for me, I told him a joke every day, for six months. Six fucking months. Nothing. No laughs. I got him one day, with a joke about Rostov. Nobody can resist my joke about Rostov. But he thinks you're a funny man after one hour only.'

With food in his stomach and the warmth of the two shots of vodka that seemed to be Bocharov's usual evening refreshment, Jamie felt a little of his confidence coming back.

Whatever else UPK was or wasn't, the firm appeared to have a lot of money. It was a genuine sales opportunity, and he knew what to do with that. He pushed down the image of Terence's glassy, staring eyes. He couldn't afford to think about the bathroom in Paris, the metallic scent of blood.

He smiled at Bocharov. 'Of course, we've worked out those little issues. And my accent used to be a bit stronger. The voice-control units for our shelf-picking assemblies are really quite advanced now.'

Bocharov waved a hand, picking at his sandwich. 'I believe it. I was very impressed with the sales materials. You know, of course, that this is an urgent requirement? We need to retain our ISO certification to do business.'

Jamie nodded. 'Yes, of course.'

Bocharov shrugged. 'I like you, Jamie. I like this software, the equipment. I think it can do big things. UPK is old company. Needs to be . . . modernised. Part of making Russia and Russian businesses stronger. Competitive. We are behind. But not for long. This is a good opportunity.'

Jamie smiled and raised the shot glass again. 'Here's to opportunity.'

Bocharov blinked slowly, then raised his glass. 'To a fruitful discussion.' He downed the shot and sat back, hooded eyes narrowed as they searched Jamie's face.

'You are not what I expected, Jamie. From London I am expecting sharp suit, hair combed back, very nice tie. Saying a lot but meaning nothing. Instead I get sweaty, hungry man in khaki trousers and a damp shirt.' Bocharov slapped his knee and laughed.

Jamie allowed himself a half-smile. 'There are plenty of salesmen like that from London. Never really been my style. I'm from Edinburgh.'

Bocharov narrowed his eyes. 'But also went to Cambridge and Stanford, yes? You are a smart one.'

Jamie nodded. The last two achievements in his life he could be entirely sure were his own doing. 'I did. Learned a lot. Where I came from, not a lot of folk end up going to universities like that.'

Bocharov smiled. 'I say I am from Yaroslavl. Beautiful place. Churches with golden roofs. Many tourists from Moscow. But I come from small place, *outside* Yaroslavl. The ones from Moscow they think we are . . . what is this word, Vitaly, derevenshchina? What is the English?'

Vitaly's eyebrow lifted a fraction again. 'It means, like, yokel. Bumpkin. I like this word, bumpkin.'

Jamie felt a laugh bubble up from his chest, tension easing. 'Hah. In Scotland we call them teuchters.'

Bocharov's eyes widened and he sat forward. 'Oh, I *like* this word. Tewk— tewkter?'

Jamie gestured towards his throat. 'You have to make the "ch" sound with the back of your tongue. Teu*ch*ter. It means the same.'

Bocharov tried the word a few more times, then slapped his knee again. 'Well, the Muscovites, they think we are these . . . teu*ch*ters. But the people in Yaroslavl, they think people from *my* village are the real ones, the derevenshchina. Yaroslavl, it is a very pretty town. From the twelfth century. Many tourists go there. But not where I live. Where I live is cow shit and hard work. The tourists don't see it.'

Jamie remembered concrete blocks, grey pebble-dashed walls he grew up calling 'harling'. The long, dark stains caused by five or six decades of rain. 'Edinburgh is the same. The centre is beautiful. But it's . . . like a theme park.'

Bocharov pointed at him. 'Exactly. Like Disneyland. My village is not Disneyland. So I work my way from there to here. I serve my country. I make money for people. And I am there for the birth of the New Russia. And I will make the New Russia stronger, with everything I have planned. It is quite a life, no?'

The big man leaned back, arms spread wide either side of him, eyeing Jamie.

'It's . . . a remarkable story,' said Jamie. 'To have got where you are from where you started.'

Bocharov looked pleased, dipping his head in acknowledgement. 'And the same to you,' he said. 'I admire this. England, it is a hard place to do this. A lot of old men in good suits. But they cannot resist our money. They are survivors. They know when to back the winning horse, yes? And you, Jamie, you are winning horse.'

Jamie swallowed, his throat suddenly dry. He took a sip of the water glass by his empty sandwich plate. Bocharov was right, of course. He was successful because he was useful and he made money. But how much of it was Jamie himself? His regular meetings with Terence had been more than just check-ins. He got nudges, subtle and not so subtle, to go after particular jobs, to make connections at the right time. Terence had always been there, always watching.

'So . . .' said Jamie, sitting forward. 'There's some scoping work to be done. A lot of detail for me to go through with your operations people?'

Bocharov reached forward and picked up the remaining half of his sandwich. He took a large bite and sat back, chewing thoughtfully. 'Yes. But not today. We leave for Stone Town tomorrow morning, I think. We will meet some of my people there. A very fine hotel, you will like it. We will do the details at my house. It is in the north of the island. Very beautiful place. Have you been to Zanzibar before?'

Jamie shook his head. For some reason he'd thought everything was going to happen in Dar. Now he was going somewhere he'd dreamed about as a young man. Somewhere he'd never got to, once he'd become a Legend. 'I wanted to travel more, when I was younger. Work got in the way.'

Bocharov shrugged. 'You don't want to travel with backpack, filthy like a soldier. See the world in style, my friend. It is a better way.'

The Russian waved towards the door. Jamie was being dismissed. 'Tonight you get some sleep. Vitaly will wake you in time for the boat. You are at the end of this floor. Not as big as my room. But very nice.'

Jamie stood up, crumbs cascading from his khakis. He felt a slight shiver from the air con, the sweat long since dried from his shirt. 'Thank you for such a warm welcome, Mr Bocharov.'

Bocharov inclined his head. 'Call me Arkady, please. See you tomorrow, Jamie. Or maybe I call you Yakov. It is the Russian name closest, I think.'

Jamie finally allowed himself a proper smile. 'It would be an honour.'

Bocharov's face was perfectly flat, the bright green eyes following Jamie as he walked towards the door, Vitaly turning to follow. 'Good night, Yakov. Welcome to Tanzania.'

18

Nicola

Indian Ocean, off the Tanzanian coast: now

For once, they crossed to Zanzibar in near-flat calm. Nicola took advantage and stood out on the rear deck, enjoying the feel of the sun on her face.

Bocharov and his entourage had boarded the motor yacht MV *Kerch* early that morning, then swiftly zipped out of the estuary and into the Indian Ocean. They had followed as quickly as they could.

There were three ways to get to Zanzibar by sea. A private boat, for the rich like Bocharov. The slow ferry for most of the locals and backpacking tourists on a budget. And, for triple the price, one of the fast catamarans, shaving an hour off the travel time. But if there was the slightest bit of chop, the fast ferry could be a rough trip.

Today, though, they had perfect conditions. Nicola looked down at her hands, tight on the polished steel of the guardrail. The ocean stretched away on all sides, pure aquamarine. Mainland Tanzania was a low, dark line on the horizon, while Zanzibar emerged slowly from the heat haze.

The old harbour of Stone Town was visible now, the powdery bulk of the old Portuguese fort, sand-coloured buildings lined up against the water, the ferry piers jutting out, fishing dhows bobbing in the water. Impossibly picturesque. The rest of Stone Town, mile after mile of low concrete buildings, acacia trees and dust roads, was rarely visited by tourists. If she knew Bocharov, he'd be sticking to the part of the city that made for a good Instagram backdrop. Probably in one of the nicer hotels with a harbour view.

The unease she'd felt yesterday as they'd watched GARNET arrive had doubled after the call with Althrop. They'd agreed she should continue for now, while Althrop tried to secure the lost files and salvage the programme. GARNET was more at risk than before, but there was nothing specifically tying the attack to Bocharov. Yet. And the operative was a seasoned field man. One of their best, Althrop had said. He was probably lying low, biding his time before making contact.

Sylvan appeared at her elbow and leaned on the rail, gazing across the water as the ferry began its turn towards the terminal.

'What's the plan, boss? You got a contact drill established with GARNET? I've got sources in most of the hotels around the Old Town.'

Nicola nodded. 'Could be any number of reasons he's not made contact yet. But we need to figure out where they've gone first. A party of Russians isn't going to fade into the background in Stone Town harbour. If GARNET can get away on his own, he'll do a bit of lingering, run a couple of flags up. He knows we're watching. And he's been in tight spots like this before.'

'And what about the risk from London?'

Nicola bit her lip, staring out across the water. 'Althrop said the data's encrypted and they're trying to get it back. GARNET'S cover should be solid for as long as that stays true. So we crack on with the original plan.'

Sylvan nodded. 'Roger that. We've got a couple of good street operatives here, locals. Brought some kit for them. I'll get them wired up while you get accommodation sorted. I know a good place. I'm guessing Bocharov won't be here long though. The big man likes his swimming pool and his croquet lawn, back at the compound.'

Nicola smiled as they drew alongside the pier, remembering the copious detail in the mission prep. That must have been Sylvan's doing. It felt good to have a team working with her, to be back on task.

She leaned down and picked up her bag. 'Let's start with finding the Russians.'

19

Jeremy

Peckham High Street, London: now

It had taken seventeen hours of number-crunching, but their sister services had come up trumps. Sally Lime's discovery of the 5G dongle surreptitiously inserted into a highly secure, air-gapped SIS work terminal had sparked something of a panic across every part of the British intelligence establishment, from Thames House to Cheltenham and beyond.

Working together, they'd narrowed down the destination IP address to a single Edwardian three-storey above a launderette in Peckham. But it was split into at least six flats, two per floor. Full of families, kids. Going in with a tactical squad was the last resort. For now, they would watch and wait while Sally Lime and her fellow keyboard warriors tightened the digital noose on the building.

There were six of them crammed into the tiny bedsit above a pub that rented rooms on Airbnb. Jeremy had thought this kind of place had been regulated out of existence back in the seventies, but clearly the skyrocketing price of all kinds of accommodation in the city had brought the bedsit back.

Two watchers from Thames House crouched by the window in perfect silence, binoculars and a mounted scope trained on the building across the junction. Two other teams were watching the back of the building and the street in both directions, while half a dozen front-runners and tailenders waited outside, moving in their slow, careful loops.

Jeremy was slumped on the folded-up sofa bed, while Lime sat at the tiny kitchen table on some kind of fishing stool the surveillance team had brought with them. She was typing steadily, swearing under her breath with endearing frequency.

The worst thing was the waiting. Knowing that the package was possibly in that building, that they could end it right there if they knew which flat to target.

Just like his marriage a half-decade before, it was the prospect of losing what he'd built that made Jeremy realise how little value he had been placing on it. A few days before, he'd seen the Legends Programme as a prison of his own making. Now he was fighting to keep dozens of people safe, people he'd made promises to.

His attempt to recreate Legends from memory still wasn't yielding much, but he felt less hopeless as time went on, dates and places and names coming back to him as he typed more. Operatives he'd vetted, Legends he'd taken out to dinner. The mixture of emotions on their faces and in their body language as he explained the Faustian nature of the programme.

He'd just got to his older recruits, those now joining the active pool. He wrote down Jamie Tulloch's name, remembering the recruitment run to Cambridge and the weekend in Wales. That had been the first time Alex Bowen had come along. She'd visited several times since, never letting much slip about what the Langley take was, whether they were attempting something similar. Then, three years ago, silence. Polite enquiries were met with stonewalling from the liaison types. At the time, he'd shrugged. It was part of the game. Career handlers like Alex went off the map sometimes. And with the rise of the New Russia in the sorry aftermath of the Ukraine war, there was plenty for both of them to handle, in the field or otherwise.

He looked down his list of active case officers. Terence Stringer was still offline. That was odd, but again not unprecedented. Perhaps the handover in Paris had been a little bumpy and Stringer had decided to drop out of sight for a day or two, make sure there was no back-tracing possible to Vauxhall Cross. If he'd suspected countersurveillance from Bocharov's people, or even the DGSI, France's counterintelligence service, Stringer would double back a few times before coming in from the cold. He was a seasoned case officer with the skills and resources to do just that.

But, something niggled. Jeremy looked through his issued phone for Stringer's secure comms number, then sent a brief message.

AEGIS ACTUAL, CHECK IN.

The message turned grey, then a small red icon popped up. 'Not deliverable? What the fuck does that mean?' muttered Jeremy.

Lime looked up from her laptop. 'Using secure messaging? It means they didn't get a response from the target device, so they scrubbed the message. Device might be turned off, or it might be compromised. Either way, you don't want a bunch of messages stacking up.'

Jeremy saw the question in her eyes. 'One of our case officers. Still hasn't checked in.'

Lime looked back down at her laptop. 'On the op I've been working on? With GARNET?'

'Yes. Asset is on task, so my case officer did the handover, but he's not been offline for this long afterwards before.'

Lime's eyes narrowed. 'Think it could be related? Your handler going offline right when someone's sneaking data out of our secure servers?'

Jeremy felt the sick feeling intensify. Stringer as a foreign asset? He couldn't see it. He'd known the man since his twenties. But then they'd been saying the same thing of every mole and turncoat since the Cambridge Five.

He tapped at his keyboard, trying to ignore the turmoil in his gut. 'Something to consider. Speaking of data. Any joy?'

Sally Lime grinned. 'A bit. GCHQ have given us packet monitoring on every router in that building. There's a lot of encrypted stuff,

E2E comms like WhatsApp. But that's standard. There is one unusual thing though.'

Jeremy raised an eyebrow.

'Top-floor apartment, on the right side. Absolutely *nothing* in there. No router traffic, no network-cell requests, nothing. It's a black hole. Nearly every home in the country has *something* that's networked these days. A house with absolutely nothing coming in or out, *that's* weird.'

Jeremy leaned forward and peered out of the window, as if he could see more with his ageing eyes than the two Security Service specialists with their giant binoculars. 'Could be an older person, someone without a phone line, no internet. Those people do still exist, you know. Or just an empty flat.'

Lime snorted. 'Not in this part of London. Nothing sits empty for long. And I'm willing to bet it isn't a Peckham grannie in there.'

One of the surveillance team coughed and turned around, a young white woman, red hair in a ponytail. She'd introduced herself as Blake when she'd arrived. 'Just got a glimpse, sir. Someone inside just twitched the curtain. IC1 male, late twenties, brown hair, blue shirt. He just did a visual sweep of the whole street, quartered off, very methodical.'

Jeremy felt his shoulders drop a few centimetres. There was someone in there. Their targets hadn't moved on yet. The trail was still hot.

Sally Lime grinned, clearly thinking the same thing. 'If our data's still in London, it's in that flat.'

20

Jamie

Royal Acacia Hotel, Stone Town, Zanzibar: now

'This is a pretty amazing place, Mr Boc— Arkady.'

They were leaning on the hardwood railing that encircled Bocharov's private balcony. Bocharov looked over his shoulder at the low curve of Stone Town harbour, the long seafront beyond. He nodded slowly, stretched expansively in his blue linen shirt, unbuttoned to the chest hair.

'It is very beautiful. Before I start with UPK, I had been to Africa before. But not this kind of place. I love it now. It is a good place to be rich.' He turned and pointed towards a pair of low couches shaded by a canvas awning. 'Come, sit. We will have some coffee, some breakfast. This hotel makes good pancakes. Like the American ones. Very fluffy.'

Vitaly sidled away to put in the room-service order, then came back with coffee and stood with his hands folded, eyes sweeping the horizon. His head snapped up at a high whine overhead. Jamie's eyes followed and saw the tiny speck of a tourist's drone making its way along the beach. Below, a young woman walked in the surf, the drone following her every move.

Bocharov shook his head. 'Drones. They use them for their videos. I hate the fucking things.'

Vitaly gave a slow nod. 'In Kherson, we used to pull the pin on a grenade, when they were overhead. Insurance policy. If you get hit, grenade goes off. Better than bleeding for hours in a muddy hole. Drone goes away, put the pin back in. Or sometimes I throw at the Ukrainians.'

Jamie took a sip of his coffee, unsure what to say to that, or even where to look. He swallowed hard.

Bocharov laughed. 'Best not to scare our new friend here with the war stories, Vitaly.' He sipped his coffee and let out a satisfied sigh. 'I like to get here early, get across the sea before it gets too hot. But I need a lot of coffee after this early start.'

Jamie was also appreciating the caffeine boost. He'd slept poorly, fighting the anxiety that had been with him since Paris, then waking every time Vitaly or one of his men paced past in the corridor outside. Jerking awake with the fear of what might have happened to GARNET ringing around his head like he was a freshly struck bell.

Part of his mind was still in Paris. He'd scanned as many sources as he could find on his phone that morning. Nothing. No news stories or vague allusions to security alerts. No chatter on social media. The coffee tasted suddenly bitter as he realised that could mean Terence's body was *still there*, beginning to rot in that hot little room. He swallowed back a sudden acidic tang of bile and put the coffee down.

'Today, you will meet my team,' said Bocharov. 'It is good timing, this ISO thing. I have many of my top people here anyway, for some . . . important meetings. So we can . . . what is that thing the English say, kill birds with a rock?'

Jamie stifled a laugh. 'Two birds with one stone.'

Bocharov frowned. The flat, emotionless green eyes looked him up and down. 'Is funny, when I say things wrong?'

'No, of course not. It's just that Russians have a reputation for . . . you know, straightforward execution. And that *is* a more direct way of saying the same thing.'

Bocharov nodded. 'It is true. Us Russians, we do what is necessary, no messing around.' He shrugged. 'Sometimes, mistakes. But we repeat, until the thing is done.'

Bocharov looked up and raised a hand to someone. Jamie twisted in his chair and saw a thin, pale man with little round glasses come on to the terrace. He looked like an accountant.

'Yakov, this is Yevgeny Olenev. He is not part of your deal, but I like everyone to meet each other. It is better for later, by the pool.'

Jamie nodded to the sallow-faced man as he sat down on the opposite couch, next to Bocharov. He didn't smile, so Jamie took the hint and didn't either. The two men exchanged a few words in Russian, Bocharov leaning back to listen closely. Towards the end of the exchange, Jamie could have sworn he heard the words 'Canning Town', which made him blink. But it must be just a Russian word that sounded like the district in East London, surely? He kept his face neutral, looking between the two men. Olenev gazed at him, lizard-like, still and watchful. Bocharov looked up at his bodyguard.

'Vitaly, where are the ladies this morning?' Bocharov said.

'On the way, boss.'

The food began to arrive from room service, wheeled in on a two-tier cart by a hotel waiter in a starched white shirt. He laid out a half-dozen plates; stacks of American-style pancakes, bacon, granola, yoghurt, fruit. Jamie's mouth watered at the sight of it all.

Bocharov gestured. 'Please, have some. If we wait for the ladies, we will starve, yes?'

This turned out to be a little uncharitable. Three women arrived on the terrace as Jamie was still transferring pancakes and fruit to his plate. They swept past him in a backwash of expensive perfume, silk shawls fluttering, darting in to plant kisses on Bocharov's cheek and settling in around the table with a ripple of Russian, Italian and French. Jamie blinked at the sudden stillness. It was like being in the middle of a lake when a flight of birds landed.

'Sophia, Elena, Natasha, this is Jamie. He is from Scotland. He is . . . for business here,' said Bocharov.

Cordial handshakes and unreadable eyes hidden behind large sunglasses. The women began to assemble their own breakfast plates, talking in quiet Russian to one another. Sophia and Elena were both long-haired brunettes with near-identical white and tan blouses and skirts. Natasha was a blonde with shorter hair and wore a black wraparound dress. She had watchful eyes that swept across the food options, slim hands carefully selecting food that she arranged with photo-ready precision on her plate. She gave Jamie a small smile as she leaned back on the couch, feet pulled up under her.

Jamie sipped at a fresh cup of coffee and worked his way through a plate of pancakes, wondering what the hell he was doing here. He'd had plenty of breakfasts with clients in anonymous business hotels, but this was the first time he'd done it by the Indian Ocean with someone who could plausibly be called a warlord.

'So, Jamie,' said Olenev, sitting forward. 'Arkady tells me that you sell warehouse equipment and software, yes?' His accent was also Russian, Jamie guessed, although far stronger than Bocharov's. Less time on the expat circuit, perhaps. He wondered what this man did for a living. Something told him it wasn't accountancy, despite the immediate sense that Yevgeny Olenev knew exactly where every penny, cent and kopek of his money was.

'That's right. Supply-chain automation and inventory management. All real-time. Takes the guesswork out of things. Makes your inventory more resilient to supply-chain shocks. I'm sure I don't need to explain the value of that to a Russian.'

Olenev's eyebrows shot up, then he barked a sudden laugh that made Natasha, sitting beside him, jump in her seat.

'I like him, Arkady. Funny man.'

Jamie shrugged, confidence coming back on the familiar ground of logistics and software and hard numbers. 'It's true. The collapse showed how fragile supply chains can be, all over the world. Especially in Russia. If you don't know what you have, or how fast it's leaving your warehouses, or if that data is out of date before you get it, how can you plan?'

Olenev shrugged. 'You are selling to Arkady, not me. But it is good to meet you, Jamie. I was not pleased when Arkady tells me there is someone new coming. But this is unavoidable, he must do for the ISO certification, yes?'

Jamie nodded. 'That's right. It's time sensitive. And there's a lead time on the installation and integration work.'

Olenev leaned back and finally smiled, but it was a cold and humourless smile of appraisal, not one of welcome. He was satisfied he had the measure of Jamie. 'You will have a good time, then. Arkady and I, we have not always seen eye to eye. But he has been very kind host. You will be looked after. Only the best for Bocharov, eh?'

Jamie gestured to the food in front of them, the hotel terrace they sat on. 'I mean, I'm feeling pretty spoiled already, Mr Olenev.'

'Yevgeny. Call me Yevgeny. But you have not seen Arkady's place in the north yet. It is . . . compound? But very nice compound. Like holiday park.'

Bocharov grunted. 'It's good for security. If I live behind fence, it should be nice, yes?'

Olenev nodded and sipped at the cup of black coffee that was the only thing he'd taken. 'You've earned your rewards, my friend. We all have. This is the afterlife. Valhalla, like the Kievan Rus' had.'

Bocharov chuckled. 'In Valhalla you don't have to do Zoom calls.'

After breakfast, Vitaly led Jamie down two floors to the hotel's business suites, a collection of blandly corporate meeting rooms that were quite out of character with the hardwood, sandstone and Instagram-ready Zanzibari art everywhere else in the hotel. Instead, the office suite had laminate floors, pine-veneer desks, printers and the ever-present corporate smell of hard-wearing nylon carpeting.

Bocharov arrived shortly after with another Russian Jamie hadn't met yet, plus a dark-skinned man in his fifties.

'Jamie, this is Anton Komarov, the UPK logistics manager for East Africa. And this is Moses Omondi, who runs our warehouses in Kenya and Tanzania.'

As soon as they'd sat down and Jamie had introduced himself,

Bocharov became absorbed in something on his laptop screen. Social media, judging by the occasional flickers of satisfaction and envy that flitted across his face.

Komarov was a younger man, blond hair cut short. Too young to be one of Bocharov's old comrades. A perfect representative of the New Russia. Prepared to smile, even at foreigners. His accent was almost traceless, Russian-inflected internet English.

'We won't be going into any real contractual negotiations until we're at Mr Bocharov's villa tomorrow. But Moses does have a few initial queries he needs to ask. Does that sound good to you?'

Jamie nodded. This was familiar ground. He could quote the relevant standards backwards and forwards.

The two men peppered him with questions for nearly three hours as the sun peaked and began to drop back towards the horizon. He had an answer for everything, pivoting smoothly from answer to answer. Terence had said this would be an easy deal, but they still put him through his paces. This wasn't exactly selling double glazing over the phone. Perhaps GARNET could have done this job, but Jamie was certain he was doing it better.

Finally, Bocharov looked up from his laptop and checked his watch.

'A late lunch, now, I think? Then we will give Mr Tulloch the afternoon off while I continue with the boys here. No point being in Zanzibar if you don't see a little of it.'

Jamie looked up sharply, then realised he couldn't seem too eager to get out from under the watchful eye of Vitaly and his goons.

'Sure, yeah, that would be great.' He searched his memory for itinerary items from a long-ago backpacking trip he'd planned but never taken. 'I hear the night market here is worth visiting.'

Bocharov made a face. 'Too much fish, for me. There is music at the old fort sometimes. A few bars for the tourists. Don't do anything not worth doing,' he said, wagging a finger with a leer that might have been admonishment or encouragement.

Jamie chuckled a little and sat back. 'I'll make a few notes after our conversation and join you in a moment. Back upstairs?'

'Da. See you up there,' said Bocharov, levering his bulk off the chair with surprising grace. He nodded to the other three men. 'Leave everything here. We have room until six.'

The two men filed out after Bocharov, and Jamie stared at his laptop. He typed a few sentences, then glanced out at the sky, still a blue so bright it made him narrow his eyes, even through the smoked-glass window.

Somewhere out there, someone else would be waiting for him. Well, waiting for GARNET anyway. Maybe SIS thought everything was fine. Or they already knew about Terence and they were trying frantically to find him. Either way, he had to make contact, warn them about Terence's murder. Then he could get the hell out of Zanzibar and back to his old life.

Suddenly, the apartment in Chelsea didn't seem such a gilded cage. It was home. His own bed and a door he could lock that didn't have a pacing Russian mercenary on the other side. A powerful longing coursed through him, for the London skyline, for the carbon tang of the Tube in the early morning, for the stultifying normality of the damp sandwiches and mediocre coffee.

As he thought about his next move, how he might be able to make himself known to the SIS team that must be on the island by now, his eyes settled on Bocharov's open laptop, the screen turned away from him. It was a Mac, a very recent and high-end Pro model.

Jamie felt a light sheen of moisture on his palms, the roof of his mouth suddenly dry, as if the fluid in his body had simply shifted half a metre in a few seconds.

He shouldn't look. He was in a very nice hotel by a beautiful beach, but the men upstairs were ruthless murderers. He might end up washing up on that same gorgeous beach if he wasn't careful. Tragic boating accident. It was amazing what could happen when you tangled with men like Bocharov.

Jamie took a sip of water, his heart beating loudly in the quiet room. He put the glass down. It would be stupid to look. But what if he could salvage something here? Do even a small fraction of what GARNET might have done? Do something that might make the memory of that dreadful bathroom rattling around in his skull even slightly worth it?

He'd be a fool not to take a tiny wee look, at least.

Jamie stood up and stretched, then paced to the window, eyeing the corners of the room, looking for cameras. The walls were frosted glass on two sides, a narrow clear strip showing the white walls of the corporate suite beyond. A pair of trousered legs strode past, someone heading to a meeting in one of the other rooms. Then there was silence.

He turned around, very slowly, simply a man thinking very carefully about an important business deal.

Bocharov's laptop was powered on, the screen still lit. Of course. A man like Bocharov would hate typing his password again and again. Jamie had known a dozen like him. Taking home million-dollar secrets on a poorly secured personal phone. Downloading contracts to their kid's iPad over coffee shop Wi-Fi.

Jamie took two steps forward, then tapped the trackpad of the laptop with his knuckle. The screen lit up to maximum brightness, showing Bocharov's desktop. A dozen folders in an untidy heap on one side of the screen.

Now or never. Jamie took two more steps back to his laptop bag, then extracted a spare USB stick. He plugged it into Bocharov's laptop, then opened the Mac's root folder for Bocharov's user account. Command C to copy. Command V to paste, straight into the USB.

A progress bar popped up: 14.8Gb of files. Not a lot, but not a quick minute or so. The time estimate refreshed. Three minutes. He checked his watch and noted the time.

Jamie moved the progress bar to the very bottom of the screen, then lowered the laptop lid a little. He went back to his own laptop and swallowed a mouthful of room-temperature water from his glass.

One minute down. Two minutes to go.

If he could get that USB stick in an inside pocket, somewhere Vitaly wouldn't find it in a pat-down, he could get lost in the shadows and the firelight of the night market. Lots of people, lots of stalls. Plenty of ways to disappear for a few minutes if he needed to.

He checked his watch again. One minute to go.

Footsteps. A pair of khaki-clad legs strode past outside. Going to another room, he thought, just before the legs stopped and the handle of the meeting-room door began to turn.

Jamie froze. Could he step across the room? Pull the stick?

The door opened. It was Komarov. He smiled at Jamie. 'Mr Bocharov wanted to look at some figures over lunch. Just grabbing my iPad. You got a proposal all done for us, yes?'

Jamie laughed, hearing the strain in his own voice, hoping that Komarov didn't. 'I wish I could do it that quickly. Lot of options to consider, bulk pricing, you know . . .'

How long was left on the copying process? Was the laptop muted? Jamie gripped the edge of the table, eyes fixed on the blond Russian. He glanced at his watch. Maybe thirty seconds? His pulse throbbed at his throat.

Komarov nodded and smiled as he picked up his iPad. 'Of course, of course. I was joking.'

A tiny silence descended as Komarov looked at him, broken only by the soft, springy chime as the copying process completed on Bocharov's laptop.

Komarov frowned. 'Are you all right, Mr Tulloch? You look a little pale.'

Jamie managed to nod. 'Y— yes. Just feeling a little off. The two-hour time difference, you know. Messes with my appetite.'

Komarov nodded. 'I know the feeling. The stomach takes a while to adjust to a new country, even when you're eating in places like this. Just take it easy at the night market tonight, okay?'

Jamie forced a smile on to his face. 'Of course. Wouldn't want to have food poisoning while we're at Mr Bocharov's place, would I?'

Komarov shook his head. 'Absolutely not. Food poisoning and infinity pools don't really mix.' He laughed at his own joke loudly enough that Jamie jumped, then he strode out of the room, calling back over his shoulder. 'Food will be in ten minutes. See you up in the suites.'

The door closed and Jamie let out a long, shaky sigh.

He ejected the USB and pocketed it. It felt heavy with the transgression he'd just committed.

Bocharov *must* be a threat. Otherwise SIS wouldn't be using GARNET, an asset with a cover story years in the making, to investigate him. But what if he handed over the USB and it was nothing but Bocharov's rejected Instagram selfies?

It didn't matter. He'd tried. Perhaps he could salvage something from this whole shitshow, something that might mean Terence Stringer hadn't died in vain, choking on his own blood on the floor of an airport bathroom.

He went to the window again and looked out over the harbour, the curve of buildings, quite different now the light had changed. The bright hulls of fishing skiffs bobbed in the water, alongside the long, low curves of dhows, most with their sails pulled down. Two were on their way out of the harbour, sails ascending and snapping out to catch the wind. On the harbour wall, dozens of small figures jostled and pushed, then went plummeting into the water. Zanzibari boys competing to backflip and make the biggest splash.

For the first time in many years, he thought about home. Not London, but Edinburgh. And not the jewellery-box Gothic of the city centre, the castle and the bagpipe music blaring from shopfronts. Instead, he thought of the harled concrete housing blocks and damp grey-green of the empty parks, the rumbling buses and water out of the tap that tasted like nothing at all. He didn't want to go back, but he felt a pang for it anyway. To be anywhere but here.

21

Nicola

Forodhani Gardens, Stone Town, Zanzibar: now

Every stall in the night market was bridged by intense white strip lights, pointing straight down into piles of delicious-looking food. Flaring gas stoves lit the faces of men and women in white aprons and chef's hats. Clouds of fragrant steam rose into the clear night sky.

The low mutter of five hundred conversations became a dull roar as Nicola approached the seafront park where the night market was held, pierced by the calls of the stallholders holding up sample trays and sticks of grilled meat, seafood, chapatis and samosas. Graeme Sylvan was a dozen steps behind her, his deep tan and frayed board shorts blending him perfectly into the crowds of Western backpackers thronging the stalls.

To her left and right, Sylvan's two local operatives, Farida and Tumo, weaved through the crowd. They slipped between stalls, Farida in a colourful wrap, Tumo in jeans and a polo shirt, eyes watchful, earbuds in that would pass for the Bluetooth headphones you could get from any hole-in-the-wall phone shop in East Africa. Both had grown up in the vast maze of streets that surrounded the ancient core of Stone Town. They stopped and started, murmuring in Kiswahili to the vendors, trying things from the offered plates.

All four did a slow circuit of the market, keeping well apart, not looking at each other, a dragnet pulled through the channels, intent on finding operative GARNET. Still no check-in from his burner phone. Not unusual, if he was in close contact with his target. But it was another finger on the scales, pushing them down towards the uneasy balance point, the fulcrum where a mission flipped from viable to compromised.

Earlier that evening, a bribe to the concierge of Bocharov's hotel had got them the vague suggestion that the Russians were eating 'somewhere near the market'.

She was almost certain Bocharov and his entourage would not be enticed by the delights of fist-sized falafel, skewers of roasted seafood and 'Zanzibar pizza' on chapati bases, but if GARNET was going to get away from Bocharov's security team at any point, this is where he would come.

She thought she'd seen him twice already. A flash of dark hair in the darkness, between two stalls, a blue-shirted back turning quickly towards the lights of the seafront road. Both times the figure had been gone when she'd turned to confirm. She was seeing her agent everywhere and nowhere all at once.

'Okay, let's go round again,' Nicola said softly, looking out over the dark waters of the harbour. Here and there, fishing dhows with their sails stowed bobbed low, swinging gas lamps in their prows lighting the water in pools of rippling light. Figures moved in the darkness on the sand, pulling in more boxes of fish, voices calling out as men in chef's hats bought them straight from the shoreline.

'Possible target, twenty metres,' said Tumo, his voice deep for his slight frame. 'By the cane-juice guy.'

Nicola's eyes snapped to the stall. It was easily spotted by the long sugar canes racked up, the steady thump of machetes cutting them into short lengths, ready to be fed through the heavy steel wheels of the pressing machine by a rotating cast of teenage boys in sweat-soaked vests. They cut and fed, filling the sugar-rimmed glasses with the pale yellow cane juice and passing it out to a shifting crowd of customers with practised flicks of the hand, collecting shillings and dispensing change. It was a fast, fluid dance, designed to catch the eye and reel in the tourists. And it worked. The narrow gaps between stalls were busy, with dozens of Westerners packed in close.

There, just to the left of the cane press, apparently fascinated by what he was seeing, was operative GARNET.

Or at least someone the right height, build and hair colour.

Nicola tapped her earpiece again. 'I have eyes on. Keep your distance. I'm going to get closer, get a positive ID.'

She saw Sylvan move to her left, taking up a blocking position by the nearest gate. Tumo was already halfway across the park, heading towards the other exit. Farida was closer, ready to back her up if she needed it.

She wandered closer, smiling at the imprecations of a stallholder, bought a Zanzibar pizza, chopped into small squares, to give her a prop. She popped a couple of the crisp squares into her mouth, savouring the melted cheese inside. She really had to come back here one day, when she wasn't on an op.

GARNET stood perfectly still, absorbed in the work of the cane juicers. He wasn't doing the checks she'd have expected from a seasoned operative. No backward glances, no head on a swivel finding reasons to look in every direction, constantly assessing his personal threat envelope.

This guy looked like some random business tourist, in blue shirt and slacks, a day's stubble visible in the low glare of the LED strip lights.

She was less than a metre away now, the target's back within reach. Nicola started to raise her arm, but before she could extend her fingers the man's head snapped to the left, focusing on a cluster of people at the nearest gate. He turned and plunged into the crowd.

'On the move, heading east towards the harbour wall,' said Sylvan in her ear.

'Yep, I'm on him,' she murmured, a half-dozen steps behind. 'Did he see me?'

'Negative,' said Sylvan. 'Something spooked him. Getting eyes on. Wait out.'

There was a moment of silence, the sound of fabric rubbing the mic as Sylvan changed position. 'Russians, boss. Three of 'em. Bocharov's men, I think.'

'They looking for our boy?'

'Don't think so. Looks like they're just here to eat. But it's spooked him.'

'He's at the wall, going for the south exit,' said Tumo.

'Going left,' said Farida, splitting away and angling through the densely packed stalls.

'We can't lose him in the side streets. Who's got eyes on?' said Nicola. She'd lost the blue shirt in the swirls of people. A stallholder stepped into her path, a pyramid of mouth-watering katlesi deep-fried beef balls glistening on a platter in his hand. She gave him a tight smile and edged past, shaking her head. But GARNET was gone.

'Fuck, lost him. Anyone at the south end?'

Silence, then Tumo's voice again, crackly with distance, his breath catching. He must have darted out of the park and sprinted to keep GARNET in sight.

'I can see him. He's headed towards Kenyatta Road.'

Nicola swore under her breath again, sweat prickling her back. Kenyatta was one of the wider thoroughfares cutting through the ancient stone streets of the Old Town, but there was a dark side passage, alley or doorway every metre or two. No better place to duck out of sight.

'Keep your eyes on him. Grab him if you have to. We can't lose him.'

22

Jeremy

Peckham High Street: one hour ago

The sun was low to the horizon by the time the tactical team was ready to go. Eight men arrived, spaced out over an hour, each with a kitbag full of equipment. They suited up quietly, buckling on armour and helmets, checking pouches, loading magazines and talking in low voices.

The watchers at the window kept up a constant commentary. The target had started regular checks, appearing at the window about every fifteen minutes. Jeremy ordered the front-runners and tailenders pulled back, out of sight, effectively sealing the road from either end. Just before the tactical team went in, Met officers would do the same, but far more visibly.

'We go after the next check he does, which will give us an absolute maximum of fifteen minutes to get across the road and through the door and secure the stairwell. Faster is better,' said Jeremy as they readied the final brief. The eight-man tactical team nodded, their faces impassive, almost bored. Lime was still working on her laptop. She flipped her screen around to show the team what they were looking for.

'We need to secure stuff like this – SSD drives. Plus laptops, phones, any network hardware you see. And if you see a big box of what look like oversized cassette tapes, that as well. Try not to shoot any of it.'

The officers grinned under their helmets and visors.

Jeremy was pulling on a ballistic vest as he spoke. 'We'll be just behind you to bag and tag everything. We're both tactically rated. We'll wait on your go to enter the property though.'

The sergeant in charge of the detachment stepped forward with two thigh holsters and SIG Sauer pistols. 'Things could get dicey in there, sir. Tight corners. Keep these holstered unless you have an immediate threat. Roger?'

Jeremy nodded, passing one to Sally and fastening the other around his leg. He checked the chamber, loaded a magazine and holstered the weapon. 'Roger that. Let's get going.'

The soldiers made their last preparations, weapon slings looping over heads, magazines fitted to their carbine rifles and sub-machine guns.

'Target at the window,' murmured Blake, the watcher. 'Okay, he's done. Curtain's back down.'

Jeremy raised his radio to his mouth. 'All stations, Gridiron Actual. Bluestone, I say again, Bluestone,' he said, using the codeword that would begin a carefully planned chain of actions from the units all around them.

They followed the tactical team down the narrow stairwell, booted feet rumbling on the concrete steps. The troopers stacked up to one side of the entrance hall, then the pointman pulled the door open and glanced out into the street.

'Clear, moving.'

The team filed out, staggered herringbone fashion, weapons up to cover the windows above. They went straight across, aiming for the target building's door.

Jeremy and Sally followed. Jeremy itched to have his pistol in his hand. He hated being out in the open like this, pistol holstered, a hundred windows looking down on him. In either direction police officers ushered people away, blue-and-yellow-striped police vehicles pulled up to block the road. They had to get in before whoever was inside realised the street had been cleared. A strange silence descended as the vehicle traffic dropped and the voices of several hundred people were pushed away.

'Ready to breach at street level. Go silent,' said the team leader over the radio. The pointman knelt, covered by two others aiming at the windows above. He extracted a thin plastic sheet from his belt kit, like the ones locksmiths used for simple Yale locks, then slid it into the frame. With barely a click it popped open, as easily as breathing. Many stairwell door locks in Peckham were more of a mild deterrent than an actual security measure.

The pointman pushed inwards, gloved hand on the wood, his G36C pulled in tight. He leaned against the frame and spoke over the radio.

'Door left, door right. Open front, stairs. No tangos.'

The team filed inside, dispersing to each side of the ground-floor hallway, weapons up and sweeping, covering arcs in the tight space. Jeremy followed close behind with Sally, fighting the urge to crouch against the wall, to make himself small and harder to hit. As a young man, he'd adored his tactical training, the exciting rush of clearing a building with the thunder of blank rounds. But several times since, he'd seen what a bullet could do to the human body.

'Moving to first floor.'

The team rose from their crouches and moved up the stairwell, slow and careful in the half-light filtering down from a skylight three floors above. The tiled stairs curved around in tight right-angle turns, worn tiles showing the passage of thousands of feet over the decades. Another landing, another two flat doors.

'First deck clear. Bravo, go firm on these doors. Collapse to third deck on my go.'

Two of the soldiers murmured acknowledgements and peeled off, covering up and down the stairs. The other six moved up, Sally and Jeremy following closely.

On the second floor, they left another two troopers. If any of the other occupants of the block chose this moment to step outside, they could be grabbed and hustled back inside. But the minutes were ticking down until their target took another look outside. They'd already taken four minutes. There were a thousand variables to manage, but the only one they could see was time.

On the third floor, the remaining four troopers dropped quickly into crouches, covering the apartments on each side. Their target was on the right, an anonymous blue door with a brass number 6. No name, no bell, a letterbox jammed with pizza flyers and Chinese menus.

'Bravo, Charlie, this is Actual. Collapse now,' said the sergeant. 'Point, check the frame.'

The pointman nodded and crept forward, gloved fingers sweeping around the doorway, looking for hidden switches or sensors. He pulled a tiny goose-necked camera from one of his pouches and slid it under the door, unfolding a grainy black-and-white screen from the side.

'Hallway, door left, door right, open front. No tangos visible. Nothing on the back of this door.'

Bravo and Charlie arrived and tucked themselves in behind their comrades, eyes watchful. Jeremy glanced at his watch. Eight minutes.

The pointman turned and spoke. 'Pretty solid mortice-lock door, S'arnt. Could try a hinge breach with the shotgun or do it minty fresh.'

Jeremy smirked, despite how tense he felt. The tiny breaching charges that would destroy a door lock *did* look surprisingly like over-sized breath mints.

'Mint it. Then roll straight through. We'll take open front, Delta behind us, Bravo and Charlie left and right doors respectively. Roger?'

All eight nodded silently.

'Go for breach,' said the sergeant, settling in beside the doorframe and pressing himself against the chipped paint.

The pointman nodded, then pulled a charge from another pouch. He fixed it carefully into place over the lock, then looked back at the rest of the tactical team.

'Stand by, fire in the hole.'

With a swift jerk, he pulled the device's fuse striker and stepped to one side, pressing himself against the wall on the other side of the door.

Jeremy covered his ears and pressed himself to the stairwell wall. The detonation was curiously muffled, although they all felt the pressure change as the shockwave rippled over them. When Jeremy blinked and opened his eyes again, the flat's door was swinging inwards, the space where the lock had been a smoking hole. The bolt clattered to the floorboards inside.

The black-clad figures streamed past him, through the gap, moving so quickly that Jeremy had trouble seeing what was happening. He heard loud bangs to the left and right: the team clearing rooms with flash-bang grenades.

He crouched, feeling completely powerless. His whole programme was inside that flat, currently being shaken by ringing thumps. But, so far, no gunfire.

A chorus of 'Clear' began to come back over the radio. Left room clear. Right room clear. Hallway clear. Jeremy inched closer to the front door, peering inside, trying to see through the white haze generated by the repeated flash-bang detonations.

Where the hell was the target?

'Kilo Actual, this is Whisky Two. Movement at building rear. IC1 male climbing out of the window. No shot. I say again, no shot, over.'

Jeremy heard a muttered curse from the sergeant. 'All callsigns, Kilo Actual. Continuing to clear. We'll meet you on the back roof. One room remaining.'

Jeremy flexed his hands inside his tactical gloves, moving forward until he was by the front-door frame.

'Jeremy . . .' Sally began, her hand on his shoulder. 'We should back off until we—'

'IED, IED!'

The hallway was suddenly full of black-suited troopers, sprinting towards them through the haze of flash-bang smoke. It swirled, wreathing them. Jeremy felt himself tumble backwards, a headlong scrabble towards the stairs, his thoughts a single frantic scream of urgency.

When the detonation came it was louder than anything he'd ever heard. A cloud of blackness rushing forward, dust and bricks and flying debris. He tumbled backwards, down the stairs, all thought lost, surrounded on all sides by rushing, falling, screaming.

Then there was nothing.

23

Jamie

Stone Town: now

Had he been spotted? Was he being followed?

Vitaly the bodyguard was hard to miss, which was why even Jamie, with zero training, had spotted the big Russian arriving at the night market with a couple of his shorter, nastier friends. They didn't *look* like they were on the hunt for Jamie, but of course they wouldn't. If their job was to keep tabs on him, they would appear to be there for their own reasons, just a trio of hardened killers out for a cheeky Zanzibar pizza after the boss had gone back to the hotel.

Jamie was more certain with each step. They'd been looking for him. He was being followed and they *knew* he wasn't who he said he was.

He drummed his fingers on his shirtsleeve as he walked, squinting in the darkness of the shadowed Old Town street, buildings looming on either side. His hand went to the small bulge of the USB drive in the pocket of his shirt. Still there. Every few metres, a bright LED street-lamp attracted a small cloud of mosquitoes and flies. He moved between the pools of light, the edges of cracked paving under his feet. Overhead, wooden balconies leaned out, shutting out the night sky. A shutter banged open behind him and he jumped.

The thing was, he *was* who he said he was. But he also wasn't. He was doing the job GARNET had been sent here to do, only badly, without any support, with no idea what the *fuck* he was supposed to be looking for, or why.

He glanced behind him. A few figures moved in the darkness, people passing on cross-streets. Someone called from a doorway in Kiswahili, then switched to English when Jamie got a little closer. The voice belonged to a gangly teenager in shorts and a blue vest top who was smiling and gesturing towards an even narrower side street. Beyond, a red sign glowed.

'Tourist? Good bar? You want to find a drink?'

Jamie shook his head silently and pushed past.

He should double back. That's what spies did, right? If the Russians *were* following him, he could lose them in these narrow streets. Return to the night market. There were lots of people there. It made sense SIS would be watching a big, busy place like that, if they were even here on the island. If they knew he was even on Zanzibar.

Had GARNET had some other way to contact his handlers? A phone? A computer? There had been nothing on Terence when he'd found him. Jamie's own personal phone was back in London, just as the instructions had said. So he just had his work phone. And what was he going to do with that? Ring up Geoff, Head of Sales, at home in Woking, and say, 'Sorry to disturb boss, I'm being followed through the streets of Stone Town in Zanzibar by Russian mercenaries and I think I'm fucked'?

No. He was on his own. Going for a walk just in case someone from SIS might be looking for him. Great fucking plan, pal.

Jamie turned left, taking the opportunity to glance behind him again. Two figures moving with purpose, both in shadow. Was it Vitaly's two favoured team members, the near-identical shaven-headed mercenaries, both from Chelyabinsk, who he'd christened Grumpy and Sleepy? He couldn't see. Couldn't risk stopping.

After he turned the corner he quickened his pace. Maybe he could dart down another side street, get out of sight, slip past them. It was the only thing he could think of. Panic crept down his spine, starting at his shoulders. Why were they following him? Had they figured out what he'd done with the USB drive? Were they going to take it back by force? Take him out? A tragic mugging-gone-wrong in a Zanzibari backstreet?

He turned again, this time into the narrowest street yet. A white plastic sign for a shop of some kind glowed a few metres ahead of him. Three young men sat on the steps, talking quietly, voices carrying through the night air. Now he was in the peripheral silence of Stone Town, away from the bustle of the harbour area, he could hear the distant night market. A moped of some kind whined past a street or two over, the sound echoing from the stone around him.

He looked behind once more. Nobody there. Maybe he was going to be okay.

The three young men lapsed into sudden silence as he passed. Then the closest to him nodded slowly. 'Habari,' he said, his words loud in the quiet of the narrow street.

Jamie managed a mumbled 'Nzuri', which was all he could remember. Then he was past them.

A dozen steps further on, halfway down the narrow passage, a huge stone doorway loomed. It held one of the carved wooden doors that Stone Town was so famous for. The doorway was deep and dark, the beautiful carvings nearly invisible in the dimness. A spark of curiosity rose in him, a long-buried wish to see this place, to put his hands on the centuries-old carved wood. He stepped forward, into shadow.

A hand came out of the darkness and gripped his wrist.

24

Nicola

Stone Town: now

By the time Nicola got there, Tumo had GARNET pinned in a doorway. Three youths further down the narrow street were standing up off the steps of a shop, backlit by the glow of its sign.

'Trouble? Is there trouble, friends?' they called in English.

'No trouble, no trouble. Our friend is a little bit drunk,' Nicola called out in Kiswahili, inflected with enough of her English accent that the tension immediately broke. Just a mzungu who couldn't hold his cheap Safari beer, like most of them. She saw three smiles and the young men turned back to their places on the steps.

'Get him around the corner,' she whispered to Tumo, who had one hand clamped over the agent's mouth and another twisting his arm behind his back. They hustled GARNET into a dark and silent alley that led slightly uphill. Barred windows overlooked them on every side. She didn't like this. Too exposed. Too many angles to cover.

'GARNET, I'm AEGIS Three One, your field handler. Calm down. My friend here is going to let you go. Don't run, got it? We're friends.'

The man's eyes were wide in the shadows, but she saw the way his shoulders dropped, muscles relaxed, the moment she said 'field handler'. This wasn't a good sign. Why the hell was an experienced agent so jumpy after barely a full day in the field? What exactly had spooked him so badly?

'You've been off comms. What's the issue? Emcon around the target?'

GARNET blinked in the half-light, looking between Nicola and Tumo. He opened and closed his mouth like a beached fish. What the hell was wrong with him?

Farida came around the corner and he jumped again. Nicola flicked a hand. 'You're a couple out for an evening stroll. Keep watch on the cross-street, go.'

Tumo and Farida linked arms and headed back to the broader street where they'd caught up to GARNET.

'Three Two, this is Three One, location?' she said.

Sylvan came back a second later. 'Two streets north of you, I think. No activity. Russians are still at the market.'

'Head back there, keep an eye on them.'

'Roger.'

GARNET put a hand on her forearm. His palms were clammy.

'I'm not GARNET.'

Nicola took a step back, a dry queasiness in her throat. Had they ID'd the wrong person? Chased down some random tourist? Had she blown an entire op with the simplest of mistakes?

'I'm sorry, what?'

'I'm not GARNET. I'm Jamie Tulloch. The Legend. I'm not supposed to be here.'

It was the last piece of a jigsaw slipping into place, although instead of quiet satisfaction, she felt horrible clarity. It made sense now. The tugging at the back of her mind that something wasn't quite right. How jumpy Not-GARNET had seemed every time she'd had him on scope. The fuzzy match with her memory of what the man was supposed to look like. All of it.

She was on a live op, in Africa, surrounded by deadly, utterly ruthless Russians, with an untrained fucking civilian.

Nicola took another step back and leaned against the dusty stone of the building behind her. She was still barely a metre from GARNET—from Tulloch. But he wasn't an asset, not any more. He was a giant, terrifying liability.

'Why are you here, Jamie? What happened?'

Tulloch had calmed down when she'd identified herself, but she saw him wind himself right back up again as he waved his hands, apparently not sure where to start.

'I— I was early. For the flight. I— when we landed in Paris . . .'

She stepped forward and put a hand on his shoulder. 'Take a breath, mate. What happened? Give me the basics.'

Tulloch nodded, stepped back, took a long breath, eyes on his feet. He looked up at her.

The story came out in a monotone, as if speaking without emotion might dull the horror of it. 'My flight to Paris was cancelled, so they put me on another one, earlier. I showed up at the handover an hour ahead of time. Terence was dead when I got there, on a toilet floor, for fuck's sake. No sign of GARNET. I got out of there. I left him behind. I didn't know what else to do.'

His voice cracked on the last couple of words and she squeezed his shoulder, mind racing.

'I'm Nicola, all right? That's my real name. I was GARNET'S handler, but he's off grid and you're here, so I'm going to make sure we both get out of this. Got it?'

He took another shuddery breath, then nodded. 'Okay.'

'You're sure he was dead?'

'Very sure. His throat was cut. There was – there was a lot of blood. I checked his body and there was nothing on him – no wallet, no passport, no phone, nothing.'

Nicola leaned against the wall, reappraising the man in front of her. Not many people would have the presence of mind to do something like that when they found a body. Especially the body of someone they knew and trusted. What did that mean though, the body being stripped of ID? Was this some kind of counter-intel op? Who would be doing it? And why attack in an airport, one of the most heavily surveilled places on the planet?

Nicola's fingers traced the powdery surface of the stone wall behind her. Stringer's body being stripped might explain why they'd had radio silence from GARNET. 'So you didn't have any secure comms? No way to talk to us?'

Tulloch shook his head. He stood a little straighter, the quaver gone from his voice now that he had someone to actually talk to. 'If Terence had a phone or something he was meant to give to GARNET, it wasn't on him. I'm supposed to be on a beach in South America right now. Instead, I've been selling software to Russians.'

Nicola frowned. 'Successfully?'

Tulloch gave her a shaky grin. 'Aye, actually. And Bocharov seems to like me. Sees himself as a teuchter-made-good or something. Kindred spirits, I guess. Even though I'm not a teuchter, just a wee bam from the schemes.'

Nicola blinked. 'I understood about half of that. But it sounds like you've got a bit of their trust?'

Tulloch chuckled. 'They're scary Russians. Don't think they trust anyone. But, yeah, I think *they* think I'm harmless. Software nerd that's a bit more relatable than most of the linen-suit-wearing twats they send out on jobs like this.'

Despite herself, Nicola found a laugh rising unbidden. 'Sounds like you're doing okay. And you made contact with us, even if we had to chase you down.'

'I thought you were the Russian guys. I saw them in the market, thought they were following me.'

Nicola nodded. 'Points for observation, spotting them and reacting so fast. But it looks like they were just out for some seafood skewers and Nutella chapatis. They're still back there.'

Tulloch squatted down, leaning back against the wall. He looked up into the dim starlight above. 'So what the hell do we do now? Bocharov wants to take me up to his private compound tomorrow.'

Nicola tapped her fingers against the stone. How much could she tell him? It would be an extremely bad idea to tell Jamie Tulloch his cover, as himself, relied solely on the encryption on some stolen hard drives. Better to make sure he would be cautious, give him some of the brief GARNET would have had.

Nicola leaned forward. 'Jamie, these guys are killers. Bocharov was called malen'kiy myasnik, in the Donbas. It means "the little butcher". He killed POWs, ran torture facilities.'

Tulloch visibly paled, even in the semi-darkness of the alley.

'So what's he doing in Africa then?'

Nicola shrugged. 'They're heavily involved in the arms trade in and out of North Africa, and every insurgency and brushfire war south of the Sahara to boot. Illegal mining, people trafficking, drugs, straight-up mercenary coups, you name it.'

'So you can get me out, right? We can head off tomorrow? Called back to London, maybe? They'll find another supplier. We have competitors.'

Nicola felt a stab of uncertainty. The mission brief had been very specific. Bocharov was up to something. Something really bad. Every indicator pointed towards big things going down this week. They would only have one chance at this.

'I need to speak to London. It might do more harm than good to pull you out straight away. We don't want to spook them, put you at risk. Right now, you're safe. You're not an agent. You really *are* a software sales guy. If they look into you, they're looking into the real you. Your cover is perfect because it's *actually* you.' She swallowed the lie by omission, guilt tugging at her. But knowing those encrypted drives were out in the world wouldn't help him.

Tulloch shook his head. 'Isn't all that supposed to have switched over to GARNET? Terence told me they'd scrub my old photos, put ones of him up. Clear ones, in case anyone's looking. Bocharov even said I looked younger than my LinkedIn photo, for fuck's sake.'

Nicola cursed under her breath. Tulloch was right. They'd need to swap that back. If they even *had* photos of Tulloch on file right now. From what Althrop had told her on the phone the day before, there was almost nothing left of the programme after the attack on its servers. Could this all be connected? Or was her mission collateral damage in some kind of wider attack?

'Will this help? Make a decision, I mean?' said Tulloch, holding something up. The dim street light glinted on a sliver of metal and plastic. She took it. A USB stick.

'What's this?' she said, turning it over in her hand.

'A complete copy of the root folder of Bocharov's laptop, taken this afternoon,' said Tulloch.

Nicola blinked. 'I'm sorry, what?' she said.

'We were in negotiations. They went for a late lunch. He left his laptop open. I saw a chance and I took it. Nearly got caught, but only nearly.'

Nicola let out a low huff of amusement. 'Fuck me. You're full of surprises, Mr Tulloch.'

25

Jeremy

Vauxhall Cross: now

'A gas leak? Is the press buying that?'

Jeremy hunched forward, pressing an ice pack to his right temple where a chunk of doorframe had clocked him. Sally Lime was in the next room, still working despite the half-inch gash in her scalp that had needed six stitches.

'They have to, we've D-noticed it,' said Jeremy around the ice pack. 'There was some social media footage, but GCHQ took it down.'

Stephanie Salisbury, section chief for the Africa Desk and Nicola Ellis's boss, sat back in her leather-effect chair. 'So they know something's up, then. Christ, what a mess. Casualties?'

'One of the tac squad took a nasty bit of shrapnel; he's in surgery still. But they got out quickly. We were insanely lucky. Flat below is a write-off, but there was nobody home. And the target apartment was completely wrecked.'

Salisbury nodded. 'We need to decide what we're doing more broadly here, Jeremy. Every second that data spends out of our hands there's a greater risk in recovering it or keeping any aspect of Legends alive. Including our active operatives.'

Jeremy nodded and put the ice pack down. 'The target had an escape route planned. Once he was off the rooftop we lost him. The watchers got some good stills of his face though. I've got Sally Lime working with GCHQ and Thames House, to see if we can get anything out of the data trail they left. But we need more time.'

Salisbury stood up and went to the window. 'I'm covering as much as I can, Jeremy, here with the other section chiefs and in Whitehall. But the JIC are getting jumpy. Penetration of the Cross. "Gas explosions" in Peckham.'

Jeremy sighed. 'Everyone's trying to cover their arses, and we need to move *quicker*. I need help here, Stephanie.'

Salisbury smoothed the jacket of her suit and nodded. 'I'll see what I can do. If the higher-ups can't see a pathway here, they'll burn it to the ground. Full deniability. Every Legend cut off.'

Jeremy felt sick at the idea of that. But he managed to stand up and nod.

In his jacket pocket, his secure phone buzzed. He pulled it out. Ellis calling him back. He frowned. 'I have to take this, Stephanie, apologies.'

Outside, he answered the call.

Nicola Ellis sounded tense. 'Jeremy, I just saw the news. The thing in Peckham. That's where you were, right?'

'Yes. An IED. We're playing with some serious people here, it seems.'

Nicola's sigh told him he was about to learn just how serious. 'It looks like Terence Stringer is dead, Jeremy. I made contact with GARNET this evening, in Stone Town. But it's . . . it's not GARNET.'

Jeremy felt the strength go from his legs. He flopped down on to a couch. There were too many things in those three sentences for him to process in one go. Stringer dead? Not . . . not GARNET? He rubbed at his forehead.

'Run that by me again?'

'The person on site with Bocharov is Jamie Tulloch, your Legend. He found Terence Stringer's body, stripped of any ID or assets, in Paris. No sign of GARNET or anyone else. He made a run for it, and now he's here.'

'Oh. Oh, fuck.' Jeremy leaned forward, fighting a dizziness that seemed to be coming straight from his churning stomach.

A case officer dead. An operative missing. And one of his Legends in the hot seat, right at the centre of a mission that had been months in the planning, with one of the most dangerous men on the planet. Jesus Christ.

He swallowed back the sick feeling, took a breath. Wheels were already spinning as his field instincts took over, plotting a path through the chaos.

'All right. Well. We'll make enquiries with the French, get a field team out to the airport. If this was a hit *and* a covert clean-up airside at a major airport, we're going to have to speak to the DGSI. Shit.'

Nicola was silent for a moment. 'What do you want me to do here, Jeremy? There's no contingency plan for something like this.'

Jeremy squeezed his leg, focusing on the pressure of his fingers around the knee joint. It was an interrogation resistance technique that Terence himself had taught him, bored on a long observation mission in Yemen in the nineties. He'd been using it more and more recently, when the sheer number of things he was trying to control threatened to overwhelm him.

'Okay. First things first. Is Jamie okay?'

'Yes. He's . . . well, he's playing himself. He knows the material better than literally anyone. But if your targets manage to break that encryption, his cover will be blown.'

Jeremy suppressed a smile. He could well imagine the quiet, watchful Scotsman 'playing himself' in a meeting room somewhere in Stone Town. But Ellis was right about the encryption. Right now it was the slim thread by which his entire programme, and Jamie Tulloch's life, was dangling.

'We can start planning an extraction then. He doesn't have the skills he needs—'

'He— he did manage to get us something, actually,' said Nicola softly. 'He had ten minutes alone in a room with Bocharov's laptop and he got a full dump of the main document directories. Locally stored emails as well. It's a lot of stuff. I've got my local team combing through it.'

Jeremy blinked and sat forward. 'Wait, he copied Bocharov's laptop?'

'Enough to be useful. So far, we've got some itinerary information, a list of names attending his compound over the next two weeks. We're definitely seeing traces of something bigger. Tulloch did well to grab it. But he's scared, Jeremy. He shouldn't even be there. And we have no idea where GARNET is. He's off the board, could have been grabbed by the same operative that killed Stringer.'

'What's your read on this, Nicola? Is it linked? The attack on the Cross? The bomb in Peckham? Bocharov? Wherever the hell GARNET's gone?'

There was a long silence on the other end of the line. 'The timing seems too close to be coincidental. And yesterday at breakfast, he heard a reference to "Canning Town" between Bocharov and Olenev. I think Thames House will want to look into that.'

Jeremy sat up at that. If Bocharov was planning something in London . . .

This might be what he needed to keep the nervous fingers of the Joint Intelligence Committee away from the kill switch. 'Send me what you have from the laptop dump – we'll see if we can get some big guns on it, data-wise. And I'll speak to Thames about Canning Town. That might give us a lead, if these things are linked.'

'On it, boss,' she said. He heard the sound of typing in the background and briefly imagined Nicola in a guest house somewhere, phone jammed against her shoulder.

He looked down, took a breath. 'We'll play things light with Jamie, but we'll keep him in there. No unnecessary risks. Eyes and ears only.'

Another long silence. When Nicola spoke again, it was the pragmatic, neutral voice he'd come to expect from her. But even he couldn't miss the hesitation behind the words.

'I think I can give him enough skills to stay out of trouble, if I get him for a few hours tomorrow. And I gave him a burner, so he's not entirely off the grid now. But he's a civilian, Jeremy. We can't forget that. He didn't sign up for this. And if someone *does* have GARNET in a basement somewhere, Jamie could be compromised at any time, encrypted records or not.'

Jeremy rubbed his temples. Even hours later, his ears were still ringing from the blast in Peckham. And now he was imagining GARNET in a basement somewhere, just like he'd been himself in Bishkek, eyeing a tray of pliers and hammers in the dusty light. Denying, denying, denying. How long would William Price hold out, if someone did have him?

'I understand the risks. I wouldn't normally ask you to do this. And a month ago I wouldn't have dreamed of putting a Legend into a live mission. That's not how any of this is supposed to work.'

'But . . .' said Nicola.

'But we're under attack here. This could be something big, Nicola. And it could be linked. We have no choice. Right now, Jamie's all we've got.'

26

Jamie

Stone Town: now

Next morning, the port was already busy, fishing skiffs motoring into the beach, dhows gliding silently out to sea. A light breeze ruffled the palms lining the wide promenade. Jamie followed Mizingani Road, past the park where he'd fled the night market. It was all packed up now, the park returned to lush, sand-dusted greenness. A few figures lounged on benches, reading newspapers or staring at their phones, enjoying the shade of the acacia trees.

Past the park, the promenade narrowed and followed the curve of the shore. He walked with the sea to his left, tide coming in, fishermen in the surf pulling in boats. He felt his neck prickle in the heat of the sun, as though someone was watching. He glanced back, looking for the tall figure of Vitaly or one of his men, but there was nobody, just a few early tourists strolling. A white man in a baseball cap and sunglasses sat on one of the concrete block benches under a palm tree. The man sat across the road from the pillared hardwood balconies of a four-star tourist hotel, taking in the incredible view of the sea.

For just a moment, Jamie imagined himself on a trip like that, free to go where he liked, do what he liked. The trip that Terence had promised, where he would get to try on another life for a few weeks. But instead he was here, playing himself. He turned away and kept walking.

Mercury's Bar was sparsely populated with hung-over tourists pick-ing at club sandwiches and plates of chips. As he got closer, he heard the strains of 'Fat Bottomed Girls' and suddenly understood the name.

Nicola Ellis was waiting for him at a table on the edge of the beach terrace.

'Interesting choice,' he said as he sat down.

She shrugged. 'Who doesn't like Freddie Mercury? National hero here, just about. And it's a nice view.'

Jamie squinted into the brightening sun. 'It is that. So what are we doing here?'

'Drinking some coffee, first. Then we'll take a short walk back to our guest house. Graeme and I have some kit we need to give you, as well as some advice and briefings on where you're going with Bocharov.'

'Vitaly told me we're leaving just before lunch.'

'Vitaly is Bocharov's head of security? The big guy?' she asked, taking a note on her phone.

'Yes,' said Jamie. 'Although they're all pretty big.' A waiter came and took Jamie's order, then returned shortly after with a latte, a per-fect acacia leaf stamped into the foam.

'You really can get exactly the same coffee anywhere you go these days,' Jamie said, looking down at his drink.

Nicola smiled. 'Tell me about it. I think I've slept on the same Ikea sofa bed in sixteen countries so far.'

Jamie gazed towards the port terminal. A tourist ferry was pulling slowly away from the dock.

'I thought about getting on one of those, this morning. Before you texted. Just packing what I had, leaving this whole mess behind. Let you lot sort it out.'

Nicola appraised him over the dregs of her coffee. 'And why didn't you?'

He shrugged. It was a good question. Not one he was sure he had an answer to. 'I made an agreement.'

She put her cup down, eyes unreadable. 'Not for this. You agreed to limitations on your life, not risking it. And I want you to be very clear that you *are* risking it.'

He nodded. 'Does Jeremy know this is happening? Or is this your call?'

She shook her head. 'Jeremy made the decision. I told him what happened in Paris. They're looking into it. But your USB stick has given us a lot to work with.'

Jamie drank some of his coffee. It was strong. 'What do you mean, they're "looking into it"?' he asked. 'There was a body. In an airport bathroom. It should be all over the news by now. What the hell happened to him?'

'There's ways,' she said, draining the last of her coffee. 'To clean up something like that. Bribes. Insiders with keys.'

'What about GARNET? What the hell's happened to him? Did whoever killed Terence get him as well?'

Nicola shifted back in her seat, eyes guarded. 'There's a risk, yes, that he's been captured. Compromised in some way. But we don't know that. Still, if you were any normal operative, we'd scrub the op. Cover blown. But your cover *is* you. In some senses, you *can't* be blown. If you stick to eyes-and-ears, you could see a lot, but keep the risk low. I know seeing Terence like that was a shock. But you have to focus on what's in front of you, right now.'

Jamie twisted the cup in his hand. He had seen what he'd seen. Would never forget it, in fact. But she was right. If he was going to do this, he had to give it his full focus. And thinking about Terence, or a man who looked like himself having his teeth pulled out in some filthy cell somewhere, wouldn't help. He drained his coffee.

Nicola stood up and shoved some shilling notes under her coffee cup. 'Come on, we'll talk as we walk.'

They were twenty metres along the beachfront when she slipped her arm through his. He managed not to flinch at the sudden human contact, the first for some time that wasn't a pat-down, an apologetic squeeze of the shoulder or a restraining arm around his neck.

'We're a couple, just out for a nice morning walk in Stone Town.'

'Got it,' he said, eyes forward. 'What if Bocharov's guys see us?'

'Then you met an old friend. Or did some fast and charming work over a coffee with a nice tourist lady you met.' Nicola's shoulder was warm against him, even in the rising morning heat. He glanced over at her, this no-nonsense woman from SIS. Short, sandy-brown hair pulled back in a ponytail. A practical khaki shirt and ripstop travel trousers. A lightweight blue scarf, sandals on her feet. She looked every inch the experienced traveller. The kind young backpackers would ignore and locals would offer their better prices to.

She spoke as they walked, eyes straight ahead. 'The USB was valuable. We got a good snapshot of Bocharov's email activity, his calendar, a bunch of shipping data. All of it shows we're building towards something, this week, while you're at his compound.'

'So you want me to keep my eyes peeled?'

'Exactly. People you meet at the compound, how they introduce themselves, accents, clothes. Vehicle licence plates. Any equipment you see. Positions of guards and patrolling routines.'

They crossed the road and passed two buildings, both with beautiful wood-and-metal balconies overlooking the main road. Then they were back in the narrow passages of the Old Town. This area, near the port, was much thicker with small hotels, cafés and handicraft shops for tourists. Every few yards someone would step out of a doorway and call to them as they passed. Nicola smiled and nodded and replied in fluent Kiswahili, placing her hand across her heart and bowing a little to each man or woman she spoke to.

'You've spent a lot of time here?' said Jamie as they turned a corner into a shaded lane, then crossed a small, open square with an acacia tree in the centre. Young men lounged on the steps of a building, playing chess on a folding wooden board. They glanced up without interest at the two passing tourists.

'Zanzibar specifically? No. A few trips on leave. I've mostly been on the mainland. Mombasa, Nairobi, Dar. And in the back country and the border areas. But I've worked in the region for six years.'

'Must be an amazing job.'

She glanced over at him. 'You see some pretty hard things in this line of work, Jamie. Deal with terrible people. You think you're ready for that?'

He looked ahead as they reached another crossroads and turned left, into an alleyway so narrow they had to go single file in places to squeeze past those coming the other way.

'I'm not sure, to be honest.'

'We're not going to ask you to do what GARNET might have done. This is eyes-and-ears only. No more stunts like you pulled with the laptop. Just observe, remember and report. You'll have the tools *if* you do need to capture an image or record something. But your safety comes first. You're there to sell UPK some software and then leave, like the salesman you actually are.'

Jamie nodded. 'I can do that, I think.'

They passed a hole-in-the-wall gift shop. Carved giraffes in black hardwood, colourful prints, beaded bracelets and hair ties and scarves draped across white metal stands.

'Think of it,' said Nicola as the street widened a little and she was able to take his arm again, 'as a particularly nice all-expenses-paid trip at a resort that just happens to cater to military-age Russian males. Which describes half the resorts in Turkey and Thailand anyway.'

He smiled at that. 'Sounds lovely.'

'Don't underestimate Bocharov, or especially his men. They all served together. Survived the war. Did some *really* terrible things. Vityaz's main revenue source is extracting cobalt from the DRC and gold from Mali. The mercenary side of things is mostly to protect that. And UPK is just one part of Bocharov's little empire. You're going to see *all kinds* of interesting people at that villa of his.'

'I think I can do this,' said Jamie, not sure if he believed it as he said it. 'I've been to sales conferences before, done a lot of networking. I can put on a front when I need to.'

'Good,' said Nicola. 'Your training, when you first signed on. What did it cover? Basic countersurveillance? Looking for tails and making contact safely?'

He nodded. 'It's been a long time though. I don't think I remember half of it.'

She smiled then, as they reached a wider street. This one held three tourist hotels, including one at the end which Nicola pointed out. 'That's us. Jambo Life Guesthouse. And yes, I can tell.'

'Tell what?'

'That you don't remember your training. We've had a front-runner and two tails on us since we left Mercury's.'

Jamie's stomach dropped to the stones under his feet. 'The Russians?' he said, a tight note of paranoia in his voice that he hated as soon as he heard it.

Nicola squeezed his arm. 'No, Graeme and our two locals. Graeme's been ahead of us the whole time. In plain sight.'

Jamie followed her nod and saw a rangy man in board shorts and a khaki shirt leaning against the wall outside the guesthouse. He raised one hand in a mildly mocking wave.

Nicola nodded the other way and two Zanzibari locals emerged from a doorway at the end of the street. It was the man and woman from the night before, obvious now he knew. They nodded to Nicola and walked away.

Nicola gave him an encouraging smile. 'We'll practise some stuff on our way back. But, for now, we need to get you kitted out and prepped.'

27

Nicola

Indian Ocean, off Zanzibar coast: now

Once they were sure they were clear of countersurveillance, Nicola and Sylvan had driven up to the resort closest to Bocharov's compound that afternoon and got settled, settling into a new role as a tourist couple. When Nicola decided she wanted to get eyes on Bocharov's lair, Sylvan suggested hiring a boat from the resort's pier. It cost nearly as much as the room. Nicola physically winced as she paid with one of her cover identity cards. This would be fun to explain in mission debriefing.

At least it was a *very* nice boat.

Graeme Sylvan lounged on the cream leather bucket seats, nestled between long strips of hardwood decking. Nicola stood at the wheel, guiding them gently out towards a marker buoy they'd spotted from the dock.

She curved the boat in towards the buoy, then cut the engine and drifted the last few metres. Graeme was already unpacking their gear.

Nicola tied off the boat's painter to the buoy with a quick hitch knot, then dug suncream out of her bag and started applying it. Even after years working in East Africa, a couple of hours bobbing in the Indian Ocean with no shade would still burn her if she wasn't careful. She offered the tube to Sylvan and he took it, nodding towards the scope as he slathered cream on his neck and forehead.

'Let's keep it low profile. Chances are slim that they're keeping an eye specifically on us – there's boats anchored out here all the time. But if they see one too many lens glints, they might get out the Dragunovs.' He put the sun cream back in her bag and mimed shooting with the Soviet-era sniper rifle.

Nicola eyed the distance to the beach critically. It was well over a kilometre. 'Effective range on an SVD is about eight hundred metres. I think we're fine.'

Sylvan raised an eyebrow. 'Nic, I was joking. They're not going to start plinking at us. Not unless we try a beach landing and we're visibly armed.'

She sighed. 'Sorry, too many years bobbing around off the Horn. We should probably eat that lunch before it gets too warm.'

While Sylvan opened the hamper the hotel had made up for them, Nicola sat down and put her eye to the scope. She focused on the distant compound.

'You weren't kidding,' she said softly. 'It is a bloody fortress.'

Sylvan nodded. 'Triple fence line. Motion and thermal sensors. Twenty-four-hour overflight from a Kvazimachta tethered drone that Bocharov took with him when he got out of Crimea. They're always watching with that thing, for a good couple of kilometres in every direction. Plus a couple of Mavics they use to buzz anything suspicious.'

'And how many guys?'

'Platoon strength at least, all the time. Probably more like a company this week. They've got barracks blocks that will hold that many. Got their own pool and everything.'

Sylvan handed her a sandwich on delicate white bread, the crusts cut off. She wolfed it down. She was hungrier than she'd realised.

Nicola squinted through the scope again. 'And Jamie will be in the main building?'

'Yes, that's all guest accommodation. Security lives down in the Nissen huts near the fence line there.'

She moved the scope, trying to compensate for the slow swell of the waves. The house looked like a set of concrete terraces, overhanging balconies and jutting extremities that curved around a central infinity pool, with decking on three sides. It was an oligarch's playhouse, a place to see and be seen.

'Big place,' she said.

'It's your basic Russian Versailles, yep.'

She looked at Sylvan, one eyebrow raised. 'Didn't have you pegged as a history buff, Graeme.'

'Same basic idea, right? Neutralise your underlings and their plans by making them live with you.'

'And you see Bocharov as, what, Louis XIV?'

Sylvan shrugged. 'More like a viceroy or something. Regional governor. Russians love places like this. Burmese triads do too. And the only difference between a place like this and a stone-built country mansion in Hertfordshire is how recently the cash to fund it was extracted.'

She smirked at that and went back to the scope. 'I somehow doubt a place like this is going to end up with a gift shop and a National Trust ticket booth.'

Sylvan shook his head as he finished his sandwich. 'Nah, colonial outposts like this tend to meet a different end. The Russians are doing what we did, just a couple of centuries later. And with satphones. They'll get kicked out eventually, once they've taken everything worth taking. Might take the Chinese a bit longer to get the boot, since they're actually building roads and railways.'

'And post-colonial theory as well,' said Nicola, reaching out and punching Sylvan lightly on the shoulder. 'Good to know I've got someone with a bit of insight on my team.'

Sylvan grinned and threw her a cold can of Coke. He cracked one for himself. 'When you spend half your life watching very bad people doing terrible things in countries you've come to love, you start to ponder. Especially when you've got hours sat in cars, hotel rooms and now fucking boats with nothing to do *but* think about how fucked it all is.'

Nicola considered the tanned field man from the other side of the boat. 'You really love it here, don't you? Not just being in the field. You love the country.'

Sylvan shrugged. 'There's never been much for me back home. Left as soon as I could. The Army, then this. But there's something about Tanzania. I suppose I do love it. Seeing places like this,' he said, tilting his can of Coke towards the dark blot of the compound and narrowing one eye, '. . . squatting on the landscape, it's depressing. Given half a chance, men like Bocharov would turn the entire world into armed compounds for them and slums for everyone else. I hate the pricks.'

'Well, with any luck,' said Nicola, finishing her drink and crumpling the can, 'we'll get something that takes Bocharov out of the picture. That's the mission.'

They lapsed into silence, aside from the odd question from Nicola on what she could see through the scope. Sylvan took over for a little while as she used small tactical binoculars to get a broader view. He pointed out the fence that extended all the way to the waterline, sectioning off a good kilometre of the beachfront. He walked her through the shift patterns and the double roving guard that moved inside the first and third fence line. Not the second though. A local contact had reliably informed him that particular strip was heavily mined, brutal little PMN-2 anti-personnel mines under the scoured sand.

They spent another hour watching the patterns of vehicles arriving and departing as the guest list for the week filled out. At one point a helicopter roared up the coast, an AgustaWestland in gold and silver livery. It flared and landed on the roof of Bocharov's house. Sylvan snorted.

'Oh, I forgot about that. Helipad on the roof of the main block, 25,000kg-rated; it'll take a bloody Chinook. Overkill for dinky little business choppers like that. I guess Bocharov wants the option to land a couple of Super Hinds there if he fancies it.'

After another hour, they were both reddening, despite drinking all the water that had been packed with the picnic and reapplying sun

cream every thirty minutes. Nicola decided it was time to head back
as the sun dropped towards the horizon.

'Good to get a proper look at it,' she shouted over the thrum of the
boat's inboard engines.

'What do you reckon?' Sylvan asked. 'Now you've seen it.'

Nicola shrugged. 'I reckon if Jamie gets in trouble in there, he's
screwed. GARNET, we could probably arrange some exfil, give him
a covert weapon to get himself out of trouble and get to a fence line.
But Jamie's a civilian, with none of those skills. We'd need a battalion-
sized combined arms group to take that place. And I doubt we're
getting inside covertly without six months of set-up, even with your
local operatives.'

Sylvan shrugged at the wheel, the breeze tugging at his shirt as they
picked up speed. 'We had a couple of months' warning, hence the brief
I managed to work up. But you're right: not long enough to get past
their security. And the place is fully staffed anyway. They're not hiring.
They pay well enough that hardly anybody quits.'

'I'm worried. About this op. About Jamie. Whether he's got what it
takes, even just for an eyes-and-ears job,' Nicola said, looking down at
her handwritten notes.

'Come on now,' said Sylvan. 'It's my job to be the sceptical cynic.'

She laughed as they approached the long floating dock of their
resort. A couple of other rental boats bobbed alongside. The man who
had hired the boat to them was nowhere to be seen, but there was
somebody else waiting on the dock. He was a slim, dark-skinned man
in his late thirties dressed in chinos and a neatly pressed short-sleeved
blue shirt. His hair was trimmed short and he watched them through
rimless glasses as they pulled into the dock. Nicola threw him the
painter, since he was just standing there.

'Beautiful afternoon,' she said. 'Mind tying us off?'

'Of course,' said the man, his accent local. Nicola looked him over
more closely. It was unusual for locals to come to resorts like this,
unless they worked there or owned the place. The man knelt and

looped the painter around a dock cleat with practised efficiency, tying it off neatly. Then he stood and extended a hand to Nicola as she stepped off the boat, a flight case in her other hand. He smiled at her. His hand was cool.

'Did you have a booking for the boat?' she said.

Sylvan climbed out of the boat with the other flight case and the picnic basket. 'Sorry if we were out too long, mate. Might be a few sandwich crumbs in there as well.'

The man chuckled and placed his hand across his chest, gave both of them a small bow. 'Oh no, I'm afraid this is a small misunderstanding. I am a guest here, but I was not waiting for the boat. I was waiting for you.'

Nicola caught the tension in Sylvan's shoulders at the same moment her neck prickled. She flexed her fingers around the grip of the flight case and began judging distances, insteps, pivots and twists.

'Not sure what you mean by that, friend,' said Sylvan, stepping forward.

'I would like to know,' said the man, taking a half-step back and gesturing towards the terraced restaurant of the resort above them, 'if you would consent to having dinner with me. And telling me what your interest is, exactly, in Arkady Bocharov.'

28

Jeremy

King Charles Street, Whitehall, London: earlier

'Wow.'

Jeremy's voice echoed in the glass-roofed Durbar Courtyard of King Charles Street, home of the Foreign, Commonwealth and Development office.

'Frankly, Stephanie, this whole place feels way above my pay grade,' he stage-whispered.

Stephanie Salisbury was half a step ahead. She glanced back as they crossed the mosaic marble floor of the courtyard, aiming for the grand staircase and the Locarno Suite, where the Joint Intelligence Committee had camped for the day.

'You're de facto operating at that level now, Jeremy, whether you like it or not. This is a critical breach. Now do me a favour and act like it.'

Jeremy felt a brief sting of shame but didn't allow it to reach his face. 'Of course. I apologise.'

Salisbury glanced back again. 'Look, Jeremy, there's nobody better placed for this right now. You were there in Peckham. You have people on the ground in Tanzania. It's my desk and Ellis is my officer, but you're the one handling the detail. And JIC *loves* to dig into the detail.'

Jeremy frowned as they reached the edge of the courtyard.

'Speaking of digging, what about Stringer, in Paris?' he asked. 'I can't get an answer from the Europe Desk. I copied you in, about liaising with the French.'

'Don't worry,' Salisbury said, favouring him with a red-lipstick smile. 'I'm following it up personally. I've got some contacts in DGSI that I can lean on. Once they start prodding Paris Station we'll get some movement, I'm sure of it. Believe me, Jeremy, I'm as anxious as you are to see the AEGIS operation succeed and get Nicola and your agent out of there safely. I'm sorry you may have lost one of your case officers though. I met Stringer a few times. He was a good man.'

Jeremy noted the past tense and cleared his throat. All he'd told anyone at SIS so far was that GARNET had reported an incident in Paris and Stringer was a suspected casualty. As far as anyone outside his own small team knew, Jamie Tulloch was somewhere in South America and GARNET was on task in Tanzania. Jeremy tried not to think too hard about where William Price might *actually* be. The last thing he wanted in his head before a grilling by the Joint Intelligence Committee was images of broken thumbs, smashed teeth and fingernails torn out at the root.

Jeremy coughed and looked down at the polished tiles. 'I just hope we can recover a body.'

They reached the Locarno Suite. A long rectangular hardwood table ran the length of the room, polished to a low shine. Wall-mounted lamps and gilded chandeliers lit the room with a yellowish light. Gilded crests and emblems of a dozen countries were set into the plaster ceiling. Low couches and sideboards lined one wall, while the other was broken only by an empty marble fireplace. A beautiful Edwardian mantel clock kept slow and steady time.

'This is . . . grand,' said Jeremy as they took their seats.

'Great Office of State.' She smoothed the creases from her skirt and jacket. 'Refurbished in the eighties, I believe. They'd split it up into plasterboard cubicles, if you can believe that. No respect for tradition, in those days. They wanted to *demolish* the place at one point. Thank God they didn't. We'd have been left with some grim Brutalist slab, no doubt.'

The large double doors at the end of the room opened and a dozen people filed in. Every one of them was several pay grades above Jeremy. The kind of person whose official headshot graced monthly emails he deleted unread, with subject lines like 'An update from Clive'.

The committee settled in around the table, as Salisbury stood and pressed the flesh with peers from other agencies, including the Security Service, GCHQ, the Army's Intelligence Corps, the Home Office and several others Jeremy couldn't identify. The chairwoman was talking to the CIA head of London Station, a square-jawed white man in a blue suit he vaguely recognised from a joint operation fifteen years before. Back then he'd been a junior case officer. Apparently he'd done a better job of clambering up the greasy pole than Jeremy had.

The chair tapped her water glass. Dame Philippa Collingwood was another relatively young high-flyer. She had worked her way up through at least three major government departments before coming to the JIC with her freshly minted honorific, still in her early fifties. She peered down the table through rimless bifocals.

'Thank you, everyone. Apologies for bringing you all in on a Sunday, but we have an active incident, as you'll have seen from yesterday's events in Peckham. I'll yield the floor immediately for a review with Stephanie Salisbury, who's joining us in her capacity as head of the Africa Desk at SIS and JIC liaison for this operation. Stephanie?'

Salisbury stood, smoothed her jacket down and smiled around at the gathered intelligence worthies. She glanced at the papers on the polished mahogany in front of her. 'Thank you, Madame Chairwoman. SIS is currently engaged in an operation on British soil, with the full cooperation and support of the Security Service and the Metropolitan Police, to identify and detain those responsible for a serious security breach at Vauxhall Cross, and to recover the physical data assets taken during the initial attack.'

An older man with carefully parted hair who reminded Jeremy of a younger Winston Bascomb sat forward and frowned. 'So the data *is* recoverable?'

Salisbury nodded. 'We believe so. Obviously, the longer it remains out in the world, the more risk there is. But we have good reason to believe that the attackers have stored the stolen data on physical drives. It's possible they don't want it out on the dark web any more than we do.'

'Why not?' said a soldier in a dark khaki dress uniform and bright white belt. Senior Intelligence Corps liaison, Jeremy guessed, by the colour of the beret neatly folded beside his briefing papers. 'If the aim is disruption of some kind?'

'I'll hand over to Jeremy Althrop, senior case officer and lead for our Legends Programme, to give you the details on that.'

Jeremy rose slowly to his feet, feeling eyes on him from every corner. At the end of the table, the chair woman cleared her throat. 'Aides, leave the room, please. This is an eyes-only topic. Grade Emerald.'

Six younger men and women in sharp suits and blazers rose from the low couches against the wall and exited swiftly, while Collingwood swept her eyes around the room. 'Anyone not read in on this subject? Good, excellent. Please continue, Mr Althrop.'

Jeremy cleared his throat and looked down at the table, wishing he'd written some notes. Now more than ever he could feel the fuzziness at the back of his mind, age catching up with him. He'd become so *used* to having information at his fingertips, to just letting it sit out there in the clouds and the servers and the hard drives. Now, when the moment came to it, he was struggling to remember what exactly it was that he'd built.

'Thank you, Madame Chairwoman. My team has been working with the Security Service and GCHQ since the incident in Peckham.'

The Met Police liaison in the room shifted in her seat at this. Jeremy tried not to look at her. At least one of their officers was still in hospital after the explosion.

Jeremy stood up a little straighter and continued. 'We're closing in on suspects for both the physical and digital breaches. And we're chasing down the male suspect seen by our surveillance teams in Peckham.'

The Cabinet Office liaison sat forward, his cufflinks clinking against the polished wood. 'And your live Legends ops? Is there a link?'

Jeremy glanced at Stephanie Salisbury. This was dangerous ground. But he couldn't ignore it.

'Yes, sir, I believe so. The timing seems too close to be coincidental. Within a forty-eight-hour period, we had an operational mishap in Paris, the attack on our servers and a live op in East Africa observing key changes in target behaviour.'

'I'm sorry,' said Collingwood, 'could you possibly clarify your use of the word "mishap", Mr Althrop? Was this part of the assessment passed to the JIO?'

Salisbury inserted herself smoothly, leaning forward. 'It's unconfirmed for the moment. We're following up. But there was a possible loss of a programme asset.'

Collingwood sat back, mild shock on her face. 'Not one of the civilians?'

Jeremy shook his head, both hands planted on the table. 'No, ma'am. One of my case officers. As Stephanie said, unconfirmed.'

'Surely the best course here is disavowal?' said a deep, booming voice from the opposite end of the table. Jeremy looked up and into the eyes of Sir Roger Flannery, senior Home Office liaison. A huge man, former Oxford Blues rugby player, wrapped in Savile Row pinstripe.

'With respect, sir, we'd be burning years of effort. Dozens of assets. Prepwork and live operations.'

Flannery shrugged elegantly. 'To my eye, it's *already* burned. Unknown operatives, probably of a foreign power, running around in South London letting off *IEDs*, for Christ's sake. While toting around the details of one of our most secret programmes on a *USB stick*. And we're no closer to finding them than we were twenty-four hours ago.'

'The data is encrypted, and we're—'

'And now you tell us,' Flannery continued, turning the water glass in his hand, 'that you've lost officers in the field, on a NATO ally's territory, or you *think* you have, but you can't be sure. I'm willing to bet you haven't told the French either.'

Jeremy saw the opening and darted for it, thankful for the earlier update from Stephanie.

'No, sir, we have. The DGSI has been informed and is helping us get the right CCTV footage and access we need to find our officer.' He glanced at Salisbury for support, but she said nothing, staring straight ahead at Flannery.

'My point is not whether you're following procedure talking to our allies, Althrop. My *point* is that your programme is irreparably damaged. I believe disavowal and withdrawal of field assets is the best option at this stage.'

'It's a good thing, then,' said Jane Bailey, the SIS liaison sitting two down from Flannery, 'that SIS is not subordinate to the Home Office.' Bailey wore a smile, but even Jeremy could see the bared teeth just behind it. She operated at the level of C, SIS's chief. She was the designated pit fighter when it came time to defend the turf of the Secret Intelligence Service against threats of all kinds.

Flannery turned his bulk towards Bailey and gave her a slow smile. 'No, but the environs of leafy *Peckham* absolutely are. This can't go on, Jane. You know it, and I know it. Best to cut it off now, while we still have some measure of control. Cauterise the stump. A year from now, it'll be a rumour, or a suspected Russian provocation, or both.'

The American in the blue suit sat forward. 'If I may, on behalf of the US government?'

Collingwood nodded and the man stood up. 'For those who don't know me, I'm Dan Litchfield. New in the job at Nine Elms,' he said, referring to the hyper-modern crystalline cube of the American embassy compound just south of the river.

Litchfield glanced at Flannery and smiled. 'We understand the concerns raised by Sir Roger and we're standing ready to assist in whatever way we can, especially with ELINT or satellite assets. But we'd also like to strongly recommend the protection of Legends. We're aware of some critical factors at this time, with an unacceptable risk to global security if those particular operations are compromised.'

Jeremy swallowed. How much did the CIA know about the Bocharov operation? Shit, about Jamie? What did they know that he didn't, about what Bocharov might be up to on Zanzibar?

Jane Bailey nodded to Litchfield. 'Thank you, Dan. As ever, we appreciate the support and insight of our American colleagues. Any intelligence you feel able to share about ongoing operations would help our teams on the ground immeasurably.'

Litchfield sat back down, giving a small, non-committal tilt of the head, which might look like a nod in certain lights. Nothing in the record or the minutes indicating assent, of course.

Bailey turned her gaze back to Jeremy, studiously ignoring the glare from Sir Roger to her right. 'At SIS, we believe there are both immediate operational benefits here, as well as long-term investments to be recouped. These outweigh the reputational risks of continuing the recovery operation. As Mr Althrop mentioned, the data is encrypted, so there's a good chance we can successfully recover it and our Legends assets won't be blown. Mr Althrop, what is your plan of action in the next twenty-four to forty-eight hours?'

Jeremy straightened. Here was something he could answer. No manoeuvring or doublespeak.

'I have technical specialists working with Thames House on two main objectives. The first is to trace the person or persons who placed intrusion devices inside the Cross. The second is to find the man who escaped the safe house in Peckham. I expect us to make significant progress on both of those objectives in the next day and to have made arrests within forty-eight hours. Our operation in Tanzania has already given us key leads on both.'

Stephanie shifted in her seat beside him, perhaps at the firmness of the commitment he'd just made. Given his 'key leads' were a murmured reference to Canning Town and the not exactly smoking-gun contents of Bocharov's laptop, he could hardly blame her.

'And the situation in Africa? Whatever *that* is?' said Sir Roger, the irritation at having lost this first skirmish written in every line of his face.

Stephanie sat forward. 'Our asset needs time to get close to their target. But I'm confident they will get us what we need to tie this together.'

Dan Litchfield's eyes widened, very slightly, at that assertion. Jeremy caught the look, and they held each other's gaze for a moment. But he could read nothing in the flat gaze of the American.

'Thank you, Mr Althrop, Ms Salisbury, for your time. Unless anyone else has any questions? No?' Collingwood nodded towards the double doors at the back of the room. Jeremy and Stephanie got up to leave. As the door closed behind them, Roger Flannery's voice rose in a protest best described as a harrumph, followed swiftly by the mild tones of the chairwoman. The matter was put to bed. For the next two days, at least.

'Well done, Jeremy. Pretty good for a first-timer,' said Stephanie as they walked along the sunlit baroque beauty of the upper mezzanine. They stopped and looked down one of the grand staircases. A small group of fast-track graduates was being shepherded up the stairs, gazing around them in awe at the sheer grandiosity of the building.

Jeremy leaned against the rail. 'Thanks. Tough customers.'

'Oh, that was nothing. A mild grilling at best. If you don't deliver what you said you would in there, that's when it'll get tougher. And I won't be able to help you a great deal. This op is on my patch, with one of my best people in the handler's seat, but it *is* a Legends gig. I'm sorry to say, if GARNET gets burned, then you *will* be the one shouldering the blame.'

Jeremy nodded and exhaled slowly. 'That's how it's supposed to work. It's just different when you can actually *see* the chopping block.'

She turned to look at him. 'Judging by what you said in there, GARNET is already active? I haven't seen any summaries coming through. How long do you think until we're getting usable product from him?'

Jeremy's palms were suddenly quite damp. He'd kept the knowledge of the operative's disappearance limited to himself and Nicola's team so far. But this was the first time he'd been asked about it directly.

He cleared his throat, considered his wording. 'We're in Bocharov's orbit now, yes. He's headed to a secure compound in the north of the island. Ellis and her team are observing from close by.'

Salisbury frowned. 'Going to the compound wasn't anticipated in mission planning?'

Jeremy's stomach was doing flips. Should he come clean about Jamie? About just how fucked they all were?

Something in Stephanie Salisbury's acute, evaluating gaze told him no. She was on side, for now. A contingent ally as he fought to save his programme, his career and quite possibly the lives of his field operators. But that look told him all that was balanced very finely indeed. If Salisbury thought this mess was going to affect her directly, he had no idea which way she might break.

'It was, but Bocharov has nearly doubled the security detail on site. The team is discussing new exfil routes, that kind of thing. Ellis is very confident.'

Even as he said it, he deeply hoped he wasn't dropping the young field officer into a bucket of shit. She was just there to do a job. And now he'd lied to her boss.

Salisbury gave him one last assessing look, then a small nod. 'Very good. Keep me posted. I have a meeting on the top floor here. I'll see you back at the Cross. And I'll follow up again about Paris for you.

We'll fix this together, Jeremy.' Another smile, then she turned and walked away, heels clicking on the marble floor.

Jeremy sagged back against the stone balustrade. He wasn't sure how long he could keep this up.

In his jacket pocket, his secure phone rang. Sally Lime.

'Sally. Please tell me you have some good news.'

29

Jamie

UPK compound, north-east Zanzibar coastline: earlier

Jamie had expected fences.

In his years in software, he had been to more than a few high-end villas, beach houses and island getaways. He'd seen many different kinds of fence. Elegant wrought-iron railings backed by beams of infra-red light to detect prowlers. High walls topped with rounded anti-ladder overhangs. Chain-link fences with razor wire artfully hidden by mani-cured hedges. Motion sensors. Floodlights. Security cameras. A panic room deep inside the house somewhere. Every wealthy client he'd ever visited had eventually shown him their panic room. They seemed strangely proud of them. Rich enough to be a target.

But he'd never seen anything like Arkady Bocharov's compound on Zanzibar.

Jamie spotted the outer fence line when they were still more than two kilometres out, gleaming wire reflecting in the low afternoon sun. Every hundred metres or so, a tall pole held a circlet of glinting cam-eras and sensors.

As they got closer, he made out two more fences, each separated from the last by a dozen metres of sand and rolls of razor wire. It looked like the Berlin Wall, or a prison camp. He'd seen military installations with less formidable perimeters.

'Some place,' he said to Vitaly, slouched in the front passenger seat of their air-conditioned Range Rover. Next to Jamie one of Vitaly's men sat in rigid silence. Bocharov and Olenev were in the car behind, discussing something 'time-sensitive', the young women he'd met at breakfast in the one behind that. A final Rover brought up the rear with the luggage and two more of Vitaly's roving security detachment.

'Good angles,' said Vitaly, looking back at Jamie. Once they'd left the environs of Stone Town, the security men had slipped on assault vests and produced compact sub-machine guns from compartments built into the dashboards and boots of the Range Rovers. 'Easy to defend.'

'Expecting trouble?' said Jamie, trying to make the question as casual as he could. 'I thought Zanzibar was pretty safe, with all the tourists.'

Vitaly glanced back again, over the top of his aviators. 'Mr Bocharov is person of interest. Success brings enemies. Some are worse than others.'

Jamie nodded as they slowed down, pulling to a stop beside a guardhouse set into the first fence line. The local guard leaned into the vehicle, saw Vitaly and gave him a nod, then waved to another two guards to open the gates. They wore the same khaki and grey quasi-uniforms as the Russian mercenaries, though the local guys wore dark blue baseball caps and carried much older wooden-stocked rifles. They pulled forward, passing through the three fence lines. Jamie stared at the empty sand between each line, the razor wire and cameras. No way anybody was sneaking through that.

Vitaly twisted in his seat as the gates closed behind them. Inside the compound, the single road that wound towards the centre was smooth tarmac.

'Welcome to Rayskiye Vrata, Mr Tulloch, the UPK hospitality location for East Africa and Mr Bocharov's private residence.'

Jamie managed a weak smile, peering through the window at the expanse of green lawns ahead of them, the pools of shade under acacia and palm trees, the swimming pool and the tiered, three-storey modernist villa at the centre of it all. The house looked like it could plausibly survive a missile strike, all concrete and sharp angles.

Overhead, a tiny black dot hovered in the deep blue of the sky. Something seemed to drop from it, whisper-thin, like a hair on a camera lens.

'What's that?' Jamie asked, pointing through the vehicle's windscreen.

Vitaly's lip curled as he leaned forward to look up. 'Kvazimachta. Tethered drone. For security. It has a cable, so it can stay up for a week. I hate the fucking things.' He sat back.

Jamie looked at the livid white scars on Vitaly's neck. He must have very good reason to hate the high whine of drones overhead.

'What does it mean?' Jamie asked, as they passed a small group of men and women lounging by the infinity pool. Their heads turned to follow the entourage as Bocharov swept past.

Vitaly grunted and looked back again. He shifted the sub-machine gun in his lap and frowned. 'What does what mean?'

'The name. Rah-skee . . .'

Vitaly grinned. It was the first time Jamie had seen a genuine, unmoderated smile on the man's face. 'In English, it means "Heaven's Door". Believe me, it is not a lie.'

Part Three

COMPOUND

30

Jeremy

Vauxhall Cross: now

When he got back to the Cross, Jeremy found Sally Lime in a fourth-floor secure meeting room, hunched over her laptop, a fresh bag of Doritos by her elbow.

'Those things will kill you, you know,' he said as he pushed through the heavy soundproof door.

Lime didn't even look up from her laptop. 'Jez, this is Stuart Alden,' she said, gesturing to her left. She took another Dorito and popped it into her mouth with an audible crunch. 'Vauxhall Cross internal security. He's got some news for us.'

Jeremy swivelled and nodded hello to the man who had been sitting out of sight on the other side of the table. Alden was in his late forties, in a navy jacket and open-necked shirt. He had greying hair, a lean jawline and watchful blue eyes. He stood and shook Jeremy's hand.

'I think we've met,' said Jeremy. 'When the Real IRA took that potshot at us with an RPG back in 2000.'

Alden smiled. 'That was my first week, if you can believe that. Hell of a baptism of fire.'

Lime stabbed at her keyboard with an air of finality, then looked up at them both. 'When you've finished reminiscing about the late-medieval period, you might want to hear what Mr Alden's found.'

Alden reached into a bag next to his chair and extracted a thick manila folder. He dropped it on to the conference-room table with a thud.

'That looks like some serious paperwork,' said Jeremy.

Alden nodded. 'Summary DV files on 322 security, cleaning, maintenance and reception staff with access to the floor in question,' he said, referring to the extensive 'Developed Vetting' process that everyone who worked at SIS had to undergo.

'And you've found something?'

Alden frowned. 'More an *absence*. It was Sally's idea to look for staff who haven't badged in since the attack on your servers.'

Lime sat forward. 'This op had a lead time, right? That 5G dongle was in place for a couple of weeks, but whoever put it there must have been working in the building for months, possibly years. I built a spreadsheet so we could cross-reference an absence record dump from HR with badge ID access patterns.'

Alden opened the manila folder and pulled out the top sheet, then slid it across the table to Jeremy. An image at the top showed a white woman in her late twenties or early thirties, hair in a short brown bob, wearing a blue polo-neck shirt.

Jeremy picked up the cover sheet and peered at it. 'Sarah Grey. Heating and ventilation maintenance.'

Alden nodded. 'Access to every part of the building as a result. No flags in her vetting. She's been part of a four-person team running the systems in this building and our other London locations for two years.'

'Right, so why pick her out? If there're no flags?'

Lime plugged a cable into her laptop and brought up a spreadsheet and a dot graph. 'Our Sarah is a real grafter. Twelve-hour shifts for most of those two years. Not a single sick day.' She swiped her finger along the trackpad, panning across columns of numbers, badge entry and exit timestamps.

'Then, three weeks ago, she starts pulling weird hours. Callouts, according to her run sheets. Secure areas where she's had HVAC issues reported, but she works at night, mostly alone, to "minimise disruption", allegedly.'

Alden sat forward. 'We think that was her trying to find a gap in the electromagnetic shielding panels, where she could get a 5G signal. When that stuff was put in, they were worried about shortwave radios and Chinese signals intelligence. The designers of this place never imagined we'd have gigabit over-the-air internet barely twenty years later.'

Jeremy looked down at the photograph on the personnel file. Sarah Grey stared back at him, unreadable. 'And there's no CCTV footage of these late-night callouts?'

Lime shook her head. 'Nope. All of them wiped. Targeted, based on the timestamps and the camera locations. She's been casing the joint for two straight years. She'd have known where every camera was, who was watching them in Building Control, when they'd be at their doziest. It's a hell of an op.'

Alden tapped the files. 'She's the only one with a matching pattern. That's all still circumstantial, though heavily so. But the damning part is that she's disappeared. Badged out of here via the employee car park fifteen minutes after your servers melted down, with no CCTV record. Hasn't been back in since.'

Jeremy felt the prickle of a hot trail, a clear breadcrumb they could follow. 'What have you done with this so far?' he said to Lime.

'Nothing yet. I wanted to talk to you first.'

Jeremy nodded. 'I'm going to talk to a couple of my contacts, and I'll ask them about Sarah Grey too. With any luck they'll have found something on our friend from Peckham and we'll be able to link them. Before I do that, though, can I have a word, Sally?'

Alden stood up and gathered his files, then headed out of the door. Lime tilted her head. 'What is it? You think there's someone else involved?'

Jeremy nodded. 'Has to be. This woman's a seasoned operator. Worked here in plain sight for two years, pulled off this data theft. But if I'd been reviewing this DV file, I wouldn't have cleared her. Too much access, too many unanswered questions. And she couldn't have written her own work orders.' He gestured at the screen on the wall. 'There's a mole, I think.'

Sally blew out her cheeks and exhaled slowly. 'It would have to be someone senior, to get her through Developed Vetting, get all those late-night work orders signed off.'

Jeremy smiled. 'I bet you can find whoever it is. But that's not why I asked for a word.'

'What is it?' she said.

Jeremy slid a USB stick across the table. 'I need you to do an update. You worked on the GARNET mission prep, right? Swapping all the social media and web assets before the op started?'

'Yep,' she said, picking up the USB and slotting it into her laptop. 'So what's this?'

'New images. I need you to keep this to yourself, but GARNET has gone missing.'

Sally blinked behind her glasses. 'I thought it was the case officer who was missing? Stringer?'

Jeremy rubbed at the stubble on his chin. 'He's missing too, presumed dead. But GARNET never showed up for the handover.'

Lime's eyebrows knitted in confusion. 'So who the hell— oh.' She'd opened the USB stick and was staring at the screen. 'Tell me these aren't pictures of Jamie Tulloch. Tell me you haven't put a Legend into a live op.'

'We didn't have a choice.'

'Jesus, Jeremy. *Jesus.*' She leaned forward, peering at the screen. 'All our records were lost in the breach, so these are, what, pics the field handler took?'

Jeremy nodded. 'He's in close contact with the target, and he seems to have passed for now. But he's heading to a location with a lot more people. Lots of curious people googling, I'd guess. We need every-thing to match.'

She rubbed her forehead with the tips of her fingers, then gave him a short nod and started typing. 'All right, I'm on it. But this is a risk, so you know. I'm going to have to amend a bunch of server logs, which I already amended when we swapped in the GARNET images. We're only supposed to do this twice – on insertion and then successful exfil. This'll be four times. Four chances for someone to notice something. I can't control browser caching, Jeremy. I'm not superhuman.'

Jeremy half shrugged, and grimaced at Lime. 'That sounds . . . dif-ficult? I'm sorry?'

Lime sighed. 'Who knows about this?'

'So far, you, me, the team on the ground. That's it. I'll take the heat, if it comes to that. But he's going in eyes-and-ears only. Strictly the basics.'

Lime sat back, fingers still rattling on her keyboard. 'Senior fellas like yourself love to say "I'll take the heat", then become mysteriously absent when things get a bit toasty. This is serious shit.'

'I know. And all I can do is promise I won't do that. But there's something here. Something big. And Jamie's not doing too badly. He got us that data dump yesterday. And that tidbit about Canning Town.'

'An untrained civilian got a full laptop dump from a primary target? Colour me impressed,' said Lime, pushing her glasses up. 'Speaking of. Thames House called. They want you over there sharp-ish to look at some CCTV analysis. Apparently they got a lead out of everything we gave them yesterday.'

Jeremy nodded and stood. 'I'll head over there now. Let me know when the new images are in place.'

Lime smiled and sat back. 'What do you take me for? Already done.'

*

They kept him down in reception at Thames for nearly fifteen minutes. Eventually Michelle Cavendish appeared, crossing the black-and-white chequered tiles of the grand entrance hall in a blue skirt suit. She smiled ruefully as she approached, pale skin framed by dark brown hair, a tiny touch of grey at the temples.

'I'm so, so sorry, Jeremy. A lot of new information earlier, so I've been in back-to-back meetings. You know how it goes.'

He stood up and shook her offered hand, smiling to show he very much did know how it went. 'Of course. Your team sent a request, said they had something for me?'

'Yes, absolutely, come on.'

They climbed the red-carpeted stairs to the second floor, Michelle just ahead, her arm wrapped tightly around a tablet and a manila folder. She glanced back at him.

'Any joy tracking down your infiltrator?' she asked as they got to the landing and turned down an anonymous grey corridor. Door after door with inscrutable numbered codes, as if the whole building was a library, each door a book with a code along the spine.

'Yes, actually. We've got a pretty solid lead. We're chasing it down now.'

She glanced back again and gave a small nod. Need to know. And she didn't. Not yet.

'Perhaps our little breakthrough can help locate whoever it is a little quicker. In here.'

She opened a door exactly like all the others and ushered him into a low-ceilinged space set up as a temporary ops room. There were large monitors on two of the walls showing grids of CCTV footage. A long desk in the centre of the room was covered with laptops, sheafs of printout paper, coffee cups and empty Red Bull cans.

'Ah,' said Jeremy, glancing at his watch, 'nothing like the smell of taurine in the evening.'

The two analysts sitting at the laptops turned and grinned together. Michelle swept a hand across them. 'Jeremy, this is Anjali and Luke.

They're the grid-matching team assigned to your case. You pair, this is Jeremy, from SIS. He's going to be on the sharp end for what you've found. Anjali?'

'Yep, two ticks, let me put it on the monitors,' the young brown-skinned woman said, in an East London accent if Jeremy was any judge. She grabbed a cable and plugged it into her laptop, then stood up and pointed to two spare chairs.

Jeremy and Michelle sat down and swivelled to face the screen, where the grid of CCTV was replaced with a dizzying array of open windows, applications and progress bars. Jeremy briefly regretted not bringing Sally with him. The problem with these kinds of things was often simply not knowing which questions to ask.

With a few swift clicks, Anjali hid half the windows and brought up a pin-sharp CCTV still. Jeremy saw the broad, unsmiling face of a man with close-cropped military-style hair, a dark jacket and a back-pack over one shoulder. Judging by the background, he was in some kind of small newsagent's.

Anjali gestured at the image. 'So, we started with the data dump your field operatives got, looking for cross-matches from the overheard Canning Town reference. That was a critical lead. Canning Town came up sixteen times, across several emails and some PDF files. Which is a bit weird for some Russian guy in Africa.'

Jeremy frowned. 'It is. So you started looking there?'

Anjali nodded. 'We got this footage from the Met's Crimelink pro-gram. They get direct feeds from privately owned security cameras that have signed up in high-crime areas. Very successful in detecting patterns of petty crime, apparently, shoplifters and so on. This is from a newsagent's in Canning Town, this afternoon. Your suspect, desig-nated Target Boxwood.'

She tapped her keyboard and another image appeared. The same man, in a different T-shirt. Same jacket, same bag. 'This is from earlier today. Once we had a match to the observation footage from Peckham, we checked other Crimelink cameras, plus the street cameras in the area.'

'And you have a solid match on our suspect . . . on Boxwood?' said Jeremy.

Anjali nodded. 'Biometrics match about 93 per cent to 97 per cent, depending on the light and the angles. That's as close as you can get without sticking a camera right in someone's face.'

'So what's he doing in Canning Town?' asked Michelle.

Luke, a pale, gangly, curly-haired redhead in a short-sleeved shirt, sat forward and tapped his laptop, bringing up a satellite map of East London on the other large monitor. 'We ran timestamp and direction-of-travel analysis. He's doing an irregular loop around the Bidder Street area. Looks like short supply runs out to local shops and cafés, or maybe some kind of countersurveillance.'

Jeremy frowned. 'What's around there?'

Luke zoomed the map. 'Mostly light industrial. Breaker's yards, warehouses, garages, a couple of nightclubs, greasy-spoon caffs.'

'Okay, so where's he going back to?'

Michelle pursed her lips. 'That's why we asked to see you. Once we had the positive grid hit, we put a field team in late this afternoon. And we found them.'

Anjali brought up a half-dozen surveillance images, including several aerial shots. 'We also put up a drone an hour ago, once we were sure this was the place.'

Jeremy sat forward. The drone images showed a low, two-storey warehouse with dusty grey walls, roofed in corrugated steel with acrylic skylights. A couple of blurred, ground-level shots were presumably from a passing vehicle. Two SUVs were parked in the small yard at the front of the warehouse. It was separated from the main road by a wall, then a scrap-metal yard, dense with stacks of crushed cars and vans. A clear path through the wrecked vehicles led to the inner gate and the warehouse.

Jeremy frowned. 'What I don't understand is why Boxwood would risk going out at all. Unless he's in there on his own.'

Anjali shook her head. 'He's definitely not. But once we saw who *else* was in there, it made sense. He's the least risky option for them.'

Jeremy's eyes widened. 'A man who blew up a top-floor flat in Peckham? The *least* risky?'

Anjali tapped the laptop again, and a final image appeared. This was another overhead shot from the drone, this time at an angle, looking down into the small yard in front of the warehouse. A third SUV had joined the first two and the metal gate had been dragged across, hiding the vehicles from the street and the scrapyard next door.

'Is that—' started Jeremy, blinking in confusion.

Michelle nodded grimly. 'Four extremely well-armed, former SVR operators? Yes. Yes, it is.' The name of the old Russia's former covert foreign intelligence agency sat heavy in the room.

Jeremy sat back as Anjali punched up profiles on the three men and one woman busily unloading rifles, boxes of ammunition, flight cases and black nylon grip bags of equipment from the back of the SUV.

'This group was identified as an active SVR cell in Turkey six years ago, before the Russian collapse. None of them were scanned or tracked at the border. We've checked known aliases and cover identities. Nothing. It's like they just materialised in East London. They might have come in through people-smuggling routes. Or paid someone off in the Border Force. Either way it's not great.'

Jeremy swallowed, thinking of a third option: that an SIS mole had cleared them and had the records wiped. Then he frowned. 'The SVR doesn't exist any more. As far as I was aware, they cut most of their deep-cover cells loose during the collapse. They all melted away or went to the private sector.'

Michelle shrugged. 'Well, they're here now. Whether they're working for the New Russia or someone else, they're on my patch.'

'With enough ordnance to equip a full platoon, looks like,' said Jeremy, rubbing at the stubble on his chin. 'Jesus.'

'Or mount a terrorist attack. Are we looking at a Mumbai or Paris situation here, Jeremy? This is an immediate and present danger. I will have to escalate.'

He nodded. 'Agreed. We need to make sure they don't leave that warehouse, with that kind of hardware. Plus, the data Boxwood has means they've got the lives of every one of my agents and my civilian assets in their hands.'

Michelle nodded. 'We notified UKSF Command as soon as we got this drone shot. Tactical teams from 22 SAS are en route. SO15 and SO19 are also on board and drawing a cordon. We'll have them bottled up in around an hour. UKSF want time to plan an assault, given the potential risks. They're recommending early tomorrow morning.'

Jeremy glanced at his watch. It was past 7 p.m. already. A wave of tiredness threatened to overwhelm him. He'd been awake for . . . well, too long.

Michelle caught the slump of his shoulders and stood up. 'Okay. Everyone in this room needs some sleep, including me. Let's aim to get there for 0500. In the meantime, go home.'

The two analysts nodded and started packing up.

Outside in the corridor, Michelle turned to him, concern in her eyes.

'Are you doing all right, Jeremy? You look done in.'

'I'm running on not much sleep. Or food, come to think of it,' he replied, leaning back against the grey wallpaper.

'Who did you piss off, exactly?' she asked, folding her arms.

'What do you mean?'

'Someone infiltrates the Cross and burns your programme records. Someone *else* blows up a flat in Peckham so they can get away with, presumably, the only copy. Now you've got an armed cell, apparently linked to a Russian mercenary chief in East Africa, sitting there in bloody Canning Town. And they're harbouring one of the people who stole your data.'

Jeremy closed his eyes. 'That's only the half of it. My live op is compromised too. Although I think we might be able to salvage it.'

Michelle squeezed his shoulder. 'I'm just saying. To my eye, this looks deliberate. A concerted attempt to kill off Legends. Possibly *you* as well. You'd do well to think about who your enemies might be, and why they're trying quite so hard to destroy everything you've built.'

31

Jamie

Rayskiye Vrata, Zanzibar: now

They searched him twice. The first time was before he entered the villa proper, Vitaly patting down his arms and legs just as he'd done in Dar. The second time was far worse, because it was a lot more thorough.

'Apologies, Mr Tulloch. This is standard this week, I'm afraid. Enhanced security environment,' said Vitaly as he pulled Jamie's packing cubes, laundry bag, laptop and everything else out of his roller case. 'We are doing this with all of the guests.'

Jamie stood to one side in his luxuriously appointed suite, watching the big Russian poke and prod and unzip everything. Vitaly's sub-machine gun swung on its sling behind his back, black metal shining under the suite downlights.

'Place like this, security needs to be tight, right?' he managed. He could feel the pulse at his throat, like he was being slowly choked.

Vitaly nodded to himself as he picked up a black nylon zipped cube that contained Jamie's cables, chargers and other technology. It also contained the equipment that Nicola had given him.

Jamie stood stock-still, resisting the urge to dart forward and snatch the cube out of Vitaly's hands. His breath stopped in his chest, the room narrowing to a point as the Russian unzipped the pouch.

Inside, the slim tube of a laser microphone jostled against a charging brick for his laptop, the burner phone and covert smart-phone Nicola had given him and two button-like bugs, each about the size of a pound coin.

Vitaly tipped the bag on to the bed. 'You have lot of cables,' he said, picking each one up, carefully looped and secured with Velcro straps.

'Really wish everything would just use USB-C,' said Jamie, a fixed grin on his face. 'It's a pain carrying all of these around.'

Vitaly snorted and nodded. 'Last week, Artem buys phone in Dar with micro-USB socket. I ask him, is this for time travel, back to nineties. Durak.' He shook his head, then his hand went to the burner phone. 'But you have old phone too. What is this for?'

'Local SIM cards. Always a good idea to have a back-up that works on the older networks.'

Vitaly nodded. 'Smart. You have a lot of phones.'

Jamie stepped forward and pointed them out in turn. 'Work phone, travel back-up, personal phone. I've got that turned off until after I've finished these negotiations. No distractions.'

Vitaly picked up the two bugs. 'Are these . . . what are these?'

'Spare battery units. For my rangefinder.' Jamie swallowed, his throat suddenly as dry as the savannah they had driven through to get here.

Vitaly's eyes flicked down to the bed. He picked up the long tube of the laser microphone. 'What do you have a rangefinder for?' He turned the device over in his hands. 'Is military?' The big Russian's eyes came up and searched Jamie's face.

A prickle of sweat formed on the nape of Jamie's neck, despite the cool blast of the air conditioning. He chuckled and shook his head, hoping the plunging fear in his guts wasn't showing on his face.

'It's for golf. To work out the distance to the green, you know? I play a bit of golf.'

Jamie swallowed again and smiled. He did not play golf. Knew absolutely nothing about it either, apart from greens, clubs and sand traps, which was only because he had colleagues who *did* play golf and never shut up about it.

Did Vitaly like golf? Did Russians play golf? Had he just fucked himself?

'Where are your clubs?' said Vitaly, turning the rangefinder over in his hands.

'Company wouldn't cover the baggage fee,' said Jamie, unsure where the lie had come from quite so fluidly. He felt like he was tap-dancing on the edge of a cliff, barely holding his balance. 'Does Mr Bocharov play? I wasn't sure.'

'No, he hates golf. Prefers hunting, if business discussion is needed. Best if everyone is armed, eh?'

Jamie blinked at the stone-faced Russian, then saw the glimmer of a joke in the other man's eyes. It never quite turned into a smile, but Jamie managed to find a laugh somewhere.

'This is fine, Mr Tulloch,' Vitaly said, tossing the laser mic back on the bed. 'Apologies for the disruption.'

'That's fine, really. What's the plan for this evening?'

'Tonight is a drinks reception around the pool after sunset. Buffet food inside. You will meet some of the other guests and have good time.'

Vitaly pulled the sub-machine gun he had slung behind his back forward and rested his hands on it. 'In the meantime, you can check out the villa. Please don't go down past the edge of the gardens. Rest of the compound is a secure zone. Okay?'

'Yes, noted,' said Jamie, giving a small salute with three fingers. 'I'll be careful. Don't want to get on the wrong side of Security.'

Vitaly gave him a slow nod, then turned and left the room.

Jamie had already sat down, exhaled loudly and buried his head in his hands before he realised the room might have microphones and cameras in it.

He froze, blinked at his palms then turned the sagging release of tension into a long, exaggerated yawn, reaching back and stretching out his arms.

'Oh man, I'm tired,' he said to the empty room.

Trying not to move too fast or too slow, he gingerly packed up the surveillance gear and put it back in the nylon cube full of cables. Best not to carry any of that with him while he explored the villa.

He stopped and thought for a moment, then plucked out the smartphone Nicola had given him. To a casual observer, it was a bog-standard Android phone, loaded with a convincing assortment of apps, photos, music and games. It had been pre-loaded with dozens of selfies of GARNET, but Nicola had deleted those, leaving just the holiday snapshots, saved internet memes and pictures of other people's pets that you'd expect on anyone's phone. Jamie remembered looking at the pictures of GARNET in that hot little guesthouse room in Stone Town after Nicola had taken half a dozen photos of him for London to do something with.

'I suppose he does look a little like me,' he'd said.

Nicola had taken the device and started deleting the images, swiping away GARNET's face over and over again. 'Yeah, well. He's burned, if he's still alive. We don't need any of these shots. But we do need some more of you.' She'd handed the device back. 'Maybe take a few yourself. Hotel-balcony selfies. Look like a guy enjoying himself in the African sunshine.'

Jamie had chuckled. 'I *am* enjoying myself, a bit, when I forget why I'm here.'

Nicola had looked up at that. 'Hold on to that. In this job, you've got to divide yourself in two. The top layer, Jamie Tulloch, software salesman, he's having a great trip, yeah? Biggest deal of his life, fancy high-end resorts, exciting and unusual clientele. *That* guy is loving every minute of this.'

Then she'd shown him the series of presses and taps he'd need to unlock the secondary secure operating system hidden behind the first, with its own camera app, messaging and secure document storage.

He stood in his room in Bocharov's villa and practised the sequence, making sure he could do it in a second or two, and reverse it with the triple click of the home button on the side of the phone. Once he'd managed to switch it into covert mode and back three times, each attempt taking a little less time, he was satisfied.

He looked at the messaging icon. The phone was in airport mode, all wireless connections turned off. Nicola had warned him to keep the phone offline until he needed to check in. He flicked the cellular network on and typed out the agreed codeword.

PRIMROSE

Arrived, settled, safe. Nothing to report yet.

He turned airplane mode back on and pocketed the device, then walked out on to his room's balcony, high on the third floor of the villa, overlooking the tiers that dropped down to the U-shaped pool area below. Tanned bodies, men and women both, lay along the pool edge and on long, hardwood loungers with luxuriant white padding.

Time to see just who was here at Rayskiye Vrata.

The villa was enormous. The three floors he could see from outside were only the top layer, with another two levels below ground. The centre of the building's ground floor was dominated by a huge, double-height lounge area with bifold doors open to the outside, plus enormous hardwood shutters pulled down to keep the temperature cooler. Low couches and coffee tables were circled in loose groups, and a few people sat talking.

Faces looked up as he passed and gave him small nods. Jamie returned them, unsure who any of these people were. Business contacts? Gangsters? He walked through to the pool.

It was curving, teardrop-shaped, ending in the flat infinity edge that looked out over the compound. Strings of softly glowing lights hung from the palm trees and bushes artfully arranged around the pool. Between the trees there were loungers and more tables, mostly unoccupied, but here and there serious-looking men in khaki trousers and linen shirts sat talking, cradling expensive-looking cocktails.

Men like Vitaly were everywhere. Three at the end of the garden, walking in slow circles. At least one by every door. They all carried the same sub-machine guns, and pistols in thigh holsters, though they mostly had the weapons slung at their sides. But it gave the whole place an air of unreality, like they were waiting in the US embassy at Saigon in '75. Or indeed, Kabul in '21.

'You the English guy?' said a voice, American, male, deep, from the shadows to his left. Jamie peered into the dimness between two palm trees. A figure was sitting out of the light, the glow of a cigarette in one hand. The shadow took a drag and the orange pinpoint lit a pair of aviators, a flat line of a mouth and a jaw lined with greying stubble.

'Scottish. Jamie Tulloch.' He stepped towards the table and extended his hand.

The American raised both of his hands in a parody of fear. 'Woah, sorry, man. I know the Scotch get touchy about that shit. Like the Canadians. Cody Klein.' He levered himself out of the chair and held out a beefy hand.

Klein's handshake was vice-like, but Jamie got the sense the big man was holding back. He didn't see a thirty-something pasty Scots-man as any sort of equal or threat, so he didn't get the full death grip. But Cody Klein was definitely the sort of man who thought 'winning' a handshake mattered.

Klein settled back into his seat, which was only just big enough for him. He wore black multi-pocketed cargo trousers, tactical boots and a safari shirt with the sleeves rolled up. The ashtray beside him held at least three spent cigarette butts.

Jamie half smiled. 'Scotch is the whisky. Scots are the people.'
'Huh?'

'Never mind.' Jamie looked at the other man in the half-light. American. Possibly ex-military. Jamie had met enough men like this to know they generally liked to talk. Brag, even.

He sat down on the other side of the small table. 'Arkady told a few people I was coming?'

'First-name terms already?' said Klein, stubbing out his fourth cig-arette and immediately extracting a fifth from a packet in his leg pocket. 'Must like you. Yeah, he told a few of us. Said you was here for some software thing, for UPK.'

'That's right. Warehouse and logistics. We're helping UPK meet its ISO standard.'

Klein lit the cigarette and sat back. 'Fascinating. You enjoying yourself? Checking out Zanzibar? Hell of a place, right?'

Jamie nodded. A server appeared from the gloom with a tray of drinks and offered it to Klein, who waved the man away. Jamie took a glass of chilled white wine.

'It is when you're staying in places like this.'

Klein chuckled. 'Damn right. Only way to live, this part of the world. Can you imagine living in this kinda place without AC? Fuckin' worse than the South.'

'Millions of people do. That where you're from? The South?'

Klein took another drag. 'Shit no. Brits can't read an accent worth shit. I'm a mountain boy, Southern Colorado. Pueblo. Mile High State. Whole damn state is higher than your highest mountain. You know that?'

Jamie sipped his wine. 'Aye. Ben Nevis. I climbed it once, in school.'

Klein shook his head. 'Where I'm from, we don't have fuckin' schoolboys climbing our highest mountains.'

Jamie ignored the jibe and gazed out across the pool. It glowed, lit from beneath, blue-green in the darkness. Despite their bulk, men like Cody Klein always had extremely thin skin. It didn't take much to get under it.

'So, what do you do for Arkady? You sales? Marketing?'

The big man actually flexed his shoulders. 'Fuck no,' said Klein. 'We run security ops on UPK's mining operations in Mali and the DRC. Gold and cobalt. Profitable sideline for them, on top of the manufacturing.'

Time to confirm Klein's obvious opinion of him, invite a little more flexing. 'That sounds . . . scary, to be honest. Been doing it long?'

Klein gave him a look of barely disguised pity. Good. Best if he kept thinking of Jamie as an easily impressed beta lightweight. He'd be more likely to run his mouth that way. 'A year. I was anti-piracy before that, in the Gulf. And USMC before that. Three tours in Afghanistan.'

Jamie smiled. 'I was just thinking, this compound, all the guys with guns walking about. Feels a bit like how I imagine the embassy must have been, before it all fell apart.'

The indulgent smile left Klein's face and he picked up his half-drunk beer. 'Nah. No mortar fire. No crowds at the gates holding their fuckin' kids up to you. No VBIEDs coming down the roads trailing fuel from all the bullet holes. This is a *resort*, man.'

'You were there?'

'Yeah, I was there. Fuckin' sucked. But I got my discharge, got on the private circuit. All the fun parts, less of the bullshit.'

'I'm surprised Russians would choose to work with American security contractors. You know, after everything.'

Klein waved away the argument. 'That's ancient history. Arkady's a New Russian through and through. Or so he tells me. He likes money. I like money. Everything else is nothing to do with me. You work cobalt mines in Africa, my friend, you gotta be focused. Bring that American work ethic, know what I'm saying?'

He stubbed out his cigarette. Jamie let the silence lengthen. 'Anyway. Here to re-up our contract for the next fiscal. Bocharov likes to get everyone together like this a couple times a year. Do business. Drink a little. Eat a lot. Fuck, if that's your thing.'

Jamie blinked.

'Guess not. Wife at home?'

'No, no, I just . . .'

Klein rolled his shoulders. 'Not the confident type. I get it. Let you into a little secret. These girls? Bocharov pays 'em to be here. Maybe not in cash, but they don't pay for those five-thousand-dollar hand-bags and dresses with their Instagram follows, know what I mean? So they'll probably fuck you. If you ask nice.'

Jamie took a sip of his wine. He'd been around enough crass

businessmen high on their own power to have heard similar before, but normally it was alluded to, not said outright. Klein smiled smugly and lit another cigarette.

The bulky shape of Arkady Bocharov came along the edge of the pool. 'Ah, Klein,' he said, stepping towards them. He was in a white linen suit with a bright red shirt. Yevgeny Olenev was a few loungers back, trailing Bocharov, squatting down and talking quietly to two girls sitting on the edge of the pool. They were leaning back and laughing, although Jamie saw them exchange a look with each other as Olenev stood and walked towards Bocharov.

'Arkady. Pleasure, as always. Just getting to meet your software guy. Filling him in on these soirées of yours.'

Bocharov boomed a laugh. Several people looked up and smiled along with whatever it was the boss was finding funny. 'Painting a terrible picture of my morals, I am sure.' Bocharov pointed to Jamie. 'You don't listen to this man. He is a very good security man, but horrible person.'

Klein put a hand across his heart. 'You wound me, Arkady.'

'It's fine,' said Bocharov, turning to indicate Olenev as he got to them. 'I need horrible people. Why else am I talking to Olenev?'

Olenev's face cracked into a hard scowl, but it was almost instantly replaced with a smile and a laugh. 'What is it the Anglos say? Takes one to know one?' he said.

As Bocharov turned away, the scowl crept back on to the other man's face. Jamie filed that away for later. Bocharov was the boss here. But clearly not everyone liked him all that much.

'Anyway,' said Bocharov, 'Yakov is an innocent. Just here to sell his software. Do not be filling his head with bad stories. Although, if you do want a little' – Bocharov tipped his head and gave Jamie a considering look – 'whatever, all you have to do is ask. UPK looks after its guests.'

Cody gave a deep chuckle beside him, and Jamie shifted in his seat. 'Thanks. I'll keep that in mind.'

Bocharov smiled, slow and leering. 'Good. Time to get this party started.'

The lounge had been laid out with three long, cloth-covered trestle tables, each weighed down with an astonishing variety of food. There were plates of pickles, salads, American-style miniature burgers, vol-au-vents, pierogis, tiny metal buckets of thick-cut fries. Plus local food like ugali, spiced chicken curry, Zanzibar 'pizza' on chapatis. The cuisine was extremely scattershot, as though Bocharov had paged through some kind of huge menu and picked two dozen things at random.

'Love the food at these things,' said Klein next to him, taking three of the tiny burgers. 'Chefs here do a good slider. You get sick of chicken and fucking fries, working in the DRC.' He spooned some ugali on to his plate, a dense maize-based staple of Tanzanian food a little like polenta, then ladled chicken curry over it. 'Look forward to this shit for weeks.'

Jamie filled his own plate, then assessed his options.

He started by following Klein. The big man was busily wolfing down his sliders. He had a bottle of Tusker beer clutched in one hand and took gulps from it after every other bite.

Jamie nodded towards the other guests. 'Met many of these folks before?'

'Sure,' said Klein around a mouthful of burger. 'All kindsa people. You got UPK factory guys. Vityaz guys, though we're not supposed to call them that these days.' He took a swig of his beer, then burped loudly. A young woman in a sparkling blue dress of sequins and silks gave him a disgusted look, which Klein countered with a grin and a leer.

'Vityaz? Weren't those guys . . .'

'Mercs. Ukraine war. But these guys are house-trained now. They handle cross-border stuff. Convoys, that sort of thing. Not my area. And of course, personal security for Bocharov.' Klein leaned in close.

'And, I hear, the odd special piece of work. Rivals, you know?' He mimed a gun to the head.

Jamie widened his eyes, roleplaying the shocked vanilla businessman finding himself in the big leagues for the first time. But inside his guts were roiling. Had a Vityaz man been at Charles de Gaulle? Did Terence spend his last seconds looking into the eyes of someone in this room?

Klein grinned and took a spoonful of his ugali, clearly enjoying the reaction. 'Serious people, man. Make the wrong moves, not just your stock price hits the deck, y'know?' He chuckled, clearly pleased with himself.

Jamie wasn't sure if the queasy smile he offered the American was entirely acting.

A tall, slim man with short grey hair and thick, clear-framed glasses stood off to one side of the room. He was deep in conversation with Yevgeny Olenev, the two blonde women with them standing with hips cocked and bored faces, talking to each other in what sounded like Afrikaans to Jamie's ear. Maybe Dutch.

Jamie swallowed, pushing away thoughts of Terence and his dead eyes. 'What about that guy?' he said.

'Guest of honour, from what Bocharov tells me. Think he's Swiss? Big arms guy. Luca Brunner. Shadier end of the market though. Grey stuff. MANPADS outta Ukraine, kamikaze drones, lotta rifles. But I hear he's moving up in the world. Salvaged MBTs from the last couple of wars, refurbed T-80s and T-90s.'

'I don't actually know what most of that means.'

'Guns and tanks, man. He sells guns and tanks.'

Jamie picked at his food, trying to settle the nerves in his stomach. This was just another sales conference, like a hundred he'd been to before. Except the small talk was about heavy weaponry instead of EBITDA margins.

'Hey, Natasha,' grunted Klein. Jamie turned and saw one of the three young women he'd shared breakfast with in Stone Town. Natasha had swapped her black dress for a green one and her silk scarf for a diamanté-studded hair clip that swept her blonde hair back from her forehead.

'Cody!' she said, giving the American a hug, a champagne flute clutched in one hand. 'Oh, I am so glad you're here. These things are always *so boring* when you're not,' she whispered, leaning in close to them. 'Hello, Jamie. The drive from Stone Town was okay?'

'Yes, thank you.'

'Good to see you too, Tash. How was Dar?'

Natasha rolled her eyes. 'Oh, you know, very important man doing very important things. We went to Kipepeo for two days. It was very nice.' She flicked a dismissive hand towards Vitaly, standing silently by the bifold doors. 'No men, no guns. But it is nice to be here again. I love the pool here.'

Klein grinned. 'Gonna be a hell of a party. I'm gonna get more sliders. Didn't get a chance to eat before I flew outta Kinshasa. Nothing but beer and cigarettes since I got here.'

Natasha squeezed the man's cheeks and pouted. 'Oh, lapachka, how have you survived?'

Klein laughed and strode back to the buffet. Natasha turned to Jamie.

'You know Mr Klein well?' he asked.

Natasha smiled. 'Oh, yes. He is fun. Not like the others.'

Jamie looked away. 'Seems quite similar, in some ways.'

Natasha shrugged and folded her arm across her waist, holding her champagne flute aloft with the other. She sipped from it. 'In this world, the bar is low, Jamie. Very, very low. Cody is good man who does bad things sometimes. The rest, they are all just bad.'

Jamie took in her profile against the glowing lights: the snub nose, the blonde hair swept back. She felt his gaze and turned big, mascaraed eyes on him. 'What about you? What are you doing here, Jamie? Are you a bad man too?'

He was about to say something, though he had no idea what, when a flutter of movement on the other side of the room saved him.

Bocharov emerged from the crowd with a tray of his own, this one crowded with tiny glasses. As he crossed the lounge, he spun slowly, the tray high above his head. Then he held up a hand. The chatter dropped. And so did the lights. From a hidden sound system, a deep bass beat filled the room.

'Now,' Bocharov called out over the music, 'let's fucking party!'

32

Nicola

Ocean Jewel Resort, north-east coast of Zanzibar: now

Once they'd sat down and ordered, the man lapsed into silence. He regarded both of them over steepled fingers, eyes watchful behind his rimless glasses. Nicola was glad of the sharp South African white wine. It took the edge off the pulse of adrenaline that Bocharov's name had brought on.

Her phone buzzed and she slipped it out of her pocket.

PRIMROSE

Tulloch was in place. She wasn't sure if that was a relief or not.

'So . . .' she began, as the waiter put down the plates and backed away.

'You are wondering who I am? And whether you can be honest with me?'

'Wondering who you're talking about,' said Sylvan. 'Bocharov? Sounds Russian. Haven't seen any Russians here. We're just here on holiday, mate.'

'Please, Mr Lenahan, which I am sure is not your real name, I know why you are here. Let us drop the pretence, yes?'

'You start,' Nicola said, spearing a sweet potato chip and dipping it in the spinach artichoke dip she'd ordered. She took a bite and chewed thoughtfully. 'What's *your* interest in *us*, exactly?'

The man took a sip of his wine, then sat back. 'I am Adil Komba. I work for the Tanzanian Intelligence and Security Service, here on Zanzibar. TISS for short. This is my . . . patch, is the phrase?'

'What, like MI5 or whatever?' said Sylvan, keeping up the gormless-tourist act. Nicola put her hand on his arm.

'I think we can drop it. He knows we're not tourists. Though of course I can't confirm or deny what you think we are.'

Komba shrugged. 'You're Kate Askwith, FCDO officer. So your diplomatic passport says. I would be very sad to make you persona non grata, should that prove untrue. And of course, your physical description is curiously close to at least three reports I have of a British officer working in Kenya and Somalia. I would not wish to look into some of the things our brother services there have reported to me. That terrible business in Nairobi, for example.'

Nicola's hand stilled halfway to her glass. A local guy, showing up a little too early for his warehouse shift. Lying there in the dust with an arms dealer's bullet in his guts.

She'd been gone for twenty minutes before the Kenyan NIS had shown up. But there must have been a camera. These days, there was always a fucking camera.

She completed the movement and picked up her glass, swirling the wine. The sun was a deep bronze line on the horizon and would soon be gone. A light breeze came in from the water and cooled Nicola's bare shoulders, delicious after the afternoon in the burning sun. She sipped, then spoke over the rim of the glass.

'Veiled threats are still threats, Mr Komba. What is it you want from us?'

Komba tilted his head to peer at her. 'I have already said. I want to know what you think you are doing. This is not London, my friends.'

'It's not St Petersburg either, but Bocharov seems to be doing what he likes,' said Sylvan, a note of distaste in his voice.

'We are well aware of Mr Bocharov,' said Komba. 'Of who he is and what he does. Bocharov is a vulture, picking at Africa where he is permitted to. He brings a few legitimate jobs, yes. But mostly he brings death and misery.'

'I'm glad we agree on that much,' said Nicola. 'So you're warning us off, is that it? You're building some kind of case against him?'

Komba smiled slowly, turning the wine glass in front of him. 'I could not comment on this. But we are not blind. We know there is something happening here, this week. You do too, otherwise you would not be here.'

'So what are you proposing? Why collar us like this? Aside from the opportunity to have a nice meal?' she said as the waiter returned with their mains. She took a long sip from her iced water, then started eating, eyes on Komba.

After a long moment, he also began eating, a rib-eye steak. 'The food *is* very good here. It is a nice resort. Brings a lot of money to the island. Big companies come in, they build places, they take most of the money out of Tanzania. But this place is Zanzibari-owned. I like it.'

He took another bite and chewed for a moment, then washed it down with some more wine. 'We do not want Bocharov on Zanzibar. But his company has skirted the law for a long time. And we think he will leave soon, in any case. Go back to Russia. There is some kind of deal. We don't want you to disrupt that. If you do, maybe he stays, takes more. Does more damage.'

'Your plan for getting rid of Russian mercenaries is just hoping they go away?' said Sylvan, snorting. He sat back and took a long swig from the beer the waiter had brought him. 'Ask the DRC how that worked out. Or Mali. Or the CAR.'

'The difference between us and the Central African Republic is that we are not paying mercenaries to keep us in power, Mr Lenahan. This has been a bad idea since the Ancient Greeks.'

Nicola sighed. 'Can we stop with the geopolitical dick-waving? I can tell you're both smart realists with your fingers on the pulse. Tell us what you want, Mr Komba. In plain terms.'

Komba's eyes widened at the language, but then he laughed, a quiet, wheezing sound. 'Very good. Smart realists indeed.' He finished his wine and set the glass down with a click.

'Keep your distance. As you say, you are simply tourists. That means you do not attempt to enter Mr Bocharov's compound. You do not bring any British air assets anywhere near this island. And you do not attempt to recruit local help.'

Sylvan tried not to react, but Komba caught the glance he gave Nicola. 'Yes, we know about your two street runners in Stone Town. Keep them *away* from here.'

'And what, you'll take care of it? You're on the case?' said Sylvan.

Komba frowned. 'You think you can run our country better than we can, Mr Lenahan? This is a common affliction among the London and Washington set, I find.'

Nicola picked up her wine glass. 'No, but we also think the risks are greater than you appreciate. Sit back and watch this deal happen, whatever it is, and it could have consequences. Big consequences.'

Komba raised an eyebrow. 'You have something actionable? We are notional allies, Miss Askwith. Commonwealth members. Is there something you wish to share with the TISS? I am right here.'

Decisions on intelligence sharing and joint operations were so far above her pay grade they may as well be in the stratosphere. She had to play this carefully.

'Nothing concrete, yet. But that's why we're watching.'

'You can keep watching. But from a distance. You are guests in this country. Diplomatic guests in your case, Miss Askwith. But guests all the same.'

33

Jeremy

Canning Town, London: earlier

The sky was beginning to lighten when they got to Canning Town, pulling in behind the low brick buildings of a commandeered textile warehouse. Jeremy stopped as he climbed out of the SUV that had brought him, breathing crisp pre-dawn air. In the distance an early DLR train rumbled past, wheels screeching as it turned south towards Woolwich.

Inside, shelves and tables usually filled with rolls of fabric instead held the monitors and whiteboards of a temporary command centre and the blinking laptops and stacked equipment cases of the tactical teams.

A small huddle of counterterrorism specialists from SO15 and 22 SAS was in one corner, examining architectural drawings of the target. Live drone footage played on one of the big monitors, a flickering thermal view of the warehouse. Indistinct blobs of white moved inside. One stepped outside and the image sharpened. The cold outline of a rifle was clearly visible, slung at the man's side.

Jeremy spotted Sally Lime, already plugged in at a table with Michelle's team from Thames House. She waved him over.

'ISR is all set up, drone coverage, 5G man-in-the-middle so we can see if they try to call anyone. The works.'

Jeremy nodded, catching about half of the jargon. 'So they can't get the data out?'

'Nope,' said Lime. 'Not without physically carrying it.'

'Mr Althrop?' said a deep voice. Jeremy turned to see one of the 22 CT team members, a captain, by the rank slide on his black combat jacket. The man held out a hand. 'Captain Wilton, 22 SAS. I believe you're our SME on this target?'

'Well, he nearly killed me yesterday,' said Jeremy, shaking the man's hand. 'Along with Sally here and eight SO19 officers.'

The captain's eyebrows rose. 'You went in with the tac team?'

'Not far behind.'

'Well, we won't be doing that today, sir. Some serious customers in that warehouse. I'll be asking you to steer *well* clear until the building's fully secured.'

'Absolutely,' said Jeremy. 'What do you need from me now?'

'A briefing on the target. And any thoughts you have on Boxwood.'

'Lead the way, Captain,' said Jeremy.

The sixteen men waiting around the whiteboards ranged in age from mid-twenties to mid-forties. Most were compact, wiry men with hair thinned from hundreds of hours in sweaty combat helmets, faces lean from months in the field. They were not the musclebound supermen of the popular imagination. Quite the opposite. Jeremy could have walked past any single one of them in the supermarket and not thought twice about it. Just like the best of SIS's operators, they faded into the background. Invisible men fighting invisible wars.

Captain Wilton pointed at a printed still of Boxwood on the top left of the board. 'This is our primary target, responsible for that little dust-up in Peckham yesterday. No ID yet, but he or someone he's working with wired that place with explosives like a pro. Our main risk here is that they've done the same to this place, so I'll want demo specialists up front for entry-point checks. We're looking for pressure switches, fishing line, grenades in tin cans, the full shitty detail. You know the drill.'

Wilton nodded towards Jeremy.

'This is Mr Althrop, from SIS. He was in Peckham yesterday. Can you give the team a brief on what we're securing?'

Jeremy nodded and stepped forward. 'These people pulled off a critical penetration of a secure facility two days ago. They got out data from air-gapped servers that could compromise dozens of operations, as well as risking the lives of SIS operators and civilians.'

'They've still got the data on them?' said one of the men, a dark-skinned sergeant in his early thirties cradling a Diemaco C8 carbine rifle. 'Sergeant Brierley, sir. Signals specialist.'

'We believe so. Solid-state drives. It's unclear why. Blackmail, some kind of targeted attack – we don't know yet.'

Brierley nodded. 'I'll keep an eye out for SSDs and other kinds of storage, sir. If they're using decent kit and nobody shoots the drives, we should be able to get them back for you.'

'What about the other members of the team?' asked a younger soldier, eyes tracking across the four other profiles on the board.

'Short version is they're all ex-Russian SVR and probably military before that. Seasoned operators. Don't underestimate them.'

Captain Wilton stepped forward. 'All right, time to get reading, lads. Commit these faces to memory so you can ID. It's going to be watch and shoot in there. Current plan is jump off in one hour, just after sun-up. Run over the floor plans again, work out the angles with your oppos. Final brief in thirty minutes. Roger?'

The men acknowledged and turned to their tasks, grouping up into bunches of two, three and four to conduct their final checks, talking in low voices as they loaded magazines, slipped on armoured vests and checked their equipment.

'Inbound contact,' called Anjali from the other side of the warehouse. Every head swivelled to face the monitors. They were still showing the drone view of the yard, but now there was a large, warm heat signature entering from the right.

'SUV, two people inside. Looks like more arms.'

They watched as the vehicle swung into the yard and three figures emerged from the warehouse, all of them carrying weapons.

'We got enough light yet to go off thermal?' said Captain Wilton. Luke nodded and tapped at his keyboard. The image switched to a dim, true-colour, stabilised view.

'Can we zoom?' said Jeremy.

Luke picked up a controller. A half-second later the drone's camera reacted, zooming in jerkily. Luke flicked the thumbsticks of the controller, re-centring the image. Now they had a clear view of the open boot of the SUV. The two new people, a man and a woman in black jackets and cargo trousers, were pulling heavy green flight cases out of the vehicle. One of the operatives knelt and opened the case.

Beside him, Captain Wilton sucked in a breath. 'That's a fucking FIM-92.'

Wilton caught Jeremy's glance. 'Better known as the Stinger. These are the upgraded ones. We sent a couple of thousand of them to the Ukrainians. Looks like a few got loose.'

Jeremy swallowed. At first he'd thought they were looking at some kind of provocation operation, men with rifles, bombs perhaps. But that kind of hardware could mean downed jets over central London. Jeremy's two daughters would be at school in a few hours, dropped off by their mother right under the flightpath for City Airport. What the hell were Boxwood and his team trying to do?

34

Jamie

Rayskiye Vrata: now

'Jamie?'

He looked up blearily from his laptop. Komarov stood by the window, sipping on his third large coffee of the morning. They'd started early. Back in London, the sun would barely be up. He still wasn't quite used to the two-hour time difference, and the hangover didn't help.

'Sorry, what? I was double-checking the question list for the pick-and-pack discussion.'

Komarov smiled indulgently. 'Tough to concentrate with a hangover. I know the feeling. I asked if you had a good night last night?'

'Yeah, yeah, it was great,' Jamie replied, remembering Bocharov twirling under the flashing lights, another tray of shots on his outstretched fingers. 'Mr Bocharov has . . . impressive stamina.'

Komarov smirked. 'All the nayemnik do. They are tough bastards. The ones who got out, of course.'

Jamie looked up. 'You served?'

Komarov shook his head. 'I was too young at the start. Then working for the Defence Ministry before the collapse. Logistics. What I do now, but with bullets and bandages.'

Jamie nodded. 'UPK must be a bit different.'

Komarov smiled and sipped his coffee, then gazed out over the villa's lawns. 'UPK is doing important things, Jamie. Very important things. I'm proud to work for Mr Bocharov. To be part of this.'

Jamie picked up his cup and went to the window to stand beside Komarov. 'How long have you worked for him?'

'Two years. Before he came here he was running the steel mills in Vorsino. I was working there after I left the Defence Ministry. Russia needed a lot of steel then. A lot of rebuilding.'

Jamie nodded but said nothing. Salesmanship had not come that naturally to him, but he'd learned over the years that some people wanted to talk. Leaving a silence gave them something they had to fill.

It didn't take long.

'He did amazing things there. Great team. So when he got the UPK job, I came too. And this deal, Jamie, it is important. Modernisation is *essential*. Without it we're dead in the water. The Chinese, the Indians, even musty old UK. Everyone is doing this. Automation and data. It's the future.'

Jamie nodded again. 'A big week, he said this morning. I'm flattered that he thinks the same way you do, about this deal.'

Komarov's face twisted, just for a moment. Jamie let the silence lengthen again. It took two more sips of his coffee before Komarov's expression turned into words.

'That's part of my job. Guiding these decisions. Bocharov has the vision, but he's not a details guy. That's me. He is very busy this week, but it is' – he waved a hand – 'other things.'

Jamie waited a heartbeat, then gave a small snort of agreement. 'I met a few of the people involved last night, I think. Certainly some characters.'

Komarov nodded, warming to his theme. 'These Vityaz guys, the security people. I know it's necessary, for the kind of business we do here. But he's always distracted when there's security matters to discuss. It can be . . . frustrating.'

Across the compound, Bocharov's office annex was busy. Two black Toyotas pulled up. They rolled to a stop, red dust coating the wheel arches. Guards climbed out and took up positions, then a familiar figure climbed out.

'That's Luca Brunner, right? Wonder where he's been?' said Jamie.

Komarov was silent for a long moment, long enough that Jamie risked a sideways glance at the man. That same twist to his mouth, his eyes fixed on Brunner's back as he disappeared into Bocharov's office.

'Some things,' he said, turning away from the window, 'it is better not to see.'

35

Nicola

Ocean Jewel Resort: now

Despite Komba's warning, Farida and Tumo were already on their way. And Nicola didn't much feel like immediately acquiescing to everything the local intelligence chief had demanded. They could push the boundaries a little further.

Dinner with Komba had ended amicably enough, the TISS chief bowing to both of them and wishing them a good night's sleep.

But Nicola had slept fitfully, eventually rising before dawn to run on the beach, pounding along the wet sand before the temperature rose too high. She swam in the sea, saltwater stinging her sunburn from the previous day. Turning the options over in her head, lost in the mission as she backstroked out past the marker buoys. Sometimes it was better to be on her own when she was thinking like this, preoccupied and distant. She got the same way sometimes even after missions. Lost in thought. Reassessing what she'd done and said and how it could have played differently. Rachael had found it alluring, at first. Saw Nicola as a deep thinker, always considering carefully before she spoke. But thoughtful pauses too often became long, tense silences.

She'd towelled off on the shoreline as the sun rose, had a shower, put London and Rachael out of her mind. Now she was famished, grumpy and in need of caffeine.

They met on the terrace for breakfast. Farida inclined her head and raised the coffee pot that had been delivered to the table. 'You want some?'

'Abso-bloody-lutely,' said Nicola, sitting down beside her. Farida filled a cup and passed it to her.

Sylvan nodded hello. 'Just filling these two in on our dinner,' he said.

'We have met Komba before. In our world, he is a well-known man.'

'Glad to hear he actually *is* from TISS. I was half worried Bocharov had clocked us and paid a local to warn us off.' She sipped the coffee gratefully, then sat back in her chair and looked around the other three at the table. Sylvan grimaced.

'He's the real deal. Now I know he's watching I've clocked at least three staff keeping a closer eye than normal on us.' He nodded towards a gardener a dozen paces away, watering the low bushes that ringed the pool area. The man caught Nicola's turned head and looked away sharply, squinting into the distance as if trying to read the number on a passing bus.

Sylvan *tsk*ed under his breath. 'I think these *are* actually staff he's paying off. They're not very good. Presumably he's got trained operatives either in the local area or on the way.'

Tumo nodded, chewing on a croissant. 'It's a mix. Paid informers. Tip-offs from ex-TISS people scattered about. A few professionals. Farida and I, we did work for TISS in the past. But now we are freelance. Much more fun.'

Sylvan sat forward and put his elbows on the table, fingers interlaced. He looked over his clasped hands at Nicola. 'Anything from our boy yet?'

'Just a check-in last night.'

'I don't think we can risk another boat run today. Two days in a row, even the most dim-witted Vityaz goon is going to notice the same boat in the same place with the same people in it.'

Farida picked up her glass of orange juice and took a sip. She glanced down towards the dock, appraising the boats moored there. 'Tumo and I could rent one? Go down the coast to the beach bars?'

'No, I don't want to piss off Komba,' said Nicola. She saw the protest in Sylvan's eyes and held up a hand. 'Yet. I'm plenty willing to ignore him if we need to, but there's no sense antagonising him this early, when Jamie is only just through the door. And I think sending our two local operatives on a jolly straight past the compound would be a shot across the bows.'

'A shame,' said Farida. 'I like boats.'

'So what now? If we can't watch the compound directly and can't send these two to watch for us?' said Sylvan, draining his coffee, then picking up the remnants of his croissant and wolfing it down. 'I fucking hate waiting.'

'That's the job,' said Nicola. 'There's plenty to do though. We need to check out this place, work out who Komba's got on his payroll. Look for holes in Bocharov's security set-up. There's a way in. There always is, if you look hard enough. And a way in can become a way out, if Jamie needs one.'

36

Jeremy

Canning Town: earlier

His phone buzzed in his pocket just before sunrise, as the black-clad shapes of the 22 troopers began to move slowly through the dimness towards the warehouse gate.

'Althrop.'

'Jeremy, it's Stephanie Salisbury. What's the sit-rep?'

'We're going active now. Target Boxwood and six others, holed up in a warehouse in Canning Town. Heavily armed, including man-portable SAMs.'

'Jesus. And you're going in right now?'

'We have to, Stephanie. City Airport is a stone's throw from here. They could pop out of that warehouse and take down a 737 after their morning coffee.'

'Charlie Stick is at the gate,' said the radio operator at the ops table. 'Delta Stick stack up right side.'

The radio buzzed with digital compression as the other sticks checked in.

'Echo set.'

'Foxtrot set.'

'Targets?' said Captain Wilton over the radio.

'Four prone and still sleeping, probably still in their sleeping bags. Three moving. One close to the door.'

'Are you there, Jeremy?' said Salisbury on the phone.

'Yes, I'm here. We're going in now.'

'Is this the right call? Can we watch them? Work out who they're talking to?'

Jeremy turned away from the wall of displays. He stared out at the pink of the morning sky. 'We can't take the risk, Stephanie. This is a red-level threat, critical. Even if I wanted to stop it, I couldn't. This is a major terrorist attack in the making. Paris and Mumbai rolled into one with a half-dozen airliners added to the mix. You know how many widebody jets are over London, inside a Stinger's range, at any one time?'

'I just think—'

'Fifteen to twenty. Thirty or more at peak hours. If they want to, they can start popping off these things from SUVs all over the city. It'd be apocalyptic, Stephanie. My own fucking kids go to school right under City's flightpath. We have to go in, right now.'

'If you lose them, Jeremy. Or lose the data . . .'

'That's what I'm trying to prevent. I've already lost one good man because of these people. I won't let them hurt anyone else.'

'No, no, of course not. And I'm still following that up, don't you worry. I've got your back, Jeremy, every step of the way. Just . . . do it right. Don't take any risks. These people are lethal operators.'

'We won't. We're going in. I have to go.'

'Good luck. I mean that.'

'Thank you, Stephanie. I'll update you as soon as we have the data secured.'

He pocketed his phone and turned back to the displays. Sally Lime was hunched over her laptop, eyes flicking back and forth, a finger tracing something on her screen.

She looked up. 'Our man in the middle picked something up. Ping on the suspect's device. Encrypted message.'

'Movement. Target Alpha, near the doors, is moving. Heading for the building exit. Charlie Stick, he'll have eyes on you if he comes outside.'

'Back off, back off,' said Captain Wilton on the radio. The troopers shuffled backwards, away from the gate, just out of sight of the warehouse's small secondary door. 'Stay in cover. Stand by.'

The door opened and Boxwood stepped out into the morning, face lit by the glow of a phone. His breath was visible in the morning chill, even on the grainy drone feed. Boxwood put his phone away, then pulled a set of keys from his pocket.

'He's going for Vehicle 2,' said one of the troopers on the radio. 'He just unlocked it.'

Wilton turned towards Michelle Cavendish. 'Ma'am, do we have a green light?'

She stood with arms folded, staring up at the drone feed. 'Yes, we're green. Take that vehicle, detain Boxwood and clear the warehouse.'

'Roger, we're a go. Charlie, take the gate.'

The drone feed zoomed back out. Boxwood was halfway into the vehicle when the spiked metal gate of the warehouse yard swung open, pulled by two troopers, while another two swept through, their carbine rifles up. They crossed the long, dusty yard in three heartbeats, completely silent. Just as they got within touching distance of the vehicle, the gate scraped on the concrete behind them.

Boxwood looked up. Then several things happened at once.

The Russian dropped the phone and drew a pistol from his jacket. He fired twice, missing with both shots, but it was enough for the lead troopers to duck and return fire. Jeremy saw flashes and the spidery cracks of bullet holes in the windscreen of the SUV, but Boxwood was already inside with the door closed. The headlights snapped on and the vehicle lurched forward, hitting one of the troopers. The soldier managed to roll over the bonnet and drop to the ground, but Boxwood was accelerating fast, heading for the narrow gap in the gate.

'Delta, stop that vehicle! Charlie, Echo, Foxtrot, breach and clear.'

A large monitor to Jeremy's right exploded with movement, the individual bodycams of each of the troopers filled with flashes and shifting shadows as they sprinted for their objectives.

Boxwood rammed the gate, nearly crushing the other two Charlie troopers. They fired steadily, short, controlled bursts smashing into the fleeing vehicle, but it was too late. He was already out and on the street, tyres squealing.

'Anvil, this is Zero. Black SUV inbound to perimeter,' said the radio operator, warning the Met Police covert cordon. Jeremy heard an unsuppressed gunshot outside, then another. Police snipers on the rooftop, he guessed, trying to stop the vehicle.

'He's out, he's out. Vehicle is southbound on Newham Way. Headed for the DLR station. No eyes, no eyes.'

On the main monitor, there was a bright flash as a breaching charge went off on the warehouse door, then smoke, confusion. Shouts and swearing voices, then more flashes. Then Jeremy heard a sound he was deeply familiar with but which he'd never expected to encounter in London: the heavy, hammering beat of an AK rifle being fired on full automatic.

Jeremy stared for a long moment. People around him began moving.

Michelle was at his side. 'Our field team is heading after Boxwood, with the Met. Can you go with them? I need to contain this shit,' she said, gesturing towards the continuing flashes on the monitors. On the thermal feed, the warehouse door was bright with flame. A trooper swore and fired his weapon through a doorway. Flash-bangs went off, deadening the microphones. A half-second later, Jeremy heard the sound for real.

'Got it,' said Jeremy, pulling on his jacket and following the Thames House team out to their vehicles. On his way to the door, Sally Lime caught his elbow.

'Be careful, Jez. This is some serious shit.'

'I will. You just get me those hard drives, all right?'

She gestured towards the chaos on the screen. 'If anything survives that, I'll secure it, don't worry.'

He nodded, then ran out into the brightening morning.

37

Jamie

Rayskiye Vrata: now

After lunch, Komarov took a back seat and Jamie lost himself in technical specs. The Russian had lined up call after call with UPK facilities across East Africa. After three hours, Jamie had almost forgotten the other reason he was here, his head buzzing with figures and estimates.

'I think that's all we have for today,' said Komarov after the sixth call. He waved a hand at the reams of handwritten notes in front of Jamie, the open laptop screen filled with hundreds of figures in Jamie's estimating spreadsheet. 'But it looks like you got what you need?'

Jamie nodded. 'I think so. I might need to ask a follow-up question or two, tomorrow maybe? I won't know until I've done some collating.'

Komarov was already standing. 'Of course. Perfect. You can use this room, or sit by the pool – whatever, man. It's a big villa. Lots of places to get work done. If you need me for anything, just ask one of the staff to find me. Although I'll probably be by the pool myself.' He laughed and grinned at Jamie, almost giddy, like a small boy who had found out he was getting a summer afternoon off from school. Had he always been like this? Or had being around Bocharov made him this way?

After last night, Jamie knew the answer to that. Men like Bocharov corrupted everything they touched. They made complicity their weapon, reward and self-interest their currency. Once you were in their orbit, part of their never-ending whirl of deals, parties and subtle abuses, you were dirty by association, spattered with flecks of their naked greed and ambition.

'Yeah. Yeah, that's fine,' said Jamie. 'I'll probably just hole up in here.'

Komarov pointed at Jamie and winked. 'I'll get some food brought up for you. Can't wait to read that proposal. I'm sure it's going to blow us away.'

Jamie leaned back. 'It will certainly meet your warehousing and logistical software management needs with admirable precision,' he said, deadpan.

Komarov laughed on his way out of the door.

He spent the next two hours slotting data from the calls into his sales model. One of the house staff brought him lunch at one point. By the time he looked up from his spreadsheet, warehouse layouts and automation routes spinning in his head, the bread had dried out and the fruit juice was surrounded by a pool of its own condensation. He tucked in anyway, soothing his leftover hangover nausea with food and fluids.

Once the spreadsheet was finished, he went to the window and glanced at his watch. Just after 2 p.m.

The conference room he'd been in most of the morning was on the second floor. The building wrapped around the central pool area like two huge arms, or the spurs of a mountain range around a lake. Down below, the revellers from last night were reappearing, all still somehow beautiful and fresh as daisies.

Not for the first time since his arrival, Jamie wondered who exactly these people were. The ones directly involved in UPK's business or Vityaz were obvious. They were almost exclusively shaven-headed men in their thirties or older, mostly built like brick shithouses, deeply tanned and with faces like granite cliffs.

But there were younger men too, slim, often blond, with fashionable haircuts, eyes hidden by wide sunglasses. And so many women.

The three who had accompanied them from Stone Town were at the centre of a constellation of expatriates who seemed to be professional poolside selfie creators. Even as Jamie watched, five of them gathered around a sun lounger, phones held at arm's length. They chorused 'Skazhi izyum' together, which he'd learned last night meant 'Say "raisins"', the equivalent of 'Cheese'. But there were no awkward grimaces or half-shut eyes in these pictures. They were all pros. After a muttered consultation over the results on each of their phones, they extended their arms again for another try. Nothing but the best.

Jamie took the phone Nicola had given him out of his pocket, unlocked the secure OS and took a couple of shots, zoomed in on the people around the pool. There was probably nobody of interest in the gaggle of selfie-takers, but he guessed a few of the faces lurking stonily in the background might be of use to SIS. Confirmation of who was here at Rayskiye Vrata and why.

He scanned through the shots he'd taken, then zoomed in with a pinch. Bocharov was down there, deep in conversation with Yevgeny Olenev and another man, turned away from them. It was Brunner, now changed into a linen shirt and swimming trunks. Without Komarov in the room, he could get some better pictures.

Jamie walked to the other end of the long conference room, which gave him a side angle on Brunner's face. He zoomed in, took a shot, then zoomed out a little and got the context, the three men hunched over, heads together in conversation.

Was this enough?

Back in Stone Town, Nicola had said, more than once, that just being at Bocharov's villa would be enough. To be there, to see things, to leave when his deal was done. That he should take no risks and do nothing that might expose either himself or the Legends Programme.

'We're giving you this kit,' she'd said as they went through everything, 'so you can take advantage of opportunities that come up. Nothing is ever risk free, right? Especially not in covert operations. But if it feels wrong, if it *feels* risky, then it is. You're a civilian. You're untrained. Don't risk it, Jamie. Not for me, not for Terence, and definitely not for bloody Jeremy.'

He sat down at the conference table and paged through the images. Perhaps they could make something of this. Perhaps there was even something new in the UPK data he was gathering as part of the deal, a little detail that might tell them what Bocharov was doing with his African sinecure.

He got to the last image, taken from the most extreme left angle he could manage. In the background of the shot, he saw Bocharov's private office.

It was dark, blinds pulled down, door secured. On a bluebird-sky day like this, it seemed Bocharov preferred to do his business outside. But the office was well back from the pool area, screened by palms, acacias and low bushes.

A thought occurred to him, and he pushed it away. No risks, she'd said. Only take those opportunities where you can explain why you're there, where you can grab something in a heartbeat and return to your facade of studied innocence.

'No sweaty-palm moments, okay?' Nicola had said, leaning across the table in the tiny hotel room in Stone Town. 'If your adrenaline is spiking, it's because you're doing something fucking stupid. Listen to it and back away. Promise me that.'

Jamie sat there for a long time, looking at the photo. At the quiet darkness of that office, filled with secrets.

It was really not that far. A few dozen steps past the public areas of the villa. If he was challenged, he could claim to be looking for the gym. He could even dress the part.

He could do it. He could take a look. After all, there was no harm in just taking a wee look.

The covered walkway that led to Bocharov's office was lined with low bushes. Lilacs, baking in the sun. The gentle smell of them rose as he passed.

Once he'd checked for any obvious cameras, the lock on Bocharov's door was almost embarrassingly easy to defeat. Like most computer science students, Jamie had dabbled in lockpicking and other illicit arts at Cambridge. He'd defeated the simple Yale locks in his college hall of residence within a week or two. This wasn't much better. He slipped a supermarket reward card out of his wallet, bent one corner slightly, then slid it around the doorframe until he felt the edge of the lock's bolt. After a minute or so of careful shuffling, sliding the card up and down the frame, he heard a low click as the card slipped through and the bolt disengaged. He stopped for a second. There was nobody in sight. Just the low mutter of voices from the pool and the rumble of a jet passing overhead.

Jamie swallowed, his hand on the door handle. This was it. He could pull the door shut again and walk away. Or he could slip inside.

'Fuck it,' he murmured.

Inside, it was cool, a large square space with high ceilings, beautiful wooden floorboards and exposed hardwood rafters above, two large white-bladed fans stirring the air with desultory slowness. Largely for show, since the aircon units mounted on the rafters kept up a steady flow of chilled air into the room.

Two low black couches were placed across from each other, separated by a glass coffee table, littered with open magazines, a couple of laptops and the remains of a lunch tray. Staff might come in and clear the place at some point. Best to move fast.

The light in the room was dim, slatted blinds mostly closed and the sun high overhead. What light did come in was reflected from the buildings and the rippling water of the pool's deeper infinity edge. Nobody was in that part of the water, but he stepped to the window and closed the slats anyway.

Past the sofas, a huge ebony desk, intricately carved. Some kind of local wood, but the carvings were geometrical, almost cubist. Behind the desk, simple blond-wood shelves stretched the length of the room. They were lined with hundreds of books, mostly paperbacks, business books, thrillers. A few older, hardback books with Cyrillic text on the spines. Strange. Bocharov had not struck him as a reader. Perhaps he'd got into the habit to fill his time. Or perhaps a younger Bocharov had carried Dostoyevsky in his pack as a conscript, then escapist thrillers to while away the hours sitting in dugouts waiting for HIMARS strikes to end.

The top of the desk was a single glass-topped expanse, with a large PC monitor, keyboard, landline telephone, and a fax machine, of all things.

Plus three neat stacks of documents.

Jamie's heart rate picked up as he stepped behind the desk and took a long look at the stacks. The leftmost had three manila folders, each with a few sheets of A4 paper inside. Fluorescent yellow sticky notes hung from the paper's edge. This might be it. Something worth the risk he was suddenly very, very aware he was taking. The towel over his shoulder would be no protection if they caught him in here. But if he could get images of this, there might be something in here Nicola could use.

The middle stack was a thick sheaf of densely populated forms of some kind. Long lists, strings of letters and numbers, departure and arrival times. This looked like some sort of manifest or schedule, at a guess. But there was a *lot* of it.

The rightmost stack was the smallest. Just three pieces of paper, but they were the easiest to identify. The embossed logos of two leading Swiss banks and a third broker based in the British Virgin Islands stuck out, as did the quantities of money and account details printed in large, readable font. He'd seen documents like this before when he'd been involved in serious deals and cash transfers. Statements of funds, assurance for both parties in a high-risk deal that the money actually existed. Backed up by live previews in dedicated secure phone apps these days, of course. But an old-school guy like Bocharov would want to show he had the dollars, rubles, yuan or euros to back up his offer.

Outside, someone shouted, a yelp that could have been anger or surprise or delight. Jamie's head jerked up and he froze, right behind the desk, caught in the sudden glare of paranoia.

A loud splash reached him, someone diving or being thrown into the pool. He sagged back against the bookshelves.

The longer he was in here, the more risk he was taking. He slipped the phone out of his pocket, then took a couple of photographs of the document stacks, making sure to capture exactly where they were placed on the desk, how the files were laid on top of one another. That done, he worked through each stack methodically, opening the folders and turning over the pages one by one, photographing each side before moving on to the next.

There was enough light in the office and the camera was good enough that he didn't need to use the flash, which was a relief. Firing off two or three dozen flashes inside someone's empty, supposedly secure office was bound to attract someone's attention, even in the middle of a baking-hot day.

The first stack finished, he moved on to the second, then the third, carefully framing each piece of paper as closely as he could, checking each shot was crisp and clear. As he took the images, he turned over what they might mean in his mind. A stack of contracts that looked like a major deal for UPK. Then a huge list of shipping manifests, cargos being delivered and picked up all over the North African coastline, plus three East African ports too. Then the fund statements. There were a lot of extremely large numbers.

Perhaps this was just seedy, neo-colonial business as usual. The raw materials nobody ever thought about. Cobalt for the batteries inside every phone, laptop, tablet, earbud and rechargeable hand fan. Gold for the circuit boards and semiconductors. Oil and gas to make it all go. Metals and tobacco and coffee beans and a hundred other things, loading and unloading.

Bocharov could be just another middleman, placing himself in the flow of goods and extracting his tithe. But there was something in the way Komarov had stared out over the compound that morning, the way Vitaly watched the skies and clutched the stock of his submachine gun as he patrolled the grounds, the way Bocharov himself seemed both energised and as though his patience was wearing thin. *Something* was happening this week.

Jamie brought up the first picture and carefully rearranged the files on the desk. He held the phone up at the same height and flicked his eyes back and forth. That corner was a finger-width from the base of the telephone. Those two files were angled just shy of vertical from each other. The topmost account statement was slightly to the left of the bottom two. He took another shot, then flicked between the first and the last. Certainly good enough to pass the kind of quick glance that Bocharov would give it when he came in. As long as he avoided that subtle sense of movement, that things were not quite as they had been, it would be fine.

He stood there for a moment, staring down at the phone, then tapped the share icon and started uploading the images, one after another, in the order he'd taken them. Best to get this stuff into Nicola's hands as soon as possible. The images went one after the other, soft swooshes indicating each successful delivery. Somewhere else on Zanzibar, Nicola and her team would now have something new to work with.

Another shout rose from the pool, but this time it was several voices, somebody being egged on. A heartbeat of silence, then another loud splash. More cheering. Clearly the afternoon crowd were getting back into the mojitos and pina coladas.

Now that he'd done the deed and he wasn't focusing on lining the papers up precisely, the fear flooded back in. He pushed it down. Focus on the tools he had. The opportunities. He'd broken his promise to Nicola, because his palms were very definitely sweaty. But he was going to see this through.

Jamie slipped the phone back into his pocket and took out the tiny Bluetooth bug. It was smart enough to only talk to his phone when he queried it, hiding its presence from other devices. He peeled a white circle from the base of the device, then ducked under the desk and pressed it hard against the black wood, right under the centre. It would be out of sight of any casual glance under the desk, only half a centimetre thick. He gave the tiny microphone a tug, confirming the adhesive was secure. It would probably ruin the wood when some-one tried to chisel it off, but hopefully he would be long gone by then. And there was no risk of it dropping on to Bocharov's shoes mid-conversation.

As he clambered up from the honey-coloured floorboards, the PC on the desk caught his eye. On impulse, he reached out and tapped the space bar.

The monitor lit up, a tantalising glimpse of a Windows default desktop, then it was replaced by a lock screen and password field. User: ABocharov.

His hands were reaching for the keyboard when he stopped him-self. Access attempts would be logged. And keyboards could be set up with keyloggers. He'd already run enough of a risk with the docu-ments and the bug. Time to go.

He was nearly at the door before he remembered the blind. He went back and gently reopened it, glancing quickly out at the still-empty infinity-pool edge, then turned back to the room.

Exactly as he'd found it – quiet, empty, cool with air-conditioned air. Fans gently turning overhead, the light low. Ripples of light from the pool once again cast on the deep brown-orange of the rafters overhead.

He nodded to himself, then slung his towel back over his shoulder. He'd done something real. Seen an opportunity and gone for it. And he was going to get away clean.

Jamie cracked the door of the office and glanced out. Nobody on the walkway, or anywhere near the line of trees and bushes that separ-ated it from the pool. He was clear.

He stepped out in one fluid movement, then turned and pulled the door shut with a soft click, the lock re-engaging behind him, as though he'd never been there.

He was only three paces from the door when Cody Klein's deeply tanned and tattooed hand landed heavily on his shoulder.

'Tulloch,' the big mercenary said, turning him around with a flick of his thick wrist. 'The fuck are you doing back here?'

38

Nicola

Ocean Jewel Resort: now

Nicola's phone buzzed for a solid three minutes as the treasure trove of images from Jamie arrived, one after the other. After the first minute, Sylvan's eyes widened.

'What did he do, crack a safe or something?'

They were on the private terrace of their top-floor suite, Tumo and Farida elsewhere, exploring the resort and chatting to the local staff. Nicola was writing up a report for Althrop with no idea whether he'd have time to read it, while Sylvan worked on his extraction plan for getting out of Zanzibar in a hurry, if they had to cut and run.

She transferred the image files to her laptop and paged through them, noting the positioning shots Jamie had taken at the beginning and end of the reel. 'Clever lad,' she said under her breath. 'I didn't show him how to do that.'

Sylvan looked over her shoulder and nodded. 'If he figured that out himself, he's a smart one. What have we got?'

'All the ingredients for a major deal, looks like. Can you set up an encrypted connection back to London? I need some analyst support on this.'

Sylvan nodded and fetched his laptop and satphone. He sent a tunnel request back to SIS, then switched over to the hotel Wi-Fi for the speed it offered. His laptop did a handshake with a server somewhere in Vaux-hall Cross, then punched a military-grade VPN connection through the open Wi-Fi. Anyone eavesdropping on them through the network would see nothing they wouldn't expect from any business traveller or privacy-conscious tourist, but if they tried to get around the VPN they would find their usual tools failing them. A smart black-hat hacker working for a foreign government might wonder why two tourists in a Zanzibar coastal resort were using the privacy equivalent of a main battle tank, but TISS already knew they were here.

The files transferred to Vauxhall Cross, and Nicola and Sylvan waited as the mid-afternoon sun began to drop. An onshore breeze started up, beautifully cool after the earlier scorching sun. Nicola leaned forward, peering at the images, trying to do her own guesswork. The analysts at the Cross had tools she didn't have access to in the field: GCHQ and NSA link-ups, deep-web databases and Grade Emerald query priv-ileges. Compared to them, she was like a schoolkid trying to compile a report with Wikipedia, YouTube explainers and social media threads. They had access to the kind of deep data and context that never got near the public web.

What she could determine was that Bocharov was involved in a substantial shipping deal. The return trip would carry cobalt and bauxite ore back to Europe. The money exchanging hands, on top of the value of the cargo itself, was in the high millions of euros.

Buried deep in the detail, there was something strange. Something which stuck in her perception like a splinter in the thumb. Why were small-boat charters attached to this exchange, once the bulk of the shipments arrived in Mombasa? What could they be moving that would require so little space but needed to be moved on elsewhere without a shipping manifest? Theories unwound through her brain as she read the documents, searched shipping databases for the names and designations of the cargo ships on the manifest. Diamonds? Guns? Drugs? What were they moving?

After the second hour, Nicola moved inside, fighting glare on her laptop screen and the low sun on her skin. She made a cup of coffee from the station by the window and sat with it, staring out over the blue-green of the Indian Ocean. How many times had she been in places like this, watching and waiting? How many years of her life on the edge of this ocean, tasting its salt spray, her mind always somewhere else, gauging the threats and opportunities?

She thought of London. A café in Hampstead with breath-fogged windows and an overpriced Eggs Benedict which had gone cold and congealed as the conversation had turned from frosty exchange of views to tearful admission of defeat. She remembered Rachael's hands, tight on the edge of the table, as though she was afraid it would drift away from her if she let go.

Maybe after this op, staying in yet another anonymous business hotel for her debrief, she could fill out the form for an analyst role. Take all these years of waiting and watching and refine them, compress them down into something diamond hard she could finally use to make a mark, something that changed how things were done.

Or maybe she'd just leave the application tab open in her browser for three weeks, then close it as she booked her flight back out to the next op. Again.

Shit.

Nicola's secure messaging pinged and she pulled up the message, decrypted it and read.

'Fuck,' she muttered under her breath, then picked up the laptop and went through to the adjoining balcony. Sylvan was working in the shade of a giant canvas sunshade, a half-drunk bottle of water on the table in front of him. He was squinting at the screen, hunt-and-peck typing his way through some kind of requisition form. A field man's field man. He was probably only five or six years older than her, but he was a lifer, condemned to pound the pavements and whisper into earpieces until advancing age made him an operational liability and he was shunted sideways into a training role or support, prepping safehouses and doing bug sweeps in the embassy.

Was she on the same trajectory? Did she care?

He looked up and smiled. 'Did I hear a ping?'

She sat down heavily and spun the laptop around. 'You did. I spotted references to a small-boat shipment in the paperwork, but they've found a lot more.'

Sylvan leaned forward and peered at the screen. 'What am I looking at?'

'Four ships leaving North African and southern European ports in the last week, a couple of them taking on additional cargo. Then a stop in Tunisia that was added last minute. They transited Suez three days ago, made Mombasa yesterday morning.'

'Anything weird on the manifests?'

She scrolled through the detailed listings and bills of lading the analytical teams had dug out of the databases of shipping brokers and Kenya's customs service. 'Nothing unexpected – machine tools, roadbuilding equipment, cotton bales, machined aluminium, plastic feedstock. But the thing they flagged was the container holds on all four ships.'

'What's that?' said Sylvan. 'Been a while since I did any customs inspection stuff.'

'Every ship had a reserved last-minute hold for half an ISO shipping container. Something pretty big. Size of a small car, maybe? Then off Tunisia all four ships got visited by the same launch from the shore. Recorded in the logs.' She pointed at the flagged entries in the digital logs each ship had submitted when they arrived in Mombasa. 'All four reported taking on "spares and engine parts", all from the same company.'

'That's a bit weird.'

'Yeah, it is. Why take two full ISO containers of cargo and split it over four ships? Unless you're playing a shell game.'

'Pretty big cups for a shell game,' said Sylvan, leaning back.

She pointed at him. 'Exactly. Probably three of the four were empty. If anyone's following your progress, they don't know which ship has the real cargo. They have to watch all four, or pick one and risk missing it when you make your move.'

'And what move do you think they made?'

'Here, look, bottom of the report.' She pulled it up. The document wasn't part of the original dump of photographs that Jamie had sent them. This was a digitised report that Analysis had managed to pull from the Kenyan coastguard. Sylvan read the English summary and swore softly under his breath.

'So the Kenyans chased off a large motor launch from Ship Number 3 while they were in the queue to enter Mombasa harbour. Crew on the target ship claimed it was a hijacking attempt.'

Nicola nodded. 'I'm willing to bet the sailors from the MV *Kirin Shasa* will all be enjoying a little additional shore pay tonight in Mombasa. Someone paid them off to cover up for a smuggling run. We've seen the same trick off the Somali coast to smuggle embargoed arms into Puntland and Djibouti. "Oh no, Officer, the nasty pirate came and took away all those crates. Pay no attention to the suitcase of cash in the ship's safe." It'd be funny if it didn't work so often.'

Sylvan stood up and went to the balcony edge. He looked out over the tiered gardens, the blue curve of the pool below. In the distance, along the coast, Bocharov's compound was out of sight, but they both felt it.

He turned and leaned back against the glass. 'You think it's coming here? High risk, bringing smuggled cargo to his own place.'

Nicola tapped her pen against her lips, gazing into the middle distance as she thought it through. 'It's got to be something worth the risk. Something so valuable he's willing to bring it to Zanzibar. Or something he doesn't want to buy without seeing it first, in person.'

Sylvan nodded. 'You think he's the buyer?'

'Has to be. Whatever's on that boat, it's being brought *to* him.'

'Do we have a track on the boat? Satellite coverage?'

'You know how many small boats move up and down this coastline every day? Half of them don't even have radios, never mind shipping beacons. And you need an imaging platform with sub-metre resolution to spot them, especially if they've got their sails down or they're going slowly enough to not leave much of a wake. If they're *trying* to avoid being spotted, they might be moving at dawn and dusk, or overnight. We might only see them when they're a few hundred metres offshore. When I was doing arms-smuggling ops off Somalia, the Americans gave us twenty-four-hour MQ9 coverage of the whole shipping lane and we still probably missed three-quarters of them.'

'The ocean is big and Reaper drones are small,' said Sylvan, peering out to sea again. She saw him raise a hand and count the small vessels visible just from where they sat. Once he got to fifteen, he stopped. 'See what you mean.'

She picked up the burner phone with Jamie's number on it. 'We've got to rely on the eyes we have here. If this cargo arrives at the compound, maybe Jamie will see something. I doubt he'll get anywhere near it. But he can tell us if something large and weird gets dragged up from the beach in the middle of the night.'

'Anything since he sent those pictures? That was a risk. He must have got out clean if he sent us those shots, right?'

'Nothing,' said Nicola as she typed a message to Jamie, pushing down the bubble of disquiet that rose at the back of her mind. 'But he's smart. He'll play it safe.'

She sent the message, then added, quietly enough that Sylvan didn't hear her, 'At least, I hope he will.'

39

Jeremy

Shadwell DLR Station, London: earlier

'Eyes on,' said a voice in Jeremy's ear.

He was three carriages from the front of a westbound DLR train, doors chiming as they began to close.

'Still aboard,' said the voice, a Security Service operative one carriage up. 'Rear of carriage two.'

Boxwood had got two streets away from the warehouse before his SUV had ground to a halt, tyres shredded by gunfire, windscreen crazed with cracks and bullet holes. He'd simply ditched the vehicle on the gravel underneath the Newham overpass. A couple of early dog-walkers were staring from across the road by the time Jeremy and the team caught up.

One team had swept the street. Jeremy headed into the DLR station with the rest. They'd spotted Boxwood, sweating, at the end of the platform.

In that split second, as the operatives sidled towards the target, he'd had a decision to make. Grab Boxwood now, or run the risk of following him to see where he was headed.

Jeremy had squeezed his fists inside his jacket pockets, the electric uncertainty gripping him from the tip of his spine to the soles of his feet. Then he'd swallowed and told the team to hold.

They'd climbed aboard the next train, blending as well as they could with a few early-morning commuters heading into the financial district from the sandstone slabs of the new housing developments.

As Blackwall, Poplar, Westferry and Limehouse slid past and the train got busier, they'd closed the gap, moving slowly up the carriages. Jeremy finally worked his way up to the team leader. She was a middle-aged white woman in a dusty-looking purple coat with slightly greying hair. Only the earpiece, a modified Bluetooth earbud, was a little unusual.

'Hello,' she said, as he got within a metre or two, playacting familiarity. 'Nice to see you.'

'You too,' he said, then leaned in a little closer. 'Where?'

'Left side, before the next set of doors.'

Jeremy glanced and caught sight of Boxwood, hunched over on a side-facing seat, his arms wrapped around his torso. He wore a half-zipped grey hoodie, jeans and a white T-shirt. Even from here, he could see the light sheen of sweat on the man's forehead. Had the assault team clipped him with a round during his furious exit from the warehouse? Or was it simply the adrenaline crash after what he thought was a successful escape?

Jeremy turned away. If Boxwood had been involved in the original theft from Vauxhall Cross, chances were he'd been briefed on the Legends Programme and seen an image of Jeremy's face. He sat down in an empty seat and dialled Sally Lime.

'What's going on there?'

'Two dead, four in custody, one of them wounded. No casualties on our side. Lot of hardware in that warehouse, boss, a lot. The Met are really not happy.'

'Hard drives?'

'Still looking. Nothing so far. Laptops and phones, but no SSDs yet.'

Jeremy flexed his fingers inside his jacket again. They could grab Boxwood now, probably retrieve the hard drives he was almost certainly carrying. But then they'd lose their opportunity to roll up the whole network, to find Boxwood's contact and dig out the mole nestled somewhere in Vauxhall Cross.

The train began to dip down, heading into the dark maw of the tunnel down to Bank station and the wider Underground network. Short sightlines, tight corridors. Cameras everywhere, but if they had to involve Transport for London or wait for a tech team to access the feeds directly, they'd lose him.

Jeremy rubbed his thumb and forefinger together, still thinking.

'Still there, boss?' said Sally Lime, her voice already beginning to crackle.

'Going underground. Keep looking.'

'Got it. Be carefu—'

Then she was gone.

The watcher in the purple coat leaned down. 'What do you want to do, sir?' she said under her breath. 'Bank's a fucking nightmare for close observation.'

Jeremy nearly laughed at the incongruity of the woman's cover as a middle-aged office worker and the language of a covert operations specialist, but this woman likely knew several ways of incapacitating him, so he nodded. 'I want you on him. Russians always take longer to spot women. You have a swap-out? Front-runner?'

She nodded. 'Fellow in the blue jacket, five seats down. Workname Frank. Front-runner's already worked up to the top of the carriage. The Asian guy in the suit. That's Yusuf.'

Jeremy nodded. 'I'll be two corners back. We *cannot* lose this man. If you think we're going to, I want you to arrest him. I trust your judgement.'

'Got it, sir. My workname's Moira. Sorry, didn't get a chance to introduce myself when we sprinted out of that warehouse.'

'Stuart,' he said, falling back on an old workname he hadn't used since he first recruited Jamie Tulloch. 'Let's keep it tight and keep talking.'

The DLR train pulled into Bank with a squeal of brakes and announcements about delays on the Circle line. Boxwood was off like a shot, along the platform and turning sharply into a side tunnel. A few seconds later, Jeremy heard a low male voice, presumably Yusuf, crackly with interference. Their earbuds were piggybacking on emergency services transponders positioned throughout the station and tunnel network, but there were still gaps in the coverage, spots in the long, tile-lined tunnels where your voice would dip out or others would recede into digital crackle and hiss.

'Turning left. Heading to the escalators. Could be Central, Waterloo or street exits.'

'Roger, eyes on,' said Moira. Jeremy turned into the tunnel and joined the escalator just as Moira hit the top of it. He saw her purple coat disappear into the connecting tunnel at the top. Frank was half-way up, ready to swap with Moira if she thought she'd been made by Boxwood. So far, though, she seemed to be blending well with the busy crowd.

With a start, Jeremy realised he had absolutely no idea what day of the week it was. Judging by the suits and skirts around him at this time of the morning, it was a weekday. He glanced at his watch. Monday, apparently. The sleep he'd got the night before, waiting while the SAS prepped their raid of the warehouse, felt like it had barely touched the sides. He'd been operating on coffee, cafeteria sandwiches and Red Bull. Right now, the adrenaline of knowing Boxwood was just ahead of him was keeping his eyes cranked wide open, but he could feel the crash following close behind, like an inept tail who was close enough to spook the target.

He reached the top of the escalator and quickly crossed to the next set, following Frank. Once again, as he reached the bottom, he spotted Moira disappearing from the top.

'Lost comms with Yusuf,' said Frank. Moira came back a second later.

'I've got comms. He's betting on Waterloo and City line. I'm watching.'

There were three long heartbeats of silence. Jeremy waited, heart tight in his chest.

'No, Central line. Yusuf's doubling back. I'm taking front. Frank, you're up.'

Jeremy glanced up as they reached the top of the escalator and saw Frank, a tall white man with shaved hair, in a blue jacket, speeding up to take over Moira's position.

'Westbound Central line. He's halfway along the platform. I'm passing.'

Moira went silent for another long moment, then the signal cleared up as Jeremy and Frank reached the platform. The Central line was among the deepest and oldest of London's Underground, small tunnels that were always humid and warm, even in the depths of winter. Two dozen commuters were spread out along the platform, staring at phones or paging through books or copies of *Metro*.

Jeremy saw Boxwood immediately, perched on a metal bench halfway along the platform. The curve of the tunnel meant he could easily see Moira, settling into another bench at the far end. Frank remained standing and pulled out his phone, just another commuter on his way into central London.

Jeremy kept walking and ducked into one of the connecting tunnels that led to the eastbound platform. Yusuf came down the stairs from the Waterloo and City line and walked straight past him, not even risking a nod.

'Moira, coming to you,' said Jeremy as he walked quickly down the eastbound platform, then used another connecting tunnel to get back to the westbound. He sidled forward, then leaned against the wall to Moira's right. One minute until the next train.

Boxwood was still hunched over, a phone in his hands. He was staring at it with mute intensity.

Jeremy decided to continue the ruse from earlier, talking to Moira as though she was a colleague he'd happened to bump into on the way into work. He kept his voice low.

'I don't think he's trained for this,' he said.

'Nope,' said Moira, clasping her handbag. 'He thinks he got away clean. And there's no countersurveillance we can see, no minders following him. He hasn't doubled back or done any other kind of back-checks. Just stared at that phone.'

'Surely he should be going to ground, after nearly getting caught?'

'You'd think,' said Moira. 'He's either stupid or panicking. Or stupid *and* panicking.' She kept her eyes fixed straight ahead, never glancing at the man halfway along the platform. 'Or he's extremely *well* trained and he's going to lose us as soon as we go back topside. In which case us talking like this is a bad idea.'

Jeremy gave a stagey laugh, squeezed Moira's shoulder, then nodded and said, 'See you at the office then.' He walked further along the platform, nearly to the end. Again, the curve of the platform meant he could see Boxwood without having to turn his head. At least until the train rumbled into the station and blocked his view.

Jeremy stepped aboard as the driver apologised in advance for a delay in the Notting Hill Gate area affecting westbound trains, then the doors began to slide closed. He saw a flicker of a sharp suit, Yusuf stepping aboard at the last moment.

'He's still on,' said Yusuf's voice. 'Carriage three.'

The train picked up speed and slid out of the station, warm air rushing through the open windows between each carriage. Jeremy positioned himself to look back through the train, but Boxwood was well out of sight. He caught a flash of purple, Moira in the front-runner position, depending on where Boxwood got off.

They went through St Paul's and Chancery Lane, Yusuf and Frank watching from the open doorways each time, waiting for their target to step out. Finally, at Holborn, Boxwood stood up and waited, then stepped out on to the platform.

The watchers appeared, one after the other. Boxwood turned left, so Frank became the front-runner, walking quickly up the steps to the middle concourse. Moira was close behind, with Yusuf and Jeremy covering the other stairwell. On the middle concourse, Frank guessed right and headed down towards the Piccadilly line, with Boxwood unconsciously following.

'Likely destinations?' murmured Jeremy as they got aboard a south-bound train.

'Covent Garden or Leicester Square, to lose us in the crowds? If he knows we're following,' said Moira over the radio. 'But it's early. He'll be exposed.'

'Green Park, maybe?' said Yusuf. 'Could be a brush pass. Or a meeting.'

Jeremy nodded to himself. 'Okay, if it's Green Park, we'll need support to seal the park entrances. We can't risk him getting away again if he's meeting a contact.'

Moira responded after a moment. 'We can have a support unit from Thames there inside of five minutes, once we're above ground. Practically our backyard.'

40

Jamie

Rayskiye Vrata: now

Jamie turned slowly, the texture of his towel rough under his fingertips as he lifted it off his shoulder. He held it out to the American, a shield against suspicion.

Klein's face was blank, his eyes searching Jamie's face.

'You better have a good reason to be over here. This is a secure area.'

Jamie motioned with the towel again. 'I was just looking for the gym. Thought I'd try and keep the routine up, you know?'

Klein took a half-step back and looked him up and down. 'You got a routine?' he said.

Would Klein mistake the fear flickering over his face for offence? 'Well, I *try* to have one. Bit difficult when I can't find the gym though.'

Klein's face broke into a smile and he punched Jamie lightly on the shoulder. It was like someone had swung a sack of hammers at him.

'Nah, I'm just fuckin' with you, man. Still, whatever routine you're doing, you've gotta switch that up. Routine's nothing without clear goals. Otherwise you're just a hamster on a wheel, right?'

They began to walk back along the covered passage to the house. A trickle of cold sweat ran all the way to the base of Jamie's spine but he managed a tight smile for the mercenary.

'I'll keep that in mind.'

Klein glanced over and his face became serious again. 'You shouldn't have been over here, man. That was Bocharov's office you were stood outside. Usually a guard on it, but they're changing over right now. If Vitaly or one of his boys spotted you, you'd have been on the ground in a headlock.'

Jamie swallowed. 'Well, I'm glad it was you, then. I thought that building might be the gym. One of the staff said it was over here?'

'They told you wrong. Back of the building, one level up.'

As they reached the double doors that led back inside, one of Vitaly's men appeared, half a sandwich in one hand, his submachine gun slung at his side. He stopped mid-bite when he saw Klein, eyes widening.

'Shtoh—' he began, but Klein cut him off.

'Hey, dipshit, you're supposed to *wait* until your relief gets here before you go for lunch. How long since you wandered off, huh?'

The man switched to English, the sandwich forgotten in his hand, his face pale even under his tan. 'I'm sorry, Mr Klein. Five minutes only. My relief, he's late. I have been on since 7 a.m. I am sorry.'

Klein shook his head. 'Yeah, well, I'll have a word with your relief too. And Vitaly. I know you guys are excited about tonight, but this is some sloppy bullshit.'

The man's shoulders dropped a little as he realised Klein wasn't going to take things further, then his eyes slid over to Jamie. 'What is—' he began, but Klein sidestepped him and opened the double doors.

'He was looking for the gym. And if you'd been on your post, you'd have been able to send him back the right way. I'll find your relief for you. Don't leave your post again, got it?'

The man nodded and took another bite of the sandwich. 'Got it.'

Jamie took the hint and went through the double doors. When he glanced back, the guard was standing in the walkway, chewing the last bite of his sandwich, staring at their retreating backs.

'Good thing I was there,' said Klein. 'Misha's a fucking idiot. He'd probably have put a hole in your head through sheer panic.'

Jamie nodded, relief giving way to paranoia. Would Misha The Guard tell Vitaly about this? Would Klein?

Something Klein had said to Misha bubbled to the top of Jamie's mind. He glanced over. 'What's happening tonight? That the guards are excited about?'

Klein laughed. 'Their night off. Half of 'em, at least. They go to a beach bar along the coast, usually. Try to pick up tourist girls. They get one night off every two weeks. Usually later in the week, but Bocharov wants a full complement tomorrow.'

Jamie nodded, filing that away for later. What was happening tomorrow? 'Must get boring, being in a compound like this all the time.'

Klein grimaced. 'You have no fucking idea. At least here you can get out once in a while. No rebels in the forest with butterfly mines and rusty-ass AKs. In the DRC we were in a mining camp for six straight months without a break. Pay-off was good, but after four months I'd have killed to get out of that shithole.'

They reached a glass staircase, and Klein stopped. He pointed at a small sign, the size of a child's palm, pointing up with the words 'GYM', repeated in Cyrillic below. 'Bocharov keeps the signage subtle. Don't go wandering, you hear me? You got lucky today. Real fuckin' lucky.'

Jamie nodded again, feeling the truth of that statement in every bone of his body. 'Don't worry. I'll keep out of trouble.'

'See that you do, Scottie. See that you fuckin' do,' Klein said over his shoulder as he walked away.

41

Nicola

Ocean Jewel Resort: now

Nicola's phone buzzed an hour after she'd sent her last message to Jamie. She released a breath she hadn't realised she'd been holding as she read it.

She passed the phone over to Sylvan so he could read the string of messages from Jamie's secure phone. Sylvan's eyes widened.

'Lucky bastard. That was a close call.'

'You're telling me,' she said. 'Keep reading.'

Sylvan raised his eyebrows as he scrolled further. 'He got a bug in Bocharov's office? Wow. That could be huge. You speak Russian?'

'Yeah, pretty decently.'

'And a double-guard shift tomorrow night. That must be the shipment, whatever it is, arriving.'

Nicola got up and went to the edge of the balcony, looking down over the tiered gardens and the pool. Farida and Tumo were there, having a drink at the open-air bar, talking to the barman, working the angles. She wanted to be doing that. Getting her feet wet. She'd never been in such a constricted operating environment before, stuck in this whitewashed upscale prison, cut off from the people who lived nearby. Even the beach had a line of signs across it, warning locals not to cross over and annoy the mostly white, wealthy tourists sunning themselves beyond.

She turned around and faced Sylvan. 'Did you see the last couple of messages? About the guards going to that beach bar?'

'I did. We'd be stepping pretty hard on Komba's toes if we did that. Tangling with the Russians on their night off.'

'True. But mercs like to drink. When they drink, they talk. And the ones in Africa like to talk to girls at bars.'

Sylvan looked like he'd smelled something rotten. 'I bet they fucking do.'

She crossed the balcony and sat back down. 'Graeme, I'm a trained field handler with six years of undercover ops experience on top of my time in the Army. I've been around some extremely unpleasant men. And women, for that matter.'

Sylvan held his hands up. 'Sorry. Where I grew up there were quite a few men like that. It winds me up.'

She nodded. 'I get it. But we can't miss this opportunity. It won't come up again before that boat arrives. And we need *something* to work with.'

Graeme sat back. 'It's your op, boss. But I'd like to go with you. All four of us. You and Farida can work the bar, me and Tumo can keep an eye out, maybe see if we can do something with the Russian's vehicles. Pop a listener in their gear, if they leave it unguarded. They don't exactly have designated drivers.'

She nodded. 'You've seen them on these nights off before?'

Sylvan shrugged. 'Not directly. But the local eyes I've had on this place call their visits "kitoweo cha Kirusi", because of how they pour themselves back into their vehicles afterwards.'

Nicola laughed. 'Russian stew? Trust a Zanzibari to come up with a food metaphor.'

'They also told me about the backpackers the Russians pick up. They come down from Nungwi for the beach parties at that bar. More than one of them has shown up back at their hotel the next day with a fistful of cash and a bunch of bruises. These are not good people, Nicola.'

She gazed out over the ocean. 'I know. My entire working life is full of bad people. And not always among the opposition.'

Sylvan sat back. 'Jesus, Nic, you can just come out and say you don't like me.'

She looked over and saw the smile on the older man's lips, returned it. 'We'll go to the bar tonight. Let's get Farida and Tumo back up here and run some scenarios.'

'Got it,' said Sylvan, already up and dialling his phone. Nicola watched Farida take the call, then look up to the balcony and give Sylvan the nod.

At the other end of the bar, Adil Komba sat, perched on a barstool, leaning on the dark wood. A tall glass of something orange sat in front of him. He was a slim, exceptionally neat man. He picked up the glass and half turned on the stool, watching as Farida and Tumo left the bar and headed back up towards the hotel room.

Komba's eyes flicked up to where Nicola sat on the balcony. He raised the glass to her, then took a long drink, his eyes never leaving hers.

42

Jeremy

Green Park Underground, London: earlier

Yusuf's guess about Boxwood's destination was proved right four stops later. Their target stepped off the train and walked quickly towards the street-level exit, jogging up the metal-edged steps. Jeremy kept his eyes fixed on the grey hoodie but kept well back.

His earpiece crackled as he reached ground level, connectivity flooding back in. His phone rang. Sally Lime.

'Confirmed no drives in the warehouse. If he didn't ditch them before we found him in Canning Town, he's carrying them.'

'Got it. Get yourself to Thames House. Might need you there shortly. I think Boxwood's about to meet someone.'

'Our bug-planting heating engineer? Or their handler?'

'Hopefully I'll find out in a couple of minutes.'

'Got it, see you there,' said Lime, and dropped the call.

It was bright above ground, early-morning grey and pink giving way to blue and rising temperatures. The park was busy, but nearly everyone was moving: office workers speed-walking to Whitehall and Mayfair offices with jackets slung over their arms, many of the women in the distinctly London combination of pencil skirts, blouses and day glo Nikes for the commute. Here and there a jogger or two weaved through them.

There were only three benches along the slanting pathway towards the Canada Gate, all grouped around an ancient gas lamp. The first held an elderly couple surrounded by a halo of breadcrumbs, dozens of pigeons fluttering and fighting over the bounty. The third was occupied by a lone male tourist, gazing at a map on their tablet.

In the middle was Sarah Grey, erstwhile Vauxhall Cross maintenance worker and planter of data taps, leaning back on her bench, apparently reading a novel without a care in the world.

Jeremy clocked the young woman when he got within a hundred metres. She had changed her brown bob for a savage bottle-blonde pixie cut, but the profile and nose were unmistakeable from her file pictures.

'IC1 female on the centre bench, that's his contact. Designate . . . uh, Gandalf,' he said. 'She'll make me if I pass, doubling back.'

Jeremy heard a low snigger on the comms from Frank.

'Canada Gate secure, teams moving to the other exits now,' said Moira.

'That was quick,' said Jeremy, stepping off the path and circling around behind where Grey sat on the bench. Boxwood had nearly reached her.

'Managed to get on the Wi-Fi at Leicester Square and warn Thames,' said Moira. 'We've got two more field teams and a tac-ops unit parked up on Constitution Hill.'

'Keep them back for now. No sense spooking them. Can we get ears on that bench?'

'Dropping one now,' said Frank's voice. Jeremy watched as the big man strode past the gas lamp and the three benches, then dropped to one knee to tie his shoelace. When he walked away again, there was a directional microphone tucked inside a drinks can, nestled gently on the edge of the grass and pointed directly at the bench.

'You want the patch, sir?' said Frank.

'Yes,' said Jeremy. 'Put it on channel two.'

He flicked over to the secondary audio just as Boxwood got to the bench. The wiry hacker sat down with enough force that Jeremy heard the bench creak. Sarah Grey looked up.

'You're late,' she said in Russian. 'Where have you been?'

'Running for my fucking life,' said Boxwood.

Even from his position, nearly thirty metres away in the shade of one of the park's broadleaf trees, Jeremy saw the woman's back stiffen.

'What?'

'Location Shura is gone. All of it. Soldiers came. I got away with my life and the drives and nothing else. They shot the fuck out of my car.'

Grey leaned forward. When she spoke, her voice was a low hiss that the mic struggled to pick up. 'And why the *fuck* did you think it was a good idea to come here?'

'Because I want out of this fucking country. Bad enough I'm left to nearly die in Peckham,' he said, almost spitting the word. 'But for the second time in three days I have men coming at me with guns. I am a specialist. I write code. I do this job for the money. Your bomb nearly killed me yesterday. And now your little warehouse full of weapons brings the British. Probably SAS or something. They nearly killed me, Sarah.'

'Blyat, you probably came in hot, you stupid asshole. You've doomed us both. Give me the fucking drives. Maybe I can get clear before they get here.'

It was Boxwood's turn to stiffen his back. 'I'll give you nothing until I have a new passport and a ticket out of here. I've had enough. I want my money and I want out. Right now.'

Jeremy caught flickers of movement to his left and right. He switched back to the team channel. Moira was giving dispersal orders to a half-dozen operatives now closing the noose.

'Hold,' said Jeremy. 'Do we have armed operatives?'

'Confirmed,' said Moira. 'All of us have extendable batons. The three to your left and two to your right have handguns. Tac-ops team is sixty seconds away, on your go.'

Jeremy looked around. Too many people. If someone pulled a gun or either of their targets panicked, the best case was gunshots in Green Park at rush hour. The worst case didn't bear thinking about. He had to do this carefully.

'Everyone hold. I'm going to challenge them. You see a gun, you have my authorisation to shoot.'

'Sir . . .'

'No, if we mob them, she might pull a weapon. There's civilians in the firing line. Keep back. Listen in. Move in on my go.'

'Roger, standing by.'

Jeremy stepped back on to the path, covering the distance to the lamp and the three benches quickly. His heart hammered, but he felt steady, the old field instincts channelling the adrenaline. He could do this.

As he approached, the pigeons fluttered, pecking and scrabbling at the breadcrumbs. The woman of the older couple gave him a smile.

Sarah caught the movement too late. She looked up as Jeremy's shadow fell on her and blinked into the morning sun.

'Hello, Sarah,' he said. 'I'm Jeremy. I'm afraid you're both under arrest.'

Grey's hand began to move towards the bag on the bench, but Jeremy shook his head. 'Look around you. If you pull a weapon right now, all you'll do is scare these nice people and possibly get yourself killed. There's no way out.'

The hand hovered halfway to her bag while Sarah Grey turned her head slowly from left to right. Her eyes flicked between the figures around them, the ring of operatives suddenly moving with a purpose, drawing into a tight circle around the benches.

Boxwood slumped back against the bench, his eyes blank. 'I fucking knew this would happen,' he murmured in Russian.

The tension left Grey's shoulders and she closed her eyes, the hand dropping into her lap. 'I'm a British citizen,' she said softly. 'And I want a solicitor.'

Jeremy smiled and waved a hand towards the Canada Gate and, beyond it, the basement levels of Thames House. 'We'll see what we can do.'

43

Jamie

Rayskiye Vrata: now

It didn't take long for the bug Jamie had planted in Bocharov's office to start picking things up.

Jamie sat on his bed, the covert phone on his lap, a pair of headphones plugged in, scrubbing through the recordings he'd downloaded. The bug was sound-activated, so the first thing he heard was his own retreating footsteps across the polished floorboards, then the muffled beginning of the encounter with Cody Klein. He deleted that one.

The next two recordings were loud white noise, both with timestamps that matched when Jamie had been doing his token workout in the well-appointed gym. He listened closely, frowning, scrubbing back and forth, until he heard the distinct click of a power socket and muttered Kiswahili. A cleaner.

The first Russian conversation came a few minutes after the cleaner left. This would have been about the time Jamie was showering and changing.

The first voice was Bocharov's, deep and fluid. He seemed to be laying out some kind of explanation or theory, his phrases punctuated with careful pauses and emphasised words. Not for the first time since arriving, Jamie silently wished he'd picked up a bit of Russian.

The second voice was Olenev, interjecting every so often in a strained, querulous tone. At school, there had been a kid called Iain Pine. He was better known as Pine the Whine, for the way he objected to nearly everything anyone said around him, almost on principle. Olenev sounded like Pine, buzzing across Bocharov constantly. Even without understanding the language, Jamie could hear the growing irritation in the other man's voice.

The third voice he guessed was Luca Brunner. Each time he spoke, Olenev quietened. His Russian was smooth but accented, Swiss German gutturals making it sound like he was reading from a textbook.

Then there was a fourth voice. It wasn't someone that Jamie had heard before. He furrowed his brow as he listened. The Russian was halting, the pronunciation of words laboured. Deep down, he felt a strange twinge every time the man spoke. Like an old friend you hadn't seen for years overheard on a bus, or a familiar voice cutting across the buzz of a party in full swing.

The recording ended with a round of what sounded like agreements, then the click of the closing door as the four men left the office.

Jamie checked the file size. It was a big file, which would take a while to send. But he had a feeling it would give Nicola and her team something important to chew on.

He opened up the messaging app, attached the audio and sent it.

My listener caught this conversation. Bocharov, Olenev, Brunner plus one unidentified. Maybe a Russian speaker can get something out of it?

As he waited for a response, he paged back through Nicola's earlier messages. Something was arriving at the compound, probably by sea and probably tomorrow. He was to keep an eye out for anything that might help identify the cargo, or where it was stored.

Jamie stood up and went to the window. Early evening, the sun dropping towards the western horizon. Acacia trees dotted the rising slope behind the compound, casting long shadows.

He turned to look to the north. In the far distance, just where the long, straight beach began to curve, he saw the lights of a beach bar turning on. That must be where Vitaly's men would be going later.

The phone buzzed.

File received. Take no further risks. Eyes and ears only. Do not enter secure areas of the compound.

He sent back a thumbs-up emoji, then smirked down at the phone. This time last week he'd been sending emojis and GIFs in the chat app they used for work. Now he was on an island in the Indian Ocean, sending emojis to his field handler. Because, apparently, he was a spy now.

He had been on the fringes of the secret world since that first conversation with Jeremy at university. But he'd never taken any risks, only lived under restrictions. Doing the job GARNET was meant to do felt like a release. When he wasn't frozen with fear, or desperately wishing he was at home, he found himself oddly happy. This must be why people did this. Adrenaline-seeking with a side of duty and purpose. It was certainly a change from writing sales PowerPoints.

Down by the pool, the party crew was assembling again, the low beat of music starting. The pool lights came on, turning the curving shape of the water into a glowing blue teardrop.

Jamie turned off the bedside lamp, then went back to the window and stood, waiting for his eyes to adjust. He wasn't used to the swift onset of night in the tropics yet, the way that it fell like a curtain over the landscape. But just now was the brief twilight, the sky glowing amber, shadows lengthening.

His eyes roved across the swimsuited men and women below. No Bocharov. No Olenev. No Brunner. And no fourth man. Where were they?

He stood there for long minutes as the sun disappeared, eyes roving over the whole compound. From his third-floor room, with floor-to-ceiling glass on the northern and western sides, he could see most of the western side of the compound.

He strolled out on to the balcony, which let him see properly to the east, to the deep blue-black expanse of the Indian Ocean, lit now by the last dying rays of the sun, the wavetops a fading bronze as they caught the light.

In front of the beach there was the triple fence line, then the security buildings, low curves of dark green metal.

There was also the boathouse.

He'd spotted it the morning before, as they'd driven in. It was a huge structure, mostly wood, but with a corrugated-steel roof. Vitaly had told him it was where they kept all the toys for the guests: jet skis, sailing dinghies, a couple of speedboats and water-skiing gear, giant rubber rings for towing screaming girls and flipping them into the water. 'My favourite part of the job,' Vitaly had said, that ghost of a smile on his lips again.

There was a long gravel road that extended from the boathouse to the fence line and its three gates. A couple of local guards stood in a pool of light at the gate, leaning on the concrete gatehouse.

If anything was coming in by sea, it would probably end up in the boathouse. From here, it looked unguarded, for now. If he could get a peek inside, maybe he'd spot something he could pass on to Nicola. And it was far enough away from the security buildings and the fence line that he could claim to be taking a sunset walk, if someone challenged him.

He gripped the railing and shook his head. Nicola had said no more wandering. Too risky. And she was right. Klein had nearly caught him in Bocharov's office. Probably the only reason he hadn't taken it any further was because Jamie simply didn't fit his idea of a security risk, the pasty-faced, jittery software guy from Scotland.

But there was that fourth voice. Someone new. He stared at the boathouse, curiosity and fear duelling inside him. Perhaps it wouldn't be *that* risky. The boathouse wasn't *really* in the secure part of the compound. If he was quick, if he kept to the shadows, he could be down there and back up without anyone noticing. And if he could spot this fourth man, it might help Nicola work out what the hell Bocharov was up to. Plus, he *had* to know for himself. Something about that voice . . .

Jamie gathered up the phone, the other short-range bug and the laser microphone and tucked them deep into his pockets. After a moment's thought, he added his headphones, in case he needed to use the laser mic.

He went down the three flights of stairs to the ground-floor lobby, but skirted around the pool area. Too many eyes down there, including Cody Klein's.

He was coming to the end of the lawn that wrapped around the villa's easternmost spur when he heard a cough from the gathering gloom.

'Where are *you* going?' said a soft voice.

Jamie peered into the darkness. A stone bench, surrounded by an arch of magnolia flowers. And, sitting in the shadows smoking a cigarette, Natasha.

'Just, you know, fancied a walk?' said Jamie. 'Before it got too dark.'

Natasha smiled and shifted along the stone bench a little. 'Come, sit.'

Jamie took the offered seat. Natasha held out a pack of cigarettes, but he shook his head. 'Don't smoke.'

'Very sensible,' she said. 'Your business deal, it's going well? Warehouse software, right?'

He nodded. 'Very well. I think we should have everything wrapped up in a day or two. Then back home to rain and grey skies.' A half-hearted chuckle. Christ, talking about the weather.

Natasha gave him a sidelong smile. 'I like London. And not just for the shops. I like the parks. And the museums. When we go there, I get time on my own. It is very nice. Vitaly and Arkady, they think it is safer there. They only send one man with me and he is very polite. Not like these.' She gestured with her cigarette towards an armed silhouette stalking past Bocharov's office on the other side of the pool. 'These men are pigs.'

'So you don't like coming to Zanzibar?'

'No, I do,' she said, exhaling a long plume of smoke. 'I just wish I was here for myself. Without' – she waved a hand again – 'all this. Perhaps one day. But you never answered me. Where are you going?'

Jamie straightened up. 'I did. I said I was going for a walk.'

Natasha shook her head. 'Most of the compound is off limits. Vitaly didn't tell you this?'

Jamie gave her a forced smile. 'Oh yes, he did, of course. I thought I'd just walk around the building. Look at the sea from the other side.'

Natasha nodded. 'This is probably okay. But Jamie. It is dangerous here. There are scorpions in the bushes. Stay on the path. And be careful.'

Once he'd said goodbye to Natasha, Jamie slipped past the end of the villa's easternmost spur and across the lawn, down to the hard-packed dust road that led towards the security sub-compound. The barracks blocks were lit from within, a tinny beat emanating from the open door of the closest. The lucky chosen men from Vitaly's team getting ready for their night off.

The boathouse was about fifty metres further along the road. Racks of life preservers and wetsuits were drawn up outside, drying off after the day's activities. The side door was slightly ajar. Through the two windows either side of the door, he saw figures moving in the dim interior light.

He was about ten metres from the door when it scraped closed.

Jamie swore and stepped to the side of the road, into the shade of an overhanging tree, his heart hammering. The heat of the day was fading, but it was still stiflingly hot and humid, the air blood-warm. He swallowed, throat dry. Natasha's warning echoed in his mind.

Scorpions in the bushes. Stay on the path.

Someone was in there. Someone who didn't want to be overheard.

Jamie crept closer, keeping well out of the pool of brightness from the LED floodlight above the door. He positioned himself behind a trailer with an upturned dinghy on it, made sure he was still in shadow, then slowly raised his head above the curve of white fibreglass.

The first profile he recognised inside the shed was Bocharov. The man was unmistakeable, even in the half-light. He stood to the right, gesturing towards something that Jamie couldn't see.

To the left, he saw Olenev. And a third figure, just out of sight behind the door. Whoever this was, he had been the one to close the door.

He pulled out the laser microphone. It was about the length of his hand, from index finger to base of the palm. He turned it over, looking for the power switch. Seventy per cent battery. Three hours of audio.

Satisfied, he thumbed it on and pointed it at the ground. No visible light. Good.

Jamie put in one headphone and gingerly raised the laser mic above the curve of the dinghy's hull, aiming it at the window. It took a half-second for the device to calibrate against the glass, then he heard Bocharov's voice, sounding as though he was talking through a tin can. But he was perfectly audible, even though he was speaking in Russian.

'—eto budet ochen' bezopasno, konechno . . .'

Another voice broke in. The fourth man.

'—I'm sorry, really. Can we speak in English? I was at my limits with Russian before, and I'm not following this.'

Jamie blinked. The man had a Scottish accent. Softer than his own. Perth, maybe? Or Stirling.

Bocharov let out a stifled grunt, which could have been frustration or patient agreement. 'Of course. Anything for our newest friend. I was saying that we use this normally for securing special cargo. Things we don't want the house staff or any of Vitaly's men to get too curious about. Double thumbprint lock, heavy-gauge steel reinforced with titanium rods.'

'So we can put the cargo in here while the deal goes through?'

'Exactly,' said Olenev. 'We can code one of the thumbprints to Brunner's man instead of ours, so he knows it's secure, but we can't get to it. The verification may take a few hours, both for the accounts and the material. Then we make the transfer, he authorises the thumbprint back to us, the cage opens and the material is ours. Then back to Mother Russia.'

'You have transport for the second leg?' said Olenev.

'All arranged,' said Bocharov. 'One of Brunner's contacts. We can't risk Suez twice. Brunner's contact will get it to Omsk, by air. Then from there to the target. Then a new day will begin for all of Russia. New leadership and new strength.'

Olenev spoke again. 'Brunner's boat is waiting offshore. But he's getting nervous. He wants the deal done by tomorrow night at the latest. And we need to talk about our little friend. Klein says he's clean, but I do not buy this. Why would he no-show at the handover and then come here? These Legends, they understand how the programme works, no?'

The third man, the one with the Scottish accent, spoke again. He stepped forward a little and Jamie saw his profile, but still couldn't make out his face.

'I was as surprised as you to see him in Dar. But there's no reason to worry. I think he's here purely because he didn't know what else to do. We can take him out of the picture, after the deal, then I can—'

Jamie's heart was hammering as he realised the men were talking about him, but he still heard the distinct clink of metal on metal a metre or two behind him. He froze, the hand holding the laser mic trembling slightly. He turned his head.

Vitaly stood three paces away, an AK rifle levelled at Jamie's head.

'Mr Tulloch,' the big Russian said softly. 'You need to come with me.'

44

Nicola

Stevie's Beach Bar and Grill, north-east
coast of Zanzibar: now

It didn't take the Russians long to become the heart and soul of the
party at Stevie's. They insisted on choosing the music and occupying
three whole benches to themselves.

Eventually, the DJ gave in and put on the pounding electro the
Russians kept asking for. They filled the dance floor, beer bottles in
each hand, punching the sky and howling at the moon.

Stevie's lay in a shallow bay, set back from the water's edge, a grass-
thatched, open-sided building with dozens of circular tables inside.
But the dance floor was a wide square of churned sand that extended
all the way to the ocean, ringed with cane chairs, wooden picnic
benches and palm trees.

Lights strung between the trees and the buildings pulsed in time to
the beat. A laser mounted on the front of the bar spun and twisted,
bathing the dancers in flickering red and green. With each song, the
giant speakers mounted on each side of the dance floor seemed to turn
up a notch.

Sylvan kept his distance, staying by the bar with Tumo, nursing a
beer. Sylvan wore his usual shorts and battered shirt outfit, while
Tumo had donned one of the colourful patterned shirts popular on

the island. He leaned across the bar and spoke quietly to Sylvan, two friends or business acquaintances on a night out. But Sylvan kept glancing towards where Farida and Nicola had placed themselves, on the edge of a gaggle of twenty-something backpackers, close to the tables the Russians had occupied.

Nicola put one hand to her ear and spoke quietly, as though to Farida. 'Graeme, stop looking in my direction. They're either going to think you're competition or twig something's off. Start thinking about the vehicles.'

Sylvan's head turned away and he took another long pull from his beer. 'Sorry. Just can't stand these arseholes.'

'We'll be fine.' She took her hand away from the earpiece and brushed her hair back over it. The newest ones were tiny, but it was still best to conceal them if you could.

'Graeme is a worrier,' said Farida, turning her head to look out over the dance floor, her braided hair sliding from her shoulder. 'But he's right. These men are dangerous.'

Nicola nodded. 'I know. This is intel-gathering only. Chat to a few drunk Russians. See what we can find out. We're just enjoying a girls' night. Komba's people will be watching, so we can't go further than that.'

Farida nodded. 'I've seen two people I know from Stone Town since we got here. They're definitely keeping an eye on us.'

Two of the Russians seemed to be engaged in a handstand contest of some kind. As she watched, one collapsed sideways into the sand to a chorus of jeers from his comrades.

'Why don't you work for Komba?' Nicola asked.

Farida shrugged. 'I do, when the money's good enough. Zanzibar is full of spies. Drugs, arms deals, governments watching each other. It is a . . . crossroads?'

Nicola nodded. Zanzibar wasn't her patch, usually, but she'd been on the edges of enough ops to know how often the popular holiday island served other purposes.

Farida shrugged again. 'It's a good way to make a living. And most of the time, not too dangerous. I keep my distance, I report back. Sometimes it is for businesses, sometimes for governments. Many people want to watch each other.'

Nicola bit her lip as she looked out over the ocean. The moon was beginning to rise. Not quite a full moon; if it had been, the beach would be a lot busier.

'I've thought about private work myself. I love this job. But it . . . takes a toll.'

Farida reached across the table and gently squeezed her forearm. 'You should. You are good at it. And more money for less risk is better, no?'

Nicola smiled. 'Maybe.' She drained her beer. 'But we've got a job to do tonight. Ready to back me up?'

'Yep, ready.'

They started by heading to the bar for a fresh round of drinks, replacing the beers with salt-rimed frozen margaritas. Nicola swigged occasionally from a water bottle in the bag at her hip as they circled the dance floor, edging closer to the Russians. She could act the part of a drunk tourist later, if she needed to, but for now the water would help keep her head clear.

They joined the young backpacker group, dancing in the darkness with the lasers and pulsing lights overhead. The backpackers were nearly all young women, Americans and Canadians mostly, although there was the odd bare-chested, board-shorted bleached-blond young man among them. They spun and twisted in the light, shouting over the music. Nicola overheard a couple of abortive attempts at pick-up lines directed at the young women and had to turn away to hide her smile.

Eventually, they worked their way to the edge of the backpacker group and began to turn slowly towards the Russians.

They were all men in their twenties and thirties. Most of them must have been teenagers or barely into their twenties during the war, but all seemed to have served. Nicola caught the sledgehammer-wielding skeleton tattoo of ex-Wagner men a couple of times, plus the livid white scars of fragmentation wounds. Almost everyone who had fought in Ukraine had a few of those, from the constant shelling, drone-dropped munitions and liberal use of grenades.

She pushed down her distaste as two of the men clocked her and Farida and leered openly. They leaned back in the moonlight, tipping back their beer bottles, eyes following the curve of Farida's body in jeans and a halter top, then switching to Nicola, taking in her white tank top, slim-fit jeans. It was her night-off outfit, one that usually made her feel great. But the steady pressure of the men's eyes made her bare shoulders prickle. Images of Rachael flickered through her mind, laughing and drinking and dancing in flashing dance-floor lights, Rachael with her long red hair. What would she do, if she were here? If she saw Nicola, doing what needed to be done, getting close to these murderous, dangerous men?

She pushed the thought away, sipped her margarita, salt and lime sharp on her tongue.

One of the two men danced straight past them, glancing at Nicola and Farida and then heading for the younger women. Nicola glanced at the other man, a little older, and gave him a small shrug and a frown. He took the bait and closed in, leaning in close to speak into her ear. His breath smelled of stale beer.

'Please excuse Sergei. He does not recognise beautiful woman when he sees her. He prefers silly little girls.'

Nicola smiled at the man and turned towards him, continuing to dance. 'And you do recognise a beautiful woman?'

He put a hand to his chest. 'Of course! I am Anton. I appreciate all kinds of ladies.'

He was slurring his words slightly. She gave him another smile but kept dancing. After a moment, she leaned over and gave him a conspiratorial nod. 'This beautiful woman is called Lisa. That's Neema.'

Anton glanced at Farida. 'You have local friends? She is Zanzibari. I can tell.'

Nicola nodded. 'I work here. For a charity in Stone Town. We are taking a little break.'

Anton grinned. 'I work here too! Private security. Along the coast. I've been here for six months. It's a great place, yes?'

She began to steer them towards the edge of the dance floor. Anton followed, grinning. When one particularly deep bass line ended, she stepped lightly to one side and sat down at an empty table. Farida took the hint and went to the bar to get more drinks, while Anton immediately slid on to the bench opposite.

'When I was a little younger, I would dance all night. But I need the odd break these days,' she said.

Now that they were closer to the bar and the yellow light cast from inside, she could see Anton was older than the other mercenaries. His left temple was bisected by a thin white scar, the kind that came from a wire fragment. The Ukrainians had dropped thousands of trench-buster drone grenades. The grenades used tiny, segmented curls of sharp wire that split into hundreds of fragments when they exploded. She'd seen the same kind of scar on a dozen faces over the past few years. Anton smiled and leaned forward.

'Me too. And the hangovers, much worse now. I have to pace myself. The young guys, they had a half-bottle of vodka each before we came. Too much for me.'

Nicola smiled and sipped her margarita. 'You had a little pre-party? Where you work?'

Anton laughed. 'Always, it is cheaper. We have barracks, where we live. With Bluetooth speakers, you can make a real good party.' He sat back on the bench and took another long swallow from his beer. 'A few years ago I could never imagine I would come to paradise like this.'

Nicola saw Farida coming back from the bar, with two new margaritas and a beer for Anton. 'Where were you a few years ago?'

Anton shrugged, a shadow passing across his face. 'Ukraine. I don't talk about it. But it was not like this.'

She nodded slowly as Farida sat down. 'Understandable. I've been on Zanzibar a couple of years. I work on roads development and rural electrification. Neema works with me.'

Farida smiled at the slightly drunk Russian. 'Where do you work, Anton?'

Anton looked blearily between the two women, then downed the remains of his beer and picked up the one Farida had put in front of him.

'I'm security. A villa along the coast. Company called UPK. Very nice place.'

Nicola leaned back, partially to get away from the stale beer smell emanating from Anton, but also so she could stay in his eyeline. He was *very* drunk, she realised, as his eyes dropped to her breasts. She gave him a smile that she hoped was not as tight and angry as she felt.

'Anton was just telling me his friends were having a party in their barracks. Before they came here.'

Another round of cheering erupted from the dance floor and Farida glanced across. 'Looks like it was a good one.'

Anton smiled, looking between them. 'It was good. Nearly got cancelled though. Would have been a disaster. The boys, they have been looking forward to this for two weeks. No nights off after today.'

Nicola lifted one eyebrow. 'Oh? Why did it nearly get cancelled?'

Anton waved a hand. 'Security alert. My boss, he comes in, he's shouting at us that we have to get our gear on, you know. But then *his* boss, the big boss, he comes by and he looks at us and he says, "They are drunk." And I am *not* drunk. Some of the younger men, yes, but I can hold my vodka. And my beer!'

He grinned again and waved the beer bottle towards the dance floor.

'So they let you go anyway?' said Farida, casting a glance across at Nicola.

'Yes, yes. Big boss, he says that it is only a small thing. No need for drunk men to pick up loaded guns, you know?'

Nicola managed a tight laugh, but underneath it her heart was pounding. 'Did someone try to get into your villa?'

Anton shook his head, one eye fixed on her. 'No, no. Small thing only. A man came to do business deal or something, I don't know. But he was spy, for UPK competition, I think.' Anton tapped his ear. 'Listening in to important conversation. Sneaking around boathouse.'

Another shadow crossed Anton's face and he pointed at Nicola, still holding the beer bottle, raising one eyebrow as he regarded her. 'Why you want to know this?' He giggled. 'Maybe you are spy too. This island. Full of spies.'

Nicola laughed and took a sip from her drink to hide the rising fear in her chest. 'A very boring spy. I think about electrical grids, mainly.'

Farida steered the conversation back to safer ground, while Nicola put down her drink and headed to the bathrooms behind the bar. On the way, she tapped her earpiece.

'Graeme, where are you?'

'Watching the Russians' vehicles. What's up?'

'We've got a big fucking problem.'

'Jamie?'

She came around the corner of the bar and saw Sylvan lurking in the shadow of an acacia tree. Across the dirt trail, three Toyota Land Cruisers were parked in an uneven line. 'Yes, Jamie,' she said softly as she got closer.

'Don't worry, they're all inside. What's going on?'

She filled him in quickly on Anton's description of the security alert at the compound.

'Definitely him, you think? Like the man said, there's a lot of eyes on Bocharov.'

'It must be. He probably thought he could figure out what was being brought in if he looked in the boathouse.'

Sylvan nodded. 'Smart. That's what I'd have done.'

Nicola could feel a thrum of adrenaline in her system. 'Except it's not fucking smart, is it, Graeme? You'd have done back-checks. You'd have got yourself somewhere secure to observe, with multiple exits. Because you're a *fucking trained field agent*.'

Sylvan held both hands up. 'Sorry, Nic. You're right. This is fucked. London shouldn't have put you in this position, and he shouldn't be in there.'

'Yeah, well, shoulda-woulda-coulda.' Nicola swore and looked at the ground. 'We've got to crash it.'

Sylvan's eyes widened. 'What?'

'If we're getting him out of there, we have to do it now. We've got an opportunity with these goons having their night out. Security is only going to get tighter. If I can get in there tonight, I can find him, get him out again.'

'Nicola, you can't be serious. It's a risk just being around these guys, never mind driving back to the lion's den with them. They catch you in there, they'll eat you alive. And we'll be fucked if Komba spots us. PNG for me, and you if you're still alive. And they'll throw Tumo and Farida in jail.'

Nicola clenched her hands, released them. 'I can't leave him, Graeme. He didn't sign up for this. Shouldn't even be in there. He's my responsibility. My joe.'

Graeme looked down at his feet. 'I'll go in. I know the compound, been studying it for weeks. I'll find him.'

'No. No offence, Graeme, but you're unlikely to get an invite back. These guys will get me past the fence line, inside the security zone. I can improvise from there.'

It was Graeme's turn to clench and unclench his fists, puff out a low breath. He leaned back against the tree, a shadow within the shadows. She could see his eyes, reflecting the light from the bar, fixed on her.

'Christ, Nic. Okay. But you're going in prepped.' He kneeled down and pulled a small backpack from behind the tree where he'd stashed it. In the half-light, she saw him pull out a handgun with a boxy suppressor, as well as a small black pouch of padded ballistic nylon.

'Standard SIG P226, suppressed. Still loud as fuck on a dark night, so don't get too trigger-happy.'

She took the weapon, checked the chamber, then tucked it inside her bag. If there was a bag search on the fence-line gate, she'd stash it under the vehicle's seats and hope she got lucky.

He handed her the padded pouch. 'Two field sedation syringes. Fine needle, it'll go through one thick layer of cloth or two thin ones. Retracts after use. It's a sixty-minute dose of a particularly brutal ketamine derivative. Thirty seconds to take effect. On top of booze, this'll be a lot, so if you have time, put these sad fucks in the recovery position before you leave them.'

She unzipped the pouch and turned the syringes so she could see them. 'Just press and go?'

'Yep, neck or thigh is your best bet, near an artery. Use them if one of these arseholes goes for you, but he'll still be able to move for a few seconds. Any doubts, use the SIG.'

She looked up at him. His eyes were locked on hers. He was biting his lip.

She put out an arm. 'I've snuck around in the dark with worse than this, Graeme. I'll be fine. Just get as close as you can and be ready. I don't know when or how I'll be coming out of that place. But I'll have Jamie with me, and I don't know what kind of shape he'll be in. We'll need transport and we'll need it close.'

He nodded. 'I'm on it.'

She squeezed his arm. 'The big-brother routine is very sweet though.'

He half laughed, half sighed. 'Jesus. Okay, go. Stay safe. Bring back our boy.'

45

Jeremy

Room 19A, Sub-level 2, Vauxhall Cross: now

Sarah Grey had said nothing for nearly twelve hours. For a while he'd wondered if she was actually catatonic. She had an unnervingly steady gaze, blinking once every fifteen seconds. He'd counted, after lapsing into silence for the twentieth or thirtieth time.

'Shall we try again, Sarah?'

She didn't look at him, but he caught the flicker of attention in the tightening of the skin under her eyes. An involuntary reaction to hearing your own name, regardless of how well you'd been trained.

'We've talked about why you came to work here. How you did what you did. We found your data tap, spotted your little edits to the camera logs. We know the *how*. But we don't know the *why*. We don't know who Sarah Grey is, or why she would choose to betray her country.'

There. Another flicker. A very, very slight lifting of the eyebrow.

'So here's what I do know about Sarah Grey. Born 1997 in Gravesend, Kent. Good grades at the local comprehensive. Got a place at Warwick University. Studied Linguistics with Russian. Dropped out suddenly halfway through your last year, retrained as a heating engineer. Student loans paid off two years later with a large single payment. Inheritance, was it?'

Another flicker. Jeremy took a sip of water and dug in on that angle.

'I suppose HVAC apprenticeships must pay well. Specialist skill. But you were clearly passionate about your academics. In your second year you spent a year in St Petersburg. You were caught there, in fact, during the war. Must have been quite the experience for someone that age.'

Grey leaned back in her chair slightly and let out the smallest possible sigh. It was just the barest widening of her nostrils, a tiny tip of the head. She tilted her gaze up to the ceiling.

Perfect. Jeremy knew someone trying to control her anger when he saw it. He stuck the knife in and twisted it.

'I'm sorry that they took advantage of that naivety. Pushed you into this job that's a waste of your potential. To serve murderous bastards who couldn't give a shit about you.'

When she spoke, the Gravesend accent was laced with anger and bitterness.

'Listen, you posh fucking prick. I know what I'm doing, why I'm doing it and who I'm doing it for. Always have. I make my own decisions.'

Jeremy leaned back, making his eyes wide in feigned shock. 'So you do speak? What was it? My assumption you were naive? Or that you failed to know your place in our fine Western meritocracy?'

She snorted. '*Meritocracy.* You know the guy who came up with that word did it in a dystopian parody, right? Look it up. Michael Dunlop Young. Except pricks like you took it and slapped it on the nobility and the divine right of fucking kings as a fresh coat of paint. Different deck, same card trick.'

Jeremy said nothing, just watched Grey. He took a sip of water. Her eyes tracked his hand. He let the silence billow out. Now the dam had broken, he knew, her words would flow downhill, finding the path of least resistance. It was astonishing, he reflected, how little people could stand to sit in silence, once some words had been said.

'And you call them murderous bastards, but from where I'm sitting, at least they're *honest.* This place, it uses people up. I've seen it. Worked here two years. You can *see* people's hair going grey. Some of them, they come in here for a briefing, then never come back again. Where'd they go? Shallow grave in Mali? Bottom of a ravine in Waziristan? How many lives have *you* taken, Jeremy? How many people have you sent out to die for the men in the grey suits in Whitehall? For what? To keep UK Plc up a few points? Keep whatever fucking joker is in Number 10 at his steady negative-thirty-two approval rating?' She folded her arms and sat back. 'Cunts, the lot of you.'

Jeremy laid out a series of photographs on the table in front of him, colour prints of the Canning Town drone shots. Then, interior shots of the warehouse after the CT team assault. In one shot, wisps of smoke drifted across a bright spear of light from a skylight. A slumped body lay directly in the shaft of light, as though pinned by it.

'What about them? Did they have to die?'

Sarah fixed fierce eyes on him. Again, she broke eye contact before he did. 'You're the ones that killed them.'

Jeremy nodded. 'Yes, that's true. They had surface-to-air missiles. Stingers. What do you think they were going to do with man-portable SAMs in central London, Sarah? How many people do you think they were going to kill?'

She said nothing, her lips set in a thin line.

'What was your mission, Sarah? Why were you meeting your contact in Green Park? What were the armed operatives at Location Shura planning?'

But he'd pushed too hard again. She clammed up, arms folded tightly against her body, eyes fixed back on the wall.

Jeremy stood up. 'Okay. Some water and food for us both, I think. Then we'll try again in a little while.'

Her eyes widened a little again. Jeremy sighed. He leaned over, planted both hands on the metal table.

'I'm not a monster, Sarah. I don't pull out fingernails or pour water on people's faces in darkened rooms.'

She sneered. '*You* don't, maybe. But you have people who do. Maybe you outsource it, but it fucking happens.'

Jeremy shook his head. 'Not if I have anything to do with it. Look, I'm under no illusions about who I am, Sarah, or who I work for. Britain is deeply imperfect. We're still trying to untangle ourselves from an empire that died nearly a century ago. We make a lot of mistakes. But we muddle forward. Every time pricks like the men who sent this team to London' – he tapped the photo of the warehouse, the weapons cases, the slumped body sliced by sunlight – 'every time they do something like this, it gets a little harder. There are people in Britain who will take any excuse you give them to drop bombs somewhere far away. Then more people die. Here and elsewhere. I want this to *stop*. Help me make it stop.'

46

Jamie

Rayskiye Vrata: now

Jamie had been in many training seminars over the years. It was about even money whether the trainer would use a slide of Steve Jobs exhorting people to make a dent in the universe or a sweaty close-up of Mike Tyson explaining that everyone has a plan until they get punched in the mouth.

After the fourth or fifth punch from Vitaly's meaty fist, Jamie had a new appreciation for that quote. Although he still didn't see how it applied to sales development training.

He reeled backwards on the chair, but didn't tip back over. The chair flexed under his weight, but it was bolted to the concrete floor of the villa's wine cellar. Jamie chuckled under his breath, blood bubbling from his nose like the vague hysteria that had been building in him since they'd dragged him in here. The worst had happened now. He was well and truly screwed. For some reason, the panic came out as laughter.

'What the *fuck* are you laughing at, funny man?' growled Vitaly, stepping back. 'Nothing about this is funny.'

Jamie spat. When the blood hit the floor, he was back in the playground, in Primary Six, one of the bigger lads from the next street over pinning him to the concrete with one hand and punching him with the other. Jamie had started giggling then too, until the bully had climbed off him, called him a psycho and walked away. Somehow he doubted Vitaly was going to do the same.

'What is funny?' said Vitaly.

Jamie nodded at the walls of the room they'd dragged him to. 'Multi-function room,' he said, and chuckled again. 'Temperature-controlled. Perfect for wine storage *and* beatings.'

A wild anger burned inside Jamie's chest. Anger with Vitaly. With Bocharov. With fucking Jeremy. But with himself most of all. How stupid could a man get? Standing there with a listening device like an idiot. He deserved every one of these punches. But maybe that was the concussion talking.

Vitaly leaned forward, smirking. 'We Russians are *practical*,' he said. Then his fist came in from the right so hard Jamie felt his spine crackle. He flexed his shoulders.

'Thanks. Neck's been a little sore,' he managed.

'Tough man, eh?' said Vitaly, standing with his legs splayed, ready to punch again. 'Think this is a joke? You are a spy. A coward piz'duk British spy.'

Jamie grinned through the blood. 'I'm Scottish, mainly. But aye, I'm a spy. You can stop hitting me if you like. I'll tell you all about it.'

Vitaly stood up and narrowed his eyes. 'You are SIS? Field agent?'

'Nope,' said Jamie. 'I'm just some guy. Literally. Made a deal, years ago. I'm like . . . kind of a reverse sleeper? My job is to *fuck off*, and then someone else does stuff like this. But . . .' He swayed and tried to sit up straighter in the chair, shuffling his cuffed hands up until he was vertical, then spat more blood on to the concrete.

'But,' he began again, 'in *my* case, I show up, and my handler's dead and there's no sign of my opposite number. So I came instead. Didn't know what else to do. Then, because I'm an idiot, I agreed to carry on. Because, and I don't know if you know this, Vitaly, but your boss is kind of a bad man.'

Vitaly's lip twitched and he clenched one bloody fist. 'Arkady saved my life three times. Took a grenade fragment for me. A good man is relative. Depends where you are and what matters to you.'

'I think if Arkady gets his way, a lot of people are going to die.'

Vitaly smiled. 'Maybe. Again, it's relative, no? If the *right* people die.'

This time, Jamie didn't see the fist that sent him into unconsciousness.

47

Nicola

Gate 2 (North), Rayskiye Vrata: now

The worst part was pretending she didn't understand Russian. The soldiers tried unsuccessfully to persuade three of the young backpackers to join them, muttering under their breath as their entreaties failed. Nicola distinctly heard two of them discussing whether they could get away with just pulling the girls into their vehicles and driving away.

Farida had followed Nicola out to the vehicles, playing the role of the distressed friend trying to talk someone out of a bad decision. Nicola was unsure how much was part of the act.

Eventually they'd pulled away in a grinding wheelspin of dust and lurching over-steer, Nicola wedged in the back of the rear Land Cruiser between Anton and another mercenary whose name she didn't catch. Although, by the time they reached the lower gatehouse of *Rayskiye Vrata*, she certainly knew about his body odour and wandering hands.

Anton kept up a steady commentary about how much money he made as a security contractor, the dacha he had his eye on, the many and manifold problems of the New Russia and what he would do if he were in charge. Half the time he lapsed into Russian and Nicola had to feign ignorance. Every time the vehicle lurched across a rut in the dirt road or veered into the scrub that ran alongside it, Anton's body pressed against hers, his skin almost feverish to the touch, wiry and straining against the thin material of his shirt.

She wouldn't have long, once they were in the security compound. She could feel the man's impatience and desperate hunger, even through the haze of drink. Her fingers clenched tightly around the small shoulder bag that held her weapon and the sedatives.

The front two vehicles cleared the gatehouse. Their driver rolled the Land Cruiser forward, nearly side-swiping the swing barrier. One of the local guards stepped forward, baseball cap pulled low, a battered AK slung from his shoulder. He peered at the driver's ID pass, then shone a torch through the gap between the seats into Anton's face.

'Get that light out of my fucking face, svoloch! *Blyat.*'

The gate guard leaned in and flicked the torch across to Nicola. 'Who is this? No pass, no entry.'

She felt Anton tense up, as though he was going to lurch between the gap in the seats or climb out of the vehicle to go toe-to-toe with the guard. The man had a broad, friendly face, his brow furrowed in concern to see a woman in the vehicle with these men. Clearly new to the job, then.

Nicola put out a hand, pressing gently against Anton's straining chest, her other hand dropping the shoulder bag to her feet. She leaned between the seats, flashed a smile and spoke to the guard in Kiswahili.

'Ndugu, I'll be here just for a short time. You don't want to tangle with these guys. They are not worth the trouble, I promise you.'

The man's eyes widened a little and he put his hand on his chest. 'It is not safe for you, to be with these men. Please, you should leave. I will get a car for you back to Nungwi, or wherever you are staying.'

She shook her head. 'I know what I'm doing. Please. It's important. Don't make a fuss.'

The guard's lips flattened into a thin line, but his eyes flicked to Anton, who was emitting a low growl and a string of muttered Russian curses.

'Miss, you have any trouble, you come here, to this gate. You find me. I am Emmanuel, okay?'

Nicola nodded, silent.

He gave a short, sharp nod, then stepped back and swept his arm up. The barrier rose and the Land Cruiser leapt forward. As they passed, Nicola locked eyes with the guard again and saw him shake his head, just a little.

They eventually skidded to a stop at the end of a row of parked vehicles. Anton clambered over the back seats to get out, nearly tripping in the dust.

The group stumbled towards one of the barracks blocks, Anton cheerfully telling his comrades to fuck off in a half-dozen colourful Russian idioms, one arm tight around Nicola's waist, a hand slipping into the waistband of her jeans. She walked quickly, anxious to get him on his own. If the other men roped them into continuing the party, it might be hours before she could get clear.

But she needn't have worried about that. Months of guard duty and isolation on the compound gave Anton a sharp, single-minded focus that even the skinful of alcohol he'd drunk couldn't blunt. They were barely through the green metal door to the barracks before he was pushing her towards a room at the end of the corridor, ignoring the string of catcalls and whistles that followed in their wake.

'You have your own rooms?' she said, hoping there wouldn't be a grumpy bunkmate waiting for them inside.

'Perk of the job, dorogoy,' Anton slurred. 'Much better than a fucking dugout in Kremmenya, da?'

He leaned heavily against the wall and fumbled in his thigh pocket for an access card. Nicola took a step back, glanced along the corridor. The others had shuffled into the common kitchen, from where she could already hear the clink of bottles. Good. She dipped a hand into the shoulder bag and stepped out of Anton's eyeline, then unzipped the sedative pouch and tugged out one of the syringes by feel. She slipped it into her trouser pocket just as Anton slapped the access card against the reader beside his door.

Best to get it over with.

Nicola stepped straight forward, following Anton's retreating back into the dim room. There was an unmade single bed to the left, a desk and locker to the right, a laptop open on it. Anton leaned down beside the bed and snapped on a reading lamp, then stood there for a moment, breathing heavily, before pawing open the drawer of the nightstand. Nicola closed the door behind her.

'Davai, davai . . .' he murmured to himself, fingers scrabbling through the detritus in the drawer.

Nicola thumbed the cap off the syringe and put a hand on Anton's shoulder. He turned around, face split with a childlike grin, a condom held triumphantly between finger and thumb.

Nicola smiled back, then gently shook her head. 'Not tonight, tovarisch,' she whispered.

Anton's brow was barely furrowed before the needle jabbed straight into his neck. He reeled backwards, batting Nicola's arm and the empty syringe away, the other hand clamped around his throat.

'Yebanaya shlyukha!' he managed, stumbling back to the bed. Nicola was already on him, pulling the pistol from her bag with her free hand and pinning the man's arms to his chest, scrabbling to get on top of him. She shoved the pistol against his forehead and stared into his eyes, hoping she wouldn't have to pull the trigger, that he would lose the strength that still coursed through his arms. He jerked under her, trying to throw her off, his eyes wide and his veins bulging with anger.

But the dose was a strong one. One breath. Two. Three. His eyes took on a glassy sheen. The spasms of his muscles lengthened and weakened until he sagged back on the bed. His eyes were still open, staring vacantly.

'Good night, mate,' she said, tucking the pistol away. She checked his airway and slid him on to his side, pulling him into the recovery position. Whatever else she might have to do tonight, she wasn't going to leave this man to die in his own spit.

She leaned back against the wall. Her heart was pounding and her hands were clammy with sweat. She wiped them dry against the fabric of her trousers, then took a couple of deep, slow breaths.

The hard part was done. She was in. Now she had to find Jamie.

Nicola took the pistol from her bag, then the remaining syringe, ready if she needed it. She ditched the bag. The sedative should come with some minor memory loss, so hopefully if Anton came back to himself, he would think he'd passed out drunk and Nicola had got cold feet and made a run for the gatehouse. She ought to have at least an hour before that was a risk.

She spotted the access card on the floor where Anton had dropped it and scooped it into her other pocket. With any luck, it would give her the run of the place. Or at least get her through some of the exterior doors.

She snapped the room's lock closed and turned off the bedside light, leaving Anton groaning softly in the darkness, then opened the sliding aluminium window frame and glanced outside. There was a strip of mown grass between Anton's block and the next, lit irregularly by pools of light from the barrack windows. Nicola dropped silently to the turf a metre below, landing with arms spread for balance. She froze for a long moment, listening closely. From the kitchen at the end of the block she heard more bottles, the hiss-thump of shitty techno, a high whoop of laughter.

Closer, in the next block, the sound of a deep, guttural snore wound out through an open window.

Nicola moved fast and low between the buildings. She got to the end of the block and looked left and right. A gravel road led down towards the beach in one direction and curved around the villa in the other. Halfway along, the dark bulk of the boathouse loomed. According to Anton, that was where Jamie had been caught. Would they hold him in there as well?

Nicola detached herself from the building and flitted across the road, darting through the shadowed gap between two overhead floodlights. She found herself exceptionally glad she'd pulled a dark shirt over her white tank top before they left Stevie's Bar.

Halfway up the road, she froze at the sound of low voices. A lighter flared briefly in the shadows. Barely ten paces from where she crouched at the base of a thorn bush, two armed men stood, taking deep drags on their cigarettes. The tobacco glowed orange, lighting the contours of their faces. Sharp cheekbones, shaved heads. Russians.

'You just coming on?' said the first one, taller, his narrow frame wrapped in an assault vest, a black AK12 slung across his chest.

'Da, had to deal with some shit with Vitaly. Took hours.'

'Mudak, what now? He got you pulling some stupid extra detail?'

'Nyet, man. Fucking guest got caught outside the villa bounds.'

'What, some of the Instagram detishki?' The smaller man pronounced the name of the app with a long, rolled 'R', the derision clear in every syllable. 'Going off to fuck in the bushes?'

'Nyet, nyet, the Britanskiy. They caught him with a bug or something. Wildest thing. Vitaly's been kicking seven shades of shit out of him in the wine cellar. Working up a sweat.'

Nicola's hand tightened on the grip of the pistol.

'Wouldn't mind a punch of that guy's face myself. Smug little fucker was lurking around the boss's office yesterday.'

The bigger man took a slow drag from his cigarette. 'You report that?'

The smaller one shook his head. 'Klein walked him off. Figured he outranks me, you know?'

The big man nodded. 'Better not to throw a punch when the fight is already over,' he said softly. 'Keep that shit to yourself. Go get some sleep. Gonna be a busy one tomorrow. And those assholes in Block A aren't going to shut up until they run out of vodka.'

Low, rueful chuckles. Then the scrape of boots on crushed stone as the two men turned away.

Nicola turned her body to move towards the villa that loomed further up the slope, but as she did, she put her full weight on her left foot. The dried-out twig under her sole cracked, loud as a gunshot in the quiet of the night compound. She winced, froze perfectly still, her head turned towards the two men.

The big man stopped, took another drag on his cigarette. 'You hear that?'

'Probably one of those big fucking tree rats. There's a few of them inside the perimeter. The ones smart enough not to go through the minefield.'

More laughter. 'Goddamn, I hate the tree rats.'

They turned away again. Nicola stayed perfectly still, her thighs burning from the effort. She waited until the two men were more than fifty paces away, leaving long, thin streamers of cigarette smoke behind them in the night air. Then she sagged to the ground.

Up ahead, the villa was visible as a large 'U' shape, the eastern wing closest to her. With any luck, there would be external access somewhere, or a window she could climb through. Sylvan's building plans had all been from the construction phase. She remembered storerooms, cleaning supply closets, staff changing areas one level below ground. The wine cellar had to be down there somewhere.

Nicola moved carefully from cover to cover, eyes fixed on the tiers of windows above her, alert for a silhouette or snapped-on light. But most of the rectangles of dark glass above her remained so. At the top she peered into the darkness, looking for the outline of a door or window.

There. Halfway along, the white-and-green glow of an exit sign, steps leading down to a half-concealed door. She tapped Anton's door card against the reader and was rewarded with a green light and a soft click as the exit opened.

Beyond, a steep, brick-lined stairwell with a blue-painted metal handrail and concrete steps, dimly lit with recessed lights. Nicola went down one flight, then turned a corner into a wider corridor, lined with shelves full of cleaning supplies. Doors led off every metre or two. This must be part of the extensive staff quarters and storage that kept Bocharov's rolling cocktail party going day after day.

She edged along the corridor, pistol held ready, checking corners and moving as quickly as she dared. Every step took her further away from the gatehouse and the relative safety of the dark, thorny scrubland outside. The further she went into this place, the further she'd have to come back out, possibly dragging an injured civilian.

Twenty more steps and she heard something. At first she took it for the low thudding of a generator or some kind of pipework. But as she moved, she heard the grunts and gasped exhalations that signalled either pain or pleasure being inflicted. Possibly both, depending on which party you were talking about.

She turned a corner at the end of the corridor and peered ahead. There, at the end of another, shorter corridor, a rectangle of light in the dimness, an open door. Beyond was a narrow, vault-like space, walls lined with racks of bottles. And under a lamp, cuffed to a metal chair, was the battered form of Jamie Tulloch.

Nicola felt her breath catch in her throat. Was she too late? Had Vitaly killed him?

Jamie's head rolled to the right and he spat on the floor. She wasn't close enough to hear what he said, but she saw a shadow detach itself from the right side of the vault and step across the light. Vitaly, stripped to his vest, his clenched fist wet and shining, limned in harsh white light.

She raised the pistol and took a step forward. Another step.

She was just about to call out, to distract Vitaly, to get him to turn away from Jamie. Then she froze.

Just below the base of her skull, she felt the cold press of a ring of metal.

'Nicola Ellis. Imagine meeting you here. Put that pea-shooter on the shelf there.'

Nicola put the SIG on the shelf next to her, then turned around, hands raised. She looked into the eyes of a man she'd never met but whose face she knew nearly as well as the battered civilian she'd sent into this place alone.

Operative GARNET gave her a slow, predatory smile.

Part Four

CRISIS POINT

48

Operative GARNET

Terminal 1, Charles de Gaulle Airport: four days ago

William Geoffrey Price, better known to most by his cryptonym of
GARNET, was many things, but incautious was not one of them. He
arrived early at Charles de Gaulle, then circled the terminal four times
before finally picking up his crash package.

The plain manila envelope was tucked behind the polystyrene roof
tiles of a toilet cubicle at the other end of the terminal, well away from
his planned meeting with Stringer and Tulloch. Inside, a clean Can-
adian passport with his face staring out from the ID page, a neat wad
of five thousand in US dollars. Plus the special item he'd asked for: a
wicked-looking close-combat belt knife with a thumb loop and slightly
curved blade. It had cost a little extra in bribes to get it past airside
security, but it was worth it to show up in Dar es Salaam not *totally*
defenceless.

Package secured and the belt knife stashed where he could reach it,
he headed to the other end of the terminal to recon the handover
location. It was a disabled toilet, big enough for all three of them to
talk, to swap clothes and hand luggage.

This handover *had* to be clean. First so that London would believe
their agent had been successfully inserted. Second so that Bocharov
would believe he'd turned that same agent. Both would be wrong.

On the first close pass, there was no sign of Stringer: the toilet door stood slightly ajar, lock disengaged. He glanced through the narrow gap as he passed, then swung around into the men's, pissed, strode back out on to the concourse. Time to settle in.

He was halfway down an early Americano before he saw Stringer. Early, as usual. Well before the Legend was due to arrive. Price felt the dampness on his palms as he drained the last of his coffee. He'd been waiting with Stringer for nearly a month now, rotating between safe-houses in London as they prepped him to take over Jamie Tulloch's life. He was deeply familiar with the sorry wee shite of a man he'd be impersonating. Familiar enough for a good deal of contempt to have been bred.

Stringer didn't spot him. That was something. Price felt a small flutter of pride that he could still outwit the old bastard when he needed to. Stringer fancied himself a field man still, even though he couldn't see much past the end of those thick, ugly glasses he wore. In the safehouse, prepping for this godforsaken op, he'd even seemed to take a paternalistic shine to Price. Regaled him with stories of the heady post-Soviet days in Berlin, digging through Stasi archives in search of treasure.

Price waited a beat, then followed.

He rapped the identifying code on the door, glancing left and right. Still very early, with hardly anyone about. The bolt shot over to green and the door opened a crack. Stringer's myopic eyes peered out at him.

'You're early,' he said, opening the door just wide enough for Price to slip through. 'Very early. He's not due to land for nearly an hour.'

Price grinned at him, giving him the full-wattage smile. He leaned back against the tiled wall.

'Want to get a coffee? Reminisce on all our lovely hours sitting in badly ventilated flats around London? I'm game if you are.'

Stringer didn't return the smile. Instead, he leaned against the opposite wall.

'I'm glad you came a little early, actually.'

Price flicked his eyes across the older man's face. The rapport from the safehouse was gone. Stringer watched him closely. He pushed his hair behind his ears and looked down at his battered shoes. 'How much do you know about cell spoofing, William?'

Stringer looked up. Something in his eyes froze Price where he stood. It was the needlepoint focus of the hawk, just before it swooped on a field mouse. Price blinked and shrugged.

'A bit. Set up a temporary cell, copy the local cell mast's ID, copy all the traffic. Trivial to do, especially for older phones. The hard part is doing anything with the data, since most of it's encrypted. That needs GCHQ muscle.'

Stringer's eyes remained fixed on his face. 'Sure does. Unless you've copied the device IDs and you can decrypt it. But you need physical access to the device. And a strong enough reason to go to the trouble.'

A twitch of half-realised intention passed through Price's right arm. His hand desperately wanted to go to the device in his coat pocket, the burner phone he'd been careful never to leave anywhere, never to have off his person. The phone he'd been using to communicate with the contact he called SCARAB, his insider at the Cross, who'd got him what he needed to do this job-inside-a-job. The person who had finally talked him around, convinced him he could extricate himself from the Legends Programme, make the money he'd always been denied in government service and leave his country stronger and smarter into the bargain. SCARAB had a plan. And that plan had unfolded in a dozen meetings and pre-arranged texts at the right time.

But he'd been in those safehouses with Stringer for a month. A man can't be alert all the time, can't stay awake or carry a mobile handset into the shower with him. It would have been the work of a moment to pull the SIM out, get the device IDs, run it through a cloner.

He'd been so careful. Texts only when he was alone, the occasional late-night call. So, so careful. But there had been no other way for SCARAB to give him what he needed. They'd had to take the risk.

Too much of a risk. Something, who knew what, had piqued the older man's curiosity. And curiosity had turned to suspicion.

Terence Stringer pushed himself away from the wall. He stood, feet spread, shoulders set square. Did the old man want to fight him?

'Who is SCARAB, William?'

'What?' said Price, still leaning against the wall. The LED lights flickered a little and he felt the twitch of an overstrained eye muscle in his right eye, a product of too little sleep and too much coffee. 'Like, the beetle?'

'Yes, like the beetle. I've got a full record, you know. Took me a while, even with a cloned SIM. Had to pull in some favours, borrow some tools. Couldn't get the call records, unfortunately, but I managed to read the text messages last night.'

Price smiled, slow and wide. 'So why am I not banged up in a sub-level cell at the Cross, with handcuffs on?'

Stringer stood perfectly still, hands loose by his sides. He really thought he had a chance to stop his protégé from leaving this god-forsaken little French toilet. Had he managed to get a gun through security? Or a knife? If Price could do it, so could Stringer.

'William, I've been doing this long enough to see most things. I know there's secondary objectives. Sealed orders. Cerberus ops where you report to more than one handler. I've been on them myself. But this isn't how it's done. I like you, William. I wanted to give you the chance to tell me what this is. Why you're not following protocol. I want you to tell me you and whoever SCARAB is haven't sold out the entire Legends Programme. That this is SIS business, and I just don't need to know about it yet. Please, tell me that's what this is. Ten years we've worked together, William. Please.'

Price kept the smile on like a mask. But the pulse in his throat made it hard to speak. He was blown. He was full-spectrum fucked and it was all because this nosy old bastard had decided that a few calls here and there, outside this safehouse or that, warranted investigation. Why couldn't he have just kept his nose out of it? All of the brotherly bonhomie he'd spent years building with Stringer was for nothing.

Stringer grimaced. It looked like he was going to cry, for fuck's sake. Then, with a flash of the eyes, the sorrow was replaced by burning anger. 'I take it by your silence that I'm right. You cheap fucking bastard. You've sold us out for what? A few tens of thousands? An apartment on the Sochi waterfront? Who are you working for? Who's SCARAB?'

Price cleared his throat and straightened up. 'I'm not going to stand here and listen to this shi—' he began, taking a step towards the door.

'No, you are. You're a serving officer of SIS, you prick,' said Stringer. He stepped forward and shoved Price against the tiles with both hands. Price blinked in shock at the older man. Didn't think he had it in him.

'I think—' Price started, but Stringer was in close, face reddening with anger.

'I'm taking you back to London. I don't care if we burn a decade of prep. I'm not putting you in, not until you've explained this shit. Or had it dragged out of you at the Cross. But you're coming with me and we're getting on the next flight back to Heathrow.'

Stringer's hands came up to grab Price's jacket collar, to pull him in close.

Before he knew what he was doing, the belt knife was in Price's right hand, half-trapped between their two bodies. Stringer's breath was hot on his cheek.

He shoved with his left hand and lashed out with his right, the wicked curved blade slicing through softness at the far extent of his outstretched arm.

Stringer's eyes went wide. Price blinked rapidly, blood spatters hot on his shirt and eyelids.

The older man staggered backwards, emitting a low, groaning exhalation, severed windpipe rattling. His hands went to his throat, blood seeping between tightly pressed fingers. He tripped and fell straight backwards, hitting the wall hard enough that his body went limp, jammed between the toilet and the wall.

The smell of blood was overpowering. Price leaned back against the wall, heartbeat hammering in his ears.

'Jesus fucking Christ,' he murmured. 'What the fuck. You stupid old bastard.'

He slid to his haunches, still leaning against the tiles. The knife dangled from the thumb loop, his hand coated with red.

He took two breaths, three. He was in some deep shit. But there was a way out. There was always a way out.

He washed the knife, trying not to look at the dead man on the other side of the sink. Then his face and hands. His leather jacket he could wipe clean. His T-shirt he turned inside out. After a couple of minutes, he no longer looked like he'd just sliced open his handler's throat. The sink was red with diluted blood, but a few minutes more careful scrubbing got rid of that.

Once he'd dried his hands, he pulled the burner out of his pocket. Would they have assets close enough to help him? He had an hour, perhaps less. If they could get the body out of here, he could run the handover with Tulloch. Claim that Stringer wasn't available. It would work. It *had* to work.

He dialled the number.

'What the *fuck* are you calling me for *now*? You're supposed to be in the pipe, not phoning me,' said SCARAB. Her voice was heavy with sleep. It was an hour earlier, in London.

'We've got a problem. Handover went bad. I need a clean-up team.'

'Where are you?'

'Charles de Gaulle. In the disabled toilet. Looking at what used to be Stringer.'

A long silence on the line. 'Get out of there, right now. Lock it behind you. I'll get a clean-up crew there, but you'll have to do the handover with Tulloch somewhere else. Get to his gate and keep a lookout for him.'

Price found himself nodding, suddenly eager to be anywhere but this tiny, tiled room that smelled of metal and death. 'Got it. I know the gate. There's another toilet like this one, at the other end. I can intercept. We shouldn't really be seen together, but I don't have an option.'

SCARAB's voice dripped with anger. 'I don't want to know what happened. But are you compromised? Did Stringer have something on you?'

'No. He thought it might be a Cerberus op. Thought you might be another handler. Couldn't believe I might have betrayed him. He was weak. Sentimental. He hadn't called it in yet. Well, that's what he said anyway.'

'For your sake and mine, we'll have to hope that's true. I can slow-walk things this end. But find Tulloch, do the swap, then get the fuck out of France.'

49

Jeremy

Corridor, Sub-level 2, Vauxhall Cross: now

Outside the room where Jeremy was grilling Sarah Grey, a row of vending machines faced a long wall of grey doors, surfaces broken only by black numbers. Padded benches between the machines gave interrogators somewhere to take a break, a few minutes away. Interrogation, at least how Jeremy had been taught to do it, was an extended exercise in empathy and emotional manipulation, a deep, exhausting synchrony of persuasion, anger, retreating, regrouping and trying again. The only thing that had come close were the long weeks when it seemed like his marriage might be saveable, 3 a.m. conversations over whisky at the kitchen table, voices low to avoid waking the girls.

He stared at the packaged sandwiches inside the vending machine, rubbing at the stubble on his chin. Remembering those conversations brought back the visceral fear from that morning, imagining the girls at school, right under the flightpath for City Airport. A bubble of nausea made the thought of a sandwich impossible, so he sat down on the bench next to the machine. Jeremy leaned forward and rested his head in his hands, rubbing at his eye sockets. His head pounded with fatigue.

Someone approached on soft-soled shoes.

'Whatever it is, please fuck off,' said Jeremy through his hands, past caring if it was the Chief of SIS herself stalking down the hall towards him.

'Um, okay. But it's good news. At least, I think it's good news,' said Sally Lime.

He looked up, bleary-eyed.

She stood on one foot, as though she was about to turn on her heel, her laptop folded under one arm.

'Sorry, Sally. I'm knackered. Got her to speak at last, but she clammed right up again. I was just regrouping. Any luck with Boxwood?'

Lime gave him a wide grin, then sat down, pushing her glasses up her nose and opening the laptop. She folded her legs under her and leaned back against the wall. 'Well, we know who he is now, anyway. Grigori Yurlov. Russian national, hacker-for-hire, veteran of an FSB cybersecurity unit, on the open market since the collapse. All these guys are guns-for-hire, except for our girl in there. She seems to be a true believer, judging by her recruitment profile.'

Jeremy nodded. 'In what, I can't tell you. But yeah. The grudge goes deep.'

Sally was typing fast, windows flying. 'So Yurlov gave us something. We've got more levers on him, as a foreign national. And he *really* doesn't want to go back to Russia. Seems like a bunch of people in the New Russia might be gunning for him, for a whole range of reasons.'

'Do we know who their insider was? Who got Grey her clearances?'

'Not yet. And Yurlov didn't have any direct contact. Sarah Grey was the cut-out. But whoever they are, they needed a bit of help to scrub the record. Yurlov wrote them a script to do the job.'

'And he gave you a copy?'

Lime grinned even wider. 'He did. It's a nasty piece of work. But now I've got the source code, I can reverse-engineer it, I think. See what it deleted. And who uploaded it. If they were smart, they did it from someone else's terminal. But we can match that up with badge records. They'll have missed something. I know it.'

'How quickly?'

Lime glanced over at him. 'The answer is always going to be "less quickly than you'd like and faster than anyone else in this place", Jez. I dunno. A couple of hours, maybe?'

Jeremy glanced at his watch. It was getting close to 10 p.m. The last report from Nicola on Zanzibar had mentioned a possible shipment, a big transaction of some kind. He'd been so focused on cracking Sarah Grey that he hadn't had much chance to properly read everything. He felt stretched, his attention in too many places at once. He was missing something.

'We need to find whoever Grey's insider is. As fast as we can. If we don't, I'm worried that we'll lose our opportunity on the Bocharov op. There's something here. I just can't ... I can't quite make it fit together.'

Sally Lime patted him gently on the shoulder. 'Eat something, boss. I'll work on this. Maybe it won't take that long.'

Her laptop chimed and her head snapped forward to peer at the screen. 'Oh, you cheeky bastard.'

'What?' said Jeremy, leaning over, fatigue falling away.

She pointed at the screen. 'They scrubbed the clearance files for Grey with this Russian worm, then deleted the logs. But just like the camera footage, our live logs caught them. You can see the edits happening. Including the terminal IDs for the initial upload.'

'And where's that?' said Jeremy.

'Fourth floor. Africa region. One of the tepid desks.'

Jeremy raised an eyebrow and frowned. 'Tepid ... desks?'

'Like hot desks, except everyone sits in the same place every day.' Lime grinned. 'Come on, you always go for that window seat. Get in fifteen minutes before anyone else to snag it. I've seen you.'

Jeremy laughed, a dry wheeze, then stood up and punched in the code for another can of Coke. He cracked it and took a sip. 'I'll need the natural light after being stuck down here. So, someone on that floor uploaded the worm. Probably the same thing that took out the camera logs, right?'

'A variant, yeah. That one went in with the 5G dongle that Sarah installed. Neat little package. But same idea.' She stood up and closed her laptop. 'I'll start backtracking through the badge IDs and internal surveillance on the adjacent floors. I'll find them.'

'And I'll keep working on our friend in there,' said Jeremy. He took a swig of the Coke. It felt sticky, coating his tongue and teeth. But he couldn't stomach coffee this late at night. 'Anything new on that analysis package we sent back to Nicola?'

'Nope, but I can check the flash traffic?'

'Do it. I want to know what the hell's going on over there. Hopefully nothing. It's the middle of the night.'

Lime nodded. 'I'm on it. Seriously, though, eat something. We're nearly there. I can feel it.'

50

Jamie

Wine cellar 2, Rayskiye Vrata: now

The next time he woke up, there were more people in the room.

Vitaly stood back against the galvanised-metal bottle racks, wiping his knuckles with a cloth. He'd managed to cut his hand, probably on Jamie's teeth. Jamie blinked and ran his tongue around inside his mouth. He still had them all. That was something.

By the door, Olenev paced back and forth, muttering under his breath in Russian. He had a rifle slung from his shoulder. Things must have escalated since they'd dragged him in here.

Bocharov sat opposite, his usual linen suit and silk shirt swapped for a more practical khaki number, black combat trousers and boots. He also carried a rifle, resting across his knees. Those piercing eyes were fixed on Jamie.

'I am very disappointed in you, Jamie. Very disappointed. They tell me you are not even trained. You are here by accident. This much I knew already. But I hoped you would not try anything so stupid as this. I hoped, truly, that I could do this deal and let you leave here. But you overheard too much. Made your little recording. You are not very good spy.'

Jamie tried to speak, but it came out as a dry croak. Bocharov signalled to Vitaly with a jerk of the head. The big man came over with a plastic bottle of water. He wetted Jamie's lips and let him swallow a couple of mouthfuls. Jamie coughed, then tried again.

'I'm still practising,' he said, then managed a half-smile around his bruised eye socket.

Bocharov blinked, then boomed a laugh that sounded oddly flat and menacing in the tight confines of the wine cellar. 'I *like* you, Jamie, really. This was not a lie. But you spied on me and my guests. You are SIS asset. This is not a good thing.'

Jamie shrugged. 'The other guy didn't show up. They asked me to watch and listen. That's all I was doing. You're obviously doing something really, really bad in this place. I mean, aside from all the illegal cobalt mining and killing people and so on. Something *extra* bad.'

Bocharov's eyes narrowed, and Jamie could have sworn he saw the beginnings of a vein pulsing at his temple. 'I make money. That is what I have always done. That is why I'm *useful* to those giving away Russia piece by piece. But not any more. I am going to take them on. Make Russia strong again. And there's not a damn thing the British or the Americans or the Chinese or anyone else can do about it.'

Beside the door, Olenev cleared his throat. 'Let's keep any details to ourselves, yes, Arkady?'

Bocharov snorted. 'He's a dead man anyway. What does it matter?'

'Operational security. And it's worked out, despite our friend's mistake in Paris. Just like I said it would.' Olenev turned to the doorway. 'Bring her in,' he called.

A moment later, a man came in, dragging a woman with a black hood over her head. Even before Bocharov rose and the woman was zip-tied to the same chair, Jamie's stomach felt hollow with dread and certainty.

The man stepped into the light of the bright lamp that had been trained on Jamie's face.

It was him. GARNET. Jamie's alter-ego, replacement, doppelgänger. The man who should have been here instead of him all along.

Jamie blinked, looking from Bocharov to Olenev and back to GARNET.

'What—' he managed, before GARNET leaned forward and plucked the hood off the woman's head. Just as Jamie had feared, Nicola blinked in the sudden light.

'Your name is Nicola Ellis,' said Olenev, stepping between them. 'You are field handler for GARNET. You were never supposed to meet this man, Jamie Tulloch.'

Nicola said nothing, eyes fixed on Olenev, mouth set in a thin line.

Olenev shrugged. 'All of this is known, Nicola. Our friend GARNET told us. He works for Mr Bocharov. He has for more than three years. What I don't understand is why you sent Jamie here to do this job. He is' – Olenev turned and regarded Jamie with a long, appraising look – 'not a suitable man. For this kind of work. What did you think he could do?'

Jamie coughed, then spat on the floor. Olenev looked down at the frothy, blood-flecked saliva, lip curling with distaste. 'I don't believe a man such as this is a threat. But Ellis here is another matter. If she is here, then there will be others.'

Bocharov grimaced. 'Where? In the compound? Do we need to search?'

GARNET shook his head. When he spoke, it was with the same lilting, Central Scotland accent that Jamie had heard before. 'I trailed them, from Stone Town onwards. There's three others I've ID'd – one SIS field station asset and two local operatives. At a resort south of here. We can't go in there without creating more problems than we'll solve. Too many tourists. Too many cameras.'

Olenev shrugged. 'We shoot these two, put them in with the cargo and dump their bodies well out at sea. The reef sharks will take care of the rest.'

Jamie felt his skin chill in the damp coolness of the cellar.

'Da, good,' said Bocharov. He turned to GARNET. 'You did well, William. Thought on your feet. And now we have these two.'

'London won't like it,' said GARNET. 'Losing another field officer. They'll look into it. SCARAB has been slow-walking the Paris investigation, but they won't be able to do that for her. Too high pro-file, internally.'

Bocharov shrugged. 'It will be too late by then. We will be well on our way. And after that, nothing that happened here will matter.'

Olenev leaned back against the shelving. 'We have one hour. I don't think we should wait. If we wake up Brunner now, we can have him there when everything arrives and get the cargo back on the boat before dawn.'

Bocharov sighed. 'It is late, Yevgeny. I am tired. You really think we cannot wait?'

Olenev shook his head. 'If this woman is here, SIS are close. We have to do this before daylight.'

Bocharov rubbed at his chin, where a faint dusting of stubble was beginning to show. 'Maybe you are right. Okay, wake up Brunner. We have a lot to do and not much time to do it.' He looked at Vitaly. 'Lock these two in here. We can put them on the cargo boat when it leaves. I want it done away from here. No evidence.'

Vitaly nodded. 'And the men?'

Bocharov frowned. 'Who is sober? All of this was meant to happen tomorrow.'

'Squad Ekho. They are the reserve tonight.'

Bocharov nodded. 'Wake them up. I want five on the boathouse, five on Brunner and his men. This needs to go smooth.'

GARNET stepped forward. 'Where do you want me?'

Bocharov smiled. 'You, I want to do your original job, instead of Mr Tulloch here. We will make a nice little package for London. Con-fusion. Disinformation. They will not know what to believe. Yevgeny will brief you.'

GARNET nodded, then followed Olenev out of the room. Nicola was still staring at Bocharov, her face stony. Jamie looked up at the big Russian. He was shaking his head.

'You know, I was not lying, Yakov. I really did like you. Even when I knew you were lying to me. But most of it was not lies, yes? You are like me in many ways.'

Jamie shuffled backwards until he was sitting properly upright against the chair back, the zip ties on his wrists biting. He snorted, inhaled deeply through his nose, then spat on the floor again, right between Bocharov's boots. When he spoke, it was with the voice he'd used back home, growing up on rain-washed concrete.

'Big man, I'm nothing fuckin' like you.'

Bocharov shrugged, shouldered his weapon and strode out of the room. Vitaly snorted, then followed Bocharov, closing the metal door behind him. With the finality of a guillotine falling, the door's bolt slid home.

51

Nicola

Wine cellar 2: now

'I'm sor—'

'Jamie, I'm really—'

They both spoke at once, both apologising. Nicola shook her head. 'You've got nothing to be sorry for. We put you in this situation. I did. You shouldn't even be here.'

Jamie shook his head right back at her. 'I was stupid. I thought I'd get something big. Something to make Terence dying worth it. But I fucked it up. Didn't check my angles, like you taught me.'

Nicola sighed. 'Jamie, when I train a field agent, I usually get five or six *weeks* to show them the absolute *basics*. A man like GARNET has been training for years. This isn't your fault.'

Jamie's head sagged back and he stared at the concrete slab ceiling for a moment. 'Are we going to die? It seems like, whatever they're planning, they don't mind killing us to keep it secret.'

'We can't think that way, Jamie. Let's keep focused on what we know. Did you get anything, before they grabbed you?'

His head came back up and he nodded. 'There's something down in the boathouse. Like a cage? So they can keep something in it while they do their deal. Whatever it is, they need to inspect it.'

Nicola frowned. She'd seen some similar things in drug deals or major black-market weapons deals: sealed containers whose ownership could be transferred with a thumbprint or a keypad code once cash was counted or fund transfers verified. A sign of high-risk cargo, low trust between the parties involved, or both.

Jamie flexed his shoulders. 'These zip ties really hurt.'

Nicola flexed her shoulders, testing whether she could move her hands. Nope. GARNET had done a textbook job, backs of the hands together behind her back, a tight zip tie to hold her arms back, then another looped to the base of the chair she sat on. Which was, of course, bolted to the floor.

She looked around the room. Nothing within arms' or legs' reach. No handy sharp edges on the chair itself. Just a lamp that was already making her eyes hurt, shelves full of dusty bottles and a bruised Scotsman staring at her.

'Isn't this where you slip a concealed blade out of your watch or something? Or a boot knife?'

Nicola laughed, despite herself. 'You've watched too many films, Jamie. We don't get issued knife watches, generally speaking. They took everything else off me.'

Jamie managed a half-shrug. 'What is . . . what is all this? Why would GARNET be working for the Russians? Does that mean he killed Terence?'

'Looks like it,' she said, shuffling upright in her chair. The pressure on her shoulders was becoming extremely painful. She leaned back, arching her back to take some of the weight off the joints.

'But why?'

'Money? Political convictions? I have no idea. I don't think any of this was planned, except maybe compromising Legends.'

'What do you mean?'

Nicola leaned forward a little more. 'I think Stringer dying was a fuck-up. If they turned GARNET a while ago, they wanted to make him a golden goose.'

Jamie grinned. His teeth were red with his own blood. 'See, you tell me it's not like the movies and then you say shit like that. What the hell is a golden goose?'

'Someone you think is working for you. Nobody wants to kill the golden goose, when the product is so good. Problem is, it's bullshit. But bullshit that *feels* right.'

Jamie nodded. 'So Bocharov's planning something big, and he's recruited an SIS Legend operative to help him keep it secret?'

'More like keeping it camouflaged. Hide it in a flood of other, semi-plausible wild-goose chases.'

Jamie nodded. 'So if it had all gone to plan, I'd be in South America right now, none the wiser. And GARNET would be sending you dutiful reports with really exciting stuff in them, but it would be bollocks.'

'Exactly,' said Nicola, her stomach hollow at the thought. She liked to think she'd have been smart enough to spot obvious disinformation, but there was the lurking suspicion that she'd have seen a career-making treasure trove in what GARNET fed her, a chance to move back to the UK, to get a Desk of her own. Would she have looked hard enough? If it sounded convincing? Would she have found the integrity to say something, if she *did* have suspicions?

Maybe. Maybe not.

After a long beat, Jamie spoke again. 'So now they're panicking, because they don't know how much I overheard? Bringing forward their deal, trying to get whatever this is away from here as fast as they can?'

Nicola nodded. 'They're going to use every tool they have. Throw out chaff. Confuse and disorient and misinform.'

Jamie groaned. 'I bet GARNET's going to pop up, pretending to be me? Like, actually me, pretending to be him, pretending to be me? London will think they can trust me, because I'm me, but it'll be him.'

Nicola screwed her eyes shut, trying to make sense of that word salad. 'That makes my head hurt.'

Jamie grunted. 'How do you think it makes me feel? I'm having a fucking identity crisis here. I'd like to know exactly who I am before I end up dead.'

Nicola grimaced. Jamie was right. However GARNET chose to mislead London, all roads led to both of them being dropped into the Indian Ocean and never heard from again. 'What did he take off you?'

'The secure phone, the laser mic and one of the wee listeners you gave me. He made me unlock the phone before Vitaly started punching.'

Nicola swore under her breath. 'That's what I'd do. If I wanted to stop anyone looking deeper into what happens tonight. Muddy the waters.' She flexed her hands, prickly numbness spreading.

Jamie had lapsed into silence. She looked up. He had his head back, dried blood crusted on his jawline. A stab of guilt lanced through her again.

This man, who had been trying to help her, far beyond anything he had signed up for, had taken a hell of a beating. And he would very possibly die before dawn on the rusted, diamond-pattern steel deck of a Kenyan motor trawler.

'Jamie, mate, can you move your arms?'

He pulled his head vertical and blinked at her. 'What?'

'You've got to keep your body moving. Keep the circulation going. I need you to be able to walk, if we get out of this.'

Jamie shrugged, the movement curtailed by the clink of zip ties against the metal chairs. 'I thought you didn't have a laser watch.'

'Knife watch,' she said, smiling.

He chuckled, then sagged forward. 'Oh, hey, that's a different kind of pain,' he said, face down, eyes on the floor. 'Variety is the spice of life. Change is as good as a rest, so they say.' His eyes drooped closed.

'Stay with me, mate,' she said, a bubble of despair rising in her chest. It broke and she swallowed, shaking her head. 'Come on, stay with me.'

She wasn't sure how much time passed after that, just each minute deepening the pain in her arms and the despair in her chest. With no clock on the wall and no way to look at her watch, she was reduced to counting heartbeats, occasionally calling out to Jamie to try and keep him awake. It was nearly silent in the narrow, dusty room, just her breath and Jamie's, intermingled. Occasionally, she thought she heard shouts in the distance, but they always faded to nothing before she could turn her head and locate the source.

Once, for just a moment, she imagined she heard Rachael's voice, the words she'd said in Hampstead.

I want you. I want this. You have to choose, Nicola. But make a choice. Don't let them do it for you.

Nothing, for a long time.

Then, footsteps. Light and quick, with a curious cadence to them. Purposeful, but measured in a way that suggested caution.

The bolt slid in the door behind her. She twisted around, but the zip ties were too tight to get her head around. She felt the change in the room's air as the door swung open, then two more light footsteps.

Jamie pulled himself back up, eyes rising to the open door. He sighed loudly and rolled his eyes.

'Oh, fucking magic. Now they've sent the bloody Yank to have a go.'

'I'm not a Yank, man,' said a deep voice just behind her. 'I'm from Colorado.'

5²

Jeremy

Room 19A, Sub-level 2, Vauxhall Cross: now

'We're closing in on the truth here, Sarah. We know they uploaded a script to remove the evidence. Your little friend Yuri gave us that. He's cooperating.'

That got another flicker. It had been nearly an hour since he'd come back in. Grey had eaten the sandwich, then gulped down most of the bottle of water. She kept a little in reserve, on the table in front of her. Smart. Husbanding her resources carefully, never assuming that food or water or rest would come at any sort of predictable time.

She took another small sip, eyes studiously avoiding Jeremy's face as she drank.

'Aren't you getting bored of this, Sarah? I know I am.'

Bugger. Admitting a human frailty of your own was a bad move. Tiredness. Hunger. Boredom. Because a bored interrogator was one who might eventually give up. He'd been trained to be infinitely patient, to always be there, ready to end the tedium and the repeated questions, if only the subject would just give up a little tiny piece of information. Just the smallest crack in the facade.

But the training only counted for so much. Because he *was* bored. And tired. And hungry. And increasingly, deep in his heart, despairing. There were too many things to chase down, too many small points of data which might turn out to be nothing. And no way to differentiate the blizzard of information from the truth that would help him disentangle this whole horrible mess.

Sally Lime put her head around the doorframe. 'Boss, got a minute?'

Outside, she stood with her laptop open across one arm. Stuart Alden from Internal Security was with her, along with two of his officers, both toting holstered handguns and sub-machine guns.

'What's going on?'

Lime nodded towards the door. 'Grey's going back to Holding, and you're coming with us to Chiswick.'

The two security officers looked to Alden, who gave them the nod. They disappeared inside the room and Jeremy heard the low, metallic click of unfastening cuffs and the gruff undertone of the officers getting Grey to her feet. They emerged with her between them, then headed off down the corridor.

'What's in Chiswick?' said Jeremy, although a disquiet was building, a certainty that he already knew.

'The home of the person who authorised Sarah Grey's hiring, fast-tracked and signed off her security clearances personally, then filed the work orders that got her into our network,' said Alden.

Lime was grinning. 'I was right. When we matched up badge IDs and cameras, you can see the pattern. It's mostly circumstantial, but I'm betting I can find hard evidence once we get there.'

'Get *where*?' said Jeremy, fighting the exasperation rising in his voice.

Alden's face was stony. 'Stephanie Salisbury, head of the Africa Desk. Who we have reason to believe is an active mole and insider for Russian non-state elements.'

Jeremy blinked. The disquiet in his belly had become a full-blown ache. Suddenly, a lot of things made sense. The delays following up Stringer's disappearance. The constant reassurances without any concrete action. Muddying the waters at every step. Stephanie Salisbury had been there all along, a helping hand that was actually choking the supply of information. But why?

'Fuck,' he managed, leaning against the grey wall behind him. 'Fuck,' he said again.

'Come on, time for kicking yourself later,' said Lime. 'We've got a tac squad on the way, but we're going to try knocking nicely. Hopefully she hasn't scarpered already.'

He followed them in a daze, up through the bowels of Vauxhall Cross to the underground parking garage two levels up. It was empty, cold and clinically lit by white LEDs, concrete grey. Four black SUVs came swinging in, doors opening before they'd fully stopped. A tactical team waited inside. Jeremy found himself sitting next to Captain Wilton, who had been in charge of the warehouse assault. Less than twenty-four hours before. It felt like a lot longer.

'We have to stop meeting like this, Captain.'

Wilton nodded. 'It's been a long day, sir. A very long day.'

They pulled out of the Cross and on to Vauxhall Bridge. As they crossed the Thames, Jeremy leaned back, looking out at the darkness of the city, the lights of boats on the river. Not far to Chiswick, and then perhaps some answers. He checked his watch. Nearly midnight.

His phone buzzed. He took it out and frowned at the screen. Unknown number. This was a secure, anonymous, mission-specific SIS phone. You weren't supposed to be able to phone them without a paired device.

'Hello?'

'Jeremy. Excuse me busting into your comms like this, but I tried every legit channel I have and I've been getting stonewalled for the last hour.'

Jeremy's mouth dropped open. He hadn't spoken to Alexandra Bowen, his CIA contact and one-time friend, in over three years. And yet here she was, calling him on the Operation AEGIS secure line. 'Alex? How the hell did you get this number?'

'Long story. Listen, we have a mutual interest in what's about to go down on Zanzibar. And I need you to know a few things, real fucking fast.'

53

Jamie

Wine cellar 2: now

'Did Vitaly tell you we were here? Ask you to put in a few licks yourself?' said Jamie, voice rising. His heart rate had tripled since the huge American had stepped into the room.

Klein reached back and swung the heavy metal door shut. He towered over Nicola, but his eyes were fixed on Jamie.

'Y'know, a guy can get real tired of being mischaracterised,' said Klein, reaching into the pocket of his heavy-duty combat trousers. When his hand emerged, the lamplight glittered on a sharp edge. 'I'm just doing a job here, man.'

Klein put one hand on Nicola's shoulder, then leaned forward, the blade flashing as he brought it up.

'Don't you *fucking* touch her!' Jamie yelled, thrashing his legs. 'Fuck you, you big Yank bastard. Take me on, come on! I'll fucking end you, ya cunt!'

Klein held up his knife hand. 'Jesus Christ, Tulloch, shut the fuck up,' he hissed. Then in one swift movement, he bent and sliced through the zip ties around Nicola's wrists.

She twisted around in her chair, staring up at the huge mercenary.

'What . . . the fuck?' she managed.

He shrugged at her wide eyes. 'Alex Bowen and the CIA send their regards.'

Klein had already crossed the room and sliced through Jamie's bonds by the time Nicola stood up. He pulled Jamie upright and put a rough-callused hand on his jaw. 'Big Vit really took it out on you, huh? I sparred with him a couple of times. Guy's got a mean right hook. You're a tough little bastard, Jamie, I'll give you that.'

'Sorry, who are you?' said Nicola.

'Cody Klein,' said Jamie. He sat forward. 'I didn't manage to get a picture of him. But he was in one of my texts.'

Nicola frowned. 'The mercenary?'

Klein grinned. 'I prefer "soldier of fortune" myself. Got that eighties ring to it, y'know. "Security contractor" is just so blah.'

Nicola stood up and flexed her shoulders. 'And you're helping us because . . .'

'Because you sad sacks are going to blow nine months of operational planning and two years of infiltration work if I don't get you off this compound. And I need your help too. Shipment just came in. I gotta verify what it is while the guilty parties are all up in Bocharov's office burning the midnight oil.'

She nodded. 'Got a weapon I can use?'

Nicola was all business again. It astonished Jamie just how quickly she adjusted to this new reality. Jamie felt like a small child in comparison, still struggling with the terrible news about Santa Claus.

'But I thought . . .' Jamie murmured.

'That I was a horrible fucking guy? You think the CIA only recruits clean-cut Yale and Harvard men? Come on, man. These are dirty wars we're fighting here. Assholes like me are the front line.' He turned to Nicola and pulled a silenced pistol from his waistband. 'This yours? Price left it on the shelf out there. Careless asshole, you ask me.'

Nicola grinned. 'Yep.' She took the weapon and checked the chamber.

'What—' he started, but Klein was already at the door.

'Time for catch-up later. Right now we gotta boogie down to the boathouse, get eyes on that shipment and then get the fuck out of here. Come on.'

Jamie started to say something, but then he felt Nicola's hand, tight on his shoulder. 'You get between me and Cody, okay? And if the bullets start flying, you get on your belt buckle and you stay there, got it?'

Jamie swallowed, nodded, then followed Klein out into the dimness of the underground corridor. A few paces later and they were outside again. Jamie had never been so glad to breathe fresh air in his life. He realised, as he squatted there in the shadow of a thorn bush, that he had fully expected to die in that musty basement.

Klein pointed along the road. 'They woke half the camp up. The ones who were still sober after your little field trip. Got 'em walking the perimeter mostly, but there's a couple of roving patrols on the road. At least five guys in the boathouse itself.'

Nicola had the pistol in both hands, her face serious, lit by the distant floodlights on the road. 'Take it low and slow?'

Klein shook his head. 'Nah. All we got going for us is speed. They get a bead on us, they'll mag-dump and that'll be that. I figure two entry points, take 'em down faster than they can react. You think you can handle that?'

Nicola rolled her eyes. 'A tour in Afghanistan, mate, then six years of anti-piracy and smuggling ops. I can handle it. Can you? You get rusty, clubbing cobalt miners over the head for a living?'

Klein's lip twisted. 'I've stayed on top of it. Train myself and my guys hard. You don't need to worry.'

'Good. Then what are we waiting for?'

They rose and started down the hillside in the dark, Jamie between them, with absolutely no idea what they were about to do.

54

Nicola

Rayskiye Vrata: now

Klein led the way, his silhouette huge in the dimness. Nicola marvelled that a man that size could move so swiftly and silently. Twice they stopped and waited in the darkness as roving patrols moved past on the road. But the Russians were intent on securing the floodlit pathways around the compound, not on poking around in the thorn bushes.

'Any of your guys on duty tonight?' she whispered, once they'd settled in just up the slope from the boathouse.

'Negative. They've been pulling duty on the gates and the house during the day. They're asleep now. None of them are assets either — they're all single-spectrum scumbags. Unlike me. I contain multitudes.'

Nicola glanced at the big man and he flashed her a white-toothed grin in the dark.

'Any idea of dispersal inside?' she said.

'I got a good look when they were bringing the case in. Eight total, I think.'

'We'll need to go fast. If any of them gets a shot off . . .'

Klein looked left and right along the road. 'No time like the present. Roving patrols are as far as they're gonna get from here.'

Nicola glanced at Jamie, squatting in the darkness beside her. 'You get down in this bush, mate. I'll stick a hand out of that door once it's safe to come in.'

'What if you both get shot?' said Jamie.

Klein nodded towards the beach gate. 'Sneak down there. See if you can make a break for the beach.'

Jamie grimaced. 'That sounds like a shite plan.'

Klein shrugged. 'Better hope we win then.' He pulled a suppressed pistol from his waistband, a chunky Glock 19, checked the action and nodded at Nicola. 'I'll go left, you go right.'

'Roger.'

They slipped down the last couple of metres of grassy bank and into the pool of light by the boathouse's side door. Nicola tried to picture the boathouse interior, then stopped herself. No sense overlaying her imagination on what lay ahead. Better to see clearly and react. Set an expectation with guesswork and you added milliseconds to your reaction time, your mind continually reconciling what you'd imagined with what you were actually seeing. Best to go in blank.

She breathed slowly. In through the nose, out through the mouth, her SIG at the high-ready, elbows tucked in tight. Twelve rounds in the magazine, eight possible targets. If she double-tapped, she could handle six of them. If she didn't miss.

Klein leaned into the doorframe, the planes of his face lit from above, harsh white. She nodded and he pushed the door open with his fingertips, then swung around the frame and inside.

She was right behind him, travelling a little further as she pushed the door in a sweeping arc. It was dim and stuffy inside the boathouse, most of the internal floodlights turned off except for three at the far end.

Two huge speedboats took up much of the space, along with four jet skis on a trailer. Racks of wetsuits hung on the walls, along with net bags filled with life preservers, diving fins, masks. A neat row of charged air cylinders lined the wall to her left.

Behind her, she heard the sound of Klein firing. In this confined space, the suppressed weapon was loud, nothing like the whispered huff of the popular imagination. Instead there was the simultaneous *click-crack* of the action snapping back on Klein's Glock and the muffled thud of the round firing itself, like someone dropping a heavy book on a concrete floor. A groan followed the first shot, but it was quickly silenced by a second shot. One down.

A shadow stepped from behind the speedboat directly in front of her, a silhouette carrying a rifle. She squeezed off two rounds, centre of mass, before she'd fully registered the target. The soldier slumped to the oily concrete, his weapon skittering away under the speedboat's trailer. Two tangos down. Six left. Ten rounds in the magazine.

A muttered curse in Russian from the other side of the boat, then a shot from behind her. The curses leapt up a notch, then another shot cut them off. Klein must be working his way along the back of the shed in the darkness, firing between the boats.

She stepped over the prone figure of the man she'd just shot. She'd caught him in the upper chest and throat. His hands were clawing at the wound, eyes wide in the dimness. He wouldn't last long.

Around the end of the speedboat, into the more open end of the shed. Folding chairs and a white plastic table strewn with cards, abandoned now, two of the chairs tipped over, their previous occupants dispersed into the shadows.

She turned to the left, sticking to the darkness, using a huge sail locker for cover. One of the Russians was waiting there, his rifle held high. But he was facing in the wrong direction, weapon tracking the sound of Klein's progress on the other side of the shed. He called out, low, speaking in Russian.

'Sergei? You still up? Who is it? Is it the Italians? What the fuck is going on?'

Nicola fired once. He pitched forward, sprawling across the sail locker, then slumped to the floor. The mercenaries were well equipped, wrapped in assault vests and modern AK-variant rifles. But they weren't wearing helmets or body armour, thinking themselves safe inside their compound.

Two more shots from Klein.

'You, get on the package,' said a voice in Russian. 'Stupid fucking Italian, the package!'

She saw a figure break cover and run towards a large metal cage in the back centre of the shed. She fired from the shadows, missing with her first shot and hitting with the second. The Italian contractor crumpled forward and slammed into the concrete, as though he'd simply been switched off.

'*Blyat*. Where the fuck is Sasha?'

Nicola kept moving. Seven rounds remaining. How many guards left?

She found two crouched behind the jet-ski trailer. Amateurish, bunching up like that. She'd shot one of them before the second reacted, twisting and bringing up a carbine AK-105. He was a slim man, balding, his face scarred. He managed to get a bead on her and fired, the flashes lighting up the interior of the shed like lightning.

She returned fire as he stepped backwards, stumbled on the corpse of his comrade. Nicola fired again and he fell, the carbine clattering to the floor.

Silence. Her ears hummed after the thunderous discharge of the AK. 'Ellis?'

Klein came around the second speedboat, his weapon held high. He saw the two bodies and lowered his weapon a touch, then caught sight of her squatting in the shadows. 'How many you get?'

'Five,' she said softly.

'Nice. I got three.'

She was already up and moving, checking the bodies. Two were still alive, but rapidly bleeding out. She paced quickly to the side door where they'd entered and stuck her hand out for a quick flash of her palm. A moment later, Jamie came scrambling in at the door.

'Jesus Christ, I heard gunshots. I thought—'

'One of them got a couple of rounds off. Did the patrols hear it?'

Jamie shook his head. 'I don't think so. I did, but I was right here.'

Klein beckoned them over. 'Either way, we don't have long. Come on. We gotta figure out which of these dipshits is the guy in charge.'

They joined Klein near the cage, Jamie's eyes widening at the carnage the two of them had inflicted in such a short space of time. He stepped gingerly around the pooling blood on the concrete.

'All right, this guy's got a name tag. You read Russian?' said Klein, pointing down at one of the men.

'You don't? I thought you worked with them,' said Nicola, turning the body over. The tag named the man as Sergei Antonov, with 'Lead Contractor' underneath in smaller text.

'Nah, never got the hang of Cyrillic. I can speak it though.'

Nicola pointed. 'This guy. Does he have a keycard or something?'

Jamie looked at the man's hands. 'When I was listening in, when they caught me, they said something about thumbprints. Biometrics.'

Klein was already at the cage, a heavy cube of blue-painted bars, each the thickness of a human wrist. No way they were getting through that without oxyacetylene torches and plenty of time.

Klein nodded. 'There's two pads though, one each side of the door.'

Nicola bit her lip, eyes searching across the boathouse. 'Dual authorisation. Someone else will need to use the other pad. Probably one of the Italians? Brunner's men.'

Klein was already dragging the body of Antonov towards the crate. 'Try that guy. He's got an Italian flag on his shirt.'

Nicola walked over to the man she'd hit while he was running. It was a neat shot, for a moving target. She grabbed his assault vest and started dragging. After a moment, Jamie took the man's legs, although his eyes kept straying to the bloody head wound. Eventually they got both bodies to the metal cage. Nicola peered through the bars and saw a large, matte-green equipment case in the centre of the floor. It was nearly two metres long and a metre wide, large enough to carry a major piece of military hardware.

'All right, on three,' said Klein, holding up Antonov's hand. Nicola did the same for the dead Italian and they pressed the men's thumbs to the pads simultaneously.

Nothing happened for a second, then the pads lit up green and the gate built into the cage unlocked with an electromechanical clunk. Jamie grabbed it and swung it outwards. All three of them stepped inside. Klein wedged the gate open with Antonov's arm.

He caught her staring at him and shrugged. 'What? You wanna get stuck in here if that gate closes behind us?'

She stifled a nervous laugh at the macabre spectacle of the dead Russian wedged into the gate, then shook her head. 'This fucking job, man, I swear.'

Klein stepped into the cage and flipped the latches on the equipment case, then knelt and extracted a phone and a small yellow box from the pockets of his combat trousers. He took a long breath, then looked back at them. 'You might wanna step back. Just in case.'

She nodded. 'What the hell is in there? We've been running traces on this shipment since yesterday and we can't work it out.'

'Nothing good,' said Klein, then lifted the lid.

It took Nicola a moment to understand what she was seeing. At first she thought it was some kind of bizarre sculpture, a sharded, irregular shape, crusted and rounded with strange growths and extremities. But then the underlying pattern became clear, broken and partial though it was.

'Is that . . .'

Klein held up a hand, then took the phone and began snapping pictures. Nicola realised that the object was encrusted with barnacles and decades of seabed detritus. Klein got in close, focusing on faded white lettering on the device's casing, stencilled long ago. Nicola leaned in herself, read the letters under her breath.

MK-41 MOD O

The numbers weren't familiar. But the sound, when Klein switched on the yellow box next to his foot and ran it over the crumpled shape inside the case, very much was.

The ticking, clicking, crackling sound of death incarnate.

Nicola took an instinctive step back, neck prickling with animal fear.

'Confirmed radiological,' said Klein, shooting a video with the phone. He focused the camera on the Geiger counter's digital readout. 'Object is confirmed as the partial core of a Mark 41 nuclear weapon, circa 1961. Also confirmed presence of Uranium-238, looks like most of the tertiary. As suspected, we have a Broken Arrow, likely from the 1963 Operation Starshine incident. Hot weapon core, with damage. Closing the case now to limit exposure.'

Klein thumbed the video off, then closed the lid.

'Dirty bomb?' said Nicola softly.

Klein nodded. 'That's what we think. It's American. We lost a B-47 off Morocco in 1963. Disappeared into the sea. Second one, actually, in that area. They lost another in 1956. USAF was so embarrassed they reclassified it as a training accident. And they didn't recover one of the nukes.'

'Which is what we're looking at?' said Jamie, his face pale in the bright light focused on the cage.

Klein stood up. 'The core anyway. But it's a twenty-five-megaton core. Biggest weapon the US ever fielded, officially. You can't set it off without a shitload of explosives, but it's a *lot* of radioactive material. And this shit stays nasty for a long, long time. We think he's going to use it in Russia.'

Nicola frowned, mind twisting at the idea, then something slotted into place. 'He's going to try and repeat the apartment bombing trick. Shit.'

Klein nodded. 'Bingo.'

'What?' said Jamie.

Klein looked grim. 'Putin. Back in '99 he was the Russian prime minister. Allegedly, the GRU staged bombings of four apartment blocks in Russia, then blamed 'em on the Chechens. Putin got himself a nice little second war, winnable this time, and *that* got him the presidency. You probably know the rest. The bombings killed three hundred people, but Putin came out of it on top.'

Somehow, Jamie managed to look even paler. 'They said something, about a target. About flying this thing to . . . to Omsk? I think they said?'

Klein inhaled through his teeth. 'That fits. Dirty-bomb some mining town in Siberia. Claim it's a US special ops cover-up or some shit. Maybe even Omsk itself. Bocharov's a Muscovy boy, he doesn't give one solitary flying fuck about the rest of Russia, as long as the money keeps coming.'

'We can't leave this here,' said Nicola, staring at the huge case.

'You got a spare forklift?' said Klein. 'Or at least four guys? Because that's a lead-lined case right there. Probably weighs six hundred pounds.'

Nicola frowned. 'If we drop a cruise missile on this place, we'll be spreading radioactive material across half the island. But we'd need a shitload of operators to take this place from the Russians. And they'll have this case out of here before we can get anything like that spun up.'

Klein shook his head. 'Not necessarily. We're close. But we've got to buy some time. Get this intel out of here and brief the assets we've got nearby.'

Nicola shrugged. 'Maybe we can hide the bodies? Lock them out?'

Jamie looked thoughtful for a moment. Then he stepped outside the cage and peered at the access pads. A moment later he laughed.

'I know these access pads.'

'What?' said Klein, head snapping up.

'These pads. They're from one of our competitors. NextSecure. Hang on.'

Jamie gingerly reached down and grabbed Antonov's arm again, then pressed his thumb to the pad. He held it there until the light above the pad turned amber, then red.

Jamie grinned. 'We can recode them. To our thumbprints. Then they won't be able to get back inside the cage. Maybe it will, I don't know, give you some time to' – he shrugged – 'figure something out?'

Klein smiled. 'Smart. Ellis, you guys recode the pads. I gotta take a couple more shots.' He bent down and re-opened the case, the phone's camera flashing.

Nicola nodded and stepped out of the cage, then repeated the trick with the Italian's hand. She stared at Jamie. 'On three?'

'One, two . . . three,' said Jamie. They both pressed their thumbs to the pads. The lights cycled from red back to amber, then eventually green. The lock cycled.

'They want back in now, they'll have to catch both of us,' said Jamie with a grin.

55

Operative GARNET

Bocharov's private office: now

Luca Brunner was not best pleased at being rousted out of bed to oversee a last-minute change to the deal he'd spent months preparing for, but his attitude soon changed when Bocharov offered to sweeten the pot with a ten per cent premium on the price.

'We need this done now. And you and your men off my compound before sunrise.'

Brunner steepled his fingers and gave a short nod. He was somehow immaculate still, even at this hour, dressed in his usual light jacket and blue shirt and wide awake. Price guessed overseeing the transfer of extremely illegal nuclear material on a windswept Zanzibar beach was an effective stimulant.

'I am ready when you are. The device is secure, with your team and mine. And we'll be out of here as soon as the funds clear, you have my word.'

The way things had played out was almost better. More authentic. With Ellis and Tulloch dead, Price could spin any story he wanted. He'd be able to get out of this shitty business. When he'd left the Army, SIS had seemed like the perfect next step, after his brief sojourn at the Foreign Office. Field work. Really making a difference. But

when SCARAB had come calling, he'd already been primed, sick of
the mealy-mouthed arse-coverers in Whitehall. SCARAB's offer
would finally let him claw back some of the decade-plus he'd lost to
SIS and, more specifically, Jamie Fucking Tulloch.

Christ, he hated that man. A jumped-up gobshite from the
schemes who had everything Price wanted and didn't even seem to
like his life that much. The deep satisfaction of seeing Vitaly hitting
him had almost been worth the absolute panic when the stupid sod
had skipped through Paris an hour early and nearly screwed up
everything.

But it was fine. Everything was going to be fine.

Bocharov typed on his laptop, authorising the funds transfer. Three
of Brunner's men stood behind the Swiss arms dealer, their rifles carefully pointed at the floor. Bocharov was flanked by Vitaly and two of
his men, also armed. When you were doing a nuclear-grade arms deal
at one in the morning, it was best to take precautions.

Price smiled to himself, then caught Olenev's eye again. The rat-faced
Russian wasn't smiling. Too much of a poker face. There was another
arsehole Price would be glad to get shot of. Betrayal was a dirty business
and he didn't much like it, even if it was his ticket out of this sordid,
secretive half-life.

'Okay, I will begin the transf—'

Vitaly's hand shot to his ear, the sudden movement causing a ripple
of shifting rifles and hissing breath. Bocharov held up a hand. 'Podozh-
dite, all of you. What is it, Vitaly?'

The big mercenary was listening. Price could just about hear the
tinny voice speaking into his ear, the crackle of static.

'Suspected gunshots. In the boathouse.'

Bocharov stood up, his chair shooting backwards. Suddenly there
was a gun in his hand, a chunky-looking Udav service pistol.

The gun was familiar to Price. He'd shown it to him, the night he'd
arrived, the threat obvious. 'Used this in the Donbas,' he'd said, smiling

when Olenev had introduced them. 'Used it a lot. On people who bullshitted me. Are you bullshitting me, William?'

Olenev had convinced him, two nights ago, that Price could be trusted. That they could still go ahead with the deal even after the fuck-up in Paris. But now, he could see that same paranoia bubbling up in the stocky paramilitary, those wartime instincts resurfacing.

'Brunner, why have you fucked me? I have your money. Right here. I hit the key on this laptop, you take your money, you go. Why would you do this?'

Brunner had both hands up, his men stepping back and raising their rifles. 'Arkady, this is not me, I swear. You said it yourself. Why *would* I do this? I want my money, and I want to get the fuck off this island. This is someone else. Something else. Please.'

The room was silent for a heartbeat, then another. Vitaly's earpiece crackled again. 'Roving patrols are closing on the boathouse. No response from Team Ekho.'

Bocharov's eyes narrowed. 'Your men?' he asked Brunner.

The arms dealer twisted in his seat. One of his guards spoke rapid Italian into his earpiece. He waited a moment, then shook his head. 'Nothing, boss. Our team is offline too.'

Brunner held his hands up. 'This has to be someone else, Arkady. The British? You said this one was SIS, right?' he asked, jerking his chin towards Price.

Olenev stepped smoothly to Price's side. 'But working for us. I suggest we get a team down there right now,' he said, turning towards Bocharov and Vitaly. 'Make sure the device is secure.'

Bocharov wavered for a half-second more, then holstered his sidearm and nodded to Vitaly. 'Do it. I want my weapon. Kill anyone you find.' He strode out of the room, followed by Vitaly, then Brunner and his men.

The room emptied except for the two of them. Olenev twisted to stare at Price. 'Is this you? Is this SIS? Have you betrayed me, you motherfucker?'

Price shook his head in disbelief. 'Of course I haven't. Everything's still on, I promise you. I have no idea who's shooting down there. Maybe one of your guards got drunk.'

Olenev shook his head. 'I doubt it. Someone has betrayed us, William. And I'm going to find out who.'

56

Jeremy

Barrowgate Road, Chiswick, London: now

Jeremy was still reeling from the call with Alex Bowen by the time the black SUVs pulled up just shy of Stephanie Salisbury's home. A covert asset inside Bocharov's inner circle. Jamie *and* Nicola captured and, hopefully, released. And worst of all, a possible nuclear threat, sitting in Bocharov's boathouse.

Jeremy sat a moment, rubbing at his temples. There were so many things he needed to escalate to four or five pay grades above his current position that he had no idea where to start.

'Sir? You want to take the lead here?'

Jeremy looked up. Probably best to start with arresting an SIS desk chief. Yes, that's the ticket. Start the day off right. He checked his watch. Just after midnight. Technically a new day.

'Yes. I'll knock politely. Maybe you can come with me, Captain Wilton. And make sure we cut off the rear exits. Let's take it cautiously.'

He climbed out of the SUV as two files of black-clad troopers jogged past. One went to the garden wall and stacked up, covering the front of the house. The other team disappeared swiftly through a high wooden gate into the presumably huge rear garden. He'd always fancied Chiswick himself, but never quite made the salary for it.

The house itself was a red-brick Queen Anne-style semi-detached villa, three floors with white-painted sash windows. A green Audi was parked up at the side of the house and the windows were dark.

Jeremy took a deep breath, then strode to the front door, Wilton at his side. The captain's rifle clinked gently against the D-rings on his assault vest, loud in the pre-dawn quiet. Jeremy knocked loudly. 'Stephanie?'

Silence. No lights turned on in response to the knock, inside or out.

He knocked again, then waited. The silence stretched out in long seconds, divided by his hammering heartbeat. Was she still at the office? Had they even checked?

Wilton coughed lightly. 'I'd suggest we take the door, sir.'

Jeremy nodded. Wilton flashed a hand-signal. One of the troopers came around the garden wall with a heavy battering ram in his hands.

'Might take a couple of hits,' said Jeremy softly. 'Senior SIS people often have upgraded security measures.'

Wilton smiled in the darkness. 'Not to worry, sir. We've kicked in a few doors in our time.'

The remaining troopers filed around the garden wall, weapons up to cover the windows above. The ram hit the door with a heavy crash.

A second, then a third crash and the door gave way, lock splintering. The rammer stepped aside and the troops went streaming in through the door.

'Movement rear,' said a voice in Jeremy's rear. 'One IC1 female, coming out the back door. No weapon visible.'

'Take her,' said Wilton, following the men in.

By the time Jeremy got through to the back garden, passing through the shadowed house as the soldiers swept it with their weapon-mounted lights and laser-target indicators, Wilton's second team had Stephanie Salisbury sat on her back lawn, arms flex-cuffed behind her. She was dressed in jeans and a pair of slip-on Chelsea boots, a hoodie thrown over a T-shirt against the chill air.

'What the *fuck* are you doing in my house, Jeremy?' she said as she caught sight of him climbing the terraced steps to the rear lawn.

'Oh, I think we both know the answer to that, Stephanie. Or is it SCARAB, to your friends?'

Salisbury managed not to show any reaction to her cryptonym being used. The one which had hidden her identity as she had slow-walked his investigation, covered up the death of Terence Stringer, betrayed her country and put Jeremy's team in danger.

The soldiers lifted her to her feet and he caught a flash of defiance on her face. 'I have no idea what you're talking about,' she said.

Jeremy shook his head. 'Sarah Grey and Grigori Yurlov say different. And we're just getting started.'

57

Jamie

Gate 3 (beach): now

'Fuck,' muttered Cody Klein under his breath.

The road up to the boathouse was busy, men streaming up from the beach gate, more coming from the security buildings nestled below the road. Shouts in Russian and Afrikaans rose from the men as they jogged back the way Nicola, Jamie and Klein had just come.

Nicola pointed to the gatehouse on the inner fence line. 'There's only two of them on the gate. We've got to go now.'

A vehicle came rolling down the road, headlights dark, heading towards the beach gate. Four guards jumped out before the vehicle had fully stopped and jogged towards the floodlit gatehouse.

'Fuck,' said Klein again.

'All right, six. Maybe we can sneak past. Some kind of distraction.'

Klein nodded. 'I'll light up that GAZ,' he said, pointing at the vehicle, some kind of boxy Russian version of a jeep. He produced a Zippo from his shirt pocket. 'You guys circle around to the right and make for the gate. I'll go to the left.'

'Got it,' said Nicola. They crept along the line of thorn bushes and acacia trees on the right side of the road, getting closer to the road and the triple fence line.

As they got closer, Jamie saw that the men were mostly local

Zanzibari guards, wooden-stock AKs in their hands. They were talking in Kiswahili to each other. The two others were Russians, eyes narrowed in the floodlights, hands to their ears as they listened to the radio chatter. Jamie glanced back up the slope. A dozen or more figures were clustered around the boathouse. They didn't have long.

On the other side of the road, Klein darted out and squatted in the shadow of the vehicle, doing something to the fuel cap. A bright flicker of flame lit his face, then he moved away again, back into the shadows. The flame appeared to go out for a second, then there was a flash and a long tongue of fire erupted from the open tank.

Jamie braced himself, expecting a loud explosion, but instead the fire spread rapidly, catching the canvas roof and the seats inside, fuelled by evaporating, burning petrol.

The guards at the gate sprinted forward, weapons raised, surrounding the burning vehicle, eyes squinting against the brightness and intense heat.

Jamie looked away, the flames leaving bright purple after-images on his eyes. He blinked and swore to himself. 'Fuck, I can't see,' he said softly.

'Come on. Look at the floodlights,' said Nicola. She grabbed his shoulder and pushed him forward. 'Move.'

They ran, keeping to the shadows until the last ten metres, when Nicola broke cover and jogged across open ground towards the gatehouse. Klein was already there, ducking under the vehicle barrier. Beyond were two more fence lines, the outer one closed with a gate that Jamie hoped didn't have any sort of lock on it.

Klein was already three steps beyond the gatehouse barrier when another man stepped out of the gatehouse, rifle levelled. He screamed something in Russian. Then he caught sight of Nicola and Jamie and swung around to cover them.

Klein raised his weapon to fire, but it was too late. The other two Russians had turned away from the burning vehicle and aimed their own weapons. They had all three of them covered, rifles pointed at their heads.

'Down, down, on your knees,' the one by the gatehouse screamed in English.

Jamie thumped down into the dust, staring out at the darkness beyond the fence lines. They had been so close. Now he could see only the harsh white glare of the floodlights, the rippling yellow-red of the burning jeep behind him. And the crunch of booted feet as the Russians approached.

The night split with gunfire, bright white flashes and hammering reports. Jamie dived to the gravel, hands clamped over his ears. It sounded like someone had fired a rifle right next to his head.

Sudden silence. A low groan from his right. He looked and saw one of the Russians struggling to sit up. Klein stepped forward and shot the man, the pistol action clacking, almost silent compared to the roar of the AKs.

Jamie blinked, his breath coming in short huffs, hands shaking. An hour ago he'd never seen anyone die in his life. Now he was losing count. But who had shot them?

He turned. The other four guards were standing in a line across the road. One stepped forward.

'Emmanuel,' said Nicola, there beside him suddenly. 'What—'

The soldier in the lead, his baseball cap low over his eyes, nodded towards himself and the other soldiers. 'We are TISS. Mr Komba is very, very angry with you. He's outside. Come, quickly.'

Jamie struggled to his feet. The figures up at the boathouse were turning and running towards them along the floodlit road.

'You okay?' said Nicola. 'Can you keep up?'

Jamie grinned, still shaky. 'Vitaly mostly punched me in the face, not the legs,' he said.

The three of them set off at a dead run, the local guards with them. They crossed the second fence line, then the third, Emmanuel producing a key which opened the outer gate. Then they were on dry sand, which soon turned into wet. Jamie kept looking behind him as he ran. The compound was lit up like Christmas, floodlights right along the fences, the villa's windows blazing.

Two figures crouched in the darkness, a hundred metres or so from the fence line. When they rose, Jamie recognised one as Graeme Sylvan, the look of relief on his face obvious when he caught sight of Nicola.

'Fuck me, Nic. What the hell have you done?' he said.

'What's he doing here?' said Nicola, nodding at the other man, dark-skinned in a windbreaker and small round glasses, who looked absolutely furious.

'He picked us up after you went off with the Russians. Then he got a phone call and brought us here,' said Sylvan.

Klein jogged to a halt. 'Mr Komba, I believe?'

Komba nodded. 'You are one of Bowen's?' he asked. 'You have an extraction plan? Because I cannot help you any more than I already have.'

Klein nodded. 'Two-fifty metres thataway,' he said, pointing along the beach.

They turned and kept running, Komba and Sylvan falling in alongside them. After a hundred metres or so, Jamie made out a low, black shape in the white surf. Klein was talking into a radio he'd produced from his seemingly endless pockets.

'Halftack, this is Mike Three, I'm inbound hot to your position for pick-up. Got hostiles on my tail. Nine friendlies. Hold your fucking fire.'

'Roger that, standing by,' said a clipped American voice.

Thirty seconds of running later they met a compact soldier in an all-black combat suit kneeling at the surf line. Behind him was a large rigid inflatable boat, pulled up with its bow on the beach and an anchor dug into the sand. Three more troopers were dispersed around the boat, covering the beach. Jamie's heart was hammering, his breath coming in ragged gasps. He found himself regretting every single skipped workout of the past decade.

'All right, let's get the fuck off this beach and back to the *Tripoli*,' Klein said.

'What about Komba and his men?' said Nicola. 'We leave them on this beach and they're fucked.'

Klein shook his head. 'They got time, they can get clear.'

As if in refutation, something cracked overhead, followed a second later by the thump of a distant weapon. Jamie ducked, swearing softly to himself under his breath. He wasn't sure what was worse, being beaten to death by an angry Russian in a wine cellar or bleeding out on the surf line of a Zanzibar beach.

'Hold your fire, hold your fire,' said the soldier squatting beside Klein. 'It's not effective yet. We can't defend this position, sir. We gotta go.'

Komba flinched as another round cracked over his head. 'Perhaps it is best if we get off this beach, sort things out elsewhere.'

Klein nodded. 'Good call. Get on.'

'Anchor in, shove off,' said the special forces soldier. One of the other men went to lift the anchor as they all pushed the boat back into the water. Jamie felt it float free and the engines rumble into life, then he clambered awkwardly over the wet, black nylon of the boat's tubes. He fell into the bottom of the boat in a painful heap as Nicola hopped nimbly over him and aimed her pistol over the side.

'Contact, one hundred metres south. We'd better move or this boat's going to have some holes in it,' she called back over her shoulder.

'Roger that. Hold on to something,' said the American at the wheel. The engines kicked in and the boat carved a tight turn in the water, spraying them all with foam and sea salt. Then they were out, smacking across wave tops, into the darkness.

58

Nicola

USS *Tripoli*, 12 nautical miles north-east of Zanzibar: now

It looked like a grey wall, somehow dropped in the middle of the ocean. The Navy RIB had soon cleared the choppy waters directly off the coast of Zanzibar. They had been bouncing over low, slow swells of waves in near-total darkness for about half an hour when Nicola first saw the dark shape breaking the horizon line. As they approached, the crewman at the boat's helm spoke softly into his radio.

'Baseplate, this is Halftack, coming in on your port side. Multiple pax aboard.'

She heard a quiet acknowledgement, then the grey wall resolved into the side of a ship, stretching at least a hundred metres in each direction. They motored in and bumped gently against the grey-painted steel. Above, a platform jutted a metre or so out of the hull. Two seamen in blue environmental suits appeared and lowered a wide ladder.

'Is this an aircraft carrier?' she said quietly.

Klein shrugged and grinned. 'Sorta. Helicopter assault ship for amphibious ops. Got some F35s on board too, Ospreys. US Navy, baby. We bring our own air force.'

They climbed up the ladder and on to the platform one at a time, timing it with the swell. At the top of the ladder they were quickly ushered through a hatch into a narrow, grey-painted passageway. A dark-haired woman in a green bomber jacket and khaki trousers waited for them. When she saw Nicola, she extended a hand.

'Nicola Ellis? I'm Alexandra Bowen, CIA. Jeremy says hi.'

Nicola wasn't quite sure what to say, so she settled for shaking Bowen's hand.

Bowen turned to Jamie, still damp from the spray on the boat, his eyes wide as he took in the ship he'd just boarded.

'And you're Jamie Tulloch.'

Jamie blinked at Bowen. 'You . . . you were in Wales. When I signed up for . . .' He gestured around him. 'Well, I mean, I *didn't* sign up for this, but you know what I mean.'

Bowen grinned. 'Good memory. You ever considered a career in intelligence?'

Bowen led them through the *Tripoli*'s Combat Information Centre, lit by low red lights, sailors bent over monitors, radar and sonar read-outs. They didn't so much as look up at the motley crew of civilians, Zanzibari security guards and tattooed ex-Marines being led past them. Nicola admired their focus.

Bowen had established an ops room in a cabin next door. More monitors and screens, but it was a temporary affair, laptops and coffee cups spread across folding tables. There was barely enough space for them all to fit. Alexandra cast an eye across the group, especially the four guards from Bocharov's compound carrying their ancient AKs.

'Mr Komba. I appreciate your help in extracting my asset. How would your guys feel about a quick meal and making those weapons safe in our armory, for now?'

Komba didn't look happy, but his men had perked up considerably at the mention of food. 'Are you in Tanzanian waters here? Because you should not be.'

'We're inside your economic zone. But territorial waters are about a mile that way,' said Bowen, pointing to the west. 'Really, the Navy has the best food of any of our armed services.'

'Very well,' said Komba. 'But I am keeping my sidearm.'

Bowen nodded. 'Of course.'

The four guards filed out, led away by a young woman in a dark blue shipboard uniform. Bowen sat down. 'We don't have much time. So I'd appreciate a briefing on what just happened.'

Klein quickly laid out the sequence of events that had found them sprinting down the beach towards the SEAL team that had picked them up. With each sentence, Bowen's back got a little straighter, especially when Klein passed his phone across the table and she viewed the images and video he'd taken. Once he finished, she sat back.

'This is what we were afraid of. We were prepping to go in with two SEAL task units, in about an hour. But that was before you stuck a stick in this particular anthill and stirred it up. Ah, Captain Reynolds, Commander Rodriguez, great timing.'

Two officers came through the hatch from the CIC, the first a red-haired, serious-faced white woman in her forties wearing a baseball cap with the ship's name on it, the second a wiry, slightly younger man with dark hair and sharp, watchful eyes. They both nodded to Bowen, then looked around the strange assortment of people gathered at the table. Nicola was impressed by their poker faces. She caught a glance from Jamie, his eyes wide. If it was surreal for her to be sitting on an American assault ship, how must he be feeling?

'We've got confirmed radiological material at the target site,' said Bowen as the two officers sat down. 'But the extraction of our asset went hot. That place is riled up, at least company-strength hostiles. Possible anti-air, if I'm any judge. It'll be a hot LZ. But we have to make a decision on this immediately.'

A voice spoke from one of the wall monitors behind her, making Nicola jump. Since she'd sat down, three faces had appeared. They were in Washington DC, judging by the daylight in the background.

'What are the tactical options, Commander?' said a man with greying hair and a loosened tie, on the left side of the monitor.

Rodriguez sat forward. 'Option one – proceed as planned. But we'd expected to be hitting a camp with half the hostiles asleep. The scoop-and-run we had planned for that boathouse relied on taking down the beach-side gate guards quick and quiet.'

'Seems unlikely you'll be able to do that,' said the grey-haired man.

'Correct. Option 2 is . . . well, the literal nuclear option.'

Captain Reynolds broke in. 'We're loaded for bear, sir, TLAMs with JMEWS hard-target warheads. We'd put two on that boathouse at least.'

Nicola blinked, unsure she'd heard correctly. 'You want to hit a nuclear core with a hard-target cruise missile?'

Komba, who had been following the acronym-filled conversation with an increasingly bemused look on his face, blinked in astonishment. 'Who am I talking to?' he said to the grey-haired man.

'Who am *I* talking to?' said the man.

'I am Adil Komba, Tanzanian Intelligence and Security Service. I extracted your asset for you. And you are talking about dirty-bombing the coastline of our busiest tourist island. Deliberately.'

'I'm Lloyd Haverman, Secretary of Defense for the United States. And no, Mr Komba, we are considering our tactical options. That material represents a significant nuclear escalation risk if it reaches Russian territory. They'd blame the US. And the New Russian regime is still weak. We'd have to roll a lot of sixes to get through *another* armed coup in Russia without things going sideways. So we stop this material here, where we found it.'

Komba shook his head. 'By blowing it up? In a resort half full of civilians, including some of my men. On a coastline with a dozen resorts within thirty kilometres. And an island with over eight hundred thousand inhabitants? I must tell you, Secretary Haverman, the United Republic of Tanzania would consider this an act of war by the United States.'

Bowen held up both hands. 'Woah, woah there. Let's cool it down. We don't have time to get side-tracked into an argument. Commander, I get the feeling you had at least one more option for us?'

Rodriguez nodded, then glanced at Captain Reynolds. 'The JMEWS option would rely on the shipment still being inside that boathouse. We don't know if they've moved it. And short of levelling every structure in that compound, then going in to check with a task unit, there's no guarantees.'

'We locked it. With our thumbs,' said Jamie, suddenly finding his own voice.

'I beg your pardon?' said Rodriguez, turning to look at the pale Scotsman sitting three along from him.

Nicola smiled at Jamie as he sat forward. 'The device is being held in a transit cage, locked with biometrics. We recoded it to our thumb-prints. That cage has bars three inches across. It'll take them hours to get it out of there.'

Klein slid his phone across to the Navy SEAL commander. Rodri-guez picked up the phone and swiped through the pictures. 'Okay. That makes Option 3 our best bet. That thing looks like it's wired into the compound's power grid, right?'

Klein nodded. 'Yeah. Back-up generator though. If you're thinking what I'm thinking.'

Rodriguez grinned. 'Even if the cage stays powered, it'll be harder for them to work on it in the dark. Option 3 is we drop an EK2 TLAM on them. The Enhanced Kit 2 has graphite filament scatter to take out surface power lines *and* a localised EMP burst to knock out generators and unshielded electronics. We'd have to time it so it was right before our Seahawks landed.'

Klein grinned at the blank faces around the table. 'We drop a cruise missile on them that fries their power. Then land our teams by chopper.'

Rodriguez nodded. 'We've drilled this possibility. Rest of the mis-sion profile would remain the same. One task unit on the villa and securing the road. Another securing the beachside fence line. Pop the shipment out of the cage, extract by sea. Teams get out on the helicopters.'

'But he just said it will take hours to get through that cage?' said Komba, pointing at Klein.

'We've got the keys right here,' said Rodriguez, smiling. He nodded at Jamie and Nicola. Nicola felt the glimmer of hope that this might work flutter in her chest, mixed with concern for Jamie. He wasn't trained for any of this. But she was.

Rodriguez continued. 'We take them in with us, pop the cage. If the back-up power on the cage is dead, I'm pretty sure we can get through it faster than Bocharov can. We have a few toys they don't.'

'What are the risks here, Commander?' said Haverman from the monitor.

'Delay, sir. The longer we wait, the more likely they get that shipment out of here. We can have a TLAM on target in a few minutes.'

Reynolds nodded. 'Less than three minutes' flight time from our current location.'

Haverman nodded. 'And how quickly can you prep the third option?'

Reynolds frowned. 'We don't have a Kit 2 TLAM loaded. Say, thirty minutes max?'

Rodriguez shrugged. 'I'll need at least that long to brief my teams on the amended plan and get the aircraft loaded. Flight time is fifteen minutes. We make the decision now, we can be on target inside an hour.'

Komba nodded. 'I prefer this option a great deal. We still have some assets inside the compound.'

Nicola frowned. 'More of the local guards?'

A slow smile spread across Komba's face. 'All of them. They are guarding the external fence line. The Russians have concentrated themselves on the villa, the boathouse and the security buildings.'

'Wait,' said Bowen. '*All* of the local guards in that compound are your men?'

Komba leaned back. 'Oh, the Russians were very diligent in their interview processes. They found two or three of our men in their interviews, rejected them. But we made sure *all* of the candidates were TISS.'

Rodriguez smiled. 'If you can give us the beach gate, that would be a major win.'

Komba nodded. 'We can do that. But then my men will withdraw. In the dark, one man with an AK looks much like another. I don't doubt the professionalism of the famous US Navy SEALs, but I will not risk a friendly-fire incident. My men can withdraw to the beach, help secure it for the exit of the material. I will tell them that when the lights go out, they must head there.'

Rodriguez nodded. 'Sounds good to me. You have comms with them? Can you give my pilots any additional information?'

Komba nodded. 'Of course. They are already providing me with many updates.'

Bowen looked quizzical. 'You got some kind of encrypted radio network?'

Komba laughed. 'Agent Bowen, this is the twenty-first century. We have a group chat.'

Bowen blinked, then chuckled. 'Field-expedient comms. I love it.' She looked down at her phone, then up at the monitors. 'Speaking of which, sir, I've got someone else to add to the conversation. My opposite number at SIS. Can I conference him in?'

Haverman grunted. 'Awh hell, why not. Let's make it a party.'

59

Operative GARNET

Boathouse: now

'Why can't you cut the fucking hinges off?' roared Arkady Bocharov. 'There, look! Just cut them.'

The sweating soldier holding the roaring oxyacetylene torch flipped up his welding mask and grimaced.

'Those are manganese steel, sir. I could try, but it would take hours. The rest of the cage is regular rolled steel, with titanium cores. More bars to cut, but it will be faster, I promise.'

Bocharov stood perfectly still, hands bunched, staring at the hinges on the cage's gate like he could slice them open with sheer willpower. Then he threw his hands in the air and turned away. 'Fine. Do it. Fucking do it.'

When Bocharov had discovered they couldn't open the cage with the thumbprint of his dead guard, he'd lost his temper for a full fifteen minutes, breaking the dead man's arm against the bars of the cage in his fury. Olenev had calmed him down eventually, but it had still taken too long to find the cutting gear, get it brought down and start work. It had been nearly half an hour since the firefight at the beach gate. Time was running out.

The soldier flipped down his welding mask and went back to cutting, the solid-steel bars of the cage glowing under the continual assault of the torch. They'd already gone through one tank of fuel and had only cut two bars at the top. Price eyed the remaining two tanks of fuel.

'We're not going to get through this before dawn,' he said softly to Olenev.

'In the worst case, I have a chopper coming from the mainland. It will get us out of here. We can pin the whole mess on Bocharov, just like we planned. Just a little earlier,' the other man whispered, his face impassive.

'Ah, fuck yes!' muttered the soldier with the torch. One of the bars had clattered free. 'Sir, if we just want to get the material out, we only need to cut three bars. We can put the material in another case.'

Bocharov smiled. 'A very good idea, Yuri. We can pull the lead lining out and slip it through the bars too. It will be messy, but we will save a lot of time.'

Olenev glanced at Price and spoke in a low voice. 'Or perhaps we can take the weapon after all. And leave Bocharov here. I have briefed my own men. You must handle Vitaly, if it comes to that.'

Price nodded and swallowed. Vitaly was watching the cutting intently from the other side of the boathouse, cradling a rifle in his arms. If it came to that, William Price knew his own limitations. Vitaly would be getting a bullet to the back of the head. If he played this right, he could still come out ahead. William Price always came out ahead.

60

Jeremy

Ops Room 9, Vauxhall Cross: now

Salisbury had cracked, not long after they'd got her back to the Cross. Faced with the sheer weight of evidence against her, her craven opportunism and self-interest had come bubbling out. Jeremy had wanted to stay in the room, to wrench every secret out of her himself, but things were moving too fast on Zanzibar. Sally Lime got the duty ops room up and running and coordinated with the Americans for a live link-up. Which is how he found himself staring into the face of the US Secretary of Defense at half past one in the morning.

'Lloyd Haverman. And you are?'

'Jeremy Althrop. SIS lead for the Legends Programme.' Jeremy leaned forward. One of the displays was showing a view from what looked like a US Navy ship compartment, with several people huddled around a table. 'Alex, have you got my team there?' he said, squinting at the screen.

Bowen stood up, a little closer to the camera. 'I do, Jeremy. They got out with one of my guys. Brought us some key intel.'

Jeremy nodded. 'I have a further detail to add. We have just detained an SIS employee who we believed to be working with Bocharov, running an inside operation against the Legends Programme.'

Haverman caught the past tense. 'Believed?'

'Yes, sir. It's become clear that she was actually working with Yev-geny Olenev. Stephanie Salisbury and Yevgeny Olenev were on opposite sides of the Russian border, very early in the Russia–Ukraine conflict, doing very similar work. They met in 2016, during a diplomatic trip to Moscow. That's when he recruited her. He's been feeding her infor-mation on Wagner and Vityaz operations in Africa ever since. Some of that intelligence was key in stopping some very bad things, so it's been a big part of her rise in the service. She was the one who turned one of our field operatives, cryptonym GARNET. Doubtless she had bigger plans too. But Olenev and Salisbury are at the heart of this.'

'So whose plan are we trying to stop here?' said a man closer to the camera in a combat uniform. The name tape on his chest identified him as Rodriguez. 'Bocharov's or Olenev's?'

'Both,' said Jeremy. 'But Olenev's plan relies on Bocharov's. He was planning to use GARNET to feed Bocharov to SIS and CIA. A sac-rificial lamb to calm everyone down, *after* they detonated a dirty bomb on Russian territory and seized power in the chaos. And Salisbury would be picking up the pieces on the UK side, ready to slide up the ladder.'

'We found nuclear material in the compound,' said Nicola, sitting forward. 'A Broken Arrow weapon from the 1960s.'

'Exactly,' said Jeremy. 'And there was another aspect too. Olenev wanted to sow the maximum amount of chaos, to keep NATO off balance. There was a covert cell here in London, who were going to take down a passenger jet with US missiles, possibly more than one. We managed to stop that, thanks to the intelligence that Jamie there got out of the compound. Salisbury insists she was unaware of that part, but I'm sure she'd have happily capitalised on it. Her aim was to take over as Chief of SIS eventually.'

'So Olenev was running that team?' said Bowen.

'Yes. Bocharov knew they existed, but he thought they were only there to support Olenev's attack on the Legends Programme. As did Salisbury, or so she claims.'

Haverman shifted in his chair. 'And just what did you do to this Olenev guy that pissed him off so much?'

Jeremy smiled ruefully. 'Three years ago, we had one of our most successful operations. Olenev was collateral damage. We successfully infiltrated a Legend asset posing as a pipeline engineer into an Azerbaijani oil magnate's inner circle. He found the evidence that put that man and most of the trans-Caucasus arms-smuggling network he'd established into jail and prevented a coup d'état.'

'Let me guess, Olenev was his muscle,' said Bowen.

Jeremy nodded. 'At the time it was more than half of his PMC's annual revenue. We put him under, basically. He had to sell what was left to Bocharov and the whole thing got folded into Vityaz a year ago. But he found out who was responsible from Stephanie Salisbury. When Olenev learned about Bocharov's dirty-bomb plan, they cooked up their own that screwed Bocharov, put them both in positions of power and let him take revenge on the Legends Programme at the same time.'

'So there's a good chance Olenev is going to do anything he can to get that weapon out of there, including leaving Bocharov behind,' said Nicola. 'He's a sly bastard, I'll give him that.'

Haverman grunted. 'I'm hearing nothing that changes our tactical options. We should be speeding up, if anything.'

Jeremy sat down. 'And what is the plan, exactly?'

61

Jamie

Helicopter deck, USS Tripoli: now

Jamie had been around enough rich people over the years to have taken one or two helicopter rides. But he'd never been on a US Navy assault ship's landing deck while four black-painted MH-60S Seahawks spun up their rotors. The noise was thunderous.

'Put this on, stay low, follow me directly to the left-hand side,' shouted the American next to him, holding out some kind of heavy vest. Jamie took it, surprised at the weight, then slipped it over his head. The man squatted next to him and pulled at buckles and straps until the vest felt tight and heavy on him.

'This is a plate carrier. Bulletproof vest, to civilians. It'll stop a 5.56-millimetre round, 9-millimetre pistol. Just don't get shot with anything bigger than that,' shouted the soldier.

'I'll try not to,' Jamie yelled back, his throat suddenly very dry. It was bright on deck, Navy SEALs lined up, floodlights from the *Tripoli*'s bridge outlining the helicopters and rows of soldiers in harsh silhouette. The rotor noise went up in pitch and he was buffeted with a strong wash of air from the spinning blades.

Nicola knelt beside him. She'd got her own vest from somewhere, along with a rifle. 'You sure about this, mate?'

Jamie tried to smile. 'You need me to get into the cage, right? Klein probably thought they were going to drop a cruise missile on the place, otherwise he wouldn't have let me be the one to lock it.'

She squeezed his shoulder. 'You've already done so much, Jamie. I'm sorry we're asking you to do this as well.'

Sylvan came along the line of troops and knelt beside them. Rodriguez and Klein emerged from the bright white of the floodlights and joined the impromptu huddle.

'I understand you two have some combat experience,' he said, nodding towards Sylvan and Nicola.

'Roger that. Afghanistan and Iraq, respectively. Both infantry,' said Nicola.

'Outstanding. I need you two, plus Klein here, to keep Mr Tulloch out of trouble. He needs to stay with you, no matter what. Things are going to move fast, once we get down there and the lights go out. And you, Mr Tulloch. You don't leave their side, got it?'

'Aye, got it,' said Jamie, offering them all a smile.

Rodriguez held out a net bag. 'Those are NVGs for all of you. Monoculars, I'm afraid; my guys need the full rigs. But they should let you see what's going on, at least.'

Nicola opened the bag and handed out the kit. She pointed to the thumb stud on the side. 'On, off. Got it? Don't turn it on until we hit the ground.'

The Seahawks' engines rose to a higher pitch and the pilots gave a thumbs-up to the brightly shirted deck crew, who turned and waved the Navy SEAL teams on to the helideck.

In a quick rush of booted feet, they were in, under the spinning blades, the rotor wash whipping their faces. Jamie clambered aboard, pulled by the gloved hands of the soldiers around him. They settled him into a seat in the centre of the aircraft. Someone handed him a headset and he put it on. Nicola thumped down into the seat opposite and put her rifle between her legs, muzzle pointed upwards.

He couldn't quite believe he was here. About to fly into the middle of a gunfight in a heavily armed mercenary compound to help retrieve a nuclear weapon. He swallowed and gripped the nylon straps on his shoulders. He was going to do this. It was going to be okay.

A soldier next to Jamie grinned at him. 'You one of the British advisers?' he said through the intercom.

'Something like that,' said Jamie, returning the smile.

The voice of the CIC controller crackled over the radio. 'All stations, Sentinel. I say again, Sentinel.'

The soldier grinned even wider. 'Fuckin' Sentinel.'

'What's that?' said Jamie.

The engine pitch rose again and Jamie's stomach dropped as the Seahawk lifted off the deck. Warm subtropical air gusted through the open cabin as the helicopter turned and began heading towards land.

'Mission go-word. Means we're green to head on in,' said the Navy SEAL.

'Ah, like Black Hawk Down. When they say "Irene".'

The man made a face. 'That's the Rangers. But yeah, same idea. Fuckin' Irene, man. Hey, where's your weapon, buddy?'

It was Jamie's turn to make a face. 'I, uh, don't have one. I'm a civilian. I'm not really supposed to be here.'

The SEAL laughed. 'What?'

'Long story,' said Jamie.

The helicopter pitched forward and descended to skim only a few metres above the black waves of the Indian Ocean.

62

Nicola

MH-60S Seahawk, 1.5 nautical miles north-east
of Zanzibar: now

'Greyhound away. I say again, Greyhound is away. Time to target is
three minutes. All stations, maintain three-kilometre distance from
target area.'

Nicola craned her neck to see if she could spot the incoming missile. The flight of four Seahawks had turned into a low, circling pattern,
just a little way offshore. Outside the immediate radius of the graphite
bomb and EMP burst that would fry Bocharov's compound. Close
enough to get in quickly. Even now, the guards on the ground would
be looking up into the pitch-black sky, peering past their own floodlights, trying to work out where the sound of helicopter blades was
coming from.

'One minute to target,' said the clipped voice of the CIC controller
back on the *Tripoli*.

She saw it then, flashing past barely two hundred metres away, the
afterburner on the Tomahawk cruise missile a long tongue of blue-
white flame.

'Thirty seconds to target.'

Nicola's Seahawk turned to starboard, tilting towards the compound, so she had a front-row seat for what happened next.

'Ten, nine, eight, seven . . .'

The missile, low to the ground now, streaked in from the dark of the ocean. With three seconds to go, it jerked suddenly upwards, rising to around fifty metres, directly above the villa.

She'd expected a huge detonation, but it was more like a light bulb burning out at a grand scale. Nicola caught a brief flare of light from the weapon and the crackling scatter of the graphite, designed to take out any surface power lines. Then there was a second, more muted flash.

Instantly, the compound plunged into darkness. Every single floodlight, right around the fence line, flickered and died. The lights in the villa, in the security buildings, at each of the gatehouses, went a second later.

Rodriguez's voice came over the unit radio. 'Baseplate, this is Sledgehammer Actual, good effect on target. Starting insertion. Out.'

The helicopters tilted again and formed into a long line.

'NVGs on, stand by,' called Rodriguez. Nicola slipped the monocular night-sight over her head and turned it on, then saw Jamie struggling with his.

She helped him position it over his right eye, then switched it on for him. 'Keep both eyes open. Your other eye can help you spot movement. You stick to me like *glue* when we're down there, okay? Our team is going straight for the boathouse. Once we get down there, we should only be on the ground for a few minutes, long enough to pop the cage open and then get out for pick-up. Got it?'

Jamie nodded and grinned at her. 'This is kind of exciting. Terrifying, but kind of exciting.'

The big SEAL next to him punched him lightly on the shoulder. '*That's* the attitude, man.'

'Cut the chatter, we're coming in,' said Rodriguez.

Nicola leaned out. Here and there she could see quick flashes of light. Muzzle flashes, the guards on the ground firing at the helicopters they could hear but not see above them. A round smacked into the side of the Seahawk a half-metre from her head, underlining the point.

Below, Nicola made out a line of shadows, around a dozen men in a fast-moving, orderly double column, jogging down the road towards the beach gate. Komba's men, getting out of the compound under cover of the blackout.

'Baseplate, this is AEGIS Three One,' she sent. 'I've got eyes on TISS assets. They're exiting the compound as planned.'

'Ropes away,' called the gunners on each side as they kicked the heavy, black coils of rope overboard. Nicola watched them snake down to the ground below.

'Sledgehammer, go, go, go,' called Rodriguez, his voice precise and taut.

Dark shapes rushed past Nicola and Jamie, sliding down the ropes with practised speed and focus.

More muzzle flashes, mostly from the security buildings. Nicola wanted to fire back, but she would do more harm than good by revealing exactly where the Seahawk was in the sky.

Rodriguez was speaking to the pilot. 'Set down fifty metres along this track, I'll take the advisers out on the ground.'

The pilot acknowledged, then flared the helicopter directly backwards. Nicola saw the long, straight road down to the beach gate, then the scrub and dust were rushing up to meet her.

'Advisers, go, go, go,' called Rodriguez. He jumped out too, followed by one of his troopers. The helicopter was lifting off before their feet even touched the ground, rising back into the air, rotor wash beating the dust and sand of the compound into a furious cloud.

Nicola grabbed Jamie's hand and placed it squarely on the back of her vest. 'Like *glue*. Got it?'

Jamie nodded, his face pale in the green-white glow of the night vision. 'Don't worry. It's a shite time to go for a wander,' he said, half smiling.

Rounds came in, flat snaps and thumps as the guards in the security buildings fired towards the dust cloud and the sound of rotors.

Klein was to Jamie's left, weapon raised, firing back. 'Hope my guys skedaddled,' he said. 'They're assholes, but I kinda like them.'

'We gotta move. Come on,' said Rodriguez. He ducked low and dropped off the slightly cambered road into the drainage ditch to the left. Ahead, the boathouse loomed, an absence of starlight, grey-green and grainy in the night-sight. The villa was a collection of straight lines at the top of the hill, garlanded with its own chain of muzzle flashes.

'Sledgehammer One, ready to breach.'

'This is Actual, take it,' said Rodriguez.

Up ahead, Nicola caught the muted flash and metallic clang of a breaching charge going off. Then the building lit up with the bright white of flash-bang grenades.

They met the rear security of Sledgehammer One a moment later, two SEALs crouched in the drainage ditch, firing steadily at the security buildings fifty metres away. More rounds cracked overhead and slammed into the sheet-metal siding of the boathouse, ringing it like a bell.

'Sit-rep,' said Rodriguez as he slid in beside the men.

'Charlie Team's breached and cleared. Bravo is holding the south side, we're holding the north. They're taking potshots at us, but no organised resistance yet.'

Nicola smirked in the darkness. 'The ones in the barracks are probably still drunk,' she said.

Rodriguez grinned. 'Come on,' he said, looking back over his shoulder at Nicola and Jamie. 'Time for you to do your thing.'

He led them past the boats and gear stored outside, now peppered with bullet holes, then through the side door. Inside, there were more bodies, Russian mercenaries lying in corners or slumped against walls, crumpled grey-green shapes in the darkness.

A large soldier loomed out of the darkness, the NVGs over his face giving him a strange, insectile appearance.

'We took two prisoners, sir; they dropped their weapons. But I've got bad news.'

Rodriguez went still. 'They got the cage open?'

'Better if I show you,' said the burly trooper.

They followed him through the darkness to the cage.

Rodriguez stopped dead, staring. 'Jesus Christ,' he muttered.

Nicola saw immediately what they'd done. Cut only three of the bars, which must have taken them half the time it would take to cut the six or eight they'd need to get the whole case out. Then handled live radioactive material to get it out of the cage and into a new case.

'These people are fucking insane,' she murmured to herself.

'I could have told you that,' said Jamie.

'Get anything from the prisoners?' said Rodriguez, shaking himself and turning back to his team. 'Where'd they take it?'

'Nothing so far, sir. They're scared.'

'Shit,' said Rodriguez. 'I'd better call this in. We may need that secondary option after all.'

Nicola shook her head. 'Commander, if they're moving it any kind of distance, it needs to be in a case, otherwise it'll cook anyone exposed to it. If they've put it all in a new case, it's going to be *heavy*. Like four- or five-man lift, minimum. They're still in the compound. We just have to find them.'

Rodriguez nodded. 'I believe you, but I still have to call it in. We don't know where it is right now, so we have to keep every option on the table.' He raised his hand to the transmit switch on his chest rig, but the radio crackled.

'Sledgehammer Actual, this is Charlie Two, over.'

'Charlie Two, Sledgehammer Actual, go ahead,' said Rodriguez.

'We've got the east side of the villa secured. Just got eyes on six tangos moving something big and heavy. They're on the ground floor of the villa. Possible sighting of the package, over.'

Nicola thought Rodriguez might have been looking at her when he replied, although it was hard to tell with the NVGs over his face.

'Charlie Two, move to secure that package and any exit routes. We're heading up to join you. Out.'

'Why would they take it up there?' said Jamie.

'They can't take it out by boat, we hold the beach,' said Klein, checking the chamber of his rifle. 'And we've got MQ-9 coverage for forty kilometres in every direction, so we'd take out a ground vehicle too.'

'Helipad,' said Nicola. 'They've got a combat-rated helipad on top of the villa. They've probably called in a fucking gunship.'

63

Jeremy

Ops Room 9: now

The footage from the two circling MQ-9 Reaper drones had been patched through to Jeremy's ops room just as the ground attack had started. They'd seen the flash of the EMP, then the hot white dots of the four Seahawk helicopters dropping off their payloads, IR strobes flashing on the helmets and packs of the troopers as they took the boathouse and one side of the villa.

Even with the markers clearly showing who was friendly, it was still absolute chaos down there.

Fragmented radio chatter came in over the common band, along with the tinny sound of gunfire and muted explosions.

'Bloody hell,' said Sally Lime, sitting next to him at the ops desk. 'Getting a bit hot down there.'

On screen, Secretary Haverman was still online, along with the British Defence Minister Jim Straiton, Alexandra Bowen and, looking very angry still, Adil Komba.

'Baseplate, this is Sledgehammer Actual, negative on the package at the boathouse. We have eyes on tangos in the villa, possibly trying to exfil by air.'

'Roger that,' said Bowen. 'We'll discuss tactical options and come back to you. Stand by for crash extraction if we lose the package.'

Rodriguez signed off, and Jeremy stared into the camera lens. He wondered if the people on the other end of this conference line could see the fear and fatigue in his eyes.

'We might lose this thing, folks. We have to talk other options,' said Bowen. 'Bocharov and Olenev have serious military hardware on the African mainland. I'm betting they're sending some of it. If they bring in an Mi-35 or something else with teeth, there's a good chance they'll get that cargo out of here faster than we can keep up. Once they're over the African mainland, we'll lose them. We've got Reapers with Hellfires overhead, but they're going to struggle against fast-moving air targets.'

'Why can't we just shoot the damn thing down? We've got our own air assets that can do that, surely?' said Haverman.

'We have two Apache gunships ready to launch,' said Captain Reynolds. 'We can have them over that compound inside of ten minutes.'

'Good, get 'em in the air,' said Haverman.

Adil Komba sat forward, his face close to the lens. 'If your plan is to shoot down a helicopter with nuclear material aboard, that is barely better than dropping a cruise missile on it. Possibly worse, if the wreckage is spread across a wide area.'

Straiton, the British Defence Secretary, nodded. 'We understand that, Mr Komba. We're positioning assets as an option. I have confidence in the teams on the ground to secure this material.'

Komba let out a huff of breath. 'Minister, there are *people* on this island. Hundreds of thousands of them. My men are out of the compound, but there are a dozen villages within five kilometres of this place, towns, crops being grown. I do not believe you would be so calm if I was talking about shooting down a nuclear bomb over the Cotswolds.'

Jeremy stepped closer to the monitors. He could feel the eyes of the people in the room behind him on his back. 'Sir, if I may. We know there is a fracture within the Bocharov faction. Yevgeny Olenev is planning to betray his partner, with the help of the British asset he's turned. At some point, he's going to try and get out of there and leave Bocharov and his forces behind. When that happens, we'll have our opportunity. But we need to give the teams on the ground as much time as we can. If Olenev pulls off even part of what he's planning in Russia, we're risking nuclear war. Then it won't just be Zanzibar. It'll be everywhere.'

64

Operative GARNET

Ground-floor lobby, Rayskiye Vrata: now

There was so *much* glass everywhere. The ground floor of Bocharov's villa had once had floor-to-ceiling windows, all the way along the horseshoe curve around the central pool. Now they were mostly gone, shattered by gunfire. The pool itself was wrecked, tiles smashed, water dotted with floating debris and a couple of bodies. With all the lights out, the lobby was lit only by muzzle flashes, swivelling head torches on the Russians defending, and the occasional eye-searing eruptions of the flash-bangs the Americans kept throwing.

Price crouched a little closer to a shredded sofa and glanced back over his shoulder. The case was just behind him, a Russian on each corner. Olenev was one couch ahead.

'Covering fire!' shouted Bocharov from his position by the main staircase. He waved frantically at Olenev and the case-carriers.

Six Russians, tucked behind couches and the remnants of the marble-and-wood bar, rose to their feet. Price marvelled at their calmness, each firing short, controlled bursts, faces stern and impassive as they squinted into the darkness. Unlike the Americans, they had no NVGs. They were shooting at shadows.

'Move, go, go, go,' called Olenev, making for the staircase. The four men behind Price got up, grunting under the weight of the case, then shuffle-walked as fast as they could towards the stairs. The lifts were out of the question, of course. As was running, with the weight they held between them.

Price reached Bocharov and Olenev.

'Go on, get up the stairs,' said Bocharov. 'How long until the helicopter?'

'Ten minutes, maybe?' said Olenev over the clatter of gunfire. The men with the case squeezed past. Within a moment they'd reached the first landing, then turned out of sight, hidden by the bullet-pocked panelling that lined the stairwell.

'Good. No way we can take all our boys with us. But they will spend a few months in jail here, then we can put some pressure on Tanzania from the Kremlin, once it's ours.' Bocharov grinned wolfishly. 'This will work out, Yevgeny. I feel it.'

Olenev smiled back. 'I have no doubt. See you on the helipad.'

Bocharov nodded, then turned back to the firefight. 'Vitaly, watch the left!' he shouted. 'I think there are some coming from there.'

Olenev and Price crouched and climbed the stairs quickly. At the first landing, Olenev paused. Price knelt beside him.

'What's the plan here? We're going to push him out of the helicopter?' said Price. 'Because he's a big bastard, and so is Vitaly. And I don't fancy fighting either of them in the back of a Hind.'

Olenev shook his head. 'There is a firefight going on here. A lot of bullets. Look, there is Vitaly, by the potted palm.'

Price peered into the darkness, following Olenev's pointing finger. He saw the big mercenary, illuminated by a stuttering muzzle flash from his left.

'And here is Bocharov,' he said, nodding towards the figure at the bottom of the stairs. 'Best if the Americans capture them. They've come here with helicopters and special forces; they know what we have. We will give them these two. Aim for the legs.'

Price swallowed, but he did as Olenev suggested, raising his AK and sighting it on Vitaly's squatting figure, while Olenev aimed his pistol at Bocharov's back.

They fired at the same time, the flashes bright in the enclosed stairwell, weapons booming. Both targets crumpled to the ground, Bocharov emitting a grunted scream.

Olenev was already gone, ducking around the corner and up the next flight of stairs. Price blinked into the darkness for a second longer, listening to the urgent Russian below them, Bocharov shouting for a medic.

Price turned to follow Olenev, grinning at the chaos they had sown behind them, running the odds in his head. If the helicopter came, if the battle below lasted long enough. And if the four men they'd chosen got the heavy case up to the helipad. Everything was in their grasp. They had outmanoeuvred London and Washington, got one over on the biggest, baddest Russian mercenary in East Africa. They were going to pull this off, he could feel it. And a new world waited if they did.

65

Jamie

Ground-floor lobby: now

Jamie was getting *very* good at pressing himself against walls. A rattle of gunfire from the other side of the lobby lit the echoing space with staccato flashes. The bullets showered him with chips of powdered concrete.

The Americans returned fire, their suppressed rifles chattering like pistons, in contrast to the deep booms of the Russian weapons.

'They're pulling back,' said Rodriguez, tucked behind a bullet-scored pillar at the eastern edge of the villa lobby. 'Multiple tangos, headed for the stairwell.'

'Another team went up that staircase a minute ago, sir. Think they had the case. These guys are rear-guard.'

Jamie peered around the edge of the pillar, squinting through the monocular Nicola had given him. Two familiar shapes appeared among the rushing shadows going for the staircase.

'That's Bocharov. And Vitaly,' he said, pointing to the two men. Both were limping, supported by other soldiers.

Another burst of fire scored the wall above Jamie's head and he slammed back down to the floor, fragmented glass and grit against his hands and knees.

'Confirmed, eyes on primary targets. No sign of Olenev or GARNET,' said Klein.

Nicola was squatting behind a huge planter filled with trailing vines. 'They're probably with the case. We've got to get past this rear-guard, Captain. Every second we're stuck fighting them gives Olenev a better chance of getting away clean.'

Rodriguez nodded. 'Charlie Team, take that staircase. Bravo, I need you coming in from the other side of the building. We need to bottle these guys up and get past 'em.'

'Sledgehammer, this is Reaper Two. We've got two civilian vehicles headed for the western gate. No strobes. Identify, over?'

Nicola held a hand to her ear. 'Reaper, AEGIS. They're not friendly. Likely to be Brunner or some of Bocharov's men escaping.'

There was a brief pause, then the clipped voice of the Reaper pilot broke in again. 'Roger that. Rifle, rifle, rifle. Danger close, west. Keep your heads down.'

'Fuck,' muttered Nicola.

'What does that mean?' said Jamie.

'Hellfire strike,' Nicola said as she lowered herself to the ground. The SEALs did the same, squatting low behind cover. Klein pressed against the pillar just in front of Jamie.

He wasn't prepared for the explosion when it came, a ball of fire and light that erupted behind the western side of the building. The drone-launched missile had dropped from the sky like a bolt of god-like lightning, obliterating the two vehicles and anything else on that side. What remained of the shattered windows above and around them in the ground-floor lobby blew in, showering them with frag-ments as the pulse of air and heat rocked the building. Once the sound subsided, Jamie was sure he could hear distant screaming. Maybe some of Bocharov's guests on the upper floors?

'Move! Go, go, go,' called Rodriguez. 'Get up those stairs.'

Charlie Team swarmed towards the stairwell, then moved upwards, covering the angles on each side, rifles held high. Jamie was at the back of the group, but he still saw the flashes of traded weapons fire, the crumpled shapes of dead men on the stairwell.

He followed close behind Nicola, crouched and following in a daze. Klein was at his shoulder, pivoting smoothly around corners, glancing at Jamie every so often.

'Should I wait down there?' said Jamie to Klein. 'You don't need me to unlock the cage any more.'

Klein shook his head. 'Fuck no, Scottie. This team stays together. It's dark, everyone has guns and they might drop a cruise missile on this compound any goddamn time. We want you where we can see you. Your stupid dumb luck has to run out some time.'

Nicola glanced back as they rounded the first landing. 'I told you, Jamie. Like glue. And you know the compound, you know Bocharov, you know all of this. I need you right here.'

Jamie nodded back. He was glad he wasn't carrying a weapon, since he wouldn't have the first clue what to do with it. But he still felt like a fifth wheel. And Klein was right. His luck had to be running on empty.

At the top of the second flight of stairs the landing widened into a broad corridor, leading away into the two wings of the villa. The route up to the helipad had been blocked off with stacked furniture, wrecked planters and anything else the defenders could find. Charlie Team were tucked into doorways and alcoves along the corridor, trading shots in complete darkness with the men behind the barricade.

Jamie grinned to himself. He'd just thought of something.

'Nicola,' he said. 'Hey, Nicola.' He tapped her vest and she turned to face him, her face glowing strangely in the night vision. With his unaided eye, he could barely make out her shape. She smiled at him, teeth glowing white in the night-sight.

'You okay?'

'The gym is just to the left here. I think there's a door at the other end of it. Maybe we can get round the barricade, if they haven't thought of it?'

Nicola nodded. 'Captain, you hear that?'

'I did,' said Rodriguez, turning towards them. 'Good intel. Bravo

Team, take Agent Ellis and Mr Tulloch here. I'll follow. Charlie, hold this corridor, keep their heads down.'

Jamie pointed to the heavy pair of doors a metre or two back along the corridor, a tiny sign on the wall that they had missed in the dark. Nicola took the lead, shouldering her rifle. She opened the door and the SEALs streamed through, quartering and clearing the space beyond. Without the external floodlights or the gym's ceiling lights, the only illumination came from the mounted infrared spotlights and laser targeting beams on the SEALs' weapons. Squat racks and weight machines loomed in the dark, the sweeping beams casting strange, angular shadows on the floor-to-ceiling mirrors that lined the rear wall.

'Clear,' the SEALs called as they flowed to the end of the long, glass-walled room.

Jamie moved in the centre of the group. Klein was to his right, rifle up and scanning.

'Too many fucking mirrors,' the big man murmured, audible now that the crash and shatter of the main fight in the adjacent corridor was muted a little.

'Where does this come out?' said Rodriguez.

'Connecting corridor,' replied Klein. 'Goes front to back through the whole building. Helipad stairs are to the left, right at the end, past a waiting lounge. The cross-corridor the Russians barricaded is to the right. We go left, we'll bypass them. Don't know why I didn't think of it, I'm in this goddamn gym often enough. Smart, Jamie, smart.'

Jamie smiled in the darkness.

'Outstanding,' said Rodriguez. 'Bravo Two, you hold corridor right, then collapse back to the bottom of the stairwell when we reach it.'

'Roger that,' said one of the SEALs.

They reached another set of double doors, with a darkened corridor beyond. Klein and Nicola stacked up behind the SEALs as they pushed through the door, one team going right, the other left. Jamie peered down the corridor back the way they'd just come and saw the flashes of more weapons firing. There couldn't be many Russians left on this floor, with the speed and aggression of the SEALs' assault.

His head was turned the wrong way when the fresh burst of gunfire came from ahead of them, so he didn't see the shots that knocked the SEAL pointman sideways into the wall and left him slumped, groaning in pain.

The SEAL's comrades grabbed his vest and dragged him backwards, out of the line of fire, muzzle flash lighting the corridor as they covered each other.

'Shit, they're in the waiting lounge,' said Klein.

Rodriguez crouched beside the wounded man. 'Beckett, you good?'

Beckett nodded. 'Plate stopped most of it. Fragment in my shoulder, I think. Those AKs pack a punch.'

The SEALs had spread out instinctively, avoiding the bunching that could mean a dozen casualties if the enemy fired a burst down the corridor. Jamie was tucked in a doorway with Nicola and Klein, Rodriguez across the way.

'Shit, I wish we'd got better layout maps,' he said. 'What's this lounge look like?'

Klein squatted and leaned out a little. 'Basically a wide spot in the corridor. Half a dozen couches on the left and right. Waiting area for people taking a chopper out of here. Either Olenev's got a second rearguard in there, or we've found Bocharov.'

'Klein?' called a voice from the darkness. A deep, angry voice. 'Is that you, you traitor Yankee motherfucker?'

Klein smirked in the darkness. 'Vitaly Kohanov, as I live and breathe.'

66

Jeremy

Ops Room 9: now

'It is absolute *chaos* down there,' said Haverman. 'But we have teams on the ground, inside that building. We've lost our option for a Toma-hawk strike. I won't sacrifice the lives of my troops or your goddamn spooks. But we've got to consider a splash on that helicopter.'

Jeremy grimaced. 'What's the sit-rep there? Do we have any eyes on?'

Alexandra Bowen's eyes were narrowed as she scanned through data she could see on her end. 'We're limited by what the *Tripoli*'s fire-control radars can see, plus the Seahawks we have over the compound and the two inbound Apaches. It's a patchwork. We can't see what the Tanzanians can see with their civilian radar network.'

Komba, sitting beside Bowen, was busy working at a laptop, a phone cradled on his shoulder. 'I am trying to get Air Force Com-mand to give us access. But it's four in the morning. It will take time.'

'CIC reports intermittent radar contact with something that looks a lot like an Mi-35. It's a modernised Hind gunship, fast and with enough cargo capacity for Olenev and his weapon. But it's flying NOE. By the time we get a fix on it, it's gone again,' said Captain Reynolds.

Jeremy frowned. 'NOE?'

'Nap of the earth,' said Reynolds. 'Really fast and low. Treetop height, pretty much. Some of these merc pilots are real cowboys. Saw one buzz an oil rig off Yemen by about twenty metres.'

'Do we have an estimate of time?'

Bowen nodded. 'Five minutes, tops, judging by the contacts so far. It's somewhere over the western edge of Zanzibar now. We'll have a narrow window to take that chopper out when it's right over the compound, before it lands. After that, there's a radiological risk.'

'Christ,' said Jeremy, leaning forward on the desk in front of him.

'Whatever your guys on the ground are going to do,' said Haverman, leaning close enough to the camera that Jeremy could see the greying five o'clock shadow on the man's chin, 'they better do it damn quick. The United States will not permit US nuclear material to leave that compound unless it's in our control. I've been authorised by the President to ensure that. And I will shoot that helicopter down if it takes off with that case aboard, I promise you that.'

67

Nicola

Third-floor helicopter waiting area, Rayskiye Vrata: now

Nicola stepped around the corner, into the open space between two pillars. The carbine rifle she had been carrying hung by its sling from her chest harness, both hands raised. When she got a clear view of what was waiting in the lobby, her breath stopped in her throat.

Bocharov and Vitaly were crouched behind a crude barrier they had made from two sofas pushed together. Even in the green glow of the night-sight, she could see how pale they both were, their wide eyes shining in the glow of the IR torch beams sweeping across the space as the SEALs moved across behind her.

'Stay where you are! Stop moving!' Vitaly screamed. He fired his AK, but it was a high shot, the round smashing into the ceiling above. 'Call off your fucking drones. I hear them. I see what they do!'

Nicola paused for a heartbeat. Over the pops of gunfire, the steady beat of helicopters circling the compound, there was indeed the thrumming buzz of the two Reapers overhead. They must be flying low, marking targets.

Behind Vitaly, the others they had gathered emitted a low moan of fear. There were six of them. Guests at the villa, Nicola guessed. Maybe one or two of them were Bocharov's girls, the ones who followed him from place to place.

'Hold your fire, hold your fire,' Nicola called out, in English. 'You can't win. And Yevgeny Olenev is about to run off with your secret weapon. He's betrayed you, Arkady. You must know that by now.'

Jamie detached himself from the wall and came to stand beside her, putting himself in the firing line too. He reached up and squeezed Nicola's shoulder. Nicola managed a quick glance and a smile in his direction, but his eyes were fixed on Bocharov, staring intently through his monocular. When he spoke, his voice was different. The hesitance of the last few days was gone.

'We're giving you a chance to give up, Arkady. Please take it. You can survive this. The people you have with you, they can survive it too. But if you let Olenev out of here with that weapon, it might mean the end for all of us. Olenev would plunge the whole world into war just so he can warm his hands on the ashes. He doesn't care about Russia. He only cares about himself. Just like GARNET.'

'Is that Jamie?' called Bocharov. 'I misjudged you, my little friend. I did not think you would have the balls to come back here, to do something like this. And you brought so many friends with you.'

'Arkady, you're fucked man. Give it up,' said Klein.

'Not helping,' Nicola hissed.

Bravo Team were creeping from pillar to pillar, moving swiftly and silently. Vitaly was blinking furiously in the beam of an IR torch he couldn't see, three red dots clustered on his chest and forehead. He pulled the trigger on his rifle again, sending another cascade of splinters and plaster dust raining down on the troops.

'I've got the shot, Cap. Say the fuckin' word and this guy's toast,' murmured one of the SEALs over the radio.

Bocharov shifted, groaning in pain. Now that they were closer, Nicola could see the spreading dark wetness of a wound in his right leg.

'Olenev shot you, didn't he?' she said. 'He's been working against you from the start, Arkady. Who knows how many of your men he's turned. Help us stop him.'

Bocharov blinked, eyes unfocused in the green glow of the IR lights. 'I . . . I wanted to build a better Russia. A stronger Russia . . .' he said. Nicola could see his eyelids fluttering, blood loss taking its toll. Beside him, Vitaly's forehead was coated in sweat, his lips drawn back in a defiant snarl.

'Olenev, Bocharov, it's the same,' Vitaly said. 'Russia needs to be stronger again. Fuck you, all of you,' he roared, raising the rifle.

Nicola's hands dropped to her rifle, but she couldn't move fast enough. She ducked, darting towards the pillar to her left. But the expected thud of bullet impacts didn't come. There were five shots, loud and close, muzzle flash lighting the barricade and making her night-sight glow green-white. But they weren't from an AK. They were higher, the metallic crack of a Russian 9mm Grach pistol.

Vitaly slumped forward. Behind him, dressed in a tracksuit, the pistol held in both hands, eyes wide in the darkness, stood a tall, willowy woman with short blonde hair. Nicola saw her throat bob as she swallowed. She could hardly see what she'd done, but the long, groaned exhalation from the dying Vitaly told her that she'd hit her target.

Bocharov blinked in the darkness that came after the muzzle flash. 'Natasha, what have you done, koshka? You have killed Vitaly. You have killed him.'

Natasha took a step forward, raising the pistol at Bocharov. 'I have listened to you two talk about your wars and your strength for three years now. Swapping stories about Donetsk. Enough – enough of this shit. My grandmother was Ukrainian. She died in the first invasion. Did you know that? You would have known that if you'd ever thought to ask, you piece of shit.'

Nicola took two steps forward and spoke softly in Russian, her hands up. 'Natasha, please. Don't shoot him. He should face a court, for everything he's done. All of it. Please, give me the gun.'

Natasha sat down on the sofa opposite Bocharov, but she kept the gun in her hand. 'No. I will cover him. You go and get Olenev. That khuyló is the worst of the lot.'

Nicola nodded, even though Natasha couldn't see it in the dark. 'Thank you, Natasha.'

She turned away and pointed up the stairs towards the helipad. 'Up there. And let's get some fucking lights on that helipad.'

Rodriguez nodded and put his hand to his ear. 'All Sierra units, illuminate with spots and flares. Sniper cover, watch and shoot.'

Outside, the sky lit up.

68

Operative GARNET

Helideck stairwell: now

Price squinted against the sudden flare of light. It seemed to be coming from everywhere. Rotors thumped overhead and the glass-walled stairwell was filled with the swinging, unreal light of parachute flares and the sweeping beams of spotlights.

Two steps ahead, the four mercenaries stumbled under the weight of the lead-lined case, the contents shifting as they climbed. They were all breathing hard, the flare light glinting from sweat-coated necks and foreheads.

Two steps beyond, the slim, rangy form of Yevgeny Olenev stopped and turned.

'Come on, you bastards. A bonus for each of you when you get this damn thing to the top. And a ticket out on the chopper. Davai, we're nearly there. One more flight.'

'We're going to get fucking shot up there,' murmured one of the soldiers.

Even as he said it, the window to Price's right spidered with an incoming round. The soldier on the other side of the case grunted and collapsed to the translucent steps, blood staining the greenish-blue of the glass.

The corner he'd been carrying dropped, slamming on to the step. The other three staggered. Price swore and stepped over the wounded

man, picked up the corner. He strained, feeling the weight of it pulling at his arm. There was no way he was going to die in this stairwell,
nearly free of SIS and these stupid fucking Russians, from an American sniper's bullet.

'Snipers!' he shouted in Russian. 'Go *fucking* faster!'

More rounds cracked through the glass above their head, an entire
pane shattering on the right, spotlights sweeping across them. Warm
night air flooded in, and Price gazed for a half-heartbeat out over the
compound, marvelling at the absurd beauty of combat. Flares drifting
downward, the rolling clouds of smoke and flame from what must
have been an American Hellfire strike. Probably Brunner's men.

They turned the last corner of the stairwell and faced another
double door. Olenev had one side already open. 'There, get in there.
Behind the refuelling station. They can't shoot there without hitting
the fuel tanks. Move! Get into cover, you idiots. We're sitting ducks
here. The case, davai, fucking move!'

They crossed the helideck to the refuelling station in one long, agonis-
ing run, covering ten metres and losing another man to a sniper's round
as they did. He hit the metal grating with a sickening thud, his rifle firing
in a burst as he pitched over. Olenev took the man's place and they staggered onward. Finally they slid into cover, the case shoved ahead of them.
Olenev crouched there in the half-darkness, a spotlight illuminating his
thinning, wild hair, narrow face, wide eyes behind the spectacles he'd
somehow managed to preserve, though one lens was cracked.

'Three minutes,' said Olenev, a half-wild grin on his face. 'Three
minutes, that's all. Cover that goddamn door. We'll get out of here,
and they won't dare shoot us down, not with this aboard.'

He rose a little and pointed. Out in the darkness, beyond the compound perimeter, past the fires and the billowing smoke and the
stabbing diamond-white spears of the spotlights, Price saw the green-
and-red blink of running lights.

'There!' said Olenev. 'There she is! The best helicopter Russia ever
built. We're going to make it, boys!'

69

Jamie

Helideck: now

'Sir, we fire too close to that fuelling station, the whole helideck'll go up like the Fourth of July,' said the pilot of Sierra Two. 'You included. Gotta be a 10,000-gallon tank up there.'

Jamie crouched just behind Klein, with Bravo Team clustered at the top of the stairwell. AK rounds slammed into the doorframe and the SEALs crouched a little lower.

'How long on the inbound Hind?' said Rodriguez. 'We can rush 'em when they try to get aboard.'

'Sledgehammer Actual, this is Victor Three. Tally one bogey, Mi-35. One minute out, moving fast. Keeps breaking lock. Sucker's mowing the goddamn trees with his rotors.'

Jamie peered through the shattered, bullet-pocked glass. Somewhere out there, two Apache gunships were trying to kill the Russian helicopter, whose pilot was probably wondering what, exactly, his boss had ordered him to fly into.

Then he saw it. The Hind came in low over the western fence, rotors cutting spirals through the smoke from the burning Range Rovers. It seemed to almost graze the roof of the villa as it flared and turned, dropping airspeed, the reverberations of its turbine engines rattling the window frames.

'Contact, got it. Goddamn it, he's on the pad already. Permission to fire?'

'Negative, negative, we're danger close, nuclear risk. Weapons hold. I say again, weapons hold.'

One of the SEALs by the door rose into a half-crouch, as though preparing to sprint from the starting blocks of a particularly lethal race.

'Cap, they're going for it. Three of 'em left on the case.'

Rodriguez nodded to the man. 'Spread out across the pad. Take them down. Go!'

Four SEALs darted through the open door and out on to the metal grid of the helideck, opening fire, rifles chattering. Nicola followed, with Jamie close behind, Klein at his right shoulder.

The helideck was complete chaos.

The Russian gunship was perched diagonally across one half of the deck, close to the fuelling station. A body lay halfway to the helicopter.

Jamie caught a glimpse of GARNET in the swinging light of the parachute flares, next to the single surviving Russian soldier, both their faces bright red with exertion as they shoved one end of the heavy case into the open side door of the Hind. Olenev was already inside, pulling hard on the case's other end.

The SEALs fired and the last Russian soldier slumped to the deck. Rounds punched into the skin of the helicopter, careening wildly off the curved bubble of the pilot's canopy. The troopers advanced across the deck, spread out in a line.

'Davai! Davai!' screamed Olenev. But the case was simply too heavy for the two remaining men to easily move. It slid back on to the metal decking with a crash.

Olenev picked up the AK next to his foot and sprayed the advancing line of SEALs with gunfire, screaming in frustration. The SEALs hit the deck, returning fire. Nicola and Klein crouched, aiming their rifles.

Jamie saw his chance and went for it.

He broke away from Nicola and sprinted across the yellow H of the helideck, aiming squarely for the man who was supposed to be him, for GARNET, William Price, the shithead who had nearly got him killed a half-dozen times over. He ignored the yelp of surprise from Nicola, the shouts from Klein and Rodriguez, the flat cracks and thumps of the rifles.

GARNET didn't see him coming.

Jamie crashed into his doppelgänger, matched in height and weight, but given a slight edge by the heavy plate carrier he wore. GARNET yelped in surprise as he fell sideways, scrabbling for his rifle, flare-lit face set in a rictus of anger and fear.

'You!' he hissed. 'You wee fucking *shitebag*.' He twisted and slammed the butt of the rifle into Jamie's side. Jamie grunted and rolled.

By the helicopter, Olenev screamed in incomprehensible Russian, loosing bullets in every direction, blind-firing over the top of the case. The SEALs returned fire, bullets thumping into the helicopter.

'Ten years of my fucking life for you, you fuck,' yelled GARNET, jumping astride Jamie and punching him left, right, left. 'I was going to do big things. Served my country, fought for it. Then this *filthy* fucking job, doing the dirty work of the scumbags in Whitehall. Then they give me you, you wee prick. Well, I've had enough. Enough of you and the Legends. Fuck Althrop, fuck Ellis, and fuck you too. I'm getting *out* and I'm getting what I'm fucking *owed*.'

Jamie blocked a hammer-blow left hook and twisted his hips, rolling GARNET off him. He kicked out, connecting with the man's kneecap. GARNET howled in pain, dropped the rifle, then lashed out with a kick of his own.

Jamie slumped backwards, scrabbling for the fallen rifle, just as someone else rolled in from the right. Nicola. Somehow she'd got behind the helicopter, skirted the dangerous whirling tail rotor. She had a pistol in her hands and pointed it at GARNET.

'You're done, Price. Stand down!' she yelled.

But GARNET wasn't done. Jamie saw his hand go to a sheath on his belt and come back with a wickedly curved knife. The blade's edge glittered in the bright magnesium-white of a fresh parachute flare drifting just a few metres above their heads.

'Fuck *you*, Ellis,' he hissed, and leapt.

The rifle in Jamie's hands barked three times. He wasn't ready for the recoil, barely had time to aim, felt the stock slam into his shoulder and the rifle buck in his hands.

GARNET twisted in mid-air and slammed against the side of the helicopter, leaving a dark smear of blood on the mottled tan of the aircraft's camouflage paint. He slid to the deck, the knife tumbling from his hand.

Klein was already there, scrambling through the helicopter's cargo deck from the other side, a pistol to Olenev's neck. 'Drop it, you stupid Russki fuck,' he shouted.

Then the SEALs were on them, rushing the chopper's canopy, the pilot raising his hands and adopting a look of such forced innocence that it would have made Jamie laugh if he hadn't seen the strange look on Nicola's face. She stood under the whirling blades, hair whipped from side to side by rotor wash as the engine shut off and whined down to silence. Her hand was at her side and she looked almost confused, her eyebrows knitted together.

'Bollocks,' she said, blinking. Jamie's heart jammed in his throat as he saw the oozing swell of blood between her fingers. 'I think one of these twats managed to shoot me,' she muttered, just before she pitched to the deck at Jamie's feet.

Part Five

AFTER

70

Jamie

The Grapes, Limehouse, London:
six months, one day, ten minutes from now

A quiet Tuesday lunchtime in early September was an excellent time to visit the Grapes. It was a place Jamie hadn't been to since he'd first moved to London, so many years before. When he was still feeling out the boundaries of what he was permitted, he'd struck up a friendship with a native Londoner who'd made it on to the same graduate scheme as he had. He'd shown Jamie coaching inns and riverside pubs and all the nooks and crannies of the city.

The friendship hadn't lasted, once Terence learned about it. 'Best not to get too close, my lad,' he'd said. 'Don't want you all over the internet, do we? And you young 'uns do put absolutely bloody everything on the internet.'

The Grapes hadn't changed much. He supposed that was the point. A pub that had been there since Dickens stalked the streets of Limehouse, dreaming up child thieves and sinister figures haunting the marshlands, before concrete and brick spread over all.

Inside, a bar ran the length of a room panelled in dark wood. It was early, the bar just opened, only a few people tucked in corners talking in low voices. The barman asked him for his order and Jamie gave it, adding a gin and tonic to his pint of ale. He picked them up, then went out on to the tiny terrace.

Of course, she'd arrived early enough to snag one of the tiny tables that overlooked the sluggish waters of the Thames. She was at the bottom of a gin and tonic already, a menu open in front of her.

Nicola Ellis grinned when she saw him.

'Hello, Jamie,' she said as he sat down opposite, the river on his right, then placed the G&T in front of her.

'Got you another.'

'Very kind. Came off the meds the other week there, so I'm good to have a tipple again,' she said, emptying what was left of her first glass into the new drink. She raised the full glass and clinked it gently against Jamie's.

Jamie sat back and stared at his erstwhile handler. He wasn't sure if the prickling feeling in his breast was anger or relief, or both, mixed together. 'Nicola, I never thought I'd hear from you again. A man came to my house with an envelope and a document I had to sign. I didn't even know if you were *alive*. Not after they took you away to the sick bay on the *Tripoli*.'

She gave him an apologetic smile. 'Sorry. Covert agents who get wounded on deniable ops don't exactly have visiting hours. I've been in recovery.'

Jamie glanced across the terrace. Only one of the other tables was occupied, the couple talking quietly to each other.

'Should we be . . .'

'Discussing current events? This is an off-the-books meeting, mate. We shouldn't be talking at all. But I felt like I owed you lunch, at least, for everything you did. Including saving my life.'

'He was trying to kill me as well. All in all, I really didn't like my double. Bit of an arsehole.'

Nicola grinned and took a sip of her drink. Midday sunlight sparkled from the river and lit the side of her face with shifting golden planes.

'You can say that again. So what's next? You sticking with Tacitech?'

Jamie looked down at the table. 'Honestly, I don't know. I spent ten years waiting for something to happen. Now it has and I feel . . . lost? I'm having to figure out who the hell I am, Nicola. From scratch.'

'You and me both, mate. I haven't spent more than a couple of months back in the UK since I started this job. The last six months has given me time to think. About what I want. Who I . . . want to be. Be *with*. I screwed a lot of things up, over the years. Trying to fix them now.'

Jamie smiled. 'And?'

She didn't answer, just looked up from her drink and tilted her head with a smile, as though appraising him. Then she sat forward.

'You know, Jamie, you're a natural. You've got the guts and you've got the instincts. If you wanted to come back in, to work with Legends again, you could.'

Jamie frowned. 'As a Legend? I'm not sure the answer to an identity crisis is to go back to not having one.'

Nicola shook her head. 'No. As a handler. You've seen both sides. You're *good* at this. And we're going to need every helping hand we can get, me and Jeremy.'

'You're joining Legends?' he said, blinking in surprise.

'I'm *fixing* Legends. We got the data back, we've restored contact with everyone. But the programme has been flawed from its inception. The wait's too long. And every Legend/Operative pairing is *two* chances for someone to be turned or just fuck up. We need to be faster and lighter. The principle is sound, but we need to start by making sure our existing Legends aren't compromised. Then recruiting more of them. I could do with your help.'

Jamie looked out over the river, his pint glass slick in his hand. He narrowed his eyes against the low sunlight and let the silence linger for a long time.

'We stopped World War Three, right? Or at least a nasty Russian coup and possible civil war and all the chaos that might come from that.'

Nicola nodded, one finger wiping condensation from her glass in precise stripes of beaded moisture. 'We did. We got some breathing room.'

'Well, then, it's time for me to breathe,' he said. 'I'm not saying no, but I *am* saying not now. I need a life that's not half a secret. At least for a little while. Spend some of my pay-off. Do some of the things I couldn't, when I was a Legend.'

Nicola laughed. 'Strange, isn't it? To be in your thirties and still have no idea who you're supposed to be.'

Jamie shrugged. 'I think that's everyone, to be honest. The difference is we do it professionally.'

Nicola leaned across the table, slid a small white card towards him. 'Well, when you come back, when you know a bit more about what you want, who you want to be, you call me. Even if the answer's no. I think . . . I think I might be allowed to have friends, now. Or allow myself, anyway.'

Jamie took the card. Just a mobile phone number, handwritten in blue ballpoint. 'I think I might be allowed that too. Nice, isn't it?'

'What, having a life? Or not being a Legend?'

Jamie nodded. 'Both. A legend is something that doesn't really exist, a story intended to prove a point, deliver a message. And I'm tired of my life, my real life, being a myth.'

She raised her gin again. 'I'll drink to that,' she said.

They clinked glasses, rippling light from the river bathing them both in autumn sunshine.

Acknowledgements

Over twenty years ago, as he reviewed my outline for an undergraduate dissertation on the treatment of paranoia and fear in the spy fiction of John Le Carré and Graham Greene, Professor Peter Davidson was the first person to say to me 'one of these days, young man, you should really think about writing one of these yourself'. So, chronologically at least, the first thanks must go to him.

Thank you to my agent, Harry Illingworth of DHH Literary, who has stuck with me as I wrote three books, found a perfect pairing in Headline and juggled a triple workload in my day job, espionage fiction and my parallel career in science fiction. Harry's belief in my work has been a constant reassurance and I benefit from his guidance and support every day. Thanks also to Emily Glenister, Kirsten Lang, David Headley and the rest of the DHH team. I've also been lucky enough to meet an incredible community of other writers through Harry, who have been a huge support through the last couple of years. Hello and thank you to 'Iller's Killers' or whatever we're calling the Discord server this week.

Massive thanks to the team at Headline Books, most particularly my editor Toby Jones, who gave me an extraordinary opportunity to write this book and advocated tirelessly for it. Thank you also to Isabel Martin, Ollie Martin for incredible publicity work, Andrew Davis for the phenomenal cover, Sarah Day for meticulous copyediting and the rest of the team who worked on this book (see credits).

This book is far, far better than it would have been otherwise because of the support of my writing community. Thank you to my incredible critique group, who have changed my writing life for the better – Nicholas Binge, Lia Holland, Shauna Lawless, Ellie Imbody, Talia Rothschild, Michelle Ruiz Keil and Lee Sandwina – for their critiques, their bottomless support and their insights into this business. Thanks also to Erin Hardee, Morag Hannah, CJ Dotson, Jordan Acosta, Marco Rinaldi, Tariq Ashkanani, Ben Anning, Annabel Campbell, Cat Hellisen, Katalina Watt, Lorraine Wilson and Lyndsey Croal for beta reads, group chats, game nights, pub lunches, dinners and drinks over the last few years as I found my local and virtual writing community. Thanks also to the many other members of the ESFF, Inklings and Codex chat servers who have celebrated, commiserated, and cheered me on over the years.

A huge thank you to my oldest friends, who have endured twenty plus years of mumbled responses to 'how's the writing going?' and then managed to not (visibly) glaze over as I told them everything in excruciating detail once the answer became 'quite well actually'. Alex Douglas, Iain McDougall, Ali McLachlan, Deryck Swan, Victoria Hill-Ryder, Hayley and Luke Dalrymple, Eli and Kathryn Appleby-Donald, Beckett Hougham, Anja Tröger, Ian Brember, Ian Ramsey, Andy Hughes, Andrew Cowan, Duncan Russell, Bradlay Law and Mike Bryant – thank you to all of you.

Twenty-one years after that fateful conversation with Professor Davidson, I've achieved a dream that I've had since my teens. For every step of that journey, from the first terrible 'novel' I tapped out on the family PC in the early Nineties to the book you hold in your hands now, my family has been there. Thank you to my brothers Neil and Andrew, new brother Rory, sister Hannah, my mum Eleanor, my dad Nigel, stepmother Fran and the broader Goodman, McCulloch and Rankine clans for their love and support.

But the last and greatest thanks must go to my wife Valerie, who has never faltered in her support, her love and her belief in me and my writing. Without her, you wouldn't be reading this book. Thank you, darling. This one is for you.

Credits

David Goodman would like to thank everyone involved in the production of A Reluctant Spy

Editorial
Toby Jones
Isabel Martin

Copy editor
Sarah Day

Proof reading
Shan Morley Jones

Audio
Ellie Wheeldon

Design
Patrick Insole
Andrew Davis

Production
Rhys Callaghan

Marketing
Ana Carter
Hannah Sawyer

Publicity
Ollie Martin

Sales
Becky Bader
Sinead White
Izzy Smith

Contracts
Helen Windrath